The Same Old Story

The Same Old Story

Ivan Goncharov

Translated by Stephen Pearl

ALMA CLASSICS

ALMA CLASSICS LTD
Hogarth House
32-34 Paradise Road
Richmond
Surrey TW9 1SE
United Kingdom
www.almaclassics.com

The Same Old Story first published in Russian in 1847
This translation first published by Alma Classics Ltd in 2015

Cover design: nathanburtondesign.com

Translation and Translator's Ruminations © Stephen Pearl, 2015

Published with the support of the
Institute for Literary Translation, Russia.

AD VERBUM

Notes © Alma Classics, 2015

Printed in Great Britain by CPI Group (UK) Ltd, Croydon CR0 4YY

ISBN: 978-1-84749-562-4

All rights reserved. No part of this publication may be reproduced, stored in or introduced into a retrieval system, or transmitted, in any form or by any means (electronic, mechanical, photocopying, recording or otherwise), without the prior written permission of the publisher. This book is sold subject to the condition that it shall not be resold, lent, hired out or otherwise circulated without the express prior consent of the publisher.

Contents

The Same Old Story	1
PART I	3
Chapter 1	5
Chapter 2	31
Chapter 3	76
Chapter 4	101
Chapter 5	118
Chapter 6	151
PART II	173
Chapter 1	175
Chapter 2	204
Chapter 3	222
Chapter 4	261
Chapter 5	294
Chapter 6	313
Epilogue	347
Note on the Text	366
Notes	366
Translator's Ruminations	375
Acknowledgements	387

To Brigitte
always there to slap on the mortar
at times when the bricks get dislodged
— and this bricklayer is at his testiest
S.P.

The Same Old Story

PART I

Chapter 1

ONE SUMMER IN THE VILLAGE OF GRACHI, in the household of Anna Pavlovna Aduyeva, a landowner of modest means, all its members, from the mistress herself down to Barbos, the watchdog, had risen with the dawn.

The only exception was Alexander Fyodorych, Anna Pavlovna's son who, as befits a twenty-year-old, was sleeping the sleep of the just. The house was full of hustle and bustle. People were going back and forth, but moving on tiptoe and speaking in whispers for fear of waking the young master. At the slightest sound of a raised voice, or of anyone bumping into anything, Anna Pavlovna, like an enraged lioness, would appear and severely berate the offenders, tell them off in no uncertain terms – and even, on occasion, when sufficiently provoked, would, as far as her strength permitted, box an ear or two. The clatter coming from the kitchen was as noisy as if they were preparing to feed an army, even though there were only two members of the mistress's family: herself and her son, Alexander.

In the coach house, the carriage was being cleaned and greased. Everyone was busily at work – except Barbos, who was doing nothing, although even he had his own way of contributing to the general commotion. Whenever one of the servants, a coachman or a maid slipped past him, he would wag his tail and carefully sniff the passer-by, and the very expression in his eyes seemed to be asking: "Will someone please tell me what all this hustle and bustle is about?"

Well, what it was all about was that Anna Pavlovna was sending her son off to St Petersburg to make a career – or, as she would put it, to see and be seen. What a terrible day it was for her! And that was why she was looking so downcast and unhappy. Often in the midst of the turmoil she would open her mouth to tell someone to do something, stop suddenly in the middle of a word and remain speechless; she would turn her head aside to wipe away a tear, but if she couldn't catch it in time, she would let it drip onto the very trunk which she happened to be packing. The tears would well up from deep in her heart, where they had long been accumulating, rise to her throat and lie heavy on her chest, ready to burst into a flood any moment: it was as if she was hoarding them all to unload at the moment of parting, and would rarely shed only a single, solitary tear.

She was not the only one reduced to tears at the prospect of Sashenka's departure: his valet, Yevsei, was also deeply distressed. He would be accompanying his master to St Petersburg, and would be leaving behind his cosy nook in the house. It was in the room of Agrafena, the first minister of Anna Pavlovna's household and – what was even more important for Yevsei – her housekeeper and keeper of the keys.

Behind the bunk bed there was just enough space to squeeze in two chairs and a table, on which tea, coffee and other goodies were prepared. Yevsei had staked a firm claim on both his place behind the stove and in Agrafena's heart – and it was she who occupied the other chair.

The Agrafena and Yevsei story was an old one in that house. Like every other subject, their story was on everyone's lips and set everyone's tongues wagging, but after a while, inevitably, people lost interest and the tongues stopped wagging. The mistress herself had got used to seeing them together, and they had enjoyed a good ten blissful years. After all, how many people can count as many as ten years of happiness in their whole lives? But finally came the time to say goodbye to all that. Farewell cosy corner, farewell Agrafena, farewell the card games, the vodka, the coffee, the cherry brandy – farewell the lot!

Yevsei sat in silence, sighing deeply. Agrafena, frowning, busied herself with her housework. She had her own way of expressing her frustration. That day she poured the tea furiously, and instead of serving the first cup of strong tea to her mistress, just splashed it about as if to say "*No one*'s getting any!" and was impervious to recriminations. Her coffee boiled over, the cream was burnt and cups slipped out of her grasp. She didn't just put a tray on the table: she banged it down; she didn't just close a cupboard door: she slammed it shut. She didn't cry, but just vented her anger on everyone and everything in her path. Of course, this was in any case one of her dominant characteristics.

CHAPTER I

She was never content; everything rubbed her the wrong way; she was constantly grumbling and complaining. But that moment of fateful adversity revealed this side of her at its most melodramatic. Worse still, she even took it out on Yevsei himself.

"Agrafena Ivanovna!" he said plaintively, but gently, in a tone not quite in keeping with his long and solid frame.

"What do you think you're doing, you dunderhead, lounging around here?" she retorted, as if it were the very first time he had ever sat there. "Out of my way, I have to get a towel."

"Come on, Agrafena Ivanovna!" he repeated lazily, sighing and rising from his chair, only to sit down again the moment she came back with the towel.

"All he can do is snivel! That's the rascal I have to put up with! What a pain! Good God! – and he never leaves me alone!" she said, as she dropped a spoon with a clatter into the washing-up basin.

Suddenly, there was a shout from the next room: "Agrafena! How could you? You must be out of your mind; don't you know that Sashenka is sleeping? Starting a fight with your darling by way of a goodbye?"

"That's right, so she wants me to sit here like a corpse without showing my feelings because you're leaving!" Agrafena hissed under her breath, drying a cup with both hands as if she was trying to break it in pieces.

"Goodbye, goodbye," said Yevsei, sighing deeply. "It's our last day, Agrafena Ivanovna!"

"And good riddance! I want you to get the hell out of here; at least there'll be more room for me. Yes, clear out: nowhere to move with your legs in the way all the time!" He reached to touch her shoulder and got another earful in return. He heaved another sigh, but stayed put anyway. He knew that Agrafena didn't want him to move, and he was not at all put out.

"I wonder who's going to be sitting in my seat," he said with a sigh.

"The Devil," she snapped.

"I hope to God it won't be Proshka – and who's going to play the card game with you?"

7

"So what if it is Proshka – what's so wrong with that?" she retorted venomously.

Yevsei got up.

"Not with Proshka! God no, don't play with him!" Yevsei was clearly upset and almost menacing.

"And who's going to stop me? You, with your ugly mug?"

"My dear Agrafena Ivanovna," he began cajolingly, putting his arms around her waist – that is, if there had been the slightest sign of a waist.

His attempt was met with an elbow in the chest.

"My dear Agrafena Ivanovna," he repeated, "do you think he's going to love you like I do? He's a fly-by-night; he's after any woman who happens to pass by. Not me, oh no, I'll stick to you like glue. If it wasn't for the master's orders – well... you'd see!" As he spoke he grunted and waved his arm. As for Agrafena, her distress was too much for her, and she burst into tears.

"And you're really going to leave me, damn you?" she said in tears. "How can you come up with such nonsense, you halfwit?! Me, team up with Proshka? You know as well as I do that you can never get any sense out of him, and he can't keep his hands to himself – that's all he knows."

"You mean he's already been after you? What a bastard! You only have to say the word, and I'd soon show him..."

"Just let him try, he'd soon get what's coming to him! It's not as if there aren't other women in the house – I'm not the only one. Me team up with him! The very idea! I can't even stand being near him, he has manners like a pig. Before you know it, he's managed to hit someone, or snatch something from the master's table right under your nose."

"Look, you never know what may happen when the Devil's at work, so just in case, why not get Grishka to sit here? He's a harmless lad, hard-working and respectful."

Agrafena jumped on him: "Another one of your great ideas! Dumping any Tom, Dick or Harry on me; what do you take me for? Get out of here! It must have been the Devil himself who put me up to teaming up with a hobgoblin like you for my sins – and for that I'll never forgive myself... what an idea!"

CHAPTER I

"May God reward you for your virtue! That'll be a weight off my mind!" Yevsei exclaimed.

"So, now you're relieved," she screamed again, like an animal in pain. "You must be really happy – I hope you enjoy it!" Her lips were white with anger. They both fell silent.

"Agrafena Ivanovna," Yevsei began timidly, after a pause.

"Now what?"

"Well, I forgot; I haven't had a bite to eat the whole morning."

"Oh, so that's it!"

"Well, I was too upset."

From behind a loaf of sugar on the lowest shelf, she produced a glass of vodka and two enormous hunks of bread with some ham which she had carefully prepared for him well beforehand. She shoved it all at him in a manner you wouldn't even shove it to a dog, and a piece fell on the floor.

"There, now choke on it. I hope to God you... quietly! Everyone in the house can hear the noise you're making with your mouth."

She turned her back on him as if she hated him, and he slowly began to eat, watching Agrafena warily and covering his mouth with the other hand.

Meanwhile a coach had appeared at the gate with three horses harnessed to it. A yoke had been thrown over the neck of the shaft horse. The little bell fastened to the saddle rang with a muffled and constricted sound like a drunk who had been bound and thrown into the guardhouse. The coachman tethered the horses under the awning of the barn, took off his cap, produced from it a dirty towel and mopped his brow. Anna Pavlovna saw him through the window and her face went pale. She went weak at the knees and her hands dropped, although it was a sight she had been expecting all along. She recovered her composure and called Agrafena.

"Go and see if Sashenka is sleeping, but on tiptoe and without making a sound," she said. "My darling may have a long sleep, and it's the last day, so I'll hardly have a chance to look at him. No, wait! If I let you go, you'll just blunder in like a cow! I'd better go myself."

She went.

"Yes, you go, oh no, you're no cow!" Agrafena grumbled to herself on her way back to her room. "Some cow! You'd be lucky to have more cows like me!"

On her way, Anna Pavlovna saw Alexander Fyodorych coming towards her. He was a fair-haired young man, in the flower of his youth, health and strength. He bade his mother a cheerful "Good morning", but, suddenly catching sight of the trunks and packages, he was taken aback and moved silently to the window and started drawing on it with his finger. A minute later, he was back talking to his mother, quite untroubled, and even happily inspecting the preparations for the journey.

"Dear boy, you seem to have overslept – your face is even a little swollen; come, let me dab some rose water on your eyes and cheeks."

"No, Mummy, please don't."

"What do you want for breakfast? Tea first or coffee? I've ordered chopped meat with sour cream for you."

"Doesn't matter, Mummy."

Anna Pavlovna continued packing his linen, but then stopped and gave her son a sorrowful look.

"Sasha!" she said after a pause.

"What is it, Mummy?"

She hesitated before speaking, as if she were apprehensive.

"Where are you going, my dear, and why?" she asked timidly.

"Where to? What do you mean, Mummy? To St Petersburg, and then... and then, well, to..."

"Listen, Sasha," she said nervously, putting her hand on his shoulder, clearly intending to make one last attempt, "there's still time; think it over, don't go!"

"Don't go! How do you mean, 'don't go'? I mean, you've just packed my linen and all," he said, at a loss for words.

"The linen is packed? Well, watch this: look, now it's unpacked." In a trice she had emptied the trunk.

"What are you doing, Mummy? I was all packed and ready to go – and now this. What will people say?"

He was downcast.

CHAPTER I

"It's not for my sake that I want to stop you going, but rather for your own sake. Why go there? To find happiness? Is your life here so bad? Doesn't your mother spend her days finding ways of indulging your slightest whim? Of course, at your age, a mother's attentions alone are not enough to make you happy – and I don't expect them to. Just look around you: you're the centre of attention. And what about Sonyushka, Maria Vasilyevna's daughter? There – you're blushing! For three nights she hasn't slept, pray God her health doesn't suffer! Look how she loves you, my darling."

"Come on, Mummy, what are you talking about, she's…"

"Don't deny it, you think I don't… see. And let's not forget, she's taken your handkerchiefs to hem. 'I won't let anyone but me do them,' she says, 'and I'll sew on the name tags.' So you see, what more could you want? Stay here!"

He listened in silence, his head lowered, and playing with the tassel of his dressing gown.

"What will you find in St Petersburg?" she went on. "You think your life there will be the same as it is here? God only knows what things you will see, and what troubles you'll have to contend with – cold, hunger, penury, the lot. Bad people are everywhere, but you won't find good ones easily. When it comes to your standing, it's the same everywhere, whether in the country or in the capital. Unless you see life in St Petersburg, it will seem to you, living here, that you're the world's most important person; and it's the same in all respects, my dear! You're well educated, smart and good. I'm an old lady: all I have left is you to gladden my eyes. God willing, you'll get married, maybe have children, and I could look after them – your life would be free of trouble, and free of cares, and you could live it out peacefully and quietly, envying no one; but there, what if things don't turn out well? Then you might remember my words… stay, Sashenka, please!"

He coughed and gave a sigh, but didn't say a word.

"Just take a look outside!" she said, opening the door to the balcony. "Won't you be sorry to leave this corner of the world? A whiff of fresh air blew into the room from the balcony. From the house, a wood of linden, dog rose, bird cherry and lilac spread as far as the eye could see.

Between the trees, flowers of all colours could be glimpsed, paths ran in all directions; beyond, a lake quietly lapped its shores, bathed on one side by the golden rays of the morning sun, its surface as smooth as a mirror; on the other side, it was a deep blue, like the sky reflected in it, the surface barely ruffled. Fields sown with grain of many colours, stretching in a semicircle around the dark wood, rippled in the breeze.

Anna Pavlovna, shielding her eyes from the sun with one hand, pointed out these sights in turn to her son.

"Just look," she said, "at the beauty with which God has clothed our fields! Over there you have fields of rye from which we will reap a harvest of as much as 4,000 bushels alone; over there you have wheat and buckwheat; only this year it doesn't look as if the buckwheat will be as good as last year's crop. And look at the wood: see how big it's grown! Just think, how great is God's wisdom! The firewood from our property will bring in at least a thousand. And then there's the game as well! And it's all yours, my son – I'm just your bailiff. Look at the lake; what a delight – truly divine! The lake is positively teeming with fish like ruff, perch and carp, enough to feed us all, including the servants; the only fish we need to buy is sturgeon. Over there, your cattle and horses are grazing. Here you alone are the master, but there, maybe everyone will be bossing you around. And here you are, wanting to run away from this heaven on earth to somewhere or other where, God forbid, you may end up floundering in some maelstrom... Stay here!"

He remained silent.

"You're not even listening," she said. "What is it you're staring at so intently?"

Pensively, without saying a word, he pointed to the far distance. Anna Pavlovna looked and her face fell. In the distance between the fields a road snaked beyond the woods, a road leading to the Promised Land, to St Petersburg. Anna Pavlovna fell silent for a while until she felt strong enough to speak.

"So, that's it!" She pronounced the words despondently. "Well, my dear, have it your way! Go, if you feel so strongly that you must leave; I won't try to keep you! At least you won't be able to say that your mother held you back and ruined your youth and your life."

CHAPTER I

The poor mother! This is the reward you get for your love. Is that what you expected? Well, the fact of the matter is that mothers don't expect rewards. There's no rhyme or reason – they just love. Do you achieve greatness and fame, are you proud, is your name on everyone's lips, do your deeds resound around the world? Then your mother trembles with joy, she weeps, laughs and prays long and ardently. But you, the son, rarely think of sharing your success with the woman who bore you. Are you lacking in wit or spirit, has nature denied you beauty, are your heart and body dogged by ill health, do people shun you, and is there no place for you among them? Then so much the bigger is your place in a mother's heart, and so much more tightly does she enfold you in her arms, ill-favoured, failed creature though you are, and so much the longer and more fervently does she pray for you.

Are we to call Alexander unfeeling because he is bent on leaving home? He was twenty years old. Life has smiled on him from the cradle, his mother has coddled and pampered him, as you would expect with an only child; in his cradle his nanny crooned to him how he would be clothed in gold and never know sorrow; his teachers predicted that he would go far, and on his return home the neighbour's daughter would favour him with her smile. Even Vaska, their old cat, was more affectionate to him than any other member of the household.

Sorrow, tears, hardship were all things he had only heard about as if they were some kind of disease which had never actually manifested itself, but was lurking somewhere among the masses. That was why to him the future shone with all the radiance of a rainbow and drew him towards something in the distance, although what it was he did not know. He was beguiled by wraith-like visions luring him on, but could not grasp their substance; he heard a chorus of voices which he could not distinguish – were they singing of fame, of love? He couldn't tell, but he was aquiver with a pleasurable anticipation.

He soon came to feel cramped by the world of his home. Nature, his mother's tender loving care, his nanny's veneration, and that of all the household servants, his soft bed, the delicious treats, the purring of Vaska – all those pleasures which are so highly valued in later years, he was happy to trade in for the unknown, an unknown fraught with a seductive and mysterious delight. Even Sofia's love, first love, tender and roseate, was not enough to hold him back. What was that kind of love to him? He dreamt of a tremendous passion which knew no obstacles and crowned glorious exploits. The love he had for Sofia was a small thing compared with the great love yet to come. He dreamt also of the great services he would render his country. He had studied diligently and widely. His diploma stated that he was well versed in a dozen branches of knowledge, and half a dozen ancient and modern languages. But his greatest dream was that of becoming a famous writer. His friends were amazed by his poems. Before him there stretched any number of paths each more attractive than the last. He did not know in which direction to strike out. The only one he failed to see was the one straight ahead of him: if he had seen it, then perhaps he might never have left.

Yes, Alexander had been spoilt growing up at home, but that didn't turn him into a "spoilt brat". Fortunately nature had seen to it that he reacted in a positive way to his mother's love and the adoration of those around him – which, among other things, developed in him early in life temperamental instincts which made him trusting to a fault. This itself may even have stimulated a feeling of self-esteem within him, but, of course, self-esteem itself is nothing but a mould, and what results depends on what mixture is poured into it.

For him a much greater misfortune was the fact that his mother, for all her loving care, was unable to provide him a proper perspective on life, and had failed to prepare him for the battles in store for him as they are for everyone. But for this she would have needed certain skills, sharper wits and a wealth of experience not limited by her narrow rural horizons. It would even have been better for her to have loved him a little less, not to have spent every minute of the day thinking about him, not to have spared him every possible trouble and unpleasantness, not to have done his weeping and suffering for him even in his childhood so as to give him a chance of developing a feeling for the prospect of adversity, and a chance to learn to muster his own resources and consider what lay ahead – in a word to realize that he was a man. How could Anna Pavlovna possibly have understood all this, let alone act on this understanding? Should we perhaps take a closer look?

CHAPTER I

She had already forgotten her son's selfishness. Alexander found her repacking his linen and clothes. Amidst the bustle of the preparations for his journey, it seemed that she had totally forgotten how upset she was.

"Now, Sashenka, take a careful look at where I'm putting everything," she said. "At the very bottom of the trunk, underneath everything else, are the sheets: a dozen. Look and see whether it's all according to the list?"

"Yes, Mummy."

"Everything is marked with your name, you see – it's all dear Sonyushka's work. Without her, our own oafs would never have got it done in time.

"What now? Oh yes, pillowcases. One, two, three, four – there's a whole dozen here. And here are your shirts – three dozen. What fine linen – so lovely! It's Dutch. I went myself to see Vasily Vasilych at the factory; he chose three lengths of the very best quality. Remember, my dear, to check against the receipt whenever you get them back from the laundress: they're all brand new. You won't see many shirts like that in St Petersburg, so they may even try to fob you off with imitations: some people are such crooks – not even afraid of God! Twenty-two pairs of socks... You know, I've just had an idea, why not put your wallet with the cash in a sock? You won't need any money before you get to St Petersburg. Like that, God willing, if anything should happen and someone tries to go through your luggage, they won't find it. And I'll put the letters to your uncle in the same place – I'm sure he'll be so pleased! I mean, it's seventeen years now since we've been in touch – it's hard to believe! Here are your scarves, and here are your handkerchiefs; Sonya still has half a dozen of them. Try not to lose them, my love, they're the best cambric! I bought them at Mikheyev's for two and a quarter each. Well, so much for the linen. Now for the clothes... but where is Yevsei? Why isn't he watching? Yevsei!"

Yevsei was in no hurry to enter the room – and in even less of a hurry to enquire: "How can I be of service?"

"'How can I be of service?'" Aduyeva retorted angrily. "Why didn't you come to watch me pack? And now if something is needed on the journey, you'll be turning everything upside down looking for it! Can't tear yourself away from your girlfriend – what use are you? There's plenty of the day still left; you'll have time later. Is this how you'll be looking after your master when you're there? Now, watch me! You see, this is a good tailcoat, watch where I'm putting it! And, Sashenka, you take good care of it, it's not to be worn every day; the cloth cost sixteen roubles a length. Put it on when you're paying social calls on the right people, and mind where you sit, not just anywhere like your aunt, who practically makes a point of never sitting on an empty chair or sofa, but always manages to plonk herself down on a hat or something of the sort; just the other day she sat down on a plate of jam – what a disgrace! When you go out more casually, wear the tailcoat in dark red. Now waistcoats – one, two, three, four. Two pairs of trousers. These clothes should last you for three years. Whew! I'm tired, and no mistake. I've been running about the whole morning. You can go, Yevsei.

"Sashenka, I want to talk to you about something else. Our guests will soon be here, and we don't have much time." She sat down on the divan and made him sit down beside her.

"Well, Sasha," she began after a short silence, "now you're going somewhere entirely new and different…"

"How do you mean, 'different'? It's only St Petersburg, Mummy!"

"Hold on just a moment, wait until you hear what I have to say. God alone knows what lies in store for you, and what things you will be seeing, both good and bad. I only hope that Our Heavenly Father will give you strength; but you, my dear, whatever you do, don't forget him, and remember: without faith there is no salvation anywhere or in anything. No matter how high you rise, no matter what high society you'll be moving in – after all, we are just as good as others, your father was a member of the nobility, a major – remember to humble yourself before the Lord God, pray in happiness and in sorrow, and don't go by that old proverb: 'The common man never crosses himself until he hears thunder.' Some people, when things are going well for them, never even go near a church, but when they're in trouble – well, there they are, lighting one-rouble candles and giving alms to the poor: and that's a great sin. And while we're on the subject of the poor, don't throw money away on them, and don't give too much. There's no point

CHAPTER I

in being generous, they'll just spend it on drink and have a good laugh at your expense. I know you have a soft heart, and you would probably give away more than just small change. So please don't. God will give. Will you promise me you'll attend church and go to Mass on Sundays?"

She sighed.

Alexander remained silent. He remembered that while he was studying at the university and living in the provincial capital he wasn't too keen on going to church, and in the country he only accompanied his mother to church to please her. He was ashamed to lie, so he just kept quiet. His mother understood his silence and sighed again.

"Well, I won't try to force you," she continued. "You're still young, how can you be expected to be as churchgoing as oldsters like us? I expect your duties will prevent you, and you'll stay up late in the company of your society friends, and get up late the next morning. God will be understanding because of your youth. But don't worry, you have a mother. She won't sleep late. As long as a drop of blood remains in my veins, my eyes can still shed tears, and God tolerates my sins, if I don't have the strength to walk, I'll drag myself on my knees to the church door; I'll give up my last breath and offer up my last tear for you, my dear. I'll pray for your health, for your honours, promotions and decorations, and for every blessing that heaven and earth can bestow upon you. Surely Our Merciful Father will not reject the prayers of a poor old woman? I want nothing for myself. Let everything be taken from me, my health, my life, strike me blind, just as long as every joy, every happiness is granted you…"

Before she could finish, tears welled up in her eyes.

Alexander sprang up from his seat.

"Mummy…" he said.

"No sit, sit!" she responded, quickly wiping away her tears. "I still have a lot left to say… Now, whatever is it I wanted to say? – it's just slipped my mind… You see what's happened to my memory… Oh, yes! Keep the fasts, my dear; that's supremely important! Wednesdays and Fridays, well, God will overlook that; but Lent itself, God forbid! Take Mikhailo Mikhailych: he passes for an intelligent man, and what do we see? Whether it's forbidden or not, he gorges on meat anyway, even during Holy Week. It positively makes your hair stand on end! All right, he helps the poor; does that make his charity acceptable to the Lord? Did you know that he once gave ten roubles to an old man, who took it but turned away and spat? Everyone is very respectful in his presence, and God knows what they say to him, but behind his back, whenever his name comes up, they cross themselves as if he were the very Devil."

Alexander listened as patiently as he could, turning to look out of the window from time to time at the road in the distance.

She fell silent for a minute.

"Above all, take care of your health," she went on. "If you're taken seriously ill – God forbid! – write... and I'll make every effort to come to you. Who will be there to look after you? They won't scruple to rob even a sick man. Don't walk the streets at night, and avoid anyone who looks dangerous. Don't waste your money... please, save it for a rainy day! Spend it prudently! Money can be a curse: all evil comes from it, as well as all good. Don't squander it, don't cultivate extravagant tastes. You'll be getting 2,500 roubles from me on the dot every year. Two thousand five hundred is a tidy sum! Don't go in for luxuries of any kind, absolutely not, but don't deny yourself anything you can afford, and don't begrudge yourself the occasional treat. Don't get into the habit of drinking wine – no, it's man's worst enemy! And another thing" – here she lowered her voice – "be careful with women! I should know! Some are so shameless that they will come and throw their arms around your neck when they see someone like you."

She looked lovingly at her son.

"That's enough, Mummy; what about some breakfast?" he said with an edge of annoyance.

"Right now, right now... just one more thing..."

"Don't go after married women," she hastened to add, "there's no greater sin! It says in the Bible: 'Thou shalt not covet thy neighbour's wife.' If some woman seems to have marriage in mind – God forbid – don't even think about it! Once they spot someone with money, and good-looking into the bargain, they won't let go. But if your boss or some prominent person or rich aristocrat should take a fancy to you and wants you to marry his daughter, that would be all right – but

CHAPTER I

write to me, and I'll manage somehow or other to come and look her over just to make sure that they're not trying to saddle you with some old maid or some good-for-nothing they're just trying to get off their hands. Anyone would be delighted to reel in a catch like you. But if you should happen to fall in love yourself and it's with a nice young woman, then, well…" – and here she lowered her voice even further – "…we can forget about Sonyushka." (The old lady allowed her love for her son to get the better of her scruples.) "How did Maria Karpovna ever get such an idea into her head! Her daughter is no match for you. Just a country girl. There are better candidates who would set their caps at you."

"Sofia! No, Mummy, I will never forget her," said Alexander.

"Never mind, my love, calm down! No need to take it seriously. You'll find a position, you'll come back, and the Lord will provide; there will be plenty of brides! And if you haven't forgotten her by then – well, so be it… and so…"

She wanted to add something, but couldn't quite bring herself to say it, and then bent towards his ear and asked him softly:

"But will you remember… your mother?"

"So that's what you've been trying to say," he said, interrupting her. "Better to order whatever there is to eat, scrambled eggs or whatever. Forget you? How could you even think it! God would punish me…"

"Stop that, Sasha, don't place yourself in harm's way like that! No matter what happens, if such a sin were committed, let me be the only one to suffer for it. You're young, you're only just beginning life, you'll make friends, you'll get married – your young wife will take the place of your mother, and that's the way it is… No! May God bless you, just as I bless you."

She kissed his forehead, thus concluding her homily.

"How come no one is coming?" she said. "No Maria Karpovna, no Anton Ivanych, not even the priest. Mass must be over by now! Ah yes, someone is coming! Anton Ivanych, I think… so it is, talk of the Devil."

Everyone knows an Anton Ivanych. He's like the Wandering Jew. He has been with us from time immemorial and he is everywhere, and has never become extinct. He was a guest at feasts in ancient Greece and banquets in ancient Rome; he has, of course, also partaken of the fatted calf sacrificed by a happy father to welcome the return of his prodigal son.

Here in Russia, he has assumed various forms; the form taken by this particular person was as follows: he owns twenty souls, mortgaged over and over again; he lives in what is virtually a peasant's hut or a strange kind of structure which looks like a barn from the outside – the entrance is somewhere round the back, and you have to clamber over some logs by the wattle fence in order to enter; for twenty years, however, he has been telling everyone that, come next spring, he is going to start building a new house. He doesn't keep house, or any servants to do it for him. None of his acquaintances has ever been entertained to dinner, supper or even a cup of tea there, but neither is there anyone at whose house *he* hasn't been entertained at least fifty times a year. Formerly, he went about clothed in wide and baggy trousers and a knee-length pleated coat, now for everyday wear he sports a frock coat and trousers, and on high days and holidays he appears in a tailcoat, but God only knows of what style. He has a well-fed look, because he has no worries, no cares and nothing to upset him, although he pretends that his whole existence is weighed down with the woes and cares of others, but we all know that the woes and cares of others do not shrink us: that's just the way it is with people.

As a matter of fact, Anton Ivanych was of no use to anyone, but no ceremonial occasion, no wedding, no funeral was complete without him. He was in attendance at every formal dinner and party, every family discussion; no one could take a step without him. Lest it be thought that perhaps he was particularly helpful, or that he might be entrusted with some important errands, or perhaps offer useful advice or could handle some piece of business – absolutely not! No one would trust him with any function of that kind; he was as incompetent as he was ignorant: he couldn't help with anything at the courts either as an intermediary or as a conciliator – he was of no use whatsoever.

However, people would ask him to pass on a greeting to someone if he happened to be passing by, and this chore he performed unfailingly, and just as unfailingly would happen to be available to stay for lunch.

CHAPTER I

People would also ask him to tell someone or other that a certain paper had been received, although he wouldn't be told exactly what paper it was, or to deliver a jar of honey or a handful of seeds with instructions not to spill any, and they would ask him to remind them when it was someone's name day. They would also make use of him in matters which they thought unsuitable for a servant. "We can't send Petrushka," they would say. "Before you know it, he would get it all muddled. No, it's better to let Anton Ivanych go!" Or: "It wouldn't do to send a servant, someone might be offended; really better to send Anton Ivanych."

How astonished everyone would be if there were ever a dinner or party at which for some reason he failed to appear!

"But where's Anton Ivanych?" everyone would be asking in surprise. "What's happened to him, why isn't he here?" The dinner simply didn't feel right without him. So then they would appoint someone to go and find out what was wrong; was he sick, had he gone away? And if he *was* sick, even a family member would not have enjoyed such care and attention.

Anton Ivanych approached to take the hand of Anna Pavlovna.

"My respects, Anna Pavlovna! Allow me to congratulate you on your new acquisition."

"What acquisition, Anton Ivanych?" she asked, looking herself up and down.

"Why, that little bridge down by the gate. I see you've just had it put up? I could hear that the planks weren't bobbing about under the wheels, so I took a look, and sure enough they were new!"

Whenever he met someone he knew, he would usually start by congratulating them on something or other, be it a fast, the spring or autumn, and if after the thaw frost was on its way, then he would congratulate them on the frost, and if a thaw was on its way in after a frost – then on the thaw...

This time, however, none of these opportunities presented themselves, but he was sure to come up with something.

"Alexandra Vasilyevna, Matryona Mikhailovna and Pyotr Sergeich send you their regards," he said.

"My sincere thanks, Anton Ivanych! Are their children in good health?"

"Thank God. I bring you God's blessing; the father will be here soon after me. "Have you heard about our Semyon Arkhipych, Anna Pavlovna?"

"What about him?" Asked Anna Pavlovna apprehensively.

"Well, he passed away."

"Oh no! When was it?"

"Yesterday morning. I found out yesterday evening; some lad rode up to tell me. I left right away, and didn't sleep all night. Everyone was in tears and needed consoling, and someone had to do some organizing; everyone else was helpless with grief – except me alone."

"God in heaven! That's life! But how could it have happened? Just last week he sent his regards through you!"

"Yes, my dear lady, but he had been poorly for quite some time, and he was an old man; it's a wonder he lasted so long!"

"What do you mean, 'old'? He was only a year older than my late husband. Well, God rest his soul!" Anna Pavlovna said, crossing herself. "I'm so sorry for poor Fedosya, left alone with the children on her hands. What a terrible thing, with five of them, and almost all girls! When is the funeral?"

"Tomorrow."

"Of course, everyone has their sorrow, Anton Ivanych; here I am seeing my son off."

"What can we do, Anna Pavlovna, we're all mere mortals! We are born to suffering, as it says in the Bible."

"Please don't mind my upsetting you – we'll get over our grief together; you love us like one of your own."

"Oh my dear lady, who could I love more than you? There are so few like you! You don't know your own worth. I've so much on my plate – can't get my building project out of my mind. I spent the whole of yesterday morning wrangling with the contractor, but somehow we just couldn't agree. Then I think, I must go to her: she's all alone there, what will she do without me? She's not a young woman, her head must be whirling."

CHAPTER I

"God bless you, Anton Ivanych, for not forgetting us. I'm really not myself; can't keep a thought in my head, I'm in a total fog. My throat hurts from crying. Please have a bite to eat; you're tired, and you must be hungry."

"Thank you so much. I have to confess that on the way over I did take a drop and snatched a bite at Pyotr Sergeich's. But that doesn't really count. The father's on his way, and he'll give you his blessing! Well look, here he is at the door!"

The priest came in, together with Maria Karpovna and her plump, rosy-cheeked daughter, who was smiling, but whose eyes showed signs of recent tears. Sofia's eyes and the expression on her face clearly proclaimed: "I will love simply, unreservedly, I will look after my husband and be a nurse to him, I will obey him in all things and never appear to be cleverer than him, although how would it be possible to be cleverer than one's husband in any case? It would be sinful! I will keep house for him diligently, sew and bear him half a dozen children. I will myself feed, nurse, dress them and make their clothes." Her plump cheek, fresh complexion and splendid bosom fully confirmed her promise about children. But the tears in her eyes and the sadness of her smile lent her a less prosaic appearance at that moment.

First of all, a prayer service was conducted for which Anton Ivanych called in the servants, lit a candle, took the book from the priest when he had finished reading from it and handed it to the sexton; then he poured some holy water into a bottle, put it in his pocket and said, "It's for Agafya Nikitishna." They sat down at the table. Apart from Anton Ivanych and the priest, no one else, as was customary, touched any of the food, but Anton Ivanych did ample justice to the Homeric repast. Anna Pavlovna cried all the time and furtively wiped away the tears.

"It's time to stop wasting your tears, Anna Pavlovna, my dear lady," said Anton Ivanych with feigned indignation, filling his glass with liqueur. "After all, it's not as if you're sending him to be slaughtered."

Then, after swallowing half the contents of his glass, he smacked his lips.

"What a fine liqueur! What fragrance! Nothing like it anywhere else in our province, my dear lady!" he said in a tone of great satisfaction.

"It's... thr... three... ye... years old!" she managed to articulate between sobs. "We've op... opened it... today, just... for you!"

"Anna Pavlovna, it pains me so much to see you like this," Anton Ivanych started up again. "There's no one to assuage your grief. I would if I could, but it's beyond me."

"Judge for yourself, Anton Ivanych, my only son, and far away; I could die, and there would be no one even to bury me."

"But what about us then? What, am I a stranger to you? And what's all this about being in a hurry to die? Before you know it, you'll be married and I'll be dancing at your wedding. So let's have no more of these tears!"

"I can't help it, Anton Ivanych, really, I can't; I don't even know myself where these tears are coming from."

"You can't keep a young man like that locked up! Give him the freedom to spread his wings, and see what wonders he will work, what success he will achieve!"

"I sincerely hope you're right! But you've taken so little of the pie; do take some more!"

"Well, perhaps just this little piece, thank you. To your health, Alexander Fyodorych! And best wishes for your journey! Do come back soon – and get married too! But why are you flushing, Sofia Vasilyevna?"

"Oh, no... I was just..."

"Oh, you young people make me laugh."

"You really make people forget their troubles, Anton Ivanych," said Anna Ivanovna. "You're such a comfort. May God bless you with good health. Please have a little more liqueur."

"Of course, my dear lady: your son is leaving, we must drink to that!"

The meal came to an end. The coachman had long since loaded the luggage into the carriage, and it had been brought round to the porch. The servants came running out one after another. One carried the trunk, another a package, and a third brought a bag and went back for something else. Like flies around a drop of honey, they clustered around the carriage with everyone eager to offer help and advice.

"Better lay the trunk this way," said one, "and put the food hamper over here."

CHAPTER I

"But where are they going to put their legs?" another one put in. "Better put the trunk in lengthwise with the hamper beside it."

"That way the feather bed will slide off, if the trunk is in lengthwise; better turn it round sideways. Now, what else? Oh yes, has anyone packed the boots?"

"I don't know. Who did the packing?"

"It wasn't me. Someone go and take a look – couldn't they be upstairs?"

"Well, you go!"

"What about you – can't you see I have no time?"

"Look, here's something else; don't forget it!" one of the girls shouted, poking a package through the crowd of heads.

"Give it here!"

"Cram this into the trunk somehow: it must have been left behind," said another, standing on the footboard, holding brush and a comb in her outstretched hand.

"Nowhere to put it now," a stout footman scolded her. "Get out of the way; can't you see the trunk is right near the bottom?"

"It's the mistress's orders, but what's it to me? The hell with it!"

"Well all right, just give it here, it can go in the side pocket."

The shaft horse kept on raising and shaking its head, making the bell ring shrilly every time it did so, reminding everyone of the impending departure, while the trace horses stood still, apparently deep in thought with their heads lowered, as they contemplated the delights of the journey ahead, occasionally waving their tails or stretching out their lower lips in the direction of the shaft horse.

The fateful moment was at hand, and another prayer was said.

"Everyone sit down!" commanded Anton Ivanych. "Kindly be seated, Alexander Fyodorych. And you sit down too, Yevsei, yes, sit down!" And just for a second, he himself sat down on the very edge of a chair.

"And now, Godspeed!"

At this very moment, Anna Pavlovna burst into tears and flung her arms around Alexander's neck.

"Goodbye, goodbye, my love – when will I ever see you again?..."

Suddenly her words were drowned by the sound of another bell from a cart which came hurtling into the courtyard drawn by three horses. A young man covered in dust jumped down from the cart, ran into the room and threw his arms around Alexander's neck.

"Pospelov!... Aduyev!..." they both exclaimed at the same time, as they embraced.

"What are you doing here, where have you come from?"

"From home, I've been galloping day and night to get here to say goodbye."

"My friend! My friend! What a true friend you are," said Aduyev with tears in his eyes, "to have galloped 160 versts just to say goodbye! To think that there's such friendship in the world! For ever, right?" Alexander declared fervently, clasping his friend's hand, and crushing him in his embrace.

"To the grave!" his friend replied, grasping the other's hand even more tightly and returning his hug.

"Write to me!"

"Yes, of course, and you too!"

Anna Pavlovna did not know how to express the affection she felt for Pospelov. The leave-takings took another half-hour, before everyone was ready for the departure.

They all escorted the travellers as far as the wood on foot. On their way through the dark passageway to the porch, Sofia and Alexander rushed into each other's arms.

"Sasha! Dear Sasha!... Sonechka!" they whispered, and their words were silenced by a kiss.

"Will you forget me when you're there?" she said tearfully.

"How little you know me! I will return, believe me, and no other woman will ever..."

"Here, take this quickly – a lock of my hair and a ring."

He swiftly pocketed both.

Anna Pavlovna led the way with her son and Pospelov, followed by Maria Karpovna and her daughter, with the priest and Anton Ivanych bringing up the rear. The carriage followed some distance behind. The coachman could barely restrain the horses. At the gate, the servants crowded round Yevsei.

CHAPTER I

And cries of "Goodbye, Yevsei Ivanych – goodbye, old friend, don't forget us," rang out from every side.

"Goodbye, my friends, goodbye – remember me fondly!"

"Goodbye, Yevseyushka, goodbye my darling," said his mother, embracing him. "Take this icon, it's my blessing. Keep the faith, Yevsei. Don't let me see you joining the infidels, otherwise I'll be cursing you! Don't get drunk and don't steal, and serve your master loyally and faithfully. Goodbye, goodbye…"

She turned and left, covering her face with her apron.

"Goodbye, mother!" Yevsei muttered casually.

A twelve-year-old girl rushed up to him.

"You should say goodbye to your little sister!" one of the women urged.

"Hey, where are you going!" said Yevsei, and kissed her. "All right, goodbye, goodbye; now, off with you and your bare feet, and go back home!"

The last one left was Agrafena, who was standing apart from the others. Her face had a greenish tinge.

"Goodbye, Agrafena Ivanovna," said Yevsei, dragging out the words, and raising his voice, even stretching out his hands to her.

She submitted to his embrace, but did not return it, and just made a wry grimace.

"Here, take this!" she said, taking out a package of something from under her pinafore and thrusting it at him.

"Well, I suppose you'll be gadding about with those St Petersburg girls then!" she added without looking him straight in the eye – but that look expressed all her feelings of hurt and jealousy.

"Me, gad about?" Yevsei began. "May the Lord strike me dead on the spot – let Him pluck out my eyes, and may the earth open up and swallow me, if I ever did any such thing…"

"All right, all right!" she mumbled, not entirely convinced. "But with you, I…"

"Oh, I almost forgot," said Yevsei, and produced from his pocket a soiled pack of cards and held it out to Agrafena. "Here, take these to remember me by; you won't be able to get any here."

She stretched out her hand.

"Give it to me, Yevsei Ivanych!" Proshka called out from somewhere in the crowd.

"Give them to you! I'd sooner burn them!" And he put the cards back in his pocket.

"Come on, give them to me, you fool!" said Agrafena.

"No, Agrafena Ivanovna, do whatever you want, but I'm not giving them to you; you would play with him. Goodbye!"

Without looking round, and with a wave of the hand he sauntered after the carriage, which it seemed he could have carried off single-handedly on his shoulders along with Alexander, the coachman, as well as the horses.

"To hell with you!" said Agrafena, watching him go and wiping away the tears she was shedding with the corner of her kerchief.

Everyone came to a halt at the grove. While Anna Pavlovna was sobbing her farewell to her son, Anton Ivanych patted one of the horses on the neck, and then took it by the nostrils and shook it back and forth. The horse immediately manifested its displeasure by baring its teeth and snorting.

"Tighten the shaft horse's saddle girth – look, the pad's sliding to one side," he said to the coachman.

The coachman took a look at the pad and, seeing that it was in its proper place, didn't stir from his coach box, but just adjusted the breast band a little with his whip.

"Have it your way," said Anton Ivanych. "Anyway, it's time to go – Anna Pavlovna, time to stop tormenting yourself! Alexander – time to take your seat: you have to get to Shishkov before nightfall. Goodbye, goodbye, may God bless you with happiness, success, honours, worldly goods and everything that's good. And you, be on your way; get the horses moving and watch out for the hill and go easy!" he added for the benefit of the coachman.

Alexander, now in tears, took his seat in the carriage, and Yevsei went up to his mistress, knelt at her feet and kissed her hand. She gave him a five-rouble note.

"Listen, Yevsei, and remember: serve your master well and I'll marry you to Agrafena, otherwise…"

CHAPTER I

She was unable to complete her sentence. Yevsei climbed up to the box. The coachman, impatient because of the long delay, came to life, pulled his cap down firmly, sat up straight and took up the reins; the horses moved off at a slow trot. The coachman whipped the trace horses one by one and, plunging forward, they broke into a gallop, and the troika sped along the road towards the wood. The crowd that had gathered to see them off were left behind silent and still in a cloud of dust until the coach had completely disappeared from view. Anton Ivanych was the first to break the silence.

"All right, time to go home!" he said.

Alexander looked back for as long as he could from the coach, and then fell upon the cushion and buried his face in it.

"Don't leave me in such a state of distress, Anton Ivanych," said Anna Pavlovna. "Stay for dinner!"

"Very well, my dear lady, I'll be happy to, and perhaps I will even stay for supper."

"Then you might as well stay the night."

"But how can I, the funeral is tomorrow!"

"Yes, of course, but I'm not forcing you. Say hello to Fedosya Petrovna for me; tell her that my heart goes out to her in her grief, and I would pay her a visit myself if it were not that God, you know, has sent me my own sorrow: I've had to say goodbye to my son."

"I will, I will, I won't forget."

"Sashenka, my love," she whispered, looking round. "But he's gone, just disappeared!"

Aduyeva spent the whole day sitting in silence, going without dinner and supper. Anton Ivanych on the other hand had no trouble talking, dining and eating his supper.

Her only contribution to the conversation was the occasional "Where is my dear boy now?"

"By now he must be in Neplyuyeva. No, I'm wrong, he can't be there yet, but just approaching it. He'll stop there for some tea," replied Anton Ivanych.

"No, he never drinks tea at this time."

That was how Anna Pavlovna was mentally accompanying him on his journey. Later on – when, according to her reckoning, he must have reached St Petersburg – she spent her time praying, telling her fortune from the cards or talking about him to Maria Karpovna.

But what about him?

We shall meet him again in St Petersburg.

Chapter 2

PYOTR IVANYCH ADUYEV, Alexander's uncle, at the age of twenty had, just like his nephew, been sent to St Petersburg by his older brother, Alexander's father, and had now been living there continuously for seventeen years. After his brother's death he had stopped corresponding with his relatives, and Anna Pavlovna had heard nothing from him since the time when he had sold the small estate he had owned not far from her own.

In St Petersburg he passed for a man of some wealth, and not without reason. He was in the service of an important personage as an official in charge of special assignments, and sported a number of ribbons on the lapel of his tailcoat. He rented a good apartment on one of the smarter streets, kept three servants and the same number of horses. He was not old, but was known rather as "a man in his prime" – somewhere between thirty-five and forty. As a matter of fact, he preferred to keep his age to himself, not as a matter of petty pride, but rather on account of a kind of careful calculation, as if he were bent on insuring his life on more advantageous terms. However, there was no suggestion that behind his reticence about his age there lurked some vanity, and that this reticence would somehow succeed in impressing the fair sex.

He was a tall, well-proportioned man with pronounced features set in a lustreless dark face. He moved with an even, graceful carriage, and his manner was reserved, but pleasant – the type who is usually described as a *bel homme*.*

His face conveyed the same element of reserve, of a kind of self-possession, and his eyes would not let you see through them into his soul. It was his feeling that this would be uncomfortable both for himself and others. This was how he appeared in company. Of course, this is not to say that his face was wooden: no, it was just untroubled. Only at times did it betray signs of weariness – most probably because his work was so demanding. He was thought of as someone both businesslike and efficient. He always dressed with care and with some elegance, but always within the bounds of good taste. His linen was immaculate, his hands were white and had some substance to them, his fingernails long and clear.

One morning, after waking up and ringing, his servant brought in three letters together with his tea, as well as the news that a young gentleman who called himself Alexander Fyodorych Aduyev had arrived, and had called him – Pyotr Ivanych – his "uncle", and promised to call back some time after eleven.

Pyotr Ivanych, as was his custom, took the news calmly, reacting only with a slight quickening of his attention and an equally slight raising of his eyebrows.

"Very well, you may go," he told the servant.

Then he picked up one of the letters, was on the point of opening it, but stopped to think for a moment.

"It's that nephew from the country – that's surprising!" he grumbled to himself. "I had hoped that the people in those parts had forgotten all about me! Anyway, no need to pretend to be civil! I'll just talk my way out of it…"

He rang again.

"When that gentleman comes, tell him that when I got up this morning I got an urgent message to leave for the factory, and won't be back for three months."

"Yes sir, but what should I do about the presents?"

"What presents?"

"A servant brought them: it was the mistress," he said, "who sent them from the country."

"Presents?"

"Yes sir, a tub of honey, a sack of dried raspberries…"

Pyotr Ivanych shrugged.

"As well as two lengths of linen and some preserves…"

"Yes, I see, it must be good cloth…"

"Yes, it is, and the preserves are sweetened."

"Well, off with you, I'll come and see in a moment."

He picked up one of the letters, opened it and glanced at a page.

CHAPTER 2

It looked like that Old Slavonic-style large writing. The letter *v* had been replaced by two struck-through vertical lines, and the letter *k* simply by two lines; and there was no punctuation.

Aduyev started to read out the letter under his breath:

"Honourable Sir, Mr Pyotr Ivanych,

"I was a close acquaintance and friend of your late parents; I also used to play with you quite often when you were a child, and was frequently a guest at your parents' table. So I feel confident that I can count on your help and goodwill, and that you will not have forgotten old Vasily Tikhonych. All of us here have the fondest memories of you and your parents, and pray for you...

"What is this rubbish? Who is this from?" said Pyotr Ivanych, glancing at the signature. "Vasily Zayezzhalov! Zayezzhalov? For the life of me, I can't remember. What does he want from me?"

He continued reading.

"I don't mean to impose on you, but I do have this very humble favour to ask of you – I am sure you won't refuse. In St Petersburg, I'm sure it's not like it is for us back here. Up there, you know what's what, and everything that's going on. I've had this damned lawsuit dumped on me and it has been hanging over me for seven years now, and I can't fight it off. Do you happen to remember that grove about two versts from my village? The court made a mistake with the deed of sale, and my adversary, Medvedev, has seized on it and won't let go. There's one clause in it which he claims is forged. He's the same Medvedev who used to poach fish on your grounds; your late father drove him away in disgrace and was minded to lodge a complaint with the governor against him for his impertinence, but he was a kind-hearted man, may his soul rest in peace, and he let him go. But that rascal should never have been let off. Please be a good fellow and help me, Pyotr Ivanych, the case is now before the National Senate, but I don't know which department, or who is dealing with it, but I'm sure you can find out quickly. Go and see

the various secretaries and senators and try to influence them in my favour; tell them that I'm a victim of a mistake in the deed of sale, yes, a definite mistake; they will do whatever is necessary for you. Oh, and while you're about it, see if you can get the papers granting me an official promotion to a higher grade.

"One more thing, Pyotr Ivanych, dear fellow, a little matter of a most deserving case: please find it in your heart to offer advice, help and sympathy to a poor, downtrodden and innocent victim. There is a councillor in our provincial administration by the name of Drozhov, a man with a heart of gold, not mere flesh and blood, who would die sooner than let down a friend. When I'm in town, there's nowhere else I stay except with him. The moment I arrive I go straight to his place, and stay there for weeks at a time – God forbid that I should even think of staying with anyone else. He gives me food and drink, and after dinner we play cards until late at night. And it's a man like this that they have passed over for promotion, and they are pestering him to send in his resignation. Like a good father, please go to see those bigwigs and make them see what kind of man Afanasy Ivanych really is. Whenever there's work to be done, he does it in a flash; tell them that he is the victim of a trumped-up denunciation engineered by the scheming provincial secretary – they will listen to you – and then send me a letter by the first post. And go and see my old colleague, Kostyakov. I heard from a visitor from St Petersburg by the name of Studenitsyn, whom you probably know, that he lives at Peski; the neighbourhood kids will show you his house; and write back to me by the same post – and make an effort to find out whether he is alive, in good health, what he is doing and whether he remembers me. Get to know him and make friends with him, he's a great fellow, easy-going and a real clown. Before I finish I just have one more little favour to ask…"

Aduyev stopped reading, slowly tore the letter into four pieces, and threw them into the waste-paper basket under the desk. Then he stretched and yawned.

He took up another letter, and started to read it, once again under his breath.

CHAPTER 2

"'Dear brother, kind sir, Pyotr Ivanych!' Who can this be, calling herself my sister?" said Aduyev, looking at the signature. "Maria Gorbatova…" He looked up towards the ceiling, trying to recall…

"Who on earth can it be?… Sounds somehow familiar. Yes, now I've got it, my brother was married to a Gorbatova, so it must be her sister; yes, now I remember…"

He frowned, and continued reading.

"'Although fate has kept us apart, perhaps for ever, and there's a great gulf between us, the years have slipped away…'"

He skipped a few lines and went on reading:

"One memory I will carry to my grave was when we were strolling together around our lake, when you, at the risk of your life and limb, ventured into the water up to your knees to fetch me a big yellow flower growing among the reeds. There was some kind of sap trickling from the stalk which got our hands dirty, and you filled your cap with water so that we could wash the dirt off. That made us laugh so much, and how happy I was then! Ever since, I've kept that flower pressed inside a book…"

Aduyev stopped reading. Clearly, something in what he had read was bothering him; he even shook his head in disbelief.

He read on.

"'And do you still have that ribbon, that you filched from one of my drawers in spite of all my protestations and pleading?' I pinched her ribbon?" he said aloud, scowling. He fell silent and, skipping a few more lines, continued reading.

"'I have resigned myself to life as a single woman and am very happy with it, but no one can stop me recalling those blissful old days…' Ah, an old maid," Pyotr Ivanych thought to himself. "No wonder she can't get those yellow flowers out of her head! What else does she have to say?

"Are you married, my dear brother, and if so, to whom? Who is that dear companion who now graces the path of your existence? Tell me her name; I will love her like my own sister, and in my dreams I will join

your two images and pray for you both. And if you are not married, what's the reason – please write and tell me frankly; there's no one here to read your secrets, I will lock them in my bosom, and someone would have to tear out my heart to get at them. Please write back without delay: I'm burning with impatience to read your ineffable words...

"Well – how's that for your own 'ineffable' words!" Pyotr Ivanych thought to himself.

"'I didn't know,'" he read on,

"that dear Sasha would suddenly take it into his head to visit our magnificent capital – how lucky he will be to see those beautiful houses and shops, to enjoy such luxury and to clasp to his bosom the uncle he adores, while I will be shedding tears as I am reminded of those happy days. If I had known he would be leaving, I would have spent the days and nights embroidering a blackamoor with two dogs on a cushion for you; you won't believe how often I have burst into tears at the sight of that design; what could be more sacred than friendship and loyalty?... Now I am possessed by a single thought, and I will devote my days to it, but I don't have any good wool here. So may I most humbly request you, my dear brother, as soon as possible and from the best shop, to procure some of the highest-quality English wool for embroidering the designs which I have enclosed. But what am I saying? A most horrifying thought has frozen the pen in my hand! What if you have already forgotten us, and why should you even remember this poor unfortunate who has hidden herself from the world and sheds tears? But no, I refuse to believe that you could possibly be a brute like all other men – no! My heart tells me that amidst all the luxury and pleasure of our magnificent capital you still have the same feelings as always for all of us. It is this thought which is balm to my soul. Forgive me, I cannot continue, my hand is trembling.

"*I remain to the grave,*

yours,

Maria Gorbatova.

CHAPTER 2

"P.S. My brother, do you happen to have any nice books? If you have any to spare, please send them. As I turn every page, I will be reminded of you, and will weep, otherwise please buy some new ones, but not expensive ones. I hear that there are some good ones by Mr Zagoskin and Mr Marlinsky,* so perhaps those; otherwise, I've also seen something in the papers about a book called On Prejudice *by Mr Puzin* – please send it, I can't stand prejudices."*

After finishing the letter, Aduyev felt like throwing it into the same waste basket as the one before, but he stopped himself.

"No," he thought, "I'll keep it: there are people who value letters like this; some people even collect them, maybe I can give it to someone, and he will owe me a favour. He threw the letter into the beaded basket hanging on the wall and then picked up the third letter and began to read it.

"My dearest brother-in-law Pyotr Ivanych,
"Do you remember the send-off we gave you when you left seventeen years ago?
"Well, now it has been God's will that I should be blessing my own son on his long journey. Be kind to him, my dear, and remember our dear departed Fyodor Ivanych, whom Sashenka resembles in every way. God alone knows the anguish in this mother's heart when I saw him off on his journey into the unknown. I am sending the person closest to me straight into your care, and told him to take shelter nowhere else..."

Aduyev shook his head once again.
"Stupid old woman!" he said.

"Left to himself he might, because of inexperience, have chosen to stay at an inn, but I know how that would have upset his very own uncle, so I suggested that he go straight to you. What a pleasure it will be for you to meet him! My dear brother-in-law, please give him the benefit of your good counsel and take him under your wing; I hand him straight over into your care."

Once again Pyotr Aduyev paused in his reading, and then resumed.

"As you know, you are the only one he has. Look after him, don't pamper him, but don't be too hard on him either; you can be sure there will be others to do that. He can't count on affection from anyone except his family; he himself is a very sweet boy; once you've set eyes on him you won't want to let him out of your sight. And tell whoever his future boss turns out to be to take care of my Sasha, and to treat him above all with kindness, just as I have always treated him at home. Keep him away from wine and cards. At night, you will no doubt be sleeping in the same room. Now, Sashenka is used to sleeping on his back, and the darling moans a lot during his sleep and tosses and turns; wake him gently and make the sign of the cross over him, and he will soon be asleep peacefully. In the summer, cover his mouth with a handkerchief; he sleeps with his mouth open, and those damned flies start going inside it towards the morning. Also, don't leave him short of money if he should need any..."

Aduyev frowned, but as he continued reading he brightened up.

"I will send him whatever he needs, and I have given him a thousand roubles to take with him, only I don't want him to waste it on trifles or allow strangers to cheat him, and remember that where you are, in the capital, there are a lot of swindlers and other unscrupulous types. But now, forgive me, dear brother-in-law, I've simply grown out of the habit of writing.

"With my sincere respects, your sister-in-law,

"A. Aduyeva.

"P.S. I am sending you some gifts of produce from the country – raspberries from our garden, white honey as pure as tears, Dutch linen, enough for two dozen shirts, and some of my homemade preserves. Please eat and wear these presents in good health, and when they run out, I'll send some more. Keep an eye on Yevsei: he is quiet and

CHAPTER 2

doesn't drink, but it may be that there in the capital he will get into bad habits; if so, don't hesitate to give him a good hiding."

Pyotr Aduyev slowly placed the letter on his desk – and even more slowly picked out a cigar and, after rolling it in his hands, began to smoke it. He spent a long time mulling over what he thought of as a "stunt" that his sister-in-law had pulled on him. He carefully turned the matter over in his mind, comparing how he had been treated and how he should act in his turn. This was how his reasoning proceeded on this matter. He didn't know this nephew of his, and accordingly had no affection for him, and therefore his feelings placed him under no obligation: thus the whole matter should be decided purely on the basis of reason and justice. His brother had married and enjoyed all the benefits of married life, so why should he, Pyotr Ivanych, who had enjoyed none of the benefits of married life, assume any obligations towards his brother's son? No reason at all, of course. But on the other hand, the matter could be viewed from a different angle. His mother had sent the young man directly to him and entrusted him with his care, without even knowing whether he was prepared to shoulder this burden, or even knowing whether he was alive and in a position to do anything for his nephew in St Petersburg. This was stupid of her, of course, but since the deed had been done and the nephew was already in St Petersburg without help, without knowing anyone, without even letters of recommendation, young and inexperienced, did he have the right to leave him at the mercy of fate and strangers, without any guidance or advice? And if he were to meet with some misfortune, would he then have to answer to his conscience?

He also happened to recall how, seventeen years ago, his late brother and Anna Pavlovna herself had seen him off. Naturally, they were unable to do anything for him in St Petersburg, and he had had to make his own way, but he couldn't help remembering her tears, how she had given him her blessing like a mother, her kindness, her pies and, finally, her parting words: "When Sasha grows up" – he was then a three-year-old child – "perhaps you too, my dear, will be kind to him…" At this point Pyotr Ivanych rose and strode quickly to the entrance hall…

"Vasily!" he said. "When my nephew arrives, let him in, and go and see if that room upstairs is free, the one that had recently been rented out. If it is free, then tell them that I want to reserve it for myself. Oh yes, and these presents, what are we going to do with them?"

"Our shopkeeper saw them when they were being brought up, and he asked whether we could spare him the honey. 'I'll give you a good price for it,' he says; and he'll take the raspberries too."

"Excellent! Let him have them; but where will we put the cloth? Couldn't it be used for covers? So put away the cloth and the preserves – we can eat them, they look decent."

Pyotr Ivanych was just about to start shaving when Alexander Fyodorych appeared. He was on the point of throwing his arms around his uncle's neck, whereupon Pyotr Ivanych grasped his nephew's tender, youthful hand in his powerful grip, thereby keeping him at a distance, as if the idea was that he wanted to give himself the pleasure of taking a good look at him, rather than squelching his affectionate impulse by interposing a handshake.

"What your mother wrote was absolutely true," he said. "You're the living image of your late father: I would have recognized you anywhere. In fact, you're even better-looking. Anyway, you won't mind if I continue shaving; you just sit down here where I can see you, and we can chat."

So Pyotr Ivanych carried on doing what he was doing as if there was no one else there, moving his tongue from side to side as he soaped his cheeks. Alexander was so taken aback by this treatment that he was at a loss about how to start the conversation. He put down his uncle's chilly reception to the fact that he had not come straight to him.

"So, how is your mother? Is she well? I imagine she must have aged somewhat?" his uncle asked, grimacing into the shaving mirror.

"She is well, thank God, and sends you her greetings, and so does Auntie Maria Pavlovna," Alexander Fyodorych said shyly. "Auntie told me to embrace you," he said as he stood up, and made as if to kiss his uncle on the cheek, the head, the shoulder or indeed anything within range.

"At her age, your auntie should have more sense, but I see that she's just as foolish as she was twenty years ago…"

CHAPTER 2

Nonplussed, Alexander retreated back to where he had been sitting.
"Did you get a letter, Uncle?" he asked.
"Yes, I did."
"Vasily Tikhonych Zayezzhalov wants your help with a problem…"
"Yes, he wrote to me about it… Are there really such asses still around in your village?"

Alexander was so confounded by his uncle's response, that he couldn't even gather his wits.

"I'm sorry, Uncle…" he began nervously.
"What about?"
"For not coming straight to you, and first putting up at the coaching inn… I didn't know how to find your apartment…"

"No need to apologize. You did the right thing. I don't know what your mother was thinking of, sending you here without even knowing if you could stay here or not. As you can see it's just a bachelor's flat – just for one person – a hallway, a drawing room, a dining room, a study and a workroom, plus a dressing room, and a bathroom – there's no other room. We'd get in each other's way. Anyway, I've found a place for you to stay in this building…"

"Oh, Uncle, how can I thank you for such thoughtfulness?"

Once again he jumped up from where he was sitting in order to express his gratitude both verbally and physically.

"Be careful, be careful, don't touch me," said his uncle, "the razor's terribly sharp, and before you know it you'll be cutting yourself and me."

Alexander realized that in spite of all his efforts on that day he would never succeed in embracing and hugging the uncle he so admired, and decided to try again on another occasion.

"The room is very cheerful," Pyotr Ivanych began, "the view through the windows is of a wall, but you're certainly not going to be sitting by the window all day; if you're at home, you'll be busy doing something, and won't have time to be gazing at the window. And it's not expensive: just forty roubles a month. There's an entrance hall for your servant. You'll have to learn to live by yourself without a nanny right from the start, and how to run a household – in other words, provide your own food and drink – in a word, create a home of your own, or *un chez-soi*,* as the French say. You'll be able to invite any visitors you choose… and incidentally, when I'm dining at home, you are welcome to join me, and at other times – young people around here usually eat at a tavern, but I advise you to send out for your food: it's quieter at home, and you won't run the risk of running into undesirables. All right?"

"I'm really grateful, Uncle…"

"What for? You're family. I'm just doing my duty. Now, I'm going to get dressed and go out; I have my work, and a factory to run…"

"I didn't know you had a factory, Uncle."

"Glass and porcelain; but it's not mine alone, I have three partners."

"Is it doing well?"

"Yes, reasonably; we sell mostly to neighbouring provinces at trade fairs. For the last two years business has been booming! If we do as well for the next five years, so much the better. One of the partners is not too reliable – he only knows how to spend, but I manage to keep him in hand. Well, I'm on my way now. Why don't you go out and look around the city, walk around, have a meal somewhere, and in the evening come back here and we'll have tea? I'll be at home and we can talk. Vasily! Show him the room. And help him to settle in."

"So that's the way it is in St Petersburg…" thought Alexander, sitting in his new home. "If my own uncle is like this, then what are the others going to be like?…"

Young Aduyev paced back and forth in his room, lost in thought, while Yevsei moved around it putting things in order and talking to himself.

"What kind of place is this?" he grumbled. "Pyotr Ivanych has his own kitchen, but would you believe, the stove is only heated once a month, and the servants have to eat out. Good Lord, what strange people! And they're what people call Petersburgers! Where we come from, even dogs have their own bowls to feed from."

Alexander, it seems, was of the same opinion, although he didn't actually say anything. He went to the window, but there was nothing to see but roofs and chimneys, and the blackened, dirty sides of the brick houses… and when he compared that sight with what he had

CHAPTER 2

seen two weeks ago from the window of his home in the country, it made him sad.

He went out into the street: nothing but hustle and bustle, everyone rushing somewhere or other, totally self-absorbed, hardly sparing a glance for the people they passed – and even then it was only to avoid bumping into one another. He thought of his provincial town, where everyone you happened to run into had something of interest to tell you. Here was Ivan Ivanych on his way to meet Pyotr Petrovich – and everyone in town knew why. There was Maria Martynova on her way back from vespers, and Afanasy Savich going fishing. Over there, the constable was galloping like mad from the governor's house to the doctor, and everyone knew that Her Excellency was about to give birth, although in the opinion of the gossips and old ladies it was not nice to anticipate such events. Everyone would be asking "Is it a boy or a girl?" Young ladies would be preparing their Sunday-best caps. Over here, Matvei Matveich would be stepping out with a stout stick sometime between five and six, and everyone knew that it was for his evening constitutional, just as everyone knew that in any case he was suffering from indigestion and would stop by at the old councillor's who, as everyone also knew, would be drinking tea at that time. You couldn't pass anyone in the street without a bow and exchanging a word or two, and even if there was someone you didn't stop to greet, you knew who he was, where he was going and why, and it was clear from the look in his eye that he too knew equally well who you were, where you were going and why. And even when people who didn't know each other and had never seen each other before passed on the street, they would stop and turn around a couple of times, so that when they got home they could describe the clothes and gait of this stranger, and everyone would start speculating and trying to guess who he was, where he was from and what he was doing. But here it took only a look to make someone move out of the way, as if everyone else was an enemy.

To start with, Alexander would stare with typical provincial curiosity at every passing stranger and every respectably dressed person, thinking that they must all be some minister or ambassador, or perhaps a writer: "Could he be so-and-so?" he thought. "Or perhaps that other one?" But soon the novelty wore off – since he seemed to be running into ministers, writers or ambassadors at every step.

When he looked at the houses, that was even drearier, and he was oppressed by those monotonous stone piles which, like colossal mausoleums, seemed to form a single unending, uninterrupted mass. "I'm almost at the end of the street now," he thought, "and then there'll be some relief for my eyes," he thought, "at least a hill, some greenery or a broken-down fence." But no, once again he was confronted with the same stone façade of identical houses with four rows of windows. That street too came to an end, but only to be replaced by a further series of identical houses. Whether you looked right or left, your way was barred by house after house after house, pile of stone after pile of stone, each one the same as the one before... no empty space anywhere to give your eyes a rest; you were blocked on every side – and you felt that people's thoughts and feelings were similarly limited and confined.

Such were the first grim impressions of the provincial in St Petersburg. It was all so bewildering and depressing. No one paid him any attention: he simply felt lost here. There was no novelty, no variety of any kind to distract or entertain him, not even the crowds. His provincial parochialism declared war on everything he saw when he compared it with what he saw at home. He was lost in thought, and started imagining that he was back in his home town. What a delight it was to see! One house with a gabled roof and a little front garden with acacias. On the roof a dovecote had been built; the merchant Izyumin was a pigeon fancier and liked to race them, and that's why he went and built that pigeon loft on the roof. Morning and evening you would find him up there on the roof in his nightcap and dressing gown, whistling and waving a stick with a rag tied on the end. Another house was lit up like a torch; windows practically filled the four sides of the house, which had a flat roof and had been built long ago; you had the feeling that at any moment the house would collapse or set fire to itself; the colour of its timbers had faded to a light grey.

You would be afraid to live in that house, but people actually lived there. At times, it is true, the owner would look at the sagging ceiling, shake his head and mutter: "Will it last until the spring?" followed by:

CHAPTER 2

"Well, let's hope so!" He continued living there, not so much afraid for himself, but rather for his pocket. Next door was the eccentric house of the doctor, painted a rakish red and extending in a semicircle with two wings built like sentry boxes – and all hidden behind greenery was another house. The back of the house gave onto the street and was protected by a fence which stretched for two versts. Through the fence you could see red apples peeping out – a temptation for the small boys. The houses all kept a respectable distance from the churches, which were surrounded by thick grass and tombstones. As for office buildings, you could see that they were – well, office buildings, and no one went near them unless they really needed to, while here, in the capital, they looked no different from the buildings where people lived – and, what is worse, there were houses with shops inside them – what a disgrace! If you were walking in our town, after just two or three streets, you would begin to smell fresh air and find wattle fences, and behind them kitchen gardens, and then even an open field where spring crops were growing. Here you would find quiet and stillness – and yes, tedium; both in the street and among the people – that blissful inactivity! Everyone lives as they please, and there are no crowds; even the chickens wander freely through the streets; goats and cattle nibble the grass, and the little ones fly kites. But being here – it makes him so homesick! And this provincial sighs for the fence outside his window, for that dusty, dirty road, that wobbly bridge, the sign outside the inn. It pains him to see that St Isaac's Cathedral is superior to the one in his home town, and that the hall of the Assembly of the Nobility is bigger than the one back home. When faced by such comparisons, he maintains a resentful silence, although sometimes he dares to say that a piece of such and such cloth, or a certain kind of wine can be had where he comes from at a lower price and of better quality, and that, where he comes from, people wouldn't even look at delicacies from overseas like big crabs or shells, and that you can buy all these fabrics and knick-knacks from foreigners if you want, as long as you don't mind being fleeced by them and are content to be taken in! But how suddenly he cheers up when he compares caviar, pears and a certain kind of bread and observes that they are all better in his home town!

"You mean that's what you call a pear?" he would say. "Where I come from even the *servants* wouldn't touch them!"

The provincial feels even worse when he enters one of these houses bearing a letter from back home. He thinks that he will be met with wide-open arms, that they won't know how to welcome him warmly enough, what chair will be comfortable enough for him, how to entertain him hospitably enough; they will somehow succeed in worming out of him what his favourite dishes are. He imagines how embarrassed he will feel at the attentions lavished upon him, and how finally he will cast aside all conventional constraints and rush to embrace his host and hostess and start calling them by their first names as if they had known each other for twenty years – and they would all end up drinking liqueurs, and maybe even burst into song…

Some hope! They hardly spare him a glance: they frown, apologize for being so busy. If they need to see him about something, it has to be at a time when they are not having dinner or supper, and they have never heard of such a thing as an aperitif, or a little vodka with some appetizers. His host avoids any attempt to embrace him, and gives his guest strange looks. In the room next door, cutlery and glassware can be heard tinkling, and you would think they might invite him, but no: they do their best to hint that he should be leaving. Everything is under lock and key, and doorbells everywhere. All that seems so inhospitable! And what cold, unfriendly faces! But where I come from, you enter boldly, and if they have already eaten, they will start all over again just for the sake of the guest; the samovar stays on the table from morning until night, and even the shops don't have doorbells. Everyone kisses and embraces everyone within range. Neighbours there are real neighbours, neighbours heart and soul, and family members are true kith and kin and would die for one another… it makes your heart sink to think of it.

When Alexander reached Admiralty Square, he was dumbfounded and stood stock-still for an hour in front of the Bronze Horseman, but not with bitterness in his heart like poor Yevgeny,* but in a state of exaltation. He looked at the Neva and the surrounding buildings, and his eyes sparkled. He was suddenly ashamed of his enthusiasm for those wobbly bridges, those front gardens and those dilapidated fences. He began to feel

CHAPTER 2

cheerful and light-hearted, and he began to view the hustle and bustle and the crowded streets in a different light, and glimpsed a glimmer of hope, hope which had been suppressed by his previous dispiriting impressions, that a new life had opened up its arms to him and was beckoning him towards the unknown. His heart began to beat faster. He saw a future of noble endeavour, lofty aspirations, and stepped out boldly along the Nevsky Prospekt, seeing himself now as a citizen of this new world. His head full of these dreams, he returned home.

At eleven o'clock that evening his uncle sent to invite him to take tea with him.

"I'm just back from the theatre," his uncle greeted him, lying on his divan.

"What a pity you didn't tell me before, Uncle, I would have gone with you."

"I was in the stalls; where would you have sat – on my lap?" said Pyotr Ivanych. "Why don't you go tomorrow by yourself?"

"It's no fun being alone in a crowd – there's no one to share your impressions with…"

"You shouldn't feel like that! In time, you'll have to learn to cope, to feel and to think on your own – in short, to live on your own. What's more, you have to be appropriately dressed to go to the theatre."

Alexander inspected his clothes, and found his uncle's remark surprising.

"What's inappropriate about the clothes I'm wearing?" he thought. "A dark-blue frock coat and trousers to match…"

"I have a lot of clothes, Uncle," he said, "made by Königstein; he's our governor's tailor."

"Forget that: what you have is just not appropriate; in a day or two I'll take you to my own tailor. But that's not important. There's something more important we have to discuss. Tell me, why did you come here?"

"Well, I came… to live."

"To live? If you mean by that to eat, drink and sleep, it was hardly worth the trouble to come all that way, because you won't be able to eat or sleep the way you could at home; but if you mean something else, then tell me…"

"To make the most of life is what I meant," Alexander added, blushing all over. "I was fed up with life in the country – so monotonous…"

"Ah, so that's it! So you'll be renting a mansion on the Nevsky Prospekt, running a carriage, cultivating a wide circle of acquaintances, and will be entertaining 'at home' on certain days?"

"Well, that would be pretty expensive," Alexander responded naively.

"Your mother writes that she gave you a thousand roubles – that's not much," said Pyotr Ivanych. "An acquaintance of mine came here recently; he too got tired of living in the country, and wanted to get more out of life. He brought 50,000 roubles with him, and also has 50,000 more coming in every year. Now, he really will be enjoying life in St Petersburg – unlike you. That's not what *you* came for."

"To listen to you, Uncle, it seems that I myself don't know why I came here."

"That's close – and better expressed – and there's some truth in what you say, but still not correct. When you were planning to come here, did you really never ask yourself, 'Why am I going?' That wouldn't have been too much to ask."

"The answer was already there, before I needed to ask the question!" Alexander responded proudly.

"So why not tell me the reason, then?"

"It was some kind of irresistible urge, a thirst for some noble endeavour; I was bursting to find out what that might be, and to make a start on it…"

Pyotr Ivanych half rose from the divan, took out a cigar and pricked up his ears.

"Yes, make a start on fulfilling all those hopes and dreams teeming inside me…"

"You don't happen to write poetry, do you?" Pyotr Ivanych suddenly asked him.

"And prose too, Uncle. Shall I bring some to show you?"

"No no, some other time; I was just asking."

"But what is it?"

"It's the way you speak…"

"What's wrong with it?"

CHAPTER 2

"Well, maybe there's nothing actually wrong with it: it's just strange."

"But that's just the way our aesthetics professor used to speak, and he was considered the most eloquent of all the professors." Alexander was clearly put out.

"What was he talking about when he spoke like that?"

"About his subject."

"Ah!"

"So, Uncle, how should I be speaking"?

"A little more simply, like everyone else, and not like a professor of aesthetics. Of course, you won't get the hang of it right away, but you'll see for yourself in time. As far as I recall my university lectures and am able to construe your words, I believe what you're trying to say is that you've come here in order to make a career and a fortune, is that correct?"

"Yes, Uncle, a career…"

"And a fortune," Pyotr Ivanych added. "What's a career without a fortune? It's a nice thought, but if that's what you had in mind, you shouldn't have come."

"But why do you say that? I hope not just on the basis of your own experience?" As he spoke, Alexander was looking around him.

"Well observed! Yes indeed, I am well off, and business is pretty good. But as far as I can tell, you and I are very different."

"I wouldn't dream of comparing myself with you."

"That's not the point: you may well be ten times smarter and better than me… it's just that you're not the type to adapt to a totally new environment, and your environment back home – my God! There, you've been pampered and spoilt by your mother; how could you possibly put up with what I have had to put up with? You are undoubtedly a dreamer, but here there's simply no time for dreaming; people like us come here to get down to business."

"Perhaps I might be able to achieve something if you were to share with me your experience and offer me some advice."

"I'm reluctant to offer advice. I can't be sure about the effect of your rural upbringing on your temperament: if my advice turns out to be worthless, you'll blame *me*, but I don't mind giving you my opinion,

49

and you can heed it or not as you choose. But no, I don't think it would work. You have your own outlook on life: how are you going to change it? You're infatuated with the idea of love, friendship, happiness and the glittering prizes of life; people think that's what life is all about, my oh my! So they cry, snivel and mouth pleasantries, but never get down to business... And how can I ever hope to get you to change that outlook? It wouldn't be easy!"

"I'll try to adapt to modern ideas, Uncle. Why, just today I was looking at these monumental buildings and those ships which bring us all these gifts from foreign lands, and I started thinking about the achievements of humanity today and understood the excitement of these crowds going so purposefully about their business, and felt myself ready to join in..."

On hearing this monologue, Pyotr Ivanych raised his eyebrows expressively, and studied his nephew carefully. Alexander fell silent.

"Well, it appears to be a simple matter," said his uncle. "God knows what notions these people will get into their heads next. 'Crowds going purposefully about their business'! It would really be better for you to have stayed where you were. You could live out a wonderful life back there: you might be taken for the smartest and most eloquent fellow around – you could believe in eternal and unwavering love and friendship, in family and happiness – you could marry and live to a ripe old age without noticing the time going by, and indeed be happy after your own fashion; but by our standards here you will not be happy, and all your ideas would have to be turned upside down."

"But Uncle, surely love and friendship are sacred and noble feelings which somehow or other just happen to have fallen upon our dirty earth from above..."

"What?"

Alexander fell silent.

"'Love and friendship have fallen into the dirt'! What is this nonsense you're spouting?"

"But what I meant was: aren't those things the same whether they're here or there?"

CHAPTER 2

"Yes, we have love and friendship here too – you find those things everywhere, but they're not the same here as where you come from; in time you'll come to see this yourself... Above all, you should forget about all this 'sacred' and 'noble' business, and try to look at what these things actually are in practice: you would really be better off, and become a simpler and better person – and talk like one. But, really, it's none of my business. You're here now, and there's no turning back. If you don't find what you're looking for, you will have only yourself to blame; I'm just warning you about what in my opinion is good and what is bad, but back there, you're your own master... But let's give it a try; perhaps we'll be able to make something of you. Oh yes! Your mother asked me to provide you with money. Well, there's something I want to tell you: don't ask me for any. That always disrupts harmonious relations between decent people. But anyway, don't think that I'm refusing you money – no, and if it comes down to that, and there's no other way, then you'll just have to come to me... It's always better to borrow from an uncle than a stranger: at least, that way, there's no interest to pay. But to avoid those dire straits, I'll find you some work as soon as I can, and you can earn some money. Anyway, goodbye for now, and come and see me in the morning, and we'll discuss how to make a start."

Alexander Fyodorych was on his way out when Pyotr Ivanych said: "Listen, wouldn't you like some supper?"

"Well, yes Uncle, I wouldn't mind..."

"I don't have anything."

Alexander thought to himself, "Then what's the point of his asking me?"

"I don't have meals at home, and the inns are closed now," his uncle continued. "So this is your first lesson – and you had better learn from it. Back where you're from, people get up and go to bed by the sun, they eat and drink at the bidding of nature; when it's cold they put on a hat and earmuffs, and don't give the matter a second thought; when it's light, it must be daytime, when it's dark it must be night-time. There, when your eyes close, I'm still at work; at the end of the month I have to do the books. There, you breathe fresh air all year round; here, it's a luxury that costs money – and that's the way it is with everything! Polar opposites!

"Now, people here don't eat supper, especially at their own expense – or at mine, for that matter. That could even prove useful, because it means that you won't be tossing and turning at night, and I don't have time to tuck you in and make the sign of the cross over you."

"That will be easy to get used to, Uncle…"

"Let's hope so. But where you come from, the old ways still persist. You turn up at someone's house at midnight and they'll improvise some supper for you on the spot, isn't that right?"

"But, Uncle, I hope you won't deny that that's a traditional Russian virtue…"

"Let me stop you right there! What do you mean, 'virtue'? Those people are so bored that they will welcome any creature that shows up at their door: 'How nice to see you! Eat as much as you like, but please relieve our tedium and entertain us, help us to kill time, your very presence will give us something new to look at; and we won't stint on the food: it costs us absolutely nothing…' What a positively revolting virtue!"

So Alexander went to bed and tried to figure out what kind of person his uncle was. He remembered the whole conversation; most of it he didn't understand, and the rest he didn't believe.

"So there's something wrong with the way I speak!" he thought. "And love and friendship aren't eternal? Uncle must be making fun of me. Can there really be such a different code of conduct here? If Sofia liked anything about me, surely it was my eloquence? And her love isn't really eternal?… And people here really don't eat supper?"

He spent a long time tossing and turning in bed, his head full of disturbing thoughts, and his empty belly stopped him from sleeping.

Two weeks went by.

As the days passed, Pyotr Ivanych grew more and more pleased with his nephew.

"He does have tact," he said to one of his partners in the firm, "and that's the last thing I ever thought I would say about a boy from the country. He doesn't make a nuisance of himself, and never comes to see me unless I call him – and when he sees that he has overstayed his welcome, he leaves immediately; he never asks for money: a quiet lad. He does have some strange quirks... he's given to kissing and talks like a seminarian... but he'll get over that; and the good thing is that he hasn't saddled himself on me."

"Does he have a fortune?" his partner asked.

"No, only about a hundred serfs."

"No matter! If he has some ability, he should work out here... after all, you yourself didn't start with much, and look where you are now, thank God..."

"No! No way! He will get nowhere. With his foolish head always in the clouds, he's just not cut out for it, oh God no! He'll never get used to the way things are done here; how is he going to make a career? He should never have come... well, anyway, that's his business."

Alexander felt it his duty to love his uncle, but just could not get used to his character and cast of mind.

"My uncle seems to be a decent fellow," he wrote one morning to Pospelov,

he's very intelligent, but extremely matter-of-fact; all he ever thinks about is business and accounts... He seems totally earth-bound, and simply doesn't seem capable of raising his sights from those banal earthly concerns to the pure contemplation of man's spiritual nature. For him the heavens are securely anchored to the earth, and it looks as if he and I will never become kindred spirits. Coming here, I thought that as my uncle he would surely find me a place in his heart and warm me up from the coldness of these crowds of strangers in his affectionate embrace, and offer me his friendship – and, as you know, friendship is 'the Second Providence'! But he too is nothing but a manifestation of those same crowds. I thought I would share my time with him – never stray from his side for a minute, but what did I find? Cold advice, which he describes as practical; but I would much prefer that it was impractical, *but full of warm, heartfelt concern. It's not that he's proud, exactly, but dead against*

any demonstration of true feelings; we don't have dinner or supper together, and never go anywhere together. When he comes home, he never says where he's been or what he's been doing; nor does he ever say where he is going or why, who his friends are, what his likes or dislikes are or how he spends his time. He never loses his temper, is never affectionate, never upset and never cheerful. His heart is closed to any display of love, friendliness or any proclivity to beauty. Often you may be speaking like a prophet in the grip of inspiration, almost like our own great unforgettable Ivan Semyonych when, you remember, he thundered from the pulpit while we trembled in rapture at his fiery rhetoric and piercing gaze. But my uncle? He just listens with raised eyebrows, gives you a strange look and that special laugh of his which turns your blood to ice – and it's goodbye to inspiration! I sometimes see in him Pushkin's demon*...
he doesn't believe in love and that sort of thing; he says there's no such thing as happiness, and no one has ever even promised it, and that all there is is life, equally divided between good and evil, between pleasure, success, good health, peace and quiet and, on the other hand, pain, failure, anxiety, sickness and the rest. He says that you must simply face this fact, and not fill your head with all these useless – yes, useless! – thoughts about why we were created, and what we should aspire to – no, that's not our concern – and it's because of that that we fail to see what's in front of our noses, and don't get on with our business... business, yes that's all you ever hear from him! You can never tell whether he is experiencing some kind of pleasure, or whether he's dwelling on some purely down-to-earth matter; whether he's doing his books or at the theatre, he's just the same; he is immune to any strong emotions, and appears to have no feeling for the finer things; why, I don't believe he has even read Pushkin...

Pyotr Ivanych suddenly appeared in his nephew's room and found him writing this letter.

"I came to see how you were settling in," said his uncle, "and to talk about a practical matter."

CHAPTER 2

Alexander jumped up and quickly covered something with his hand.

"That's right, hide your secret," said Pyotr Ivanych, "I'll turn away. Well, have you hidden it? But something just fell out, what is it?"

"It's nothing, Uncle..." Alexander began, but was too embarrassed to go on and broke off.

"It looks like hair! Nothing indeed! Now that I've seen one thing, you might as well show me what else you're hiding in your hand."

Like a schoolboy caught in the act, Alexander opened his hand and revealed a ring.

"What's that? Where did you get it?"

"A material token... of an abstraction, a relationship..."

"What? What, give it here – this token."

"It's a pledge..."

"No doubt; you brought it with you from the country?"

"It's from Sofia, Uncle, a memento... a farewell present..."

"All right. And you brought it 1,500 versts all the way here?" His uncle shook his head. "You'd have done better to bring another bag of dried strawberries; you could at least have sold *them* to that shopkeeper, but these keepsakes..."

He looked at the hair and the ring in turn, sniffed the hair and weighed the ring in his hand. Then he picked up the piece of paper from the table and wrapped it around both keepsakes, crumpled it into a small ball and flung it out of the window just like that!

"Uncle!" Alexander screamed out in a fury, grabbing his hand. But it was too late. The crumpled ball flew past the corner of the neighbouring roof and fell into the canal, bounced off the deck of a barge carrying a load of bricks and into the water.

Alexander fell silent and gave his uncle a look of bitter reproach.

"Uncle!" he repeated.

"What?"

"What would you call what you just did?"

"Throwing out of the window into the canal a bunch of immaterial tokens and any other kind of useless rubbish cluttering up this room..."

"Rubbish, you call that 'useless rubbish'!"

"And what did you think it was? Half of your heart? I came here to discuss practical matters with him, and what do I find him doing? Sitting and brooding over rubbish!"

"And according to you, that interferes with practical matters?"

"Very much so. Time is passing, and I still haven't heard a word from you about your intentions: do you want to find a position, or have you chosen some other line of work? Not a word! And all because you have Sofia and her keepsakes on your mind. And if I'm not mistaken, here you are writing her a letter. Am I right?"

"Well yes... I was just beginning..."

"And have you written to your mother?"

"Not yet, I was going to tomorrow."

"And why tomorrow? So, it's your mother tomorrow, and this Sofia, whom you will have forgotten in a month, today..."

"Sofia? You think I could forget her?"

"Of course. If I hadn't thrown out your keepsakes, I suppose you might just have gone on remembering her for another month. I've just done you a double favour. In a few years, all those keepsakes would have done would be to remind you of your foolishness, and you would blush at the thought."

"Blush at the thought of such a pure, sacred memory! That would mean there's no room for poetry..."

"What's poetry got to do with such foolishness? Like that poetry, for example, in your aunt's letter! The yellow flower, the lake, some secret or other... I can't tell you how uncomfortable it made me feel; I was close to blushing, and I certainly should have got over blushing by now!"

"That's awful, awful, Uncle! So you mean you've never been in love?"

"I could never stand keepsakes."

"But that's living as if you were made of wood!" Alexander was beside himself. "That's vegetating, not living! Vegetating without inspiration, without life, without love..."

"And without hair!" his uncle added.

"Uncle, how can you so cold-bloodedly ridicule what is best in this world? That's a crime... love is the most sacred of emotions!"

CHAPTER 2

"I'm well acquainted with that sacred love of yours: at your age, all you see is a lock of hair, a dainty slipper, a garter, a touch of the hand, and this exalted love of yours runs like a shudder through your whole body – but once you give way to it, then you're in trouble… Your love, unfortunately, lies ahead of you, and there's no getting away from that – but finding a career *will* get away from you, if you don't get down to business."

"But isn't love just as serious a matter?"

"No, it's a pleasant distraction, but you shouldn't take it too seriously, otherwise it will let you down. And that is precisely what I fear for you."

His uncle shook his head and said, "I've almost found you a position; you do want one, I suppose?"

"Oh, Uncle, I'm so pleased!"

Alexander rushed to kiss his uncle on the cheek.

"You were quick to seize the opportunity!" said his uncle, wiping his cheek. "Why did I let myself be taken by surprise! Now listen; I want you to tell me what you know: what line of work do you feel equipped for?"

"I know divinity, civil, criminal, natural and customary law, diplomacy, political economics, national law, philosophy, aesthetics, archaeology…"

"Slow down! What I want to know is whether you can write decent Russian. Right now, that's the most important thing."

"What a question, Uncle – can I write Russian!" said Alexander, and hurried over to the chest of drawers and started to take out various papers, while his uncle picked some letter which was lying on the table and started to read it.

Alexander brought the papers to the table and saw his uncle reading the letter. The papers fell from his hands.

"What is that you're reading, Uncle?" he said apprehensively.

"There was this letter lying on the table – to one of your friends, no doubt. I'm sorry, I just wanted to see how you wrote."

"And you've read it?"

"Almost – everything except the last two lines – I'm just finishing it. What's the matter? There can't be any secrets in it, otherwise it wouldn't just be lying around…"

"So now what do you think of me?"

"I think that you write quite well – correctly and fluently…"

"Then you didn't read what I wrote?" Alexander asked eagerly.

"No, I think I read it all," said Pyotr Ivanych, looking at both pages. "First you describe St Petersburg and your impressions, and then you write about me."

"My God!" Alexander exclaimed, and covered his face with his hands.

"What is it? What's wrong?"

"Well, you don't seem at all bothered! Aren't you angry? Don't you hate me?"

"Not at all! Why should I lose my temper?"

"Repeat that, and set my mind at rest."

"The answer is no, no, no!"

"I still can't believe you – prove it to me, Uncle…"

"How?"

"Embrace me!"

"I'm sorry, I can't."

"Why not?"

"Because it's a meaningless gesture: it makes no sense, no – or, to use the words of your professor, my intelligence won't let me; now if you were a woman – that would be a different matter: then it wouldn't have to make any sense – it would be prompted by quite a different feeling."

"You mean your feelings would get the better of you, your emotions would have to find an outlet…"

"My feelings don't get the better of me – and if they did, I would control myself – and I advise you to do the same."

"But why?"

"Because afterwards, when you've taken a closer look at the person you've embraced, you won't have to blush at the thought."

"Hasn't it ever happened, Uncle, that you have rebuffed someone and then regretted it?"

"Yes, it happens, and that's why I never rebuff anyone!"

"Then you won't rebuff me either for my gesture, and call me a monster?"

CHAPTER 2

"Where you come from, then, anyone who writes rubbish is a monster, so there must be thousands of them around."

"But to read such bitter truths about yourself – and written by your own nephew!"

"Oh, you think you were writing the truth?..."

"Oh Uncle, of course I was mistaken... I'll correct it... I'm sorry..."

"You want me to dictate the truth?"

"Please do!"

"Well, sit down and write!"

"Alexander took out a sheet of paper and picked up a pen, and Pyotr Ivanych, looking at the letter he had read, began to dictate:

"My dear friend – have you got that down?"

"Yes."

"I won't describe to you my impressions of St Petersburg."

"I won't," repeated Alexander as he wrote the words down.

"St Petersburg has already been described long ago, and what hasn't been described you should come and see for yourself; my impressions are of no use to you, so why waste the time and the paper? I would do better to describe my uncle, because that affects me personally."

"My uncle," Alexander repeated.

"Now you write that I'm nice and intelligent – it may or may not be true, so let's split the difference and write:

"My uncle is not stupid and not ill natured, and wishes me well..."

"Dear Uncle, I can appreciate that, and I feel..." said Alexander, reaching out to kiss him.

"...although he doesn't hover over me..." Pyotr Ivanych continued dictating. Alexander, failing in his attempt, sat down quickly in his seat. "...but wishes me well because he has no reason or motive for wishing me ill, and because my mother asked this of him, and in the past she had been good to him. He says he does not love me – and quite rightly, because it's impossible to come to love someone in two weeks, and I don't yet love him, although I actually assure him of the contrary."

"How can you say that?" Alexander exclaimed.

"Keep on writing... But we are beginning to get used to each other. He even claims that one can do without love altogether. He doesn't sit

59

down and hug me from morning to night, because there's absolutely no need for that, and in any case he doesn't have the time… But dead against any demonstration of true feelings… You can leave that in, it's good. Have you got it?

"Now let's see what else you have put… No room for poetry in his soul, a demon… Go on writing!"

While Alexander was writing, Pyotr Ivanych picked up a piece of paper from the table, twisted it into a taper, set light to it and lit a cigar. He threw down the paper and stamped it out.

He went on dictating: "My uncle is neither a demon nor an angel, but just like anyone else, although not exactly like you and me. His thoughts and his feelings are earth-bound, and he thinks that if we live on the earth, then we shouldn't leave it to fly up to the heavens – which so far no one has asked us to do – and should spend our time dealing with the human business which we have been assigned to. Accordingly, he takes all earthly matters, and indeed life itself, for what they are, and not for what we would like them to be. He believes in good, and at the same time in evil, in the beautiful and in the ugly. He also believes in love and friendship, but not that they fell from heaven into the dirt, and believes that they were created along with people and for people, and therefore that is how they should be understood, and furthermore that everything should be very closely and realistically examined, and that we should not allow ourselves to be carried away in God knows what directions. He concedes the possibility of affability which, after a period of casual acquaintanceship and habituation, may turn into friendship. But he also believes that when people are apart, habit loses its force, and they forget each other, and there's absolutely nothing wrong with that. So he assures me that I will forget you, and you will forget me. To me – and no doubt to you – that seems perverse, but his advice is to get used to the idea, so that neither of us will make fools of ourselves. With slight qualifications, he feels the same way about love: he doesn't believe in enduring and eternal love any more than he does in fairies, and he advises us to follow his example in this. As a matter of fact, he advises me to think about all that as little as possible, and I offer you the same advice. It is something which he says comes of its own accord – it doesn't have to be sought; he says that there's more to life than just that, and that like everything else in life it comes when the time is right, and spending your life dreaming about that is stupid. Those who seek it, and can't stand a moment without it, are fixated on their hearts, and what is worse, doing so at the expense of their heads. Uncle likes to spend his time on business, and he advises you and me to do the same. We are members of society, he says, and society needs us; while he is working he's not forgetting himself: work brings in money, and money brings comforts, which he is very fond of. Also, it's possible that he has intentions, as a consequence of which it is likely that it won't be me who will be his heir. Uncle is not always thinking of his work and the factory: he knows some literature by heart – and not only Pushkin..."

"You, Uncle?" Alexander said in surprise.

"Yes, as you will discover some day. Go on writing!"

"He reads in two languages everything that is noteworthy in all areas of human knowledge; he likes art and has a fine collection of paintings of the Flemish school – that's his taste – and goes frequently to the theatre, but doesn't make a fuss about it or make a big show of it; he doesn't go into ecstasies over it – he thinks that's childish, and that one should restrain oneself. He doesn't impose his impressions on others, because he thinks no one needs them. He doesn't let his tongue run away with him, and advises us to follow his example. Goodbye, write to me a little less often – it's not worth your time. Your friend, etc. And of course the month and date."

"How can I send a letter like this?" said Alexander. "'Write to me a little less often'? How could I say something like this to someone who went out of his way to travel 150 versts just to say a last farewell to me! And giving him all this advice... I'm no cleverer than him; he graduated second in his class."

"It doesn't matter, send it to him anyway, maybe he'll be the wiser for it, and it will help him think about things differently. As for you, you may have completed your studies, but your true education is only beginning."

"Uncle, I don't think I can bring myself..."

"I never interfere in other people's business, but you yourself asked for my help; and here am I trying to give you a push in the right direction, and making your first step easier, while you are resisting. Well, do as you wish, I'm just giving you my opinion, and I won't put any pressure on you – I'm not your nanny."

"Sorry, Uncle, I'm ready to take your advice," said Alexander, sealing the letter as he spoke.

Having sealed the first letter, he started looking for the other one to Sofia. He looked on the table – no, not there. He looked under the table, not there either – nor any sign of it in the drawer.

"What are you looking for?" said his uncle.

"I'm looking for the other letter – the one to Sofia."

His uncle started looking too.

"Where can it be?" said Pyotr Ivanych. "I couldn't have thrown it out of the window..."

"Uncle, what have you gone and done? You used it to light your cigar!" Alexander said dejectedly, and picked up the charred remains of the letter.

"Did I really?" exclaimed his uncle. "But how could I have done? I just didn't notice; and now I seem to have burnt something precious... but come to think of it... you know what, maybe it's not such a bad thing from one point of view..."

"But, Uncle, I swear to God, it's not good from any point of view," Alexander said in despair.

"No, it really is a good thing. You won't have time to rewrite it in time for the next post – and later on, you'll have thought better of it, and you'll be busy with your work and you won't have time, and that way you will have done one less foolish thing."

"But what is she going to think of me?"

"Whatever she chooses to. As a matter of fact, it will even be useful to her. I mean, you're not going to marry her, are you? She's going to think that you've forgotten her, and she'll end up forgetting you too, and will have one less reason to blush when she's with her future fiancé, and is telling him that she has never loved anyone else but him."

CHAPTER 2

"You are an extraordinary man, Uncle! For you there's no such thing as constancy, no such thing as a sacred promise... Life is great, blissful, unending delights... it's like a smooth, placid and beautiful lake..."

"And don't forget those yellow flowers growing in it, of course!" his uncle interrupted him to say.

"...like a lake," continued Alexander, "full of mystery and allure, with so much hidden inside it."

"Like slime, my dear fellow."

"Why throw in slime, Uncle? Why are you so anxious to destroy and stamp out all joy, hope and everything that's good – and always looking on the dark side?"

"Actually, I look on the realistic side – and I urge you to do the same; that way you won't end up feeling a fool. With your outlook, life is good where you come from in the provinces, where people don't know what life is like – although they're not really people: more like angels. Take Zayezzhalov, the holy man, your auntie – such an exalted, sensitive soul – and Sofia, I imagine, is just as big a fool as the aunt, not to mention..."

"Please stop, Uncle!" Alexander was enraged.

"...not to mention dreamers like yourself always sniffing the wind for a whiff of eternal love and friendship whichever direction it may be coming from... I'm telling you for the hundredth time – you should never have come!"

"Will she really be telling her intended that she never loved anyone else!" said Alexander almost to himself.

"There you go again!"

"No, I'm sure that she will simply and with high-minded honesty hand over my letters to him and..."

"And the keepsakes," said Pyotr Ivanych.

"Yes, and the tokens of our relationship... and she will say, 'So this is the one who first stirred my heartstrings, and this is the name they responded to for the first time.'"

His uncle started to raise his eyebrows and widen his eyes. Alexander said nothing.

"So are you telling me that you've stopped playing on your own heartstrings? Well, my dear boy, that Sofia of yours is really stupid if

63

she would do something like that. I can only hope that she has a mother or someone else who would be able to stop her."

"Uncle, if you can bring yourself to describe as stupidity such a profoundly moral impulse, such a spontaneous and noble gesture, what are we to think of you?"

"Suit yourself. God knows what she would make her fiancé suspect; the wedding might even be called off, and why? Because back then you once picked yellow flowers together… No, no, that's not the way things are done. Anyway, since you can write Russian, tomorrow we'll go to the ministry; I've already mentioned you to a department head, an old colleague of mine. He told me that there's a vacancy, so there's no time to be wasted… what's that folder you've produced?"

"It's my university notes. Here, you might like to read a few pages of Ivan Semyonych's lectures on Greek art."

So saying, he was already beginning to leaf rapidly through his notes.

"Oh no! Do me a favour and spare me that!" Pyotr Ivanych responded with a frown. "And what's that?"

"These are the papers I have written which I would like to show to my supervisor. There's one in particular, the draft of a project I've worked on…"

"Yes, one of those projects which were completed a thousand years ago, or which cannot be completed and nobody needs."

"How can you say that, Uncle? It's a proposal that has already been presented to an important person, a supporter of enlightenment, and on the strength of it he invited me to dine with the rector. Here is the beginning of another project."

"Come and have dinner with me twice, only don't finish that other project."

"But, why not?"

"Because you won't be writing anything worthwhile now, and time is passing."

"What do you mean?… After all those lectures I attended…"

"They may serve some purpose in time, but for now the thing is to observe, learn and do what they tell you to do."

"But how will my supervisor know what my abilities are?"

CHAPTER 2

"He'll recognize them in a flash, he's an expert at that. Anyway, what kind of position are you looking for?"

"I don't know, Uncle, whatever would…"

"Well, there are ministerial posts, ministers' assistants, directors, deputy directors, department heads, office managers, assistant office managers, special assignments – is that enough for you?"

Alexander pondered the matter, but was at a loss to come up with an answer.

"Well, perhaps, for a start, office manager would be a good idea," he said.

"Very well then," Pyotr Ivanych agreed.

"Then after I've had a chance to get my bearings, perhaps after a month or two it could be department head…"

His uncle was taken aback. "Of course, what else!" he responded. "Then after three months you'll be a director, and in a year a minister – is that your idea?"

Alexander blushed and fell silent, and then asked, "I expect the department head told you what vacancies there were?"

"No," his uncle replied, "he didn't. Better leave it to him, we would have trouble deciding, and he's the one who knows best where to place you. Don't you say anything to him about finding it difficult to choose – and also, not a word about your projects. Furthermore, he'll be offended to think we don't trust him, and he can be quite intimidating. I would also advise you to avoid mentioning anything about 'material tokens' to the girls around here; they won't understand – and how could they anyway? It would be over their heads. In fact I had trouble understanding myself, but they would just make faces."

While his uncle was talking, Alexander was turning a package over in his hand.

"What is that you're holding now?"

Alexander had been anxiously awaiting that question.

"It's something I've been wanting to show you for a long time… some poems; you had asked about them…"

"I don't seem to remember; I don't think I asked about them…"

THE SAME OLD STORY

"The thing is, Uncle, I think office work is flat and uninspiring; it doesn't engage the soul, and the soul thirsts to give expression to its overflowing feelings and thoughts, and to share them with those closest to oneself…"

"And what of it?" his uncle asked impatiently.

"I feel I am a creative artist by vocation…"

"That is to say you want to do something else outside your work, like translation, for example. Well, that's most commendable; you mean something literary?"

"Yes, Uncle, I wanted to ask you whether there's any chance you could get something of mine placed?"

"Are you sure you have some talent? Because without it you will never be anything but an artistic drudge – and what good would that be? Now, with talent, that would be a different matter. You could achieve something worthwhile and at the same time build up some capital – easily worth the hundred souls on your estate."

"There you go again, valuing everything in terms of money."

"Well, how would you evaluate it? The more people read your work, the more money you earn."

"But what about fame? Now, fame, that's the true reward of the artist…"

"Fame is tired of pampering artists. There are too many contenders. Yes, there was a time when fame, like a woman, attached itself to any of them, but now you don't see that any more, it has pretty well disappeared, or gone into hiding – unquestionably! Yes, there is celebrity, but fame is something we virtually no longer hear of, unless it has found some other way of manifesting itself: the better a writer is, the more money he makes; anyone worse – well, I'm sorry, you don't need me to tell you.

"Nowadays, a decent writer lives decently, doesn't have to freeze and starve in some attic – although, of course, people no longer run after him in the street and point their fingers at him, as they would at a clown; they no longer think of a poet as some kind of divinity, but rather a human being who sees, walks, thinks, acts – sometimes foolishly – just like the rest of us: so what's so special about that?…"

CHAPTER 2

"'Just like the rest of us' – but how can you say that, Uncle? A poet is cast in a different mould, a higher power lies hidden within him…"

"Just as it does in others – a mathematician, a watchmaker – as well as in the likes of us factory owners. Newton, Gutenberg, Watt were also endowed with the gift of this higher power, as were Shakespeare, Dante and others. So, if I found a process by which I managed to transform our local clay into a porcelain finer even than Saxon or Sèvres, do you think there wouldn't be some higher power at work in this?"

"You're confusing the artist with the artisan, Uncle."

"God forbid! Art is its own thing, and so is craft – and creativity is common to both, in the same way as its absence. Without it, the craftsman is nothing but just that, a craftsman; and not creative, and an artist without that creative spark is no poet: he's just someone who writes things. Surely you must have learnt that at the university! Otherwise, what on earth did they teach you there?"

His uncle was already annoyed at having launched into such lengthy explanations about what he would have thought was common knowledge.

"They seem like heartfelt outpourings," he thought. "Well show me what you have there!" he said. "Those poems."

His uncle took the papers Alexander was holding and began to read the first page.

> "Whence at times, yearning and sorrow
> Envelop me in a sudden cloud
> And the heart is pitted against life…

"Give me a light. Alexander!" He lit a cigar and continued:

> "And a host of wishes are driven out.
> Why does this troubled sleep
> Suddenly descend upon my soul
> Like a dark and ominous cloud
> Of some strange unhappiness
> And cast a sudden pall upon it?…

THE SAME OLD STORY

"You're repeating the same thing over and over again in the first four lines – once you've said it, the rest is so much waffle," Pyotr Ivanych remarked, and continued reading:

> "Who can guess the reason why
> This brow, so suddenly pallid
> Is by cold tears bespangled…

"What sense does that make? The brow breaks out in sweat, but tears? Never heard of such a thing! And what happens to us then?

> "The silence of the distant skies
> Is at that instant fearsome and terrible…

"'Fearsome' and 'terrible' are one and the same thing.

> "I gaze at the sky above;
> The moon sails silently and shines…

"Of course, must have a moon, how can you do without it! And if you've put in anything about a 'dream' or a 'maiden', I give up on you.

> "And one fancies that in her
> An age-old fateful secret is buried.

"Not bad! Give me another light… my cigar has gone out. Now, where on earth – oh yes!

> "In the heavens, the fickle stars are hiding
> But tremble and shimmer
> As if in tacit agreement to keep
> A conspiratorial silence.
> And throughout the world disaster threatens,
> A grim harbinger of the evil to come,
> And a deceptive peacefulness lulls us into

CHAPTER 2

A sense of false security.
It's a sorrow that has no name…"

Pyotr Ivanych opened his mouth wide and yawned, and then continued:

"She passes and vanishes without trace,
Like a wind that sweeps the steppe
And wipes away the footprints left by the beasts in the sand.

"Now this business of beasts is entirely out of place! But what's this line you've drawn here? Oh, I see, first it was about sorrow, and now it's about joy…"
And he began to hurry through it in a barely audible mumble:

"But, it happens that at times another demon takes possession of us,
And a powerful wave of delight forces its way into my soul,
And my breast sweetly thrills in response… etc."

As he finished reading, he remarked, "Neither bad nor good, although others have got off to an even worse start – so it's worth the effort; keep writing, and apply yourself, if that's what you want, and perhaps some talent will emerge – then that would be another matter."
Alexander was crestfallen. This was not at all the response he had expected, although it was of some comfort to him that he found his uncle to be a cold character, almost totally lacking in soul.
"Here's a translation from Schiller,"* he said.
"That's enough – I see it – so you know some foreign languages?"
"I know French, German and a little English."
"Congratulations, you should have told me long before now: now we can really make something of you. A while ago, you insisted on telling me all that stuff about political economy, philosophy, archaeology and I don't know what else, but not a word about the most important thing – misplaced modesty! Now I can find you literary employment in a trice."
"Will you really, Uncle? That would really be nice of you, may I hug you?"
"Wait until I find it."

"Don't you want to show some of my work to whomever I'm going to work for, so as to give him an idea?"

"There's no need; if the need should arise, you can do that yourself, but maybe it won't be necessary. Now, give me your projects and your writings!"

"You want me to give them to you? Why certainly, Uncle," said Alexander, who was flattered by his uncle's request. "Wouldn't it be a good idea for me to make a table of contents with all the articles in chronological order?"

"No, there's no need... and thanks for the gift. Yevsei! Take these papers to Vasily!"

"But why Vasily? Don't you want them in your study?"

"He asked me for some sheets of paper to paste something on."

"But, Uncle?..." Horrified, he snatched the pile of papers back.

"But you gave them to me; what difference does it make to you what use I make of your gift?"

"You're absolutely ruthless, you spare no one!" Alexander groaned despairingly, and clutched the papers to his chest with both hands.

"Alexander, listen to me," said his uncle, tearing the papers from his grasp. "Some time in the future this will spare your blushes, and you'll thank me for it."

Alexander let go of the papers.

"Here, take them away, Yevsei!" said Pyotr Ivanych. "See, now your room is nice and tidy, no useless knick-knacks lying round. Now it depends on you whether you want to fill it with litter or with things of practical use. Let's go to the factory and take a walk, clear our heads, breathe some fresh air and watch people at work."

In the morning, Pyotr Ivanych took his nephew to the department, and while he himself was talking to his friend, the department head, Alexander was acquainting himself with this new world. His head was still full of his projects, and he was racking his brains about which major national problem would be assigned to him to resolve, and meanwhile standing and looking around.

"Exactly the kind of factory my uncle would own!" he finally decided. The foreman would take a piece of something, throw it into a machine,

CHAPTER 2

turn a handle a couple of times, and before you knew it, out would pop a cone, an oval or a semicircle; then he would hand it to another worker who would dry it over a flame; the next one would gild it, and yet a fourth worker would decorate it, and it would become a cup, a vase or a saucer. Over there, an applicant would come in from outside and, stooping deferentially with an ingratiating smile on his face, would proffer a sheet of paper. The foreman would take it, barely graze it with his pen, hand it off to someone else – who, in turn, would toss it onto a heap of thousands of other sheets of paper. It would never get lost and, stamped as it was with a number and a date, it would pass intact through twenty pairs of hands, begetting countless progeny and reproducing itself. Yet another worker would take it and slide it into a cabinet, glance at some kind of book or some other document and mutter a few magic words to the next worker, who would start scratching away with a pen. After he was done, he would hand over the mother with her new offspring to the next in line, who would scratch away in his turn with a pen, giving birth to further progeny. Farther down the line, someone else would embellish it and hand it on. And so the paper travelled ever onwards, never to disappear. Its creators might die, but it goes on and on for ever. Finally, the dust of ages would settle on it, but even then people would still come to disturb it and consult it. And day after day, hour after hour, today and tomorrow, the bureaucratic mill grinds on without a hitch, uninterrupted, never resting, as if people don't exist – nothing but wheels and springs...

"But where is the mind that quickens and drives this paper mill?" Alexander was wondering. "Is it in books, in the papers themselves or in the heads of these people?"

And where else did you see faces like these? You never seem to meet them in the street, nor do they ever emerge into the light of day. It's here, it seems, that they are born, raised and grafted onto their surroundings, and it's here that they die.

Aduyev took a long look at the head of department: a veritable Jupiter the Thunderer; he had only to open his mouth, and out would spring Mercury with a copper plaque on his chest; he had only to hold out a piece of paper, and a dozen hands would be stretching out to grasp it.

"Ivan Ivanych!" he said.

Ivan Ivanych hopped up from his seat and was standing before Jupiter in a flash.

Alexander felt intimidated, but without knowing why.

"Give me the snuffbox!" With fawning eagerness, Ivan Ivanych held open the box for him with both hands.

"Now, try him out!" said the department head, pointing at Aduyev.

"So that's who is going to test me!" thought Aduyev, looking at Ivan Ivanych's yellow face and worn and shiny elbows. "Can this really be someone who deals with matters of national importance?"

"Do you have a good hand?" Ivan Ivanych asked him.

"Hand?"

"Yes, handwriting. Here, be good enough to copy this document!"

Alexander was surprised at being asked to perform this task, but did as he was told. Frowning, Ivan Ivanych examined his work.

"Not very good, sir," he said to the department head, who took a look at the copy.

"Yes, you're right; he's not capable of producing a fair copy. So let's put him to writing out leave slips, then when he's got used to that, we could assign him to completing forms, and maybe he will work out; he's a university graduate."

Before long Aduyev himself became one of those cogs in the machine. He did nothing but write, write and write, to the point that eventually he found himself wondering what else people did with their mornings, and whenever he thought of his projects, he couldn't help blushing.

"Uncle," he thought, "you were right about one thing, inexorably right. Can it be that you were right about everything else? Could I have been wrong about those cherished, lofty ideas of mine, my eager faith in love, in friendship, in people and even in myself? Then what is life about?" He bent over the paper on which he was writing, and scratched away harder with his pen, his eyelashes glittering with tears.

"Well, fortune is really smiling on you," said Pyotr Ivanych to his nephew. "When I started out, I worked for a whole year without pay, but here you are already starting out at above minimum salary

CHAPTER 2

– 750 roubles, altogether a thousand with the bonus. A splendid start! The department head is full of praise for you, although he does say that your mind tends to wander, and you forget commas, and leave out the table of contents. So please, apply yourself, and above all concentrate on what's in front of you, and don't let your thoughts carry you up and away."

His uncle pointed upwards. From that time on, he became more affectionate towards his nephew.

"What a great fellow my head clerk is, Uncle," said Alexander one day.

"What makes you say that?"

"We've got to know each other. He's such a lofty soul, such a great sense of honour, and a noble cast of mind! And his deputy too, a mind of his own and an iron will…"

"Have you really got to know them so well?"

"Yes, indeed!"

"Hasn't the head clerk been inviting you home on Thursdays?"

"Oh yes, every Thursday. It seems that he's taken a particular liking to me."

"And has his deputy been borrowing money from you?"

"Yes, Uncle, a mere nothing. I just gave him what I had on me, twenty-five roubles, although he had asked for fifty more."

"Well, so you've started lending money!" His uncle was annoyed. "I'm partly to blame, because I failed to warn you. I just didn't imagine that you were as gullible as that, and that after knowing someone for only two weeks, you would start lending money. Well, it can't be helped, I'll go halves with you, and give you twelve roubles fifty."

"But why, Uncle? He'll pay it back."

"Some hopes! I know him. Because of him I was out 100 roubles when I worked there. He scrounges from everyone. Next time he asks you, just tell him that I want my money back, and he'll desist. And stop going to see the head clerk!"

"But why, Uncle?"

"He's a hustler. He'll get you to sit down at the card table with a couple of other card sharks, they'll gang up on you, and you'll lose your shirt!"

"A hustler!" Alexander exclaimed in astonishment. "Surely not? He always seems to be speaking straight from the heart."

"Just tell him casually in the course of conversation that I've taken all your money to keep it safe, and then you'll see how keen he is on pouring out his heart and whether he'll ever invite you again on Thursdays."

Alexander stood thinking. His uncle shook his head.

"And you thought you were surrounded by angels! 'Talking from the heart', 'a particular liking'! And anyway, how come you didn't think about it before? Don't you realize there are always predators around? You should never have come!" he said. "You really shouldn't have!"

Once, after Alexander had just woken up, Yevsei brought him in a big package with a note from his uncle.

"Now at last, here is some real literary work for you," he had written. "Yesterday I saw a journalist friend of mine; he has sent you something to try out."

Alexander's hands trembled with excitement as he opened the package. Inside there was something written in German.

"What can it be – some prose?" he wondered. "What about?"

He read something which had been written in pencil at the top.

'Fertilizer', an article for the agricultural column. Translation to be submitted as soon as possible.

He sat over the article thinking for a long time until finally, with a sigh, he slowly picked up his pen and began to translate. Two days later the article was ready and sent off.

"Excellent, excellent!" said Pyotr Ivanych a few days later. "The editor couldn't be more pleased, only he found the style a little free; but, of course, you can't expect everything the first time. He wants to meet you. Go and see him tomorrow evening at seven; he'll have another article ready for you."

"On the same subject?"

"No, something different, he told me but I forget… Oh yes, it's on potato starch. Alexander, you were, of course, born with a silver spoon in your mouth, but I'm finally beginning to believe that we can make

CHAPTER 2

something of you. Soon, perhaps, I'll be able to stop asking you why you came here. You've hardly been here a month and already everything's been going your way. There's that thousand roubles, as well as the hundred roubles a month which the editor has promised to pay you for four printer's sheets; that makes 2,200 roubles! No, that's not how *I* started out," he said, frowning slightly. "Write and tell your mother how well things are working out. I'm going to write to her myself and tell her how, in return for her kindness to me, I've been doing my best to help you."

"Mummy will be… very grateful, Uncle, and I too…" said Alexander with a sigh, but this time made no attempt to embrace his uncle.

Chapter 3

TWO YEARS HAD GONE BY. Who now would have recognized the provincial in this young man with his refined manners and ultra-fashionable clothes? He had changed a great deal and matured. The soft contours of his youthful face, the transparency and tenderness of his skin and the down on his chin had all disappeared. His shyness and timidity along with a certain graceful awkwardness in his movements were no longer there. His facial features had matured into a pattern, a pattern which revealed character. The lilies and roses had been replaced by a kind of light tan, and the down had given way to fledgling side whiskers. His diffident and uncertain tread and become firm and even, and his voice had deepened into the bass range. What had once been but a sketch had become a fully fledged portrait. What had been a youth was now a man. His eyes shone with self-confidence and boldness, but not the boldness that can be heard a mile off and comes with an arrogant glance that proclaims to everyone within range: "Watch out, don't mess with me, don't tread on my toes – or else! Understand? I'll make short work of you." No, the boldness I have in mind does not repel: it attracts. You can recognize it as a striving for good, for success, as a determination to sweep away all obstacles in its path. Alexander's old expression of eagerness and enthusiasm had mellowed into one of a certain thoughtfulness, the first sign of a wariness which had wormed its way into his psyche, and was perhaps the only effect of his uncle's homilies and the remorseless analysis to which he had subjected everything that Alexander's eyes and heart had told him. Alexander had finally mastered tact and the art of dealing with people. He no longer rushed to embrace people, especially since the time a certain person, who was given to heartfelt outpourings, had twice got the better of him in spite of his uncle's warnings, and another gentleman with a forceful personality and an iron will had persuaded him to part with a sizeable sum of money

CHAPTER 3

by way of a loan. Other people and situations had also helped a lot in this. In one place, he had noticed that people were laughing up their sleeves at his youthful exuberance and had nicknamed him "the romantic"; another time people had taken practically no notice of him because he had nothing to offer them. He gave no dinners, didn't keep a carriage and didn't play for high stakes. Previously, he would have grown sick at heart because of the painful contrast between his rosy dreams and reality, and it had never occurred to him to wonder: "What have I ever done that was noteworthy – what have I ever done to stand out from the crowd? What accomplishments do I have to my name – why should people take any notice of me?" All this was a blow to his self-esteem.

Later he came to entertain the thought that perhaps life was not all roses, but there were thorns too which sometimes pricked you – although not, of course, as painfully as Uncle made out. So he learnt to exercise some self-control and not to blurt out his feelings so often and get so excited, and also to stop letting his tongue run away with him as much, at least when he was in company.

For all that, to the deep disappointment of his uncle, he was still far from being a detached analyst of the first causes of all that troubles and perturbs the human heart. He was averse to the very idea of penetrating all its secrets and riddles.

Pyotr Ivanych would lay down the law about something in the morning, and Alexander would listen and would come away confused or deep in thought, but then in the evening he would go out somewhere and would come back a changed man; for three days he would kick over the traces – and all his uncle's theories were thrown to the winds.

The delights of the ballroom, the sound of the music, the bare shoulders, the fire of the glances, the smiles on those rosy lips had gone to his head and would keep him awake the whole night. He would dwell on that waist which he had touched with his hands, those languorous, lingering looks which followed him on his way out, that hot breath which melted him during the waltz, that muted conversation at the window to the strains of the mazurka when eyes met and sparkled, and tongues were loosened. His heart would beat faster, and he would embrace his pillow convulsively, and toss and turn from side to side.

"But where is love? How I thirst for love!" he would say. "Will it come soon? When will I know those sublime moments, that sweet torment, when will I tremble with that bliss and shed those tears?" and so forth.

The next day he would go to see his uncle.

"Uncle, what a ball the Zarayskys gave last night!" he said, his mind full of memories of the ball.

"A good one?"

"Wonderful!"

"A decent supper?"

"I didn't have any."

"What do you mean? How could you go without supper at your age! Well, I can tell that you're really getting used to the life here, maybe a little too much. How about the rest of it? Were people well dressed? Was the lighting good?"

"Yes," he said uncertainly.

"And what kind of people – respectable?"

"Yes indeed! Very much so. What eyes, what shoulders!"

"Whose?"

"Are you really asking about them?"

"Who?"

"About the girls."

"No, I wasn't asking about *them*; but never mind: were there a lot of pretty ones?"

"Oh yes, a lot... but the trouble is, they were all very much alike. You hear one of them saying something or doing something in some situation, and the next thing you know, it would be repeated by one of the others as if it were a lesson learnt by rote. There was one a little different from the rest, but still no sign of an independent character. Even the look in their eyes and their movements – all exactly the same. You would never hear an original thought, or a glimmer of a feeling – everything all covered with the identical gloss. Nothing, it seems, could make them break through that surface. Can it be that whatever

CHAPTER 3

it is will remain for ever locked inside, and never revealed to a soul? Will the corset always restrain the sigh of love and the cry of the heart in torment, or allow a feeling to break through?"

"To a husband everything will be revealed, but if what I've heard you say is right, then I suppose many of them are doomed to end up old maids. There are those who are foolish enough to reveal prematurely what they should have kept hidden and suppressed; well, later on they will pay for that with their tears: it's not a good deal!"

"There you go again with your 'deals', Uncle!"

"Just as I would anywhere, my dear boy; there are words in our language, short and to the point, 'foolish and reckless' for anyone who doesn't think in these terms."

"But to suppress a spontaneous outburst of feeling!"

"Oh, I know you are not one to suppress his feelings. In the street or at the theatre you are ready to throw yourself sobbing into the arms of someone you know."

"And what's so wrong with that, Uncle? People would just say: 'Here is a man with strong feelings, and anyone who feels as strongly as that is capable of all that is fine and noble, and not capable of...'"

"...calculating outcomes, that is, thinking things through. So that's your idea of a great personality – a man with strong feelings and powerful passions. There are any number of men like that, ruled by their emotions – easily carried away and transported by their impulses. That kind of person simply falls short of being a man, and has nothing to recommend him. The question to ask is whether he can control his feelings; if he can, then he is a man..."

"The way you see it, a feeling is something to control, like steam," Alexander observed. "Let a little escape, and then suddenly shut it off, just a matter of turning a safety valve on and off..."

"Yes, nature had a purpose in equipping man with that safety valve – otherwise known as reason – and it's a pity you don't use it more often! Otherwise, you're not a bad lad!"

"No, Uncle, it's depressing to listen to you! I'd much sooner you introduced me to that lady who was visiting."

"What lady? Lyubetskaya? She was here last night?"

"Yes, she was; I had a long conversation with her about you, and asked about that business of hers."

"Oh yes, now that you mention it…" Pyotr Ivanych took out a document from a drawer. "Take this to her, and tell her that it was only issued to me yesterday, and even then I had some trouble getting it; you heard my conversation with that official, didn't you, so make sure to explain everything properly."

"Of course I know and will explain."

Alexander took hold of the document with both hands and put it carefully in his pocket. Pyotr Ivanych looked at him.

"Why on earth did you get to know her? It's not as if she's attractive – with that wart on her nose."

"A wart? I don't remember. How did you come to notice it, Uncle?"

"You really couldn't see the wart on her nose? What do you want from her?"

"She's so nice and respectable…"

"But how could you have failed to notice the wart on her nose, and yet be so certain that she's nice and respectable? Very strange. But wait a minute – yes, of course, she has a daughter, that little brunette. Well, now it makes sense – so that's why you didn't notice the wart on her nose!"

They both burst out laughing.

"I'll tell you what surprises me, Uncle," said Alexander, "that you noticed the wart on her nose before noticing the daughter."

"Give me back that document. I'm sure you're going to let your feelings overcome you once you're there and simply forget to turn off that tap, make a fool of yourself and spout God knows what nonsense…"

"No, Uncle, I won't, but if you don't want me to, I won't take the document; now I'm off…"

He left the room.

And so matters continued to take their normal course. At his place of work, Alexander's abilities were noticed, and he was given a decent position. Ivan Ivanych too began to treat him with respect and offer him his snuffbox, since he had the feeling that Alexander, like so many others, wouldn't take long before overtaking him, and would soon be

CHAPTER 3

breathing down his neck and competing with him for the position of head of department. And then, who knows, maybe make deputy director like the other one, or even reach the rank of director like yet another one, both of whom he had started on their careers under his guidance. "And to think that I should have worked so hard for their success – and end up working under them!" he added.

At the journal too Alexander had become a person of importance. He was responsible for selecting as well as translating and correcting foreign articles, and also wrote his own theoretical articles on agricultural matters. He earned more than enough for his needs in his own opinion, although not enough to satisfy his uncle. He didn't always work for money. He had never given up the gratifying idea of some other, higher calling. His youthful energies were fit for anything. He stole time from his sleep and his office work in order to write poetry, novellas, historical essays and biographies. His uncle no longer pasted up his compositions on screens, but read them in silence, and then give a whistle or said, "Now that's better than before!" Some articles appeared under another name. It gave Alexander a thrill to hear one of his many friends praise his work – friends he had made at work, in pastry shops and in private homes. After love itself, this was the fulfilment of his fondest dream. It seemed that a glittering and triumphant future and a quite exceptional fate lay in store for him, when suddenly...

A few months had gone by. Alexander was practically nowhere to be seen: it was as if he had simply vanished. His visits to his uncle became rare, and his uncle put it down to his work and didn't bother him. However, the editor of the journal once happened to meet him and complained that Alexander was late sending in his articles. Pyotr Ivanych promised that he would find out from his nephew what was going on the first chance he had. Two days later the opportunity arose when one morning Alexander rushed round to his uncle like a man possessed. His very movements betrayed a state of pleasurable agitation.

"Good morning, Uncle, you don't know how glad I am to see you again!" he said, and moved to embrace him. His uncle was quick to take shelter behind a table.

"Good morning, good morning Alexander. Why has it been so long since I've seen you?"

"Well, I was… busy; I was working on extracts from some German economists…"

"You mean the editor was lying? Two days ago he told me you weren't doing anything – typical journalist. When I see him I'll tell him off—"

"No, please do nothing of the sort," said Alexander, cutting him off. "I haven't sent him my work yet, that's why he complained…"

"What's the matter with you? Why in such a festive mood? Is it a promotion, or you've been given a decoration?"

Alexander shook his head.

"Well, is it money then?"

"No."

"Then why are you looking so cock-a-hoop? If there's nothing, then make yourself useful, and sit down and write to the merchant Dubasov in Moscow, asking him to send the rest of the money forthwith. Read his letter – now where did I put it? Oh yes, here it is."

They both fell silent and began to write.

"Finished!" said Alexander after a few minutes.

"That was quick, well done! Let's see it. What is this? You've been writing to me. 'To Pyotr Ivanych. Dear Sir!' But he's called Timofey Nikonych! Why have you written '520 roubles'? It should be '5,200'. What's the matter with you, Alexander?" Pyotr Ivanych put down his pen and looked at his nephew, who blushed.

"Don't you notice anything in my face?" he asked.

"Nothing except a pretty silly look; wait a minute… you're in love?" Pyotr Ivanych said.

Alexander said nothing.

"So what is it? Did I guess right?"

Alexander, with jubilation written all over him and shining eyes, nodded affirmatively.

"Of course, I should have known from the first. So that's why you've been slacking off, and are nowhere to be seen. Both the Zarayskys and the Skachinys have been questioning me so insistently: 'Where has Alexander Fyodorych got to?' Well, now I can tell them – he's been in seventh heaven!"

CHAPTER 3

Pyotr Ivanych resumed his writing.

"With Nadenka Lyubetskaya!" said Alexander.

"I wasn't asking you," his uncle replied. "Whoever it might have been – it's all the same foolishness. So which Lyubetskaya is it – the one with the wart?"

Alexander cut in with some annoyance, "What's this about warts?"

"You know, the one on the nose; haven't you spotted it yet?"

"You're mixing everything up. You must be thinking of the one on her mother's nose."

"It's all the same."

"All the same! Nadenka is an angel, surely you must have noticed – it only takes one look!"

"What's so special about her? What is there to notice, especially since you say yourself she doesn't have a wart?..."

"You seem to be obsessed with that wart. Don't talk like that, Uncle! How can you say that she is like those mechanical society dolls? Just look at her face, what a quiet thoughtfulness lies behind it! She is not only capable of deep feeling, but also of deep thought... nothing superficial about her!..."

His uncle went back to scratching the paper with his squeaky pen, but Alexander went on: "In conversation you will never hear her utter a trite commonplace. Her opinions positively sparkle with intelligence! What fire there is in her feelings, and how profound is her understanding of life! Your views on life poison it, but Nadenka reconciles me to it."

Alexander fell silent for a moment, totally absorbed in his reverie about Nadenka, and then resumed.

"The moment she raises her eyes, you can see that they are the windows to a passionate and tender heart! And her voice, her voice is pure melody, pure bliss! But when that voice rings with recognition... there is no greater bliss on earth! Uncle, life is so beautiful, and I am happy!"

His eyes brimmed with tears, and he rushed to embrace his uncle with outstretched arms.

"Alexander!" Pyotr Ivanych cried, springing up from his seat. "Turn off your safety valve at once, all the steam is escaping! You've taken leave of your senses! Just look what you've done. You've committed two idiocies in just one second, you've mussed up my hair and smudged the letter. I thought you had entirely given up your old habits. It's a long time since I've seen you like this. For God's sake, go and take a look at yourself in the mirror; have you ever seen a more idiotic face in your life? And yet, you're no idiot!"

Alexander burst out laughing. "I'm happy, Uncle."

"Obviously."

"Don't you find that my eyes shine with pride? I know they do. I look on everyone around me as only a hero, a poet or a man in love can, delirious with loving and being loved..."

"Yes, just the way madmen do – or even worse... Now, what am I going to do with that letter?"

"Let me scrape it off – it won't leave a mark," said Alexander.

He rushed to the table and, with the same febrile energy, proceeded to scrub, wipe and rub the letter until he had made a hole in it. The table was tottering from the assault and knocked against the bookcase on which an Italian alabaster bust of Sophocles or Aeschylus had been standing. The revered tragedian began to sway back and forth on its unstable base from the shaking, and finally toppled from its shelf onto the floor and was smashed to smithereens.

"Idiocy number three, Alexander!" said Pyotr Ivanych, picking up the pieces. "That was worth 500 roubles!"

"I'll pay for it, Uncle, I really will pay for it; don't get upset with me for my outburst: it was sincerely meant and with the purest of motives; it's just that I'm happy, truly happy! My God, life is so great!"

His uncle frowned and shook his head. "When will you learn sense, Alexander? What nonsense comes out of his mouth!" he said, looking mournfully at the shattered bust. 'I'll pay, I'll pay,'" he said, quoting Alexander. "That will be your fourth idiocy. I can see that you are anxious to tell me all about your happiness. Well, there's no help for it. If uncles are doomed to react every time their nephews come out with nonsense, so be it. I'll give you a quarter of an hour. Just sit quietly, and try not to talk yourself into a new, fifth idiocy – and after you've done that, you must leave, I don't have the time. All right, so you're happy... and then what? Hurry up and tell me!"

CHAPTER 3

"Well, if that's the way it is, Uncle, those things can't simply be told," Alexander remarked with a modest smile.

"I was hoping I'd said enough to forestall you, but I see that you are still bent on the usual preamble, and that is going to take a whole hour. I don't have time for that, the post isn't going to wait. So instead, why don't *I* tell *you*?"

"*You* tell *me*? That's pretty funny!"

"Well, hear this then: it's funny indeed! Yesterday you saw your beauty and were alone with her…"

"How come you know about that?" Alexander began heatedly. "You're having someone keep watch on me?"

"You really think I'm paying people to spy on you? Where did you get the idea that I'm that concerned about you? What's it to me?" These words were accompanied by an icy look.

"In that case how do you know?" Alexander asked, moving closer to his uncle.

"Sit down, sit down, for God's sake, and don't go near the table: you're sure to break something. Your face is an open book, and I'll read it. So, declarations were made," Pyotr Ivanych said.

Alexander said nothing. Clearly his uncle had put his finger right on it once again.

"Both of you were behaving like fools – it's only to be expected."

His nephew responded with a gesture of impatience.

"It all started over some trifle or other when you were left alone, probably some pattern she was using," Pyotr Ivanych continued, "and you asked her whom she was doing the embroidery for, and she replied 'For Mummy or Auntie', or something like that, and you both started trembling feverishly…"

"Well, Uncle, you guessed wrong; it wasn't a pattern, we were in the garden…" said Alexander, breaking off.

"All right, then it started with a flower," said Pyotr Ivanych, "perhaps even one of those yellow flowers, but no matter – whatever your eye happens to light on – anything just to get the conversation going: in those circumstances the tongue tends to dry up. So you asked her whether she liked the flower – she said yes. Then you asked her why, and

85

she said: 'I just like it.' Then you just ran out of conversation because you both really wanted to say something different. Then you looked at each other, smiled and blushed."

"Oh come on, Uncle, don't talk like that!..." Alexander blurted out in his embarrassment.

"Then," his uncle continued inexorably, "you managed to slip in some remark about how a new world had opened up before you, and she glanced at you as if she were hearing some unexpected news, and I imagine you were stumped and thrown off track, and then just managed to recover and find something to say that made sense, like it was only now that you had understood what life had to offer, and that you had seen – what's-her-name – Maria or whatever, somewhere before."

"It's Nadenka."

"And it was as if you had seen her in a dream and had a premonition that you would meet her one day, that you were kindred souls. Then you said that from now on you would be dedicating all your writings, prose and verse... And I bet you were flinging your arms in all directions, and that you must have knocked something over and broken it."

Alexander was beside himself and burst out: "Uncle, you were eavesdropping!"

"Yes, of course, I was sitting behind a bush – as if the only thing I had to do was to run after you so as to hear all your foolishness!"

"Then how come you know all this?" Alexander asked in bewilderment.

"It stands to reason: it's been the same old story since Adam and Eve – with slight variations. Once you know the character of the dramatis personae you can predict the variations. And that surprises you – and you're a writer no less? And now you'll be making a big song and dance for the next couple of days and buttonholing everyone you meet, but please leave me out of it, for God's sake! My advice to you is to lock yourself in your room for the next few days and let off all your steam while you're there, and take out all your nonsense on Yevsei out of everyone's sight. Then you'll come to your senses a little, and take things a little further – maybe a kiss..."

CHAPTER 3

"A kiss from Nadenka – oh what a sublime, heavenly reward!" Alexander was almost shouting.

"Heavenly!"

"So the way you see it, it's purely matter-of-fact, down to earth?"

"Unquestionably, it's purely the effect of electricity: two lovers like two Leyden jars, both fully charged, discharge the stored-up energy through kisses, and when fully discharged, it's goodbye to love, and everything cools off afterwards..."

"Uncle..."

"Yes, and what did you think?"

"What a way to look at things!"

"Oh yes, I forgot: you will still be interpreting everything in terms of 'material manifestations', and you're bringing even more rubbish, and analysing and speculating while business goes by the board."

Alexander clutched at his pocket.

"What else have you got there? You'll be doing what people have been doing since the world began."

"That is to say, exactly what you did, Uncle."

"Yes, only a little more foolish."

"More foolish! In other words, what you're calling foolish is the fact that I will be loving more deeply, more strongly than you, and not mocking that feeling, and I won't be making light of it and toying with it cold-bloodedly like you... and not trying to poke holes in the most sacred secrets..."

"And you, my boy, will be loving just like everyone else, no more deeply and no more strongly, and you'll also be poking holes in secrets... the only difference being that you will continue to believe that love is eternal and immutable, and that alone will fill your thoughts – and that's precisely where the foolishness comes in – you will be storing up vastly more pain for yourself than is necessary."

"Oh Uncle, what you're saying is terrible, terrible! How many times I have sworn to myself never to reveal to you what I have in my heart."

"Then why didn't you do just that – instead of coming here and bothering me?..."

"As you must know, it's because you are the person closest to me, the only one to whom I can unburden myself when my heart is full, but it is you who so pitilessly plunge your surgical scalpel into the innermost recesses of my heart."

"It's not something I do for my own pleasure: it's you who asked me for my advice. Think of all the folly I've saved you from!"

"No, Uncle, I would rather remain forever stupid in your eyes than live with such ideas about life and people. It's too painful, too distressing! What would be the point of living like that? And I refuse to live like that – you hear me? I will not!"

"Yes, I hear you; so what am I to do? I can't take your life from you."

"Right," said Alexander. "In spite of all your predictions, I'm going to be happy, and go on loving once and for all."

"Oh no! I have the feeling that you'll be breaking a lot of my things before you're finished. Love's all very well, and no one is stopping you, but at your age love should not be your major preoccupation, at least not to the point where your work is thrown aside; yes, love is all very well, but it's work that matters…"

"Well, I'm doing these extracts from those German—"

"Enough! You're doing nothing of the kind: you're just immersing yourself in that 'sublime bliss' of yours, and the editor will drop you…"

"Let him! I don't need him. How can I be thinking of filthy lucre when—"

"Oh, 'filthy lucre', is it? Despicable, is it? You'd be better off building a shack in the hills and living on bread and water, and singing:

"A squalid shack and you,
That's my idea of heaven…

"But when you run out of 'filthy lucre', don't come running to me; I won't be giving you any…"

"I don't think I've troubled you much on that score."

"So far, thank God, you haven't, but it might happen if you give up working. Love too takes money – those fancy clothes, and all those

CHAPTER 3

other expenses... Oh yes, that's love for you, when you're twenty! Now that's what I call despicable – so despicable, absolutely no use!"

"So when *is* it useful, Uncle? When you're forty?"

"I don't know what love is like at forty, but at thirty-nine..."

"Like your own love?"

"Yes, if you like, like mine."

"That is to say, none at all..."

"How would you know?"

"Are you suggesting you're capable of loving?"

"Why wouldn't I be? I'm a man, aren't I? And am I eighty years old? It's just that if I love, I love sensibly: I don't forget myself, and don't flail my arms or knock things over."

"Sensible love! Some love that! – which doesn't forget itself for an instant, and keeps itself in check—" Alexander remarked derisively.

"Wild, animal love," Pyotr Ivanych broke in, "is unbridled, but sensible love knows how to keep itself in check, otherwise it's not love..."

"Then what is it?"

"It's an abomination – as you would put it."

"You – love!" Alexander retorted in disbelief. "You make me laugh."

Pyotr Ivanych went on writing in silence.

"Then who is she, Uncle?" asked Alexander.

"You would like to know?"

"Yes, I would."

"My fiancée."

"Your fi... fiancée!" Alexander could hardly get the word out of his mouth, as he leapt up and approached his uncle.

"Don't come any closer, Alexander, and turn off that tap!" Pyotr Ivanych snapped, seeing his nephew's eyes widening, and swiftly moved various objects closer to himself for protection – busts, figurines, timepieces and an inkstand.

"You mean you're getting married?" Alexander asked, no less amazed.

"Yes, that's what I mean."

"But you're so calm! There you are, writing letters to Moscow, talking about everything else, going to your factory, and even lecturing me with diabolical frigidity about love itself!"

"'Diabolical frigidity' – that's a new one. Where the Devil lives it's actually pretty hot, so I'm told. And why are you looking at me with that weird expression?"

"You – getting married?"

"What's so surprising about that?" asked Pyotr Ivanych, putting down his pen.

"What do you mean, 'what's so surprising'? You're getting married – and not a word to me!"

"I'm so sorry, I forgot to ask your permission."

"It's not a matter of asking permission, but I ought to have known. My own uncle is getting married, and I know nothing about it – you didn't even tell me."

"Well, I've just told you."

"Only because the subject happened to come up."

"I do my best to be relevant at all times."

"No, the point is that I should have been the first to hear your good news; you know that I love you and want to share your joy…"

"I'm totally averse to sharing – especially when it comes to marriage."

"Well, you know what, Uncle?" Alexander said eagerly. "Perhaps… No, I can't hide it from you… I'm not like you, I'll tell you everything…"

"No, Alexander, I don't have time now. If you've got a new story, why not save it for tomorrow."

"I just wanted to tell you that I may be… close to the same happiness…"

"What's that?" said Pyotr Ivanych, his interest piqued. "Now you've made me curious…"

"Ah, so you're curious? In that case, I'll keep you guessing. I won't tell you."

Pyotr Ivanych, quite unmoved, calmly proceeded to pick up the package, put the letter in it and began to seal it.

"I too may be getting married!" Alexander spoke straight into his uncle's ear.

Pyotr Ivanych stopped sealing his letter and gave him an unusually stern look.

"Turn the tap off, Alexander!" he said.

CHAPTER 3

"Joke away as much as you like, Uncle, but I'm not joking. I'm going to ask Mummy's permission."

"You... get married!"

"What about it?"

"At your age!"

"I'm twenty-three."

"And you think that's the right time? Only peasants get married at that age, and that's only when they need someone to do the housework."

"So, as you see it, just because I'm in love with a young woman, and it's possible for us to marry, it doesn't mean that I should..."

"I'm advising you not to marry a woman you're in love with under any circumstances."

"Well, Uncle, that's quite a new one, I've never heard anything like it."

"There's quite a lot of things you haven't heard!"

"I've always thought that people should never get married without love."

"Marriage is one thing, and love is quite another matter," said Pyotr Ivanych.

"So what should marriage be based on, some kind of cost accounting?"

"No, not cost accounting: more like taking account of – and it's not just money that you should take account of. A man is meant to live in the company of women; even you will find yourself figuring things out when it comes to marriage: searching, making choices from among the women you meet..."

"Searching, choosing!" Alexander repeated in amazement.

"Yes, choosing; and it's for that very reason that I'm advising you not to marry when you're in love. Love passes: it's a well-worn, banal truth."

"It's an outrageous lie, a vile calumny!"

"Right now there's no convincing you, but you'll see when you're older; for now just remember what I'm telling you. I can only repeat, love will pass, and that woman who once appeared to you ideal and perfection itself may turn out to be far from perfect, and there will be nothing you can do. Love blinds you to the lack of those qualities a woman should possess. When the time comes and you find yourself choosing – yes, you will be coldly calculating whether the woman in question possesses those qualities you want in a wife, and that's where the crucial 'accounting' comes in. And if you succeed in finding a woman like this, you will always be pleased with her because she possesses precisely the qualities you wanted. In this way, you will grow closer and closer, and eventually the relationship will become—"

"Love?" asked Alexander.

"Yes… you become accustomed to each other."

"But to marry dispassionately, without the poetry of love, without ardour, just weighing the pros and cons, what's the point?"

"So you would get married just like that, without even asking yourself what for – exactly the same way when you came here, without even stopping to consider why?"

"So you are getting married on the basis of cost accounting?" asked Alexander.

"No, but, as I told you, more like taking account of relevant factors."

"It's all the same."

"No, this cost accounting of yours *would* mean marrying for money – and that *would* be despicable, but to get married without giving the matter any thought – now that would be stupid… but now is absolutely the wrong time for you to marry."

"So when am I supposed to get married – when I'm an old man? Why should I follow some ridiculous example?"

"Like mine, for instance? Thank you very much!"

"I wasn't talking about you, Uncle, it was just a generalization. You hear about a wedding, and you go and take a look – and what do you see? A tender young thing, practically a child, who was just waiting for that magical touch of love before flowering into a luxuriant blossom, and suddenly she is wrenched from her dolls, her nanny, her childish games and dances, and let's hope that's all. Often no one is looking into her heart, which maybe no longer belongs to her. They dress her in gossamer and fine lace and adorn her with flowers, and regardless of her tears, her pallor, drag her like a sacrificial victim, and who do they stand her beside? Some elderly fellow, chances are, not too good-looking, who has already lost the bloom of youth. Either he degrades her with his lascivious glances or he looks her over from

CHAPTER 3

head to toe, thinking to himself: 'Oh yes, you're pretty enough, with a head stuffed full of frippery: love and roses – I'll soon cure her of that, it's tommyrot. No more of that sighing and dreaming when you're with me! And you'll conduct yourself with dignity.' Or even worse, what's on his mind is her estate. At the very best he will be no more than thirty. Chances are, he's bald – although, of course, he sports a decoration like a cross or a star. She is told: 'He's the one to whom you will be giving up the treasures of your youth, the first beating of your heart, your first murmurs of love, your first, those glances, those outpourings, those demure gestures of affection – in a word, your whole life.' Meanwhile, she is surrounded by a crowd of those who match her in youth and beauty and should be the ones standing beside the bride. They devour the poor victim with their eyes as if they are thinking: 'When we've run out of the freshness of our youth and the robustness of our health, and have lost our hair, then we'll get married and be awarded one of these exotic flowers...' It's horrible."

"That's crazy talk. You should know better, Alexander; you've been writing for two years now," said Pyotr Ivanych, "about manure, potatoes and other serious subjects where a disciplined, concise style is important, and here you are coming out with all this blather. For God's sake don't let yourself get carried away, or at the very least when you feel the urge coming on, just hold your tongue and wait for it to pass. You won't make any sense, and no good will come of it. You'll just make yourself ridiculous."

"But Uncle, isn't that how poets get their inspiration – by getting carried away?"

"I don't know how they get their inspiration, but I do know that fully fledged ideas come out of the head only when they have been thoroughly worked out, and they are the only ones worth anything." Pyotr Ivanych paused and then added: "And who would you have these lovely creatures married to?"

"To those that they love, who haven't yet lost the bloom of their youthful beauty – in whose hearts and minds, it's clear to anyone, life is still present; those who still have a glitter in their eyes and colour in their cheeks, and haven't lost their freshness – all signs of good health; those who won't be leading their charming companions along life's road by a withered hand, but would present them with the gift of hearts full of love for them, hearts able to understand and share their feelings, when the rights of nature..."

"That's enough! You mean young bucks like yourself. If we lived 'among fields and forests primeval',* all right, then go and marry the young buck – much good would it do you! In the first year he would go out of his mind, and then go out looking for satisfaction elsewhere, or would make the chambermaid into his wife's rival, because those rights of nature which you talk about demand change and novelty – what a wonderful scenario that would be! And the next thing you know, the wife, noticing what her husband is getting up to, would suddenly take a fancy to helmets, fine clothing and masked balls, and get back at him... and without a fortune, so much the worse! He'd be saying he couldn't even afford to eat!" Pyotr Ivanych made a sour face, then added:

"'I'm married,' he says, 'and have three children, please help me, I have nothing to live on, I'm poor...' Poor, what an abomination! No, I hope you don't fall into either of these categories."

"I'll fall into the category of the happily married husbands, Uncle, and Nadenka will fall into the category of happily married wives. I don't want to marry the way most do – with that same old song: 'My youth has gone, I don't want to be left alone: time to get married!' I'm not like that."

"You're raving, my dear boy."

"And what makes you think so?"

"Because you're just like the others, and I've long been acquainted with those others. Well, tell me why you want to get married."

"What do you mean, 'why'? Nadenka – my wife!" Alexander exclaimed, covering his face with his hands.

"So you see, you don't even know yourself."

"The very thought of it makes me feel faint. You don't know how much I love her, Uncle; no one has ever loved anyone so much – with all my heart and soul – she means everything to me..."

CHAPTER 3

"You'd do better to tell me off – or, if you have to, even embrace me; anything but just repeating that absurd phrase! How can you let your tongue run away with you like that 'more than anyone has ever loved anyone'?!"

Pyotr Ivanych shrugged his shoulders.

"So you really think it's impossible?"

"Well, thinking of *your* love, yes, it may even be possible, but a more foolish love it would be hard to imagine!"

"But she says that we should wait a year, that we are still young and should put ourselves to the test... a whole year... and then—"

"A year! Oh well, you should have told me right at the start!" Pyotr Ivanych broke in. "And that was her idea? How clever she must be! How old is she?"

"Eighteen."

"And you are what – twenty-three? That makes her twenty-three times as smart as you. It seems to me that she knows what she is doing. She's playing with you, flirting a little and having a good time, so it seems that some of those young hussies have brains in their heads! So you won't be marrying then. I thought you wanted to go ahead with it quickly, and in secret. At your age, you act on your reckless impulses promptly, and there's no time to stop you; but in a year – by that time she'll have dropped you..."

"Her – drop me – flirt! A flibbertigibbet! Her, Nadenka! Not on your life, Uncle! Who have you been living among your whole life – who have you been dealing with – who have you loved, that you should harbour such dark suspicions?..."

"I've lived among people, and I've loved a woman."

"She will deceive me? That angel, the very embodiment of sincerity, the first woman that God seems to have created entirely pure and flawless?..."

"But still a woman for all that, who will very likely deceive you."

"And next you're going to say that I too will drop her?"

"Yes, in time, you too."

"Me! You can say what you like about people you don't know, but me! You should be ashamed of yourself to think that I would be capable of such abominable behaviour. Is that how you see me?"

"I see you as a man."

"Not all of us are alike. I want you to know in all seriousness that I have given her my solemn promise to love her my whole life, and am ready to swear it under oath…"

"You don't need to tell me, I know! A decent man never doubts the sincerity of an oath he has sworn to a woman, but eventually betrays her, or cools off – and maybe doesn't even know why himself. It's not done intentionally, and there's nothing abominable about it, and no one is to blame: nature simply does not permit eternal love. Those who believe in eternal and unfailing love act in just the same way as those who don't: the only difference being that the former aren't, or at least profess not to be, aware of what they're doing; the idea being that: 'Oh no, we're above that sort of thing, we're angels, not people' – what rot!"

"Then what about married couples who start off in love, stay in love for ever and live together their whole lives?…"

"For ever! Someone who stays in love for two weeks is called fickle, but if he lasts for two or three years – then that counts as for ever! Just consider the actual constituents of love, and you will see for yourself that it's not eternal. Spontaneity, fervour, exuberance are emotions which by their very nature are not made to last. Yes, married couples do spend their lives together, but does that mean that they love each other all their lives, does it mean that they miss each other the moment they are apart, that they revel in every glimpse of each other, as if they are bound to each other in perpetuity by that first love which brought them together? What eventually becomes of those little efforts to please each other, the constant attention paid to each other, the constant need for each other's company, the tears, the raptures, all that kind of nonsense? There's a saying which sums up the coldness and sluggishness of husbands, and which is so solemnly intoned: 'Their love has turned into friendship.' Well, of course, that's no longer love! And friendship – what kind of friendship is it? The couple are bound together by common interests, by circumstances, by a common destiny – so they live together, but without that they part, and find others to love – one first, and then followed by the other; that's known as betrayal… And just between us, I'm telling you that this living together eventually turns

CHAPTER 3

into a habit which becomes stronger than love, and is rightly known as love's second incarnation, otherwise people would spend all their lives grief-stricken when deprived of their loved one by separation or death, whereas in fact they do manage to get over it; yet they kept on repeating 'for ever, for ever' – even shouting it aloud mindlessly."

"But aren't you at all afraid for yourself, Uncle? If you're right – and I'm sorry to say this – won't your own fiancée let you down?..."

"I don't think so."

"Isn't that rather conceited?"

"It's not conceit: it's a pondered conclusion!"

"Here you go again with your 'conclusions'!"

"Well, if you prefer, careful reflection."

"What if she falls in love with someone else?"

"It shouldn't be allowed to get to that point, but if such an aberration were to occur, one would find subtler ways of cooling the ardour."

"As if that were possible! Do you really think it would be within your power?..."

"Easily."

"But then all deceived husbands would have done that if it were that easy," said Alexander.

"Not all husbands are alike, my dear boy: some are quite indifferent to their wives, and simply don't notice what is going on around them, others don't want to know. Others again would like just to maintain their self-esteem, but are not up to the task, and have no idea how to set about it."

"Then how do you do it?"

"That's my secret; and in any case in your overwrought state you wouldn't be able to take it in."

"I'm happy now and I thank God, and as for what lies ahead, I don't want to know."

"The first half of your sentence makes so much sense that it could well have been uttered by someone who was not in love, and shows that you're able to make the most of the present moment. However, the second half, I'm sorry to say, is no use at all. 'I don't want to know what lies ahead' means you don't want to think about what happened yesterday and what's happening today, and you don't want to spare a thought for that, or prepare yourself for it or to protect yourself against whatever it is that might happen! I'm sorry, but that makes absolutely no sense."

"So what you're saying, Uncle, is that when a moment of bliss comes your way, you should take a magnifying glass to it and examine it…"

"No, a microscope, to stop you making a fool of yourself over that moment of bliss and rushing into the arms of everyone you meet."

"So, when a moment of sorrow comes your way," Alexander went on, "you have to peer at that too through a microscope?"

"No, through a magnifying glass! When your imagination makes your troubles appear twice their actual size, they're easier to bear."

"But why," Alexander continued indignantly, "should I destroy every chance of happiness by cold-blooded scrutiny the moment it comes my way, instead of relishing it. And why should I assume that it will let me down and slip from my grasp? Why should I agonize over sorrow before it has even presented itself?"

"However," his uncle broke in, "when it does present itself, it's precisely to that cold-blooded scrutiny that you should subject it, and the pain will pass as it has on past occasions with me and with others. I hope what I've said is useful and is something worth your consideration, and then you won't have to agonize every time something happens in life that you weren't expecting, and that you will learn to appraise matters coolly and without losing your peace of mind – to the extent possible for a human being."

"So that's the secret of your composure!" said Alexander thoughtfully.

Pyotr Ivanych remained silent and continued writing.

"But what kind of life is that? Never forgetting yourself – nothing but thinking and thinking… no, my feeling is that that's not the way it is. I prefer to live without your cold analysis, not always wondering whether disaster and danger are lying in wait or not – it doesn't matter!… Why should I anticipate trouble and poison everything?"

"Well, I keep telling him why – but he always comes back with the same story. Don't force me to make invidious comparisons with you. It's because when you foresee danger, obstacles, disaster, that's how you will find it easier to combat them, or at least endure them – you won't lose your head, and you'll survive, and when happiness comes to you, you won't rush round knocking over people's ornaments – is that clear?

"We tell him: 'This is the beginning; take a good look at it, and try to figure out from it how it's likely to end,' but he just closes his eyes and shakes his head as if he's just seen some bogeyman, and continues to behave like a child. Your idea is to live from one day to the next, as people do, and sit at the door of your shack, marking the passage of time by dinners, meals, dances and love and everlasting friendship. Everyone is looking for a golden age! Now, as I've told you, with your ideas it's all right to live in the country with some woman and half a dozen children, but here you have to work, and for that you need to think all the time and remember what you did yesterday, and what you are doing today, so as to know what to do tomorrow; in other words, keep a constant check on yourself and your doings. This is how we achieve something worthwhile in life; otherwise... But what's the use of talking to you? You're delirious right now. Oh dear, it's almost one, not another word; Alexander, go away... I don't want to listen to you. Come here for dinner tomorrow; there'll be a few other people dining with me."

"Friends of yours?"

"Yes, Konev, Smirnov, Fyodorov – you know them, and one or two others..."

"Konev, Smirnov, Fyodorov – aren't they business colleagues?"

"Yes, they're all useful people."

"And that's what you call your friends! As a matter of fact, I've never seen you invite anyone home with particular enthusiasm."

"I've told you before that the people I see most often are those who are useful, and whose company I enjoy. Now, why on earth would I waste a meal on them otherwise?"

"But I thought that before your wedding you would be celebrating your farewell with your true friends, people you care for deeply, and with whom you would get together one last time over a cup of something to reminisce about the good times of your youth and, even on parting, enfold in a warm embrace."

"Those five words of yours – 'true friends', 'cup', 'on parting' – all say things that do not – or should not – exist in real life. With what delight your aunt would throw her arms around your neck if she had read them! In actual fact, these *were* 'true friends', whereas there are others who are merely 'friends', who drink from glasses of one kind or another instead of a 'cup', and their 'warm embraces' on parting have nothing to do with a real 'parting'. Oh, Alexander!"

"But aren't you sorry to be parting from those friends, or at least seeing them only rarely?" said Alexander.

"No, I have never got close enough to anyone to feel like that, and I advise you to do the same."

"But perhaps they don't feel the same way: maybe they are sorry to be losing a good companion and his conversation?"

"That's for them to say, not me. I have lost such good companions more than once, and as you see, it hasn't killed me. So will you be here tomorrow?"

"Well, tomorrow, Uncle, I…"

"What?"

"I'm invited to their dacha."

"Really, to the Lyubetskys?"

"Yes."

"Indeed! Well, as you wish. And, Alexander, keep your mind on your work. I'll tell the editor what you're working on…"

"But, Uncle, there's really no need to do that! I will definitely finish work on those German economists…"

"Well, you'd better *start work* on them first. And be sure to remember: don't come to me for any of that 'filthy lucre' while you're totally in thrall to the charms of that 'sublime bliss'."

Chapter 4

ALEXANDER'S LIFE WAS SPLIT IN TWO. In the morning he immersed himself in his work. He rooted around in dusty files, tried to make sense of details that meant absolutely nothing to him, and counted enormous sums of money that didn't belong to him. But sometimes his head simply gave up thinking about matters irrelevant to him: his pen slipped from his fingers, and he gave himself up to that "sublime bliss" that so infuriated his uncle.

Then Alexander would lean back in his chair and let himself be transported to "green pastures", that tranquil place where there were no papers, no inkwells, no strange faces, no uniforms, a cool place where peace, quiet and bliss reigned supreme, and where in an elegantly appointed salon scented with the fragrance of flowers, a piano was tinkling, a parrot prancing in a cage. In the garden, birch branches and clusters of lilac were gently swaying. And it was *she*, the queen who reigned over all this…

In the morning, Alexander, sitting at his desk in the office, in his imagination was already on one of the islands at the Lyubetskys' dacha, but in the evening he was actually there in the flesh. Let us intrude on his blissful state and take a look.

St Petersburg was having one of its rare hot days. The sun brought the fields to life, but was having a deadening effect on the streets, heating the granite with its rays, bouncing off the stone and scorching passers-by. People were moving slowly with their heads down, and the dogs' tongues were hanging out. St Petersburg resembled one of those fairy-tale cities where everything had suddenly been turned to stone with a wave of the wizard's wand. The carriages rumbled over the cobbles. Blinds were lowered over the windows like eyes which had been closed. The wooden-block paving gleamed like parquet floors, and the heat underfoot burned the feet of pedestrians. The city was lifeless and sleepy.

Someone was wiping the sweat from his face and seeking shade. A stagecoach carrying six passengers crawled into the city, scarcely raising dust. At four o'clock, office workers were leaving their workplaces and quietly plodding their way home.

Alexander rushed out as if the ceiling were collapsing onto his head and looked at his watch – too late; he would never make it in time for dinner. He hurried to a restaurant.

"What do you have? I'm in a hurry!"

"*Soupe julienne* and *à la reine, sauce à la provençale, à la maître d'hôtel*.* Roast turkey, game bird and soufflé."

"I'll have *soupe à la provençale*, *sauce julienne* and the roast and the soufflé, and please make it quick!"

The waiter looked at him.

"Well, what is it?" he said impatiently.

The waiter rushed off and served up whatever entered his head.

Aduyev was very pleased. Without waiting for the dessert, he ran to the Neva embankment, where a boat with two oarsmen was awaiting him. After an hour he caught sight of his little plot of promised land, and strained to see into the distance. At first his eyes glazed over with apprehension and anxiety, which grew into doubt. Then suddenly his eyes lit up with joy like a sudden ray of sunlight. He made out a familiar dress by the garden fence: someone there had recognized him and was waving a scarf. Someone had been waiting for him, perhaps for a long time. The soles of his feet were practically burning with impatience.

"Ah, if only I could have walked here on the water," he thought. "They invent all kinds of rubbish, but they haven't come up with that!"

The oarsmen were rowing slowly and steadily like a machine. Sweat was pouring down their sunburnt faces; it didn't matter to them that Alexander's heart was beating wildly in his chest, and that without lowering his eyes from the spot on which they were trained, and without noticing what he was doing, he had already twice stretched one foot after another over the edge of the boat; they continued rowing just as phlegmatically as before, stopping from time to time to wipe the sweat from their faces with their sleeves.

"Speed up!" he said. "There's fifty copecks in it for you for vodka."

CHAPTER 4

They set to work with a will, rising out of their seats from the effort, with not the slightest sign of the earlier fatigue. From where had they summoned this vigour? Their oars skimmed the water. The boat slipped through the water and covered five yards in a trice. Ten more strokes – the stern described an arc, and then slid gracefully alongside the riverbank. Alexander and Nadenka exchanged smiles at a distance, without taking their eyes off each other. Aduyev stepped off the boat, missing the bank with one foot and hitting the water instead. Nadenka burst out laughing.

"Take it easy, sir, just wait a moment and I'll give you my hand!" said one of the oarsmen, but by that time Alexander was already on shore.

"Wait for me here!" Alexander told them, and ran towards to Nadenka. She smiled affectionately at him from a distance. As the boat had moved closer and closer to the shore, her breast had begun to rise and fall more and more rapidly.

"Nadezhda Alexandrovna!" said Aduyev, breathless with delight.

"Alexander Fyodorych!" she replied.

They rushed spontaneously towards each other, but stopped and looked at each other with a smile, moist eyes, unable to speak. They stood like that for several minutes.

Pyotr Ivanych cannot be blamed for failing to notice Nadenka the first time. She was no beauty, and did not command one's immediate attention. But once someone had taken a longer look at her features, he would keep looking for a long time. Her face was rarely still for longer than two minutes. The thoughts and different kinds of sensations of her extraordinarily impressionable and restless nature passed across her face in rapid succession, and the shades of these sensations mingled kaleidoscopically, creating a new and unexpected expression from one moment to the next. Her eyes, for example, would suddenly flash like lightning, catch fire, and as suddenly would hide behind her long eyelashes, and her face would suddenly become lifeless and immobile – it was just as if it was a marble statue facing you. But the next thing you are expecting is the same kind of penetrating radiance – nothing of the kind! The eyes would open slowly and quietly, and you would be bathed in the light of a demure glow from her gaze, like that of the moon slowly gliding from behind a cloud. Your heart could not help missing a beat in response to that look. The same was true of her movements: they were very graceful, but it was not the grace of a sylph. It was a grace which contained a strong element of something unrestrained and impulsive, something which nature has given to us all, but every trace of which is subsequently eroded by the civilizing process, instead of merely being attenuated. It was these traces which could so often be detected in Nadenka's movements.

She would sometimes sit as if posing for a picture, but suddenly, because of some unfathomable inner prompting, this pose would be interrupted by an entirely unexpected, and once again enchanting, gesture. The same unexpected twists and turns also occurred in her conversation – a firm opinion, followed by a pensive silence; a sudden sharp criticism followed by some childish prattle or subtle dissembling, all of which revealed her passionate, headstrong and fickle personality. Anyone would have been expected to fall for her head over heels, and Alexander was no exception. Pyotr Ivanych was a rare exception, and failed to succumb.

"You've been waiting for me – my God, how happy that makes me!" said Alexander.

"Was I? I didn't give it a thought," Nadenka replied, shaking her head. "You know I'm always in the garden."

"Are you angry?" he asked meekly.

"Why should I be? What an idea!"

"Well, give me your hand!"

She stretched out her hand, but the moment he touched it she withdrew it, and her expression changed abruptly. Her smile vanished and was replaced by something akin to annoyance.

"What are you drinking, is it milk?" he asked.

Nadenka was holding a cup of milk and a rusk in her hands.

"It's my dinner," she replied.

"Dinner? But it's six o'clock – and milk!"

"Well, of course, you must find it strange to see milk after a lavish dinner at your uncle's, but here in the country, we live modestly."

CHAPTER 4

She broke off a few morsels of the rusk with her front teeth, and took a sip of the milk, pursing her lips endearingly.

"I didn't have dinner at my uncle's: I told him yesterday that I couldn't," Aduyev replied.

"That wasn't very nice: how could you lie like that? And where have you been since then?"

"Today I was at work until four…"

"Well, it's six now, so tell the truth and own up: you couldn't resist going to some dinner in pleasant company, could you? I'm sure you had a wonderful time.

"Word of honour – I didn't go to my uncle's…" Alexander started to defend himself heatedly. "If I had, there's no way I could have got here by now!"

"You call this early? Well, you could have arrived two hours later for all I care!" said Nadenka, doing a swift about-turn, and set off on the path back to the house. Alexander followed her.

"Keep away from me, keep away from me!" she said with a wave of her hand. "I can't stand the sight of you."

"Stop clowning, Nadezhda Alexandrovna!"

"I'm not clowning at all. I really want to know where you were before you came."

"I left the office at four o'clock…" Aduyev began, "and it took me an hour to get here…"

"You see, you're still lying!"

"I had a quick bite at a restaurant…"

"A quick bite! And only one hour," she said. "You poor thing, you must be really hungry! Would you like some milk?"

"Please give me that cup…" said Alexander, and held out his hand. She stopped suddenly, turned the cup upside down and, paying no attention to Alexander, watched with curiosity as the last drops spilt onto the sand.

"You have no pity!" he said. "How can you torment me like this?"

"Watch this, watch this, Alexander Fyodorych," Nadenka suddenly broke in, interrupting him, totally absorbed in what she was doing. "See that bug, the one crawling along the path? Will I be able to hit it with a drop of the milk? Oh, I got it! Poor thing, it's dying!" she said, and then carefully picked it up, placed it on her palm and started to breathe on it.

"What a fuss you're making of that bug," he said with annoyance.

"The poor thing – don't you see it's dying?" she said sadly. "What have I done?"

She held the bug on her palm for a short time, but when it started moving, and creeping up and down her arm, Nadenka shuddered, threw it on the ground, crushed it under her foot with the words "Nasty bug!" and then asked: "So where were you"?

"But I've already told you…"

"Oh yes, of course, at your uncle's. Were there a lot of guests? Did you have champagne? I can even smell it from where I'm standing…"

"No, I wasn't, I wasn't at my uncle's…" Alexander cut in in desperation. "Who told you that?"

"Why, you told me."

"At my uncle's, I would say that they're sitting down to dinner just about now. You don't know those dinners – do you really think they're over in an hour?"

"You took two hours – between five and seven."

"So when was it that I was travelling to get here?"

She made no attempt to reply, but jumped to pick a spray of acacia and then ran off along the path.

Aduyev followed her.

"Where are you going?" he asked.

"Where? What do you mean, 'where'? What a question! To Mummy."

"But why? Maybe we'll be bothering her."

"No, of course we won't."

Maria Mikhailovna, Nadezhda Alexandrovna's "mummy", was one of those good-natured and uncomplicated mothers who think that everything their children do is wonderful. Maria Mikhailovna would, for example, order the carriage to be harnessed, and Nadenka would ask her where she wanted to go.

"Let's go for a drive, the weather's beautiful!" her mother would say.

"How can we? Alexander Fyodorych will be here."

CHAPTER 4

So the carriage would be unharnessed.

Another time, Maria Mikhailovna would sit down at her endless scarf and start sighing, take a pinch of snuff and start plying her bone knitting needles, or bury herself in a French novel.

"*Maman*, why aren't you dressed to go out?" Nadenka would admonish her.

"Go out where?"

"But we're going for a walk."

"A walk?"

"Yes, Alexander Fyodorych is coming for us. Don't tell me you've forgotten?"

"Oh, I didn't know."

"How could you not know?" Nadenka would scold her.

So her mother would abandon the scarf or the book and go to get dressed. Nadenka enjoyed total freedom. She did whatever she wished and whenever she wished – and saw to it that her mother did too. However, she was a good and affectionate daughter, although you couldn't call her an obedient one. It was her mother who did all the obeying, and was the obedient one.

"Go in to Mummy!" said Nadenka as they approached the door of the living room.

"What about you?"

"I'll join you later."

"Well, I'll go in later too."

"No, you go in first!"

Alexander went in, and immediately tiptoed out again.

"She's dozing in her armchair," he whispered.

"Don't worry, let's go in. *Maman, maman*!" she called.

"Wha!..."

"Alexander Fyodorych is here."

"Wha!..."

"Monsieur Aduyev is here to see you."

"Wha!..."

"You see, she's sound asleep. Don't wake her up!" Alexander tried to insist.

"No, I'm going to wake her. *Maman*!"

"Wha!…"

"Now, wake up, Alexander Fyodorych is here."

"Where's Alexander Fyodorych?" said Maria Mikhailovna, looking straight at him and adjusting her cap, which had slipped to one side.

"Oh, it's you, Alexander Fyodorych? Welcome! And here I was just sitting here. I must have dozed off – I don't know why; it must be the weather. My corn is beginning to act up for some reason – there's going to be rain. I fell asleep, and dreamt that Ignaty was announcing guests, but I didn't understand who. I heard a voice say that someone had come, but couldn't make out who. Then I hear Nadenka calling out, and woke up right away. I'm a light sleeper. If someone makes the slightest sound, I'm awake and looking. Please sit down, Alexander Fyodorych, are you well?"

"Very well, thank you kindly."

"And how is Pyotr Ivanych?"

"Very well, thank God. Thank you for asking."

"Why does he never visit us? Only yesterday, I was thinking how nice it would be if he came to see us some time, but no; he's busy no doubt?"

"Very busy," said Alexander.

"Haven't seen you for two days," Maria Mikhailovna went on. "One day I woke up, and asked, 'What's Nadenka doing?'

"'She's still asleep,' I was told.

"'Well let her sleep, she's spent the whole day outdoors – in the garden; the weather is fine, so she'll be tired.' Young people sleep soundly, but at my age, we don't – such bad insomnia, you wouldn't believe. I'm in very low spirits – it's probably – who knows? When they bring me coffee, I always drink it in bed – while I'm drinking it, I'm thinking: 'How come we don't see Alexander Fyodorych, could it be that he's sick?'

"Anyway, I get up, and I find that it's past eleven o'clock – would you believe! The servants don't even tell me! I go into Nadenka's room – she's still asleep. I wake her up. 'Time to get up, my dear, it's almost twelve, what's the matter with you?' I mean, I fuss over her the whole day like a nanny. I even let the governess go deliberately: we don't want

CHAPTER 4

strangers around. I don't think you can trust strangers: you can never tell what they'll get up to. No! I brought her up myself, keep a close watch on her, never let her out of my sight, and I can say that she feels this, and there's nothing she keeps from me – even what she's thinking. I know her through and through… Then the cook came to see me and we talked for an hour or so. After that I read *Mémoires du Diable* for a while. It's such a pleasure to read Soulié's books!* He describes things so beautifully! Then our neighbour, Maria Ivanovna, stopped by with her husband – so, what with one thing and another, the morning went by, and I take a look and it's already past four and time for dinner!… Oh yes, we expected you for dinner, why didn't you come? We waited for you until five o'clock."

"Until five?" said Alexander. "There was no way I could get here by then, Maria Mikhailovna, I had to be at work. Please don't ever wait for me after four o'clock."

"That's just what I told Nadenka, but of course she said: 'Let's wait a little longer!'"

"I did? Oh Mummy, come on now! Wasn't I the one who said: 'Mummy, it's time for dinner'? And you said: 'No, let's wait, Alexander Fyodorych hasn't been here for a long time, and he's coming here to dinner.'"

"Now, now!" Maria Mikhailovna put in, shaking her head. "That's really not nice of you, putting your words in my mouth."

Nadenka turned away and walked towards the flowers, and began to tease the parrot.

"What I said was: 'Where could Alexander Fyodorych be right now?'" Maria Mikhailovna went on. "It's already half-past four. But no, she says: '*Maman*, we must wait – he'll be here.' I look and it's now a quarter to five, so I say: 'Well, if you like, Nadenka, but Alexander Fyodorych has probably been invited somewhere, and won't be coming, and I'm hungry.' But: 'No,' she says, 'let's wait a little longer – until five.' And I'm starving to death because of her. Isn't that right, young lady?"

Nadenka's voice could be heard from behind the flowers, addressing the parrot: "Polly, Polly, where did you have dinner today – at your uncle's?"

"So she's hiding, is she?" said her mother. "Obviously afraid to show her face!"

"Not at all," replied Nadenka, emerging from the shrubbery, and sat down by the window.

"And she still wouldn't sit down at the table!" said Maria Mikhailovna. "She asked for a cup of milk and went into the garden, and never had any dinner. Now, look me straight in the eye, my girl!"

While Maria Mikhailovna was holding forth, Alexander maintained a stunned silence. He looked at Nadenka, but she had turned her back on him and was shredding a leaf of ivy.

"Nadezhda Alexandrovna!" he said. "Should I really be so happy that you were thinking of me?"

"Don't come near me!" she cried, annoyed because her little act had been exposed. "Mummy was joking, and you were ready to believe her!"

"Then where are the berries you had picked for Alexander Fyodorych?" her mother asked.

"Berries?"

"Yes, the berries."

"But you ate them at dinner..." Nadenka replied.

"I did what? Come clean, my dear: you hid them and wouldn't give them to me. And she said, 'Alexander Fyodorych will be coming, and I'll give you some then.' What do you think of a girl like that?"

Alexander gave Nadenka a sly but tender look. She blushed.

"She washed them herself, Alexander Fyodorych," said her mother.

"Why are you making up such a story, *maman*? I washed two or three and ate them myself, and it was Vasilisa who..."

"Don't believe her, don't believe her, Alexander Fyodorych. This morning Vasilisa was sent into town. Why pretend? It will make Alexander Fyodorych happier to think that it was you who washed the berries and not Vasilisa."

Nadenka smiled and disappeared once again among the flowers, then reappeared with a plateful of berries. She held out her hand with the berries to Aduyev. He kissed her hand and accepted the berries as if he were being awarded a field marshal's baton.

CHAPTER 4

"You don't deserve them – after making us wait so long!" said Nadenka. "I waited for two hours by the fence, can you imagine! Someone was approaching, and I thought it was you, so I waved my scarf – it was some officer, and he waved back, what a nerve!"

In the evening, some guests came and went. It began to get dark, and just the three of them were left together. Gradually this trio too dispersed. Nadenka went into the garden, and the ill-matched duet of Maria Mikhailovna and Aduyev were left together. She went on for a long time, reeling off the events of the day and the day before, as well as what she would be doing the next day. Aduyev was overwhelmed by frustration and the sheer tedium of this litany. Night was beginning to fall, and he had not yet been able to say a single word to Nadenka in private. He was rescued by the cook: his benefactor had come to ask what to prepare for supper, and Aduyev was consumed with an impatience even greater than that he had suffered earlier that day in the boat. While they were discussing cutlets and sour cream, Aduyev was able to beat a stealthy retreat. How much manoeuvring was required just to get out of range of Maria Mikhailovna's armchair! First he moved closer to the window and looked out into the courtyard, then somehow found his legs taking him towards the open door. Then slowly, barely restraining himself from making a mad dash for it, he crossed to the piano, fingered a few keys here and there and, trembling feverishly, took the music from the stand, gave it a quick look and put it back; he had enough self-control to sniff a couple of flowers and wake up the parrot. At this point he was seething with impatience; the door was so near, but it would have been awkward to walk out just like that – he needed to stand where he was for a couple of minutes before slipping out casually. But the cook had already taken a couple of steps back – one more word and he was off, and Lyubetskaya would inevitably turn to him. Alexander could stand it no longer and slithered through the door like a snake, flew down from the porch, taking several steps at a time, and after only a few strides found himself at the end of the path – on the riverbank near Nadenka.

"So you finally managed to remember me!" she reproached him, this time mildly.

"You've no idea how much trouble I had!" Alexander replied. "And you were no help!"

Nadenka showed him a book.

"I would have called you out to see this, if I had had to wait one more minute," she said. "Sit down, *maman* won't be coming out now, she's afraid of the damp. I have so much – oh so much – to say to you!"

"Oh, I have too!"

But they had little or nothing to say to each other – except for the things they had already said to each other a dozen times over. The usual things: their dreams, the sky, the stars, their feelings, happiness. Their conversation proceeded in the language of looks, smiles and interjections. The book languished in the grass.

Night fell – but what a night! Are there such things as nights in St Petersburg? No, it was not a night, but... we need another name for it, yes – half-light. Quiet all around. It was as if the Neva were asleep; now and then, the river would stir as if in a doze, and a ripple would gently slap the shore and fall back silent. A late breeze arose from somewhere or other and drifted over the slumbering waters, unable to rouse them, but just rippling the surface, refreshing Nadenka and Alexander with its coolness, or bringing with it the sound of a distant song. It passed, and all returned to silence and tranquillity, the Neva as still as someone sleeping, someone who at the slightest sound would open his eyes for an instant and immediately close them, his eyelids now heavier, keeping them even more tightly closed. Then came the sound of a distant rumbling from the direction of the bridge followed by the barking of a watchdog from where men were fishing nearby. Then, once again, silence. The trees formed a dark vault, their branches stirring all but noiselessly. Lights twinkled from the dachas lining the riverbanks.

What was it – so special – that wafted on that warm breeze? What secret was it that coursed through the flowers, the trees, the grass, bringing such inexplicable balm to the soul? Why only then did thoughts and feelings arise in the heart so different from those which arise in the presence of noise and other people? What better setting for love in this dreamland of nature – alone in this dusk, surrounded by silent trees and

CHAPTER 4

flowers? How powerfully everything conspires to bring dreams to the mind and feelings to the heart which seem so irrelevant, inappropriate, absurd and aberrant amidst the strictures and constraints of everyday life… yes, irrelevant, but still, at these moments alone, the soul has a vague inkling of the possibility of the happiness which is so earnestly sought – but never found – at other times.

Alexander and Nadenka went down to the river and leant over the railing. Nadenka, lost in thought, looked into the distance and watched the river for a long time. Their souls were overflowing with happiness, but their aching hearts were beating together in bittersweet unison, their tongues silent.

Alexander quietly touched her waist. She quietly shifted his hand away with her elbow. He put his hand back, and she pushed it back, this time more gently, gazing all the while at the Neva. The third time she made no attempt to shift his hand. He took her hand; she didn't attempt to remove it. He pressed her hand; she returned the pressure. They stood like that together in silence, but their feelings were another matter!

"Nadenka!" he said softly.

She remained silent.

He bent over her, his heart in a swoon. She felt his hot breath on her cheek and shuddered, and turned towards him – she did not step back in righteous indignation, and did not cry out! She was powerless to pretend and move away, the heady pull of love silenced reason – and when Alexander pressed his lips to hers, she returned his kiss so gingerly that it could barely be felt.

"How shocking!" a respectable mother would have scolded her. "Alone in the garden without her mother, kissing a young man!" Shocking, yes, but what can you do? There she was, responding to a kiss.

"Oh, how happy a man can be!" Alexander said to himself, and bent once again to meet her lips, this time for several seconds.

She stood there, pale and unmoving, tears glistening on her eyelashes, her breast heaving convulsively.

"It's like a dream," Alexander whispered.

Nadenka suddenly came to her senses after that moment of oblivion.

"What do you think you're doing? Have you forgotten yourself?" she burst out, and moved away from him as fast as she could.

"I'm going to tell Mummy!"

Alexander fell back to earth.

"Nadezhda Alexandrovna! Don't ruin my moment of bliss with reproaches," he began, "don't be like…"

She looked at him and, suddenly bursting into laughter, came back to him, to where she had been standing at the fence and trustingly laid her head and hand on his shoulder.

"You really love me so much?" she asked, wiping away the tear that was rolling down her cheek.

Alexander made a barely perceptible movement of his shoulders, and an expression appeared on his face that his uncle would have described as "idiotic" – and he would probably have been right, but the fact was that that stupid expression conveyed tremendous happiness!

Once again they found themselves gazing in silence at the water, at the sky and into the distance as if nothing had happened between them. They were simply afraid to look at each other; when they did finally look, they smiled and immediately turned away.

"Is there really unhappiness in the world?" said Nadenka, breaking her silence.

"So they say…" Aduyev replied pensively, "but I don't believe…"

"What kind of unhappiness can there be?"

"Poverty, according to my uncle."

"Poverty! But surely the poor must be able to feel the same way we do right now, so they can't really be poor."

"Uncle says they can't, because they need to eat and drink."

"Nonsense! Eat! Your uncle is wrong. You can be happy even without that; I haven't eaten dinner today, and look how happy I am!"

He laughed.

"Yes, in return for this moment, if they were here right now, I would give everything away to the poor, everything! Oh, if only I could give them comfort and joy of some kind!"

"You're an angel, an angel!" Alexander exclaimed ecstatically, squeezing her hand.

CHAPTER 4

"Ouch! You're hurting me!" Nadenka cried, frowning and removing her hand.

"But he grasped her hand again and covered it with passionate kisses.

"How hard I shall be praying to give thanks for this evening," she continued, "today, tomorrow and for ever. I'm so happy – and you?…"

She broke off suddenly and lapsed into thought, and her eyes glinted with a sudden trace of alarm.

"You know," she said, "people say that when something happens once, it will never be repeated. That means that this moment can never be repeated, right?"

"Oh no!" replied Alexander. "It's not true; it will happen again, even better moments lie ahead; oh yes, I have the feeling!"

"She shook her head doubtfully. Suddenly his uncle's homilies came to mind and he fell silent.

"No," he said to himself, "that can't be true; it's because Uncle has never known such happiness himself that he is so censorious and distrustful of people. Poor man! I pity him for his cold, unfeeling heart which has never known the rapture of love – and that explains his jaundiced aversion to life. May God forgive him! If only he could have seen my happiness, he would not have tried to impair it, tarnish it with his mean-spirited suspicions. I pity him."

"No, Nadenka, no, we will be happy!" he said to her. "Look around you, where everything is rejoicing in our love. God himself is giving us his blessing. How joyously we will walk through life hand in hand! How great will be our pride in our love for each other!"

"Oh, stop, please stop anticipating what lies ahead!" she cut in. "It gives me a terrible feeling when you do that. Right now, I'm actually feeling sad…"

"What are you afraid of? Do you really find it so hard to believe in yourself?"

"Yes, I do, I do!" she said, shaking her head.

He looked at her pensively for a moment.

"But why? What can possibly destroy the world of our happiness – who would want to intrude on it? It would be just the two of us: we'll keep away from others; what would we need them for? What would they need from us? They won't remember us: they'll forget us, and then there'll be no talk of sorrow or disaster to trouble us, just the way it is here and now in this garden, where there is no sound to disturb this precious silence…"

Suddenly they heard someone calling from the porch, "Nadenka! Alexander Fyodorych! Where are you?"

"Did you hear that?" said Nadenka, like the voice of doom. "Fate is trying to tell us something; this moment will never be repeated – I feel it…"

She grasped his hand, squeezed it, gave him a strange and sorrowful look and plunged into the darkness of the path.

He remained standing alone, deep in thought.

"Alexander Fyodorych!" The voice rang out again from the porch. "The meal has been waiting on the table for a long time now."

He shrugged his shoulders and entered the room.

"In an instant what was unimaginable bliss has been replaced by – the meal on the table!" he said to Nadenka. "Is this the way life has to be?"

"Let's hope it doesn't get worse!" she replied cheerfully. "The dish we're having is excellent, especially for someone who has had no dinner."

She was buoyant with happiness. Her cheeks were burning. There was a rare sparkle in her eyes. How busily she played the hostess, how gaily she chattered! Not a trace of that momentary sign of sadness remained: she was jubilation itself.

Dawn was already covering half the sky when Aduyev boarded the boat. The oarsmen, in anticipation of the promised reward, were spitting on their hands and preparing to spring forward in their seats the way they had on the way over, and ply their oars with all their might.

"Slow down," said Alexander, "and there'll be another fifty copecks in it for you!"

They looked at him and then at each other. One scratched his chest, the other his back, and their oars hardly moved as they skimmed the surface of the water, and the boat glided through it like a swan.

"And Uncle is trying to make me believe that happiness is a chimera, and nothing one can reliably trust; that life is… remorseless! Why was

CHAPTER 4

he so bent on deceiving me so cruelly? No! This is life, just as I imagined it to be, life as it should be, life as it is and always will be! There's no other way it can be!"

A fresh morning breeze was blowing gently from the south. Alexander was shivering a little, both from the breeze and from his memories. He yawned and, wrapping himself in his cloak, gave himself over to his dreams.

Chapter 5

ADUYEV HAD REACHED THE PEAK of his happiness. He had nothing more to wish for. His work, his articles for the journal were all forgotten, cast aside. He was passed over for promotion in his office. He hardly noticed it himself, but was reminded of it by his uncle. Pyotr Ivanych advised him to stop fooling around, but when he heard the words "fooling around" he just shrugged his shoulders pityingly and said nothing. His uncle, seeing that his efforts were in vain, shrugged his shoulders pityingly in his turn, and contented himself with a single remark: "Have it your own way, it's your business; just make sure not to ask me for any of that filthy lucre!"

"Don't worry, Uncle," Alexander retorted, "when there's not enough money, that's bad; a lot of money is something I don't need, and what I have is just enough."

"Well, congratulations!" added Pyotr Ivanych.

Alexander avoided him, understandably enough. He had lost all faith in his gloomy prognostications, and feared his cold view of love in general and his offensive insinuations about his relationship with Nadenka in particular. Alexander couldn't stand hearing his uncle analysing his own love for Nadenka as if the identical laws applied to all without exception, and profaning what he believed to be a lofty and sacred value. His joy and his whole rose-tinted construct of happiness he kept hidden, because of his feeling that the moment his uncle's cold analysis came into contact with it, it would crumble and turn to dust and ashes. To begin with, his uncle avoided him because he thought, "Here we go! That young man will get lazy, start pestering me for money and become a burden to me." There was something triumphant, mysterious in Alexander's manner, in the look in his eye and his whole bearing. He conducted himself with others humbly, but with dignity, but like a rich capitalist dealing with small-time traders on the stock exchange. He thought to himself: "You poor things! Which of you

CHAPTER 5

possesses a treasure as precious as mine? Which of you has a heart or soul capable of a feeling as powerful as mine?" – that sort of thing.

He was sure that he alone in the world could love as he did, and be loved as he was. Of course, it wasn't just his uncle whom he avoided, but also the *herd*, as he called it. He was either worshipping at the altar of his divinity or stayed at home, in his study, alone, wallowing in bliss, analysing it, splitting it into smaller and smaller particles. He thought of this as "creating a special world of his own" and, in his seclusion, he did indeed construct for himself a world in which he spent most of his time, going rarely and reluctantly to his office, something which he thought of as a "dire necessity", "a necessary evil" or "dismal prose", and had any number of different ways of describing. He never saw his editor or his friends.

His greatest pleasure was to commune with himself.

"Being alone with oneself," he wrote in one of his stories, "is like seeing oneself in a mirror; only in this way can one learn to believe in human greatness and dignity. How fine a man becomes communing in this way with his own inner strengths! Like the commander of an army, he reviews and scrutinizes his troops, and draws them up in a disciplined and carefully planned formation, leads them into action and creates. But how pitiful is the man who is afraid and incapable of being by himself, who is always running away from himself and seeking company, another mind, another spirit…" You might think we have here some philosopher discovering new laws for building the world or governing human existence – but no: it's just a lovelorn lad!

Here he is sitting in his Voltaire chair. Before him a sheet of paper on which he has dashed off a few lines. He is either leaning forward to make some change or to add a couple of lines, or is leaning back in his chair and thinking. A smile is playing on his lips; you can see that they have just taken a sip from the overflowing chalice of happiness. His eyelids are drooping languorously like those of a dozing cat, or his eyes suddenly gleam with a flash of internal agitation.

All around is quiet. Only in the distance from a highway can the rumble of carriages be heard, or perhaps from time to time Yevsei, tired of cleaning boots, can be heard muttering to himself, "Better not forget I bought half a copeck's worth of vinegar and ten copecks' worth of cabbage. I'd better pay up tomorrow, otherwise he won't trust me next time, the skinflint. He weighs the bread by the pound, as if it's a famine year – it's a disgrace! God, I'm worn out. I'll just finish this boot and go to bed. In Grachi, I bet they've already been asleep for ages – not like here! Perhaps one day the Lord God will let me see…"

He heaved a great sigh, breathed on the boots and set to work once again with the brush. He considered that this was his principal, if not his sole duty, and indeed that it was his boot-cleaning talents which were the measure of a servant's – and indeed a man's – worth. And he himself cleaned boots with a kind of passion.

"Yevsei, stop that! You're disturbing my work with your fooling around," Aduyev shouted.

"Fooling around," Yevsei grumbled to himself. "If anyone's fooling around, it's you, and here I am doing my work. Look how he's got his boots all dirty, and they're so hard to clean!"

He placed the boots on a table and gazed with admiration at his reflection in the glossy leather. "Try and find someone who could polish them like that!" he muttered. "'Fooling around' indeed!"

Alexander immersed himself ever more deeply in his daydreams about Nadenka, and then in his creative imaginings.

There was nothing on his table. Everything that reminded him of his former activities, his work at the office and for the journal, lay under the table, inside the cupboard or under the bed. "The very sight of that muck," he said, "scares away creative thought, which takes off like a nightingale from among the trees, alarmed by the sudden squeaking on the road of a wagon wheel that has not been oiled."

Often, dawn would find him working on some elegy. Every hour that was not spent at the Lyubetskys' was devoted to his writing. He would write poems and read them to Nadenka; she would transcribe them on good-quality paper and learn them by heart, and he "knew the sublime bliss of the poet – that of hearing his words on his darling's lips".

"You are my muse," he told her, "I would have you be the Vesta tending that sacred fire which burns in my breast; should you leave it, it would be extinguished for eternity."

CHAPTER 5

He sent his poems to the journal under an assumed name. They were printed, because they were not bad, vigorous in places and all imbued with passion and smoothly written.

Nadenka was proud of his love, and called him "my poet".

"Yes, yours – and for ever," he would add. Fame was beckoning and, he thought, Nadenka would fashion his garlands and entwine his laurels with myrtle. "Life, life, how beautiful you are," he proclaimed. "But my uncle? Why does he rob me of my peace of mind? Is he a demon sent to me by fate? Why does he poison everything that I cherish with his bile? Is it envy that makes his heart resistant to life's purer joys, or could it be sheer malevolence?... I must keep far, far away from him! He will kill my loving heart, pollute it with his hatred – he will corrupt it..."

So he ran from his uncle, kept away from him for weeks, even months at a time. And if, when they did meet, the conversation touched on feelings, he maintained a derisive silence, or else listened like a man whose convictions were impervious to all arguments. His own judgement he held to be infallible, his opinions and feelings immutable, and he resolved that henceforth he would be guided by them alone on the grounds that he was no longer a child, and because "why should only the opinions of others be sacrosanct?"* and other such reasons.

His uncle remained the same as ever. He asked his nephew no questions, and did not notice – or showed no sign of noticing – his escapades. Seeing that Alexander's position remained unchanged, that he was maintaining the same way of life and that he never asked him for money, he remained as nice to him as ever, and only ventured a mild rebuke because Alexander so rarely came to see him.

"My wife is cross with you," he said. "She had come to regard you as one of the family; we dine at home every day: why don't you come and join us?"

And that was it. But Alexander rarely visited, and anyway he had no time. He spent the morning at his office, and all the time after dinner and into the evening at the Lyubetskys', so all that remained was what was left of the night – but at night he went back to that special world of his own creation, which he continued to create – not to mention the fact that he needed to sleep a little.

His prose fiction was not proving as successful. He had written a comedy, two novellas, an essay and some travel writing. His output was astounding: his pen scorched the paper as it flew by. His comedy and one of his novellas he showed first to his uncle, and asked him to say if they were any good. His uncle read with some reluctance a few pages here and there, and sent them back marked "Fit only for use as wallpaper!"

Alexander was furious and sent his work to the journal, but both the comedy and the novella were returned. Two places in the comedy were marked in pencil "not bad" – and that was it. The novella frequently bore annotations such as "weak", "wrong", "immature", "dull", "undeveloped". At the end came the comment: "Generally speaking, we noted a certain ignorance of the heart, over-exuberance, artificiality, a stilted quality; the human person is nowhere to be seen… the principal character is an aberration… such people don't exist… not fit for publication! It should be added, however, that the author is not devoid of talent; he needs to work at it!"

"'Such people don't exist!'" thought Alexander, chagrined and dumbfounded. "But I myself am the principal character – what do they mean, 'don't exist'? Surely they don't want me to depict the banal characters you meet at every turn, who think and feel like the common herd, and act the same way – those pathetic characters who appear in those run-of-the-mill, trivial comedies and tragedies, characters with no distinctive features at all… Is art to sink as low as this?"

Alexander summoned the shade of Byron in support of the pure truth of his literary profession of faith, and invoked the testimony of Goethe and Schiller. The hero he envisaged in a drama or a novel could be nothing less than a corsair, a great poet, an artist, and he would be made to act in character.

In one of his novellas, the setting he chose was America, and its magnificent natural splendour and mountainous terrain. In its midst, a fugitive who had run away with the girl he loved. The world had forgotten them. They took pride in themselves and the nature surrounding them, and when the news came that a pardon had been granted and that they would be permitted to return home, they

CHAPTER 5

declined. About twenty years later, a European arrived there on a hunting expedition with an escort of Indians. On a mountainside he discovered a hut with a skeleton inside – that European had been the hero's rival.

How proud Alexander was of that story! With what delight he read it to Nadenka on those winter evenings – and how greedily she devoured it! And this was the story they had rejected!

He didn't breathe a word of his rejection to Nadenka. He swallowed the humiliation in silence – and no one was any the wiser.

"So, what about your novella?" she would ask. "Has it been printed?"

"No," he replied, "it can't be: there's too much in it that would seem strange and outlandish to our readers..."

If only he had known how true that was – although, of course, what he meant was the exact opposite!

"Working at it" seemed to him a strange proposition. "I mean, what is talent for?" he said. "It's a talentless drudge who has to work; talent creates easily and freely..." But then he recalled that his agricultural articles, as well as his poems, were nothing much at the beginning, and that later, little by little, they started to improve and earn some attention from the public. He began to reflect on the matter, and began to understand how wrong he had been, and with a sigh put aside his literary fiction for the time being: when his heart started to beat more evenly, his thoughts would become better organized, and he promised himself that then he would apply himself in earnest.

The days went by, days of uninterrupted pleasure for Alexander. He was happy when he kissed Nadenka's fingertips, when he sat opposite her for as much as two hours at a time posed as if for a portrait, without taking his eyes off her, relishing the moment and sighing or declaiming poetry suitable to the occasion.

It is only fair to add that at times her only response to the poetry and the sighs was a yawn. And no wonder: her heart may have been full, but there was nothing to occupy her mind. Alexander never took the trouble to nourish it. The year which Nadenka had set as the trial period passed. She was still living with her mother in the same dacha. Alexander raised the question of her promise and asked her permission to speak to her mother. Nadenka wanted to wait until they had returned to town from the country, but Alexander insisted.

Finally one evening, as Alexander was taking his leave, she permitted him to raise the subject with her mother the next day.

Alexander lay awake the whole night, and didn't go to his office. His head was spinning with the prospect of what awaited him the next day. He was working it all out in his mind, what he would say to her mother, mentally composing a speech, and preparing his thoughts, almost forgetting that it was all about asking for Nadenka's hand. But he lost his way in his musings, forgetting everything in the process. That evening he made his way to the dacha totally unprepared – which turned out not to matter in the end. Nadenka met him in the usual way in the garden, but the expression in her eyes was a little more thoughtful than usual: she did not smile, and looked altogether less composed.

"You can't talk to Mummy right now," she said, "that awful count is visiting."

"Count! What count?"

"You must know what count! Count Novinsky, you know, our neighbour; look, there's his dacha – how many times you've admired it yourself!"

"Count Novinsky! Visiting!" Alexander was dumbfounded. "What's he doing here?"

"I don't really know myself," Nadenka replied. "I was just sitting here and reading your book, and Mummy had gone out to see Maria Ivanovna. It was just beginning to drizzle, so I went inside. Suddenly a coach drives up to the porch, blue with white upholstery, the one we always saw passing by, and which you always admired. And there is Mummy emerging from the coach with some man. They came in, and Mummy said, 'Count, this is my daughter, welcome to our home!' He bowed, and I followed suit. I was embarrassed and couldn't help blushing, and I rushed to my room. But Mummy, she's intolerable, and I hear her say, 'Please forgive her, Count, she has no manners…' Then I realized that he must be our neighbour, Count Novinsky. He must have brought Mummy home with him in his carriage from Maria Ivanovna's because of the rain."

CHAPTER 5

"Is he... old?"

"Old? Not in the least. What do you mean? He's young and quite... good-looking!"

"Oh, so you had time to notice that!" Alexander was annoyed.

"Oh, wonderful! How long does it take to notice something like that? I did speak to him after all. In fact he was very nice, and asked me what I did, and talked about music – asked me to sing something, but I didn't want to: I don't sing very well. This winter I'm definitely going to ask Mummy to find me a good singing teacher. The Count says it's very much the thing these days – singing."

She said all this with much more than her usual animation.

"It was my impression, Nadezhda Alexandrovna, that there was something else you were going to be doing this winter – other than singing."

"And what was that?"

"What – you need to ask!" said Alexander with a hint of reproach.

"Ah yes... did you come here by boat?"

He just looked at her, saying nothing. She turned round and walked back to the house. Aduyev entered the room, not quite at ease. What kind of man was this count? How should he himself behave? What was this count like in company? Was he stiff, relaxed? The Count was the first to rise and bow politely as Alexander entered the room. Alexander responded with a constrained and awkward bow. Their hostess performed the introductions. Somehow Alexander took an immediate dislike to the Count, although he was a handsome man – tall, slim and blond, with big expressive eyes and a pleasant smile. His manner was simple, refined and rather amiable. He was, it seemed, the kind of man anyone would easily take to – anyone, that is, except Aduyev.

In spite of Maria Ivanovna's invitation to sit closer to them, he sat down in a corner and opened a book – very ill-mannered, awkward behaviour, and quite out of place. Nadenka was standing by her mother's armchair, regarding the Count with curiosity, listening to the way he spoke and what he was saying. For her he was a novelty.

Aduyev was unable to conceal his dislike for the Count, but the Count appeared not to notice his boorish behaviour; he was attentive to Aduyev, and tried his best to bring him into the conversation. But it was no good: he simply wouldn't talk, except to say "yes" and "no".

When Lyubetskaya happened to mention his family name, the Count asked whether he was related to Pyotr Ivanych.

"He's my uncle," he replied curtly.

"I've met him quite often socially," said the Count.

"Quite probably – it's hardly surprising," Alexander replied, shrugging his shoulders.

The Count suppressed a smile by covering his lower lip with his teeth. Nadenka exchanged glances with her mother, blushed and lowered her eyes.

"Your uncle is an intelligent and pleasant person," the Count observed with an edge of irony in his voice.

Aduyev remained silent.

Nadenka lost patience with Alexander and went to him, and while the Count was talking to her mother, whispered to him, "Aren't you ashamed? How could you behave like that when the Count was so nice to you?"

"Nice!" said Alexander, so annoyed that he spoke in a voice almost loud enough to be heard. "I don't need his niceness, and I don't want to hear that word again!"

Nadenka immediately turned and left him, and without moving watched him intently for a long time from a distance, then went back to sit by her mother's armchair and paid no further attention to Alexander.

Meanwhile Aduyev was simply waiting for the Count to leave, so that he would finally have an opportunity to talk to Nadenka's mother, but the clock struck ten and then eleven and the Count was still there talking.

All the normal subjects of conversation between people early in their acquaintanceship had been exhausted, and the Count began to entertain his host with his humour, and did so skilfully. His sallies were perfectly relaxed and spontaneous, and he made no special effort to be witty, just casually entertaining; he had a kind of special knack of making amusing conversation. He didn't even resort to actual jokes,

CHAPTER 5

but could put an unexpected twist not only on anecdotes themselves, but on some piece of news or incident, and invest a perfectly ordinary item with humour.

Both mother and daughter were captivated by his humour, and even Alexander himself had to hide his face behind a book at times because he was unable to suppress a smile, even though he was fuming inside.

The Count was able to talk equally well about any subject with tact and discretion, whether it was about people, music or foreign parts. If a man came up for discussion, he would say something caustic about him, even about himself, but he always managed to come up with something flattering to say about women in general, and some compliments for his hostesses in particular.

Aduyev thought about his literary accomplishments, his poetry, and how that subject would put the Count in the shade. The subject did come up for discussion, and both mother and daughter mentioned his accomplishments as a writer.

"That will put him in his place all right!" thought Aduyev.

Not a bit of it. The Count spoke about literature as if he had spent all his life studying the subject, and made a number of fluent and apt comments about contemporary French and Russian literary celebrities. To top it all, it emerged that he was on friendly terms with some leading Russian writers, and in Paris he had made the acquaintance of some of the French ones.

He spoke respectfully of a few, and was gently derisive of the others.

All he had to say about Alexander's poetry was that he didn't know it and had never heard of it.

Nadenka gave Alexander a strange kind of look, as if to say: "Well, my friend, it looks as if you have some catching up to do!"

Alexander looked flattened. His defiant and boorish demeanour gave way to sheer dejection. He looked for all the world like a rooster with a soaking-wet tail huddling in some corner to shelter from the elements.

The sideboard rang with the clinking of glasses and the clatter of spoons; the table was being laid, and the Count showed no sign of leaving. Alexander gave up all hope, and even accepted Lyubetskaya's invitation to stay for their supper of curds.

"The Count even eats curds!" Aduyev whispered, regarding him with hatred.

The Count ate with appetite, and continued to amuse the company with his conversation, as comfortable as if he were in his own home.

"It's his first time in this house, and he's eating enough for three – what effrontery!" Alexander whispered to Nadenka.

"What of it? He's *hungry*, that's all!" she simply replied.

At last the Count left, but it was too late to broach the subject. Aduyev took his hat and made a hasty exit. Nadenka went after him and managed to soothe his ruffled feelings.

"Tomorrow then?" he asked.

"We won't be home tomorrow."

"Well, the day after then."

On that they parted.

Two days later Alexander arrived on the early side. As he stepped into the garden he heard unfamiliar sounds coming from the living room... "Could it be a cello? No!" He moved closer. It was a male voice singing, and what a voice! Sonorous, fresh, the kind of voice no woman's heart could resist. It went straight to Aduyev's heart too, but in different way. His heart sank and was gripped by anguish, hatred and a vague, troubling presentiment. Alexander entered the house.

"Who's here?" he asked the servant.

"Count Novinsky."

"Been here long?"

"Since six o'clock."

"Tell the young lady quietly that I came, and will be back later."

"Yes, sir."

Alexander left and wandered around the dachas, hardly aware of where he was going. Two hours later he went back to the house.

"So, is he still here?"

"Here, oh yes, I believe he is staying to supper. The mistress has ordered roast grouse for supper."

"Did you tell the young lady about me?"

"I did, sir."

CHAPTER 5

"Well, what did she say?"

"The young lady didn't tell me to say anything."

Alexander went home and didn't come back for two days.

God knows what was going on in his mind and what his feelings were; finally he decided to go back.

There he is in the boat, and he stands up and catches sight of the house and, shielding his eyes from the sun, he looks straight ahead. Flitting among the trees, he glimpses the blue dress which is so becoming on Nadenka: it's the shade of blue which goes so well with her face. She always wore that dress when she wanted to look particularly attractive for Alexander. His heart leapt.

"Ah! She wants to make it up to me for her temporary lapse in ignoring me last time," he thought, "but it was really my fault, not hers. It was unforgivable of me to have behaved like that – it only makes things worse for yourself; I mean, a stranger, a new acquaintance… it was only natural; after all she was the hostess… Ah, there she is, coming out of the shrubbery on that narrow path; she's going towards the fence, where she'll stand and wait…"

She was indeed turning onto the broad path, but who was that walking beside her?

"The Count!" Alexander exclaimed aloud in dismay. He could not believe his eyes.

"What?" responded one of the oarsmen.

"Alone with him in the garden," Alexander whispered, "just the way it was with me."

Nadenka and the Count approached the fence and, without looking at the river, turned round and walked back slowly along the path. He leant towards her and murmured something. She walked on with her head lowered.

Aduyev was still standing in the boat open-mouthed, without moving, his hands stretched out towards the riverbank. He lowered his hands and sat down. The oarsmen continued rowing.

"Where are you going?" Alexander shouted at them in a frenzy as he came to his senses. "Turn back!"

"Back?"

"You want to go back?" said one of the oarsmen, his mouth wide open.

"Back! I said. What are you, deaf?"

"You mean you don't want to go there?"

The other oarsman promptly began pulling at the left oar, and then pulled with both oars, and the boat was soon moving swiftly through the water in the other direction. Alexander pulled his hat down almost to his shoulders and gave himself over to the torment of his thoughts.

He didn't go back to the Lyubetskys for two weeks. Two weeks – how long that seems to someone in love! But all that time he was waiting. Surely they would send a servant to find out what was the matter with him and whether he was sick. This was what happened normally when he wasn't feeling well, or just felt like pretending to be.

At first Nadenka would enquire on her mother's behalf for form's sake, and then she would write whatever she felt like of her own. What sweet reproaches! What tender concern! What impatience!

"No, this time I'm not going to give in so easily," thought Alexander. "I'll make her suffer a little. I'll teach her how to act with a strange man; no! No easy reconciliation this time!"

He planned a cruel revenge, imagined her repentance and how magnanimously he would forgive her and admonish her. But no servant was sent, and there was no admission of guilt. It was as if he had ceased to exist for them.

He grew shrunken and pale. Jealousy is more painful than any illness, especially when that jealousy is nourished only by suspicion and without evidence.

When the evidence becomes available, that's the end of the jealousy, and mostly the end of love too, then at least you know where you stand, but until then it's torture – which Alexander experienced to the full.

Finally he decided to go in the morning, thinking he would find Nadenka alone, and have it out with her.

He arrived. There was no one in the garden, or in the living room or drawing room. He went into the hall and opened the door to the courtyard. What a scene confronted him! Two grooms in the Count's livery were holding the reins of a pair of saddle horses. The Count

CHAPTER 5

and one of his men had seated Nadenka; the other had been prepared for the Count himself. Maria Ivanovna was standing on the porch. She was frowning, worried by what she was seeing.

"Hold tight, Nadenka!" she said. "Be careful with her, Count, for the love of Christ! Oh my! I'm so afraid, my God, so afraid. Nadenka, hang on to the horse's ear; can't you see how jumpy it is? Could be the Devil himself!"

"Don't worry, *maman*," Nadenka called out cheerfully. "I do know how to ride; watch!" She struck the horse with her crop, and it launched itself ahead and began to prance and rear on the spot.

"Hold, hold on!" Maria Ivanovna screamed, waving her arm. "Stop, you'll be killed!" But Nadenka pulled on the reins and the horse stood still.

"You see how obedient it is!" said Nadenka, stroking the horse's neck.

No one noticed Aduyev. Pale, he was watching Nadenka – who, to make matters worse, had never looked better. Her riding habit suited her wonderfully, as did the hat with a green veil, and set off her figure to perfection! Her face was animated by a timorous pride, and the thrill of a new sensation. Her face would lose its flush, but her excitement would bring it back to her cheeks. The horse was frisky, and its movements made Nadenka sway gracefully back and forth. Her slender figure quivered slightly, like the stalk of a flower in the breeze. Then a groom led the horse to the Count.

"Count, shall we ride through the grove again?" Nadenka asked.

"Again!" thought Aduyev.

"Very well," replied the Count.

The horses moved off.

"Nadezhda Alexandrovna!" Alexander, unable to restrain himself, suddenly called out. Everyone stopped dead in their tracks as if rooted to the spot and looked at Alexander in bewilderment. The scene froze for a minute.

"Oh, it's Alexander Fyodorych!" Nadenka's mother was the first to react and break the silence. The Count bowed in an affable fashion. Nadenka swiftly brushed the veil aside from her face and turned to look at him in alarm. She began to open her mouth, but immediately turned away and struck the horse with her crop. The horse took off and in two bounds had disappeared beyond the gate, and the Count took off after her.

"Not so fast, not so fast, for God's sake!" Lyubetskaya screamed. "Hold on to its ear! Oh my God! She'll fall off any moment now. What's all this mad rush for?"

No one was left in sight. All that could be heard was the pounding of the horses' hooves, and all that could be seen was a cloud of dust rising. Alexander was left alone with Lyubetskaya. He regarded her in silence; his eyes seemed to be asking her, "What's all this about?" The answer was not long in coming.

"They've left," she said, "without trace! Well, let the young people have their fun – you and I can stay and talk. How come we haven't seen hide nor hair of you for the last two weeks? Don't you like us any more?"

"I haven't been well, Maria Mikhailovna," he replied gloomily.

"Yes, I can see – how pale and thin you've grown! Sit down now, and rest. Shall I order some soft-boiled eggs for you? We won't be having supper for quite some time."

"Thanks very much, but no."

"Why not? They'll be ready in a trice; they're really fresh, the Finnish woman brought them just this morning."

"No, really, thank you."

"But what's the matter with you? I've been waiting and waiting, and wondering why on earth isn't he coming and bringing those French books with him? Don't you remember that you promised, what was it now? *Peau de chagrin*,* wasn't it? But you still didn't come, and I'm thinking to myself: 'He must not like us any more. Yes, that's it, Alexander Fyodorych doesn't like us any more.'"

"What I'm afraid of, Maria Mikhailovna, is that it's you who don't like me any more."

"How can you even think such a thing, Alexander Fyodorych? Shame on you. I love you as if you were my own flesh and blood. Of course, I can't speak for Nadenka, she's still a child: how could she have learnt to judge people yet! Every day I'm saying to her: 'How come we don't see Alexander Fyodorych these days? I keep hoping to see him.' I want

CHAPTER 5

you to know that we haven't been sitting down to dinner before five o'clock, and I keep thinking, 'He'll be here soon.' Nadenka sometimes says, 'But who is it you're waiting for, *maman*? I'm hungry, and so is the Count, I believe…'"

"And is the Count here often?" Alexander asked.

"Yes, almost every day – sometimes twice a day. Such a nice man, and he's taken a liking to us… Anyway, so Nadenka says, 'I'm hungry, and that's all there is to it; so let's start!' 'And what if Alexander Fyodorych turns up,' I say. 'He won't, you want to bet? So there's no point in waiting…'"

Lyubetskaya's words cut him to the quick.

"Is that what she really said?" he asked, doing his best to smile.

"Yes exactly that, and hurrying us to start dinner. Now I may look good-natured, but I'm actually quite strict, and I admonished her: 'You've been known to wait for him until five o'clock without eating dinner, and here you are, and simply can't wait at all – you don't make any sense! That's not nice! Alexander Fyodorych is an old friend of ours, and is fond of us, and his uncle, Pyotr Ivanych, has often shown how well disposed he is to us. It's really not nice to treat him so offhandedly. Now he may be offended and stop coming…'"

"What did she say?" asked Alexander.

"Well, nothing. But you know how she is. So lively, always on the move, bursting into song or coming out with 'He'll come if he wants' – she's so flighty! Meanwhile, here I am thinking he's going to come, but another day passes and he still doesn't come! So again I go, 'Nadenka, what do you think, is he sick?' And she says, '*Maman*, how should I know? Why don't we send someone to find out what the matter is?' Well, we were going to send someone, but somehow we never got round to it. I somehow forgot, and was relying on Nadenka to do it, but you know what a scatterbrain she is. Now she is entirely taken up with this riding. She once saw the Count riding by from her window and started nagging me. 'I want to go riding' – nothing else would do. No matter what I said, all I heard was 'I want to!' Crazy! No, in my day there was no question of riding! That was not at all the way we were brought up. Nowadays, ladies have even taken up smoking; there's a young widow living opposite – she sits on her balcony, smoking that cylindrical object all day long. People are walking and driving by, but she couldn't care less! In our day, even if it was a man smoking and the room smelt of tobacco..."

"Has this been going on for long?" Alexander asked.

"I don't really know, they say it came into fashion about five years ago; it was the French, of course..."

"No, I meant to ask, has Nadenka been riding for long?"

"About ten days. The Count is so nice, so amiable, there's nothing he won't do for us, he positively spoils her. Look at all these flowers: they all come from his garden. Sometimes I feel so embarrassed. 'But Count,' I say, 'you mustn't spoil her like this: it's sure to go to her head!' And I scold her too. Maria Ivanovna and I went with Nadenka to visit his stables. Of course, as you know, I am the one who looks after her – I mean, who better than a mother knows how to care for her daughter? I brought her up myself, and I don't think it would be immodest of me to say that anyone would thank God to be blessed with such a daughter. Nadenka even had her lessons here in this house. Afterwards we had breakfast in his garden, and now they're going riding every day. And what a splendid home he has! We saw for ourselves how tasteful and luxurious everything is."

"Every day!" said Alexander, virtually to himself.

"And why shouldn't she enjoy herself! I mean, I too was young... once..."

"And do they go out riding for long?"

"About three hours. So what was wrong with you exactly?"

"I don't know... something in the chest..." he said, placing his hand on his heart.

"Aren't you taking something?"

"No."

"That's young people for you! Everything is in the here and now, and they only start taking action when it's too late. So what exactly is it – an ache, a grumbling pain or a sharp one?"

Alexander was at a loss. "Well, all three, really!"

CHAPTER 5

"It's a cold, God help us! Don't neglect it; is that how you look after yourself?... You'll get an inflammation. And you're not even taking any medicine! You know, you should use some opodeldoc* and rub it in well before you go to bed at night until your chest turns red. And instead of tea you should drink an infusion. I'll give you the recipe."

Nadenka returned, pale from fatigue. She flung herself onto the divan, gasping for breath.

"Just look at her," said Maria Ivanovna, putting her hand to Nadenka's head, "she's all in, can hardly breathe. Drink some water, then go and change your clothes and loosen your stays. This riding is really not good for you!"

Alexander and the Count stayed for the whole day. The Count was as friendly and amiable as ever with Alexander, and invited him to visit his garden, and also to come riding with them, even offering to provide a mount.

"I don't know how to ride a horse," Aduyev responded coldly.

"Can't you really?" Nadenka asked. "But it's so much fun! Shall we go out again tomorrow, Count?"

The Count bowed.

"That's quite enough, Nadenka," her mother remarked, "you shouldn't bother the Count like that."

There was nothing to suggest that there was anything special in the relationship between the Count and Nadenka. He was equally nice to both the daughter and the mother. He never sought to be alone with Nadenka or ran after her into the garden, and looked at her and her mother in exactly the same way. That she was so spontaneous in the Count's company can be explained by the inherent waywardness and capriciousness of her temperament, and by her naivety, but also by a flaw in her upbringing, namely ignorance of social realities. Another factor is the weakness and short-sightedness of her mother. That the Count was so attentive and obliging is something that can be put down to the fact that their two dachas were so close to each other, and the warmth of the welcome he always received in the Lyubetsky home.

If looked at with the naked eye the whole thing would seem entirely natural – but Alexander was looking at it through a magnifying glass and saw much, much more in it than that casual onlooker.

"Why," he asked himself, "had Nadenka changed towards him?" She no longer waited for him in the garden, no longer greeted him with a smile, but rather as if she were afraid of him, and she now dressed with much more care. She was no longer so casual in her manner with people and was more careful about how she behaved, as if she had now become more discreet. It sometimes seemed as if there was something hidden lurking in her eyes and in her speech. What had become of her charming caprices, her waywardness, her playfulness, her liveliness? She had become serious, thoughtful and silent. It was as if something was gnawing at her. She was now like any other young woman, apt to dissemble and to lie, and careful to pay the necessary lip service to enquiries after people's health... unfailingly attentive and courteous, as required by convention. As to her attitude to himself... to Alexander! With whom... it didn't bear thinking of! His heart sank.

"There's something going on," he assured himself, "there's something behind it all, and I'll find out what it is no matter what, or however much pain it causes me...

"I won't allow a seducer
To beguile the maiden's heart
With the flames of his sighs and praise.
Nor will I permit that contemptible and poisonous worm
To gnaw through the stem of that short-lived delicate bloom
And make it wither before it flowers."*

That day, after the Count had left, Alexander did his best to snatch a moment to talk to Nadenka alone. He tried everything he knew. He took the book which she had used as a way of getting him away from her mother and into the garden, showed it to her and went down to the river, thinking that she would hurry after him. He waited and waited, but she didn't come. She was reading a book of her own

CHAPTER 5

and didn't even glance at him. He sat down next to her. She didn't look up, and then interrupted her reading for the briefest moment to ask him whether he was keeping up with literature and whether anything new had been published recently, and didn't even mention the recent past.

He struck up a conversation with her mother. Nadenka went into the garden. Her mother left the room, and Alexander rushed into the garden. Nadenka saw him and got up from her seat; instead of going to meet him, she set out slowly on the narrow path towards the house as if she was trying to avoid him. He started walking faster, and so did she.

"Nadezhda Alexandrovna!" he called out from a distance. "I would like a word with you."

"Let's go inside, it's damp here," she replied.

She entered the room and sat down next to her mother. Alexander almost felt sick.

"So you're afraid of the damp now?" he remarked caustically.

"Yes, now the evenings are getting dark and cold," she replied with a yawn.

"We'll be moving back soon," said her mother. "Alexander Fyodorych, would you mind dropping by at the apartment and reminding the landlord to change the locks on the door to Nadenka's bedroom and fix the shutter? He promised to do it, but you never know if he will forget. They're all like that – only interested in the money."

Aduyev started to take his leave.

"Don't leave it too long now!" said Maria Mikhailovna.

Nadenka remained silent.

He was already at the door when he turned to her. She took three steps towards him. His heart missed a beat.

"At last," he thought.

"Will you be coming tomorrow?" she asked coldly, but her eyes fastened on him with avid curiosity.

"I don't know, why do you ask?"

"I'm just asking, will you be coming?"

"Would you like me to?"

"Will you be here tomorrow?" she persisted as coldly as before, only more impatiently.

"No!" he snapped back.

"What about the day after tomorrow?"

"No, I won't be back for a good week, maybe... two weeks... or even longer."

He gave her a searching look, trying to read in her eyes what impression his reply had made on her.

She said nothing, but for just a moment as he answered, she lowered her eyes – but what did that mean? Was it a shadow of sadness, or a lightning glint of gratification? There was no way of reading that beautiful face cast in marble.

Alexander tightened his grip on his hat and left.

"Don't forget to rub your chest with opodeldoc!" Maria Mikhailovna called out after him. But Alexander was wrestling with another problem – how to interpret Nadenka's question? What was its purpose? Did it imply that she wanted to see him, or was she afraid of seeing him?

"What torment, what torment!" he said in despair.

Poor Alexander simply couldn't hold out, and returned two days later. Nadenka was standing by the garden fence as he approached in the boat. He was tempted to feel happy, but the moment the boat drew near the riverbank, she turned away, as if she had not seen him, and took a few tentative steps on the path, as if strolling aimlessly, and headed home.

He found her with her mother. There were two people from the town with them: their neighbour, Maria Ivanovna, and the inevitable Count. Alexander's anguish was intolerable. Another whole day passed in trivial, pointless conversation. The guests bored him stiff. Nothing they talked about so complacently was of the slightest significance; they argued, they joked and they laughed.

"They're laughing!" said Alexander. "Oh yes, it's easy for them to laugh when... Nadenka... has turned against me! It means nothing to them. A pitiful, shallow bunch. Any little thing will please them."

Nadenka went into the garden, but the Count did not go with her. For some time, they had appeared to be avoiding each other while in

CHAPTER 5

Alexander's presence. Sometimes, when he came upon them alone together indoors or in the garden, they would go their separate ways, but would not rejoin each other while Alexander was around. This new discovery dismayed Alexander, because he took it as a sign that they had something to hide from him.

The guests departed, along with the Count. Nadenka had not noticed this and did not hurry home. Aduyev left Maria Mikhailovna without excusing himself, and went into the garden. Nadenka was standing with her back to Alexander, holding on to the fence with her hand and resting her head on it, just as she had on that unforgettable evening. She did not see or hear him approaching.

How fast his heart was beating as he stole up to her on tiptoe; he had practically stopped breathing.

"Nadezhda Alexandrovna," he said, so agitated that he was almost inaudible.

She started, as if some shots had been fired near her, turned around and took a step backwards away from him.

"What's that smoke over there?" was the first thing she found to say in her consternation, pointing animatedly at the other side of the river. "Could it be a fire, or a furnace… in a factory or something?"

He regarded her in silence.

"Yes, I thought it might be a fire. Why are you looking at me like that, don't you believe me?"

She fell silent.

"And you are just like the rest of them," he said, shaking his head. "Who would have thought it… two months ago?"

"What do you mean? I don't understand you," she said, and made as if to leave.

"Don't go, Nadezhda Alexandrovna, I can't stand this torture any longer."

"What torture? I really don't know…"

"Don't pretend! Just tell me – is this really you? Are you the same person you were?"

"I'm just the same as I was!" she asserted firmly.

"How can you say that? You've turned against me."

"No. I think I'm just as nice to you, and just as happy to see you."

"Just as happy! Then why do you run away from the fence?"

"Run away? What will you think up next? I'm standing by the fence – and you tell me I'm running away?"

She gave a forced laugh.

"Nadezhda Alexandrovna, stop being evasive!" Aduyev continued.

"Who's being evasive? Why are you harassing me?"

"Is this really you? My God! Six weeks ago in this very place…"

"I was asking you what that smoke was on the other side…"

"It's horrible, horrible!"

"But what have I done to you? It was you who stopped coming – it's what you wanted… no one's forcing you…" Nadenka began.

"Why are you pretending you don't know why I stopped coming?"

She looked away from him and shook her head.

"What about the Count?" he said almost menacingly.

"What count?"

Her expression suggested that this was the first time she had ever heard of the Count.

"What count! Now you're telling me that you have no interest in him?"

"You're out of your mind!" she replied, moving away from him.

"I'm sure you're right!" he continued. "I'm losing my mind a little more every day… How can you treat so deceitfully, so ungratefully someone who loved you more than anything in this world, someone who neglected everything for you – everything… and thought he would soon be happy for ever, while you…"

"What about me?" she said, moving farther away.

"What about you?" he replied, infuriated by her cold-blooded indifference. "Have you forgotten? May I remind you that here, on this very spot, you swore a hundred times that you would belong to me and said: 'God Himself hears what I have sworn.' Well he did hear you! You should be ashamed in the presence of such witnesses as the sky, these trees and every single blade of grass – all of these can testify to our happiness; every grain of sand can bear witness to our love; take a look around you! You're a perjurer!"

She looked at him in horror. His eyes flashed, and his lips turned pale.

CHAPTER 5

"My God, how nasty you are!" she said timidly. "Why are you so angry? I never refused you, you haven't even spoken to *maman*, how do you know—"

"Speak to her after you have behaved so badly?"

"How have I behaved badly? I don't know..."

"How? I'll tell you right now; what's the meaning of these trysts with the Count, and going riding with him?"

"So am I to run away from him whenever *maman* leaves the room? And as for the riding, it means I like to go riding – it's so enjoyable... and galloping! And that sweet little horse, Lucy! Didn't you see... she knows me now..."

"And what about the way you treat me now?" he went on. "Why does the Count spend every day with you from morning to night?"

"Good Lord! How should I know? You're so ridiculous. It's *maman* who is so eager."

"That's not true. *Maman* only wants what you want. What about all those gifts – the flowers, the music, the album – they're all for *maman*?"

"Well, *maman* loves flowers. Yesterday she bought some more from the gardener."

"And what is it you talk about with him when you lower your voices?" Alexander went on without listening to her. "Look, you're growing pale because you're feeling guilty. To destroy a man's happiness, to forget, to ruin everything so quickly, so casually – hypocrisy, ingratitude, lies, betrayal! Yes, betrayal! The Count, a rich man, lionized in society, has deigned to look with favour upon you – and you melt and grovel at the feet of this cheap luminary; have you no shame? I don't want to see him here again!" he said, his voice choking with emotion. "Do you hear? Give him up! Break off relations with him so that he forgets the way to your home! I don't want..." He seized her hand in a frenzy.

"*Maman, maman*! Come here!" Nadenka screamed, breaking away from Alexander's grip, and rushed headlong along the path to the house.

He sat down slowly on the bench, clutching his head. She ran into the house pale and frightened and slumped onto a chair.

"What is it? What's wrong? Why did you call me?" her mother asked in alarm, hurrying towards her.

"Alexander Fyodorych... is sick!" She could barely force out the words.

"But why do you look so upset?"

"He frightens me, *maman* – for God's sake don't let him in: I don't want him near me."

"You gave me such a scare, you crazy girl! Anyway, what's wrong with him? Oh, I know it's his chest. Why should that upset you? It's not consumption! He should rub his chest with opodeldoc – he'll soon get over it. Of course, he didn't listen to me and rub it in."

Alexander came to his senses. His fever passed, but his pain was twice as great. Not only had he not resolved his doubts, but he had terrified Nadenka – and now, of course, he would never get an answer from her: he had gone about it all wrong.

The thought occurred to him as it does to everyone in love: "But what if it's not her fault? Maybe she really is indifferent to the Count. After all, her befuddled mother invites him every day, so what is she to do? He is urbane and agreeable; Nadenka is a pretty girl; maybe he hopes she will like him, but that doesn't necessarily mean that he has succeeded. Perhaps it's the flowers and the innocent diversions that appeal to her, rather than the Count himself? Even supposing that there is a certain element of flirtatiousness involved, surely that's pardonable? Other girls – even older girls – well, God knows what they get up to."

He gave a sigh, and a ray of joy pierced his soul. People in love are all like that, sheer blindness alternating with great insight – but still, it's always such a pleasure to find excuses for the object of one's love!

Suddenly he found himself wondering: "But how to explain her change of attitude towards me?" He turned pale again. "Why does she avoid me and refuse to speak, as if she were ashamed of something? And yesterday, a perfectly ordinary day, why did she dress so smartly? There were no other guests apart from him. Why did she ask when the ballet season would begin?" A simple question, but he recalled that the Count had casually promised to reserve a box for the season in spite of all the difficulties; that meant that he would be going with them. "Why did she leave the garden? Why didn't she come into the garden? Why did she ask one question, but not another?..."

CHAPTER 5

So once again he was assailed by all those distressing doubts which tormented him so cruelly, and came to the conclusion that Nadenka had never loved him in the first place.

"My God, my God!" he exclaimed in despair. "Life is so hard, so bitter! Give me the peace and quiet of the grave, that slumber of the soul."

A quarter of an hour later, he went back into the house, fearful and despondent.

"Goodbye, Nadezhda Alexandrovna," he said meekly.

"Goodbye," she replied curtly with her eyes lowered.

"When should I come again?"

"Whenever you like. However, we're going back to town next week; we'll let you know then…"

He left. More than two weeks went by. Everyone had returned to town from their dachas. The aristocratic salons were lit up once again. The office workers lit two wall lamps in their drawing rooms, bought twenty pounds of tallow candles, set up two card tables in anticipation of entertaining Stepan Ivanych and Ivan Stepanych, and announced to their wives that they would be "at home" on Tuesdays.

Meanwhile Aduyev had received no invitation from the Lyubetskys. He happened to run into their cook and their housemaid. When the housemaid caught sight of him, she took to her heels; clearly she was acting in accordance with her mistress's wishes. The cook, however, stood his ground.

"Have you forgotten us, sir?" he said. "We moved back ten days ago."

"I thought perhaps you hadn't settled in yet and weren't receiving guests for the moment."

"Of course we have been receiving; everyone has been over – except yourself, sir. The young lady is so surprised. Now, His Excellency honours us with his presence every day… such a nice gentleman. The other day I took him a copybook from the young lady, and he was kind enough to give me ten roubles."

"What a fool you are!" said Aduyev, and rushed away from that blabbermouth. In the evening he passed by the Lyubetsky apartment. The lights were on, and a carriage was at the porch.

"Whose carriage is it?" he asked.

"Count Novinsky's."

The next day and the day after, it was the same. Once, finally, he went in. Nadenka's mother greeted him warmly, rebuked him for staying away and scolded him for not rubbing the opodeldoc into his chest; Nadenka greeted him calmly; the Count, politely. There was no conversation.

It was the same on two further occasions. He cast Nadenka meaningful glances, but she acted as if she didn't notice – but how quick she had been to notice before! Before, he would be talking to her mother, and she would stand behind Maria Mikhailovna, facing him and pulling faces at him, and mischievously trying to make him laugh. His anguish was unbearable. The only thing he could think of was how to rid himself of this cross that he bore and had assumed of his own free will. What he wanted was to have it out with her, no matter what her answer would be. He thought that it didn't matter, even if it meant that his doubts were to become certainties.

He spent a long time trying to think up a way to arrange such a confrontation. Having done so, he went to the Lyubetskys. All the circumstances were in his favour. There was no carriage standing outside. He proceeded quietly through the hallway, and stopped for a moment just outside the door of the drawing room to compose himself. Inside, Nadenka was playing the piano. Some distance away, Lyubetskaya herself was sitting on the divan knitting a scarf. Nadenka, hearing footsteps in the room, started playing more softly and looked directly ahead; she was smiling in anticipation of the arrival of a guest. The guest appeared, and the smile instantly disappeared and was replaced by a look of alarm. Her face fell as she stood up. This was not the guest she had been expecting.

Alexander bowed wordlessly and moved on like a ghost towards her mother. He walked slowly, having lost some of his former confidence, his head hanging. Nadenka sat down and continued playing, looking back uneasily from time to time. Half an hour later Maria Mikhailovna was called from the room. Alexander went up to Nadenka, who stood up and made as if to leave.

CHAPTER 5

"Nadezhda Alexandrovna," he said dejectedly. "Wait, I won't take up more than five minutes of your time."

"I can't listen to you!" she said, and started to move away. "Last time you were…"

"Yes, that time I was at fault. This time, what I have to say will be different, and there will be no reproaches. Don't turn your back on me for what may be the last time. An explanation is necessary. After all, you permitted me to ask your mother for your hand. Since then, so much has happened that… well, I need to repeat my question. Sit down and continue playing: it would be better for your mother not to hear; I mean, it's not the first time…"

Without protest, she sat down and did as he asked. Blushing slightly, she struck some chords and in nervous anticipation stared straight at him.

"Where did you go, Alexander Fyodorych?" asked her mother as she returned to her seat.

"I wanted to speak to Nadezhda Alexandrovna about, er… literature," he replied.

"Well, speak to her, speak to her; indeed, it's a long time since you two have spoken."

He lowered his voice. "Just give me a straight and honest answer to one question, and no further explanations will be necessary… Don't you love me any more?"

"*Quelle idée!*"* she replied in her embarrassment. "You know how much *maman* and I have always valued your friendship, and how pleased we always were to…"

Aduyev looked at her and thought: "Is this really the capricious but sincere child that she was – that mischievous, frisky child? How quickly she learnt to dissemble! How quickly these feminine instincts developed in her. Were those endearing caprices really nothing but the seeds of hypocrisy and womanly wiles? And even without my uncle's tutelage, how swiftly she turned into a woman! And she learnt it all at the Count's school in a matter of a couple of months. Oh Uncle, how inexorably right you were!"

"Listen," he said in a tone of voice which suddenly ripped the mask of pretence from her face, "and let's leave your mother out of it – go back for a moment to the Nadenka you used to be when you loved me a little... and give me a straight answer; I need to know – and God knows I need to know!"

She kept silent, placed a different piece of music on her stand and concentrated on practising a difficult passage.

"Very well, I'll change the question," Aduyev continued. "Has someone – I won't say who – taken my place in your heart?"

She spent a long time adjusting her lamp, without replying.

"Answer me, Nadezhda Alexandrovna: one word from you will relieve me of my torment, and you of the necessity of an awkward explanation."

"For God's sake, stop it! What do you want me to tell you? I have nothing to say," she said, turning away from him.

Someone else might have been content with that reply and have realized that pursuing the matter further would have been a waste of time. He would have understood everything from that unspoken distress which was written on her face and revealed in her movements. But Aduyev was not content and continued sadistically to torment his victim, and was driven by a kind of savage, desperate need to drain his cup to the last drop.

"No," he said, "end this torture today; doubts, each one darker than the last, have been preying on my mind and ripping my heart to shreds. I'm at the end of my tether, and my chest is ready to burst from the pressure... I have no way of confirming my suspicions; you have to settle the matter yourself; otherwise I will never have a moment's peace of mind."

He looked at her, waiting for an answer. She still did not speak.

"Have some pity!" he began. "Take a look at me; do I look like myself? I frighten everyone, they don't recognize me... everyone pities me, you alone..."

He was right. There was a wild glitter in his eyes. He looked terrible, pale, his brow was beaded with sweat.

She cast a furtive glance at him, a look which contained a spark of something resembling regret. She even took his hand, but at once released it with a sigh and remained silent.

CHAPTER 5

"Well?" he asked.

"Leave me in peace!" she said in anguish. "You're torturing me with your questions…"

"I'm begging you, for the love of God!" he said. "End it all with one word… what good does it do to keep it to yourself? I'm still keeping a forlorn hope alive, and I won't give up. I will come to you every single day, pale and distraught… I'll importune you to tears. If you bar me from your house, I'll prowl around under your windows, I'll meet you at the theatre, in the street, everywhere like an apparition, like a memento mori. All this is foolish, even ridiculous, if anyone is in the mood for laughing, but I'm in pain! You don't know what passion is, or what it can lead to! Pray God that you never find out! So what's the use of resisting? Isn't it much better for you to speak here and now?"

"So what exactly is it that you are asking me?" said Nadenka, leaning back in her chair. "I'm totally confused… my mind is befogged…"

Convulsively she pressed her hand to her head, and immediately withdrew it.

"I am asking you if anyone else has replaced me in your heart. All you need to say is yes or no, and that will settle it – it won't take long!"

She wanted to say something, but couldn't bring herself to do so and, lowering her eyes, began to hit one key on the piano. Clearly she was in the throes of a fierce internal struggle. "Oh God!" she exclaimed in anguish. Aduyev mopped his brow with his handkerchief.

"Yes or no?" he repeated with bated breath.

Several seconds went by.

"Yes or no?"

"Yes!" Nadenka whispered barely audibly – and then, leaning right over the piano, started banging out some chords as if in a trance.

That "yes" was almost as soundless as a sigh, but it deafened Aduyev. It was as if his heart had been ripped out of him, and his legs gave way under him. He lowered himself onto a chair by the piano and sat in silence.

Nadenka glanced at him fearfully. He gave her a blank look.

"Alexander Fyodorych!" her mother cried out from her room. "Which ear is ringing?"

He didn't answer.

"*Maman* is asking you something," said Nadenka.

"What?"

"Which ear is ringing?" her mother cried out. "Tell me quick!"

"Both!" he replied bleakly.

"You're not cooperating! It's the left ear! I was trying to guess whether the Count would be coming today."

"The Count!" exclaimed Aduyev.

"Forgive me!" pleaded Nadenka, rushing to his side. "I don't understand myself either. It all just somehow happened in spite of myself… I don't know how… I couldn't deceive you…"

"I'll keep my word, Nadezhda Alexandrovna," he replied, "I won't utter a word of recrimination. I thank you for your sincerity… What you've done today is truly great. Hard as it was for me to hear that 'yes', it was much harder for you to say it… Goodbye; you will never see me again; it's the one thing I can offer you as a reward for your sincerity… but the Count, the Count!"

Tight-lipped, he made for the door.

"But," he said, turning towards her, "where will all this lead you? The Count won't marry you; do you know what his intentions are?"

"No, I don't!" Nadenka replied, shaking her head sadly.

"My God, how blinded you have been!" said Alexander, horrified.

"He can't possibly have bad intentions…" she replied in a weak voice.

"Take care of yourself, Nadezhda Alexandrovna!"

He took her hand, kissed it; his steps were faltering as he left the room. He was a sorry sight. Nadenka stood where she was without moving.

"Why aren't you playing, Nadenka?" her mother asked after a few minutes.

Nadenka awoke as if from a troubled sleep and gave a sigh.

"I'm just going to, *maman*," she replied and, turning her head pensively a little to one side, began to run her fingers tentatively over the keys. Her fingers were trembling. Clearly, her conscience was troubling her, and she was assailed by the doubts aroused by the words "Take care of yourself" that had been thrown at her.

CHAPTER 5

When the Count arrived, she was taciturn and withdrawn; there was an element of constraint in her demeanour. On the pretext of a headache, she made an early exit and went to her room. That evening it seemed to her that life had turned bitter.

At the bottom of the stairs, Aduyev's strength suddenly failed him, and he sat down on the bottom step, covered his eyes with a handkerchief and started to sob noisily, but without tears. At that moment, the porter happened to be passing through the hall, and he stopped and listened.

"Marfa, oh Marfa!" he called, heading towards his grimy door. "Come here and listen, someone is howling like some animal. I thought it was our dog which had broken its chain, but no it wasn't."

"You're right, it isn't!" she agreed, listening intently. "What the hell can it be?"

"Run and fetch the lamp – it's hanging behind the stove there!"

Marfa came back with the lamp.

"Still howling?" she asked.

"Yes! Is it some burglar who's sneaked in?"

"Who's there?" asked the porter.

No answer.

"Who's there?" Marfa repeated.

The howling continued. They both burst in. Aduyev hurried out.

"Oh, it's some gentleman!" said Marfa, watching him leave. "What on earth gave you the idea that it was a burglar howling in the hallway of someone's house?"

"Yes, well he must have been drunk!"

"Oh, an even better idea!" Marfa retorted. "You think everyone is like you? Not everyone howls when they're drunk, the way you do."

"Oh, so you think he was just hungry, is that right?" retorted the porter in his annoyance.

"What!" said Marfa, looking at him and not knowing what to say. "How should I know? Maybe he dropped some money or something..."

They both bent down and, using the lamp, began to scan every inch of the floor.

149

"Dropped something!" grumbled the porter. "Nothing can have been dropped here. The staircase is clean, and it's stone: you could even see a needle lying there... dropped indeed! We would have heard a noise if something had dropped. It would have made a tinkling sound if it had hit the stonework, and he would have picked it up. No way anything could have been dropped here. No, you can be sure a type like that would be more likely to put in his pocket. But drop something? We know those crooks. So he dropped something – but show me where?"

So they spent a long time crawling around the floor looking for money someone had lost.

Finally the porter sighed and said: "No, there's nothing!" Then he snuffed out the candle and, after squeezing the wick between two fingers, wiped them on his coat.

Chapter 6

That same night at about midnight, when Pyotr Ivanych, carrying a book and a candle in one hand and the skirt of his dressing gown in the other, was on his way from his study to his bedroom to sleep, his valet announced that Alexander Fyodorych wanted to see him.

Pyotr Ivanych frowned, thought for a moment and said calmly, "Ask him to wait in the study; I'll join him in a moment."

"How are you, Alexander?" he greeted his nephew on entering. "Haven't seen you for quite a while. There's no chance of catching you during the day – and all of a sudden you turn up here at night! Why so late? And what's wrong? You don't look at all yourself."

Alexander, without uttering a word, collapsed into an armchair in a state of total exhaustion. Pyotr Ivanych regarded him with curiosity.

Alexander sighed.

"Aren't you well?" Pyotr Ivanych asked with concern.

"Yes, I am," Alexander replied in a weak voice, "I move, I eat, I drink, so I must be well."

"You shouldn't joke about it: you should see a doctor."

"You're not the first to tell me that, but no doctor, and no opodeldoc is going to help me; my illness is not physical."

"Then what's the matter? Been wiped out gambling? Or lost some money another way?" Pyotr Ivanych enquired with keen interest.

"You can't possibly imagine anyone having troubles unconnected with money," replied Alexander, trying to smile.

"What troubles can there possibly be, if they don't cost a brass farthing, like the troubles you sometimes have?"

"That's precisely it; so now you know what's troubling me."

"You call that trouble? When everything is going well for you at home? I know this from the letters which your mother treats me to every month. And as for the office, that situation can't have got worse than it was already; they've promoted one of your juniors over you – nothing could be worse than that! You say that you're in good health, that you haven't lost any money or gambled any away... that's the important thing – any other troubles are easily dealt with; what I expect to hear next is about love and all that nonsense, I think..."

"Yes, it's love; but wouldn't you like to know what happened? Perhaps, when you hear it, you won't make so light of it, but will be horrified..."

"Very well, tell me; it's been a long time since I was last horrified," said Pyotr Ivanych with a smile, and sat down. "In any case, it's not difficult to guess what happened: no doubt you were duped..."

Alexander leapt up from his seat, thought of saying something but didn't say it, and sat down again.

"So, it's the truth then? You see, I told you so, but you wouldn't have it; it was: 'Oh no, that's impossible'!"

"Could I have felt it coming?" said Alexander. "After everything..."

"It's not a matter of feeling anything, but of foresight, or rather knowing – and, of course, acting accordingly."

"How can you discuss it so rationally and calmly, Uncle, when I..." said Alexander.

"But what's that to me?"

"Oh, I forgot, the whole city can be burnt to the ground – it's all the same to you."

"Are you kidding?! What about the factory?"

"You make a joke of it, but my suffering is no joke; I'm in a bad way – really sick."

"Do you really think that you've got so thin because of love? Shame on you! No, you *have* been sick, and now you're on the mend – and about time too! What *is* no joke is that this nonsense has been dragging on for a year and a half now. If it had gone on much longer I myself might have started believing in eternal and unswerving love."

"Uncle!" said Alexander. "Have some pity: right now I'm going through hell."

"Well, what of it?"

Alexander moved his chair closer to the desk, and his uncle began to move the inkwell, paperweight and everything else away from his nephew.

CHAPTER 6

"He comes at midnight," he thought, "'going through hell'... He's certain to smash something."

"I won't be getting any consolation from you, and I'm not asking for any," Alexander began. "I'm just asking for your help as an uncle, a member of my family... I seem like a fool to you, am I right?"

"Yes – if you weren't so pitiful."

"Oh, so that's where the pity comes in?"

"Very much so. You don't think I'm made of wood, do you? A nice lad, intelligent, well bred, reduced to such a state over nothing, over some nonsense!"

"Then show me that you have some pity for me!"

"How? You tell me that you have no need for money."

"Money again! Oh, if only my misfortune were a matter of a lack of money, I would bless my fate!"

"Don't say that!" said Pyotr Ivanych in all seriousness. "You're young, and here you are blessing your fate instead of cursing it. In the past, I have cursed my fate more than once – yes, me!"

"Please hear me out..."

"Are you going to be long, Alexander?" asked his uncle.

"Yes, I need your undivided attention, why do you ask?"

"Well, the thing is, I want some supper. I was about to go to bed without it, but now if we're going to be sitting here for a long time, then let's have some supper and a bottle of wine, and then you can tell me your story."

"You mean you can eat supper?"

"Absolutely; and you mean you won't?"

"Eat supper! You won't be able to swallow a thing either, when you know that this is a matter of life and death."

"Life and death?" his uncle repeated. "Yes, well that's very important, of course, but why don't we give it a try? Who knows, we may be able to swallow a few morsels."

He rang the bell, and his valet entered. "Find out," he told him, "what there is for supper, and bring a bottle of Lafite – the one with the green label."

The valet left the room.

"Uncle! You're in no mood to listen to my tale of woe," said Alexander, picking up his hat, "I'd better come back tomorrow…"

"No, no, it's no problem," Pyotr Ivanych insisted, holding him back by the arm, "I'm always in the same mood. If you come back tomorrow, you're just as likely to find me having breakfast – or even worse, busy with something. Better to settle the matter here and now. Supper won't interfere with that. I'll be more likely to give you the necessary attention and understand. Business doesn't thrive on an empty belly."

Supper was served.

"Now, Alexander, let's have it!" said Pyotr Ivanych.

"I really don't want anything to eat!" said Alexander impatiently, shrugging his shoulders and watching his uncle busy himself with the supper.

"Well, at least have a glass of wine; wine can't hurt!"

Alexander shook his head.

"Well, take a cigar, and tell me all about it; I'll be listening with both ears," said Pyotr Ivanych, and started eating.

"Do you know Count Novinsky?" said Alexander after a short pause.

"Count Platon?"

"Yes."

"So we know each other – what of it?"

"Congratulations on having a friend like that, the bastard!"

Pyotr Ivanych suddenly stopped chewing and regarded his nephew with astonishment.

"Well, what do you know?" he said. "You really know him?"

"Very well."

"Have you known him long?"

"About three months."

"You surprise me. I've known him for five years, and have always found him a decent chap, and no one has anything but praise for him, and here you are vilifying him."

"And since when have you been defending people, Uncle? You used to—"

"I've always defended decent people; but when did *you* start putting them down instead of calling them angels?"

CHAPTER 6

"When I didn't know any better, but now – people, people, 'what a pathetic species, worthy only of laughter and tears!'"* I realize now that I am entirely to blame for not listening to you when you advised me to be wary of everyone..."

"And I'm advising you right now that it doesn't hurt to be wary. So if someone turns out to be a scoundrel, you won't be taken in, and if someone turns out to be a decent person, you will be pleasantly mistaken."

"So tell me, where are decent people to be found?" Alexander retorted contemptuously.

"Well, let's take you and me – aren't we decent people? And since we were talking about the Count, he too is a decent fellow – as are plenty of others. Everyone has some bad in him, but no one is all bad, and not everyone is bad."

"Yes, everyone!" said Alexander categorically.

"And you?"

"Me? I at least stand out from the crowd in that, although my heart is broken, it is untainted by anything base or ignoble – my soul is riven, but unsullied by deceit, pretence or betrayal – and I shall remain uncontaminated..."

"Very well. Let's consider the matter. What has the Count done to you?"

"What has he done? Robbed me of everything."

"Can you be a little more specific? The word 'everything' could mean anything at all – perhaps money, but the Count wouldn't do that..."

"He has robbed me of something more precious than all the riches of the world."

"And what might that be?"

"Everything – my happiness, my life."

"But you're alive!"

"Unfortunately, yes! But it's a life worse than a hundred deaths."

"But tell me what exactly you're talking about."

"It's horrible!" Alexander exclaimed. "My God, my God!"

"You mean he's stolen that beauty of yours – er... what's-her-name? Oh yes, he's an expert at that; you're not in his league!" said Pyotr Ivanych, forking some turkey into his mouth.

"He will pay dearly for that expertise!" said Alexander in a fury. "I'm not giving up without a fight… Death will decide which of us will possess Nadenka. I will destroy that vile seducer – he will not live to enjoy his stolen treasure… I'll wipe him off the face of the earth!"

Pyotr Ivanych broke out laughing. "There speaks the provincial!" he said. "*À propos*, about the Count, he didn't happen to mention whether the porcelain he had ordered from abroad had been delivered? He sent away for it in the spring; I'd like to take a look…"

"This is not about porcelain, Uncle – didn't you hear what I was telling you?" Alexander burst in belligerently.

"Mmm!" his uncle mumbled affirmatively, as he gnawed on a bone.

"So what do you have to say?"

"Nothing, I'm just listening to you."

"Well, listen carefully for once in your life. I came here with a purpose: I want to set my mind at rest and resolve a million nagging questions which are worrying me… I don't know where to turn… I don't remember who I am – help me!"

"Certainly, I'm at your service, only tell me what it is you want… I'm even ready to help you out with money… provided you're not going to waste it on trifles…"

"Trifles! Hardly trifles when in a few hours I may no longer be in this world – either that, or I'll be a murderer – and you dare to sit there coolly eating your supper."

"Well, thank you very much! I believe you've had a good supper, and yet you take exception to someone else having his supper!"

"For the last two days I've forgotten what it is to eat."

"Now, *that's* really something important?"

"Just say one word: will you do me an enormous favour?"

"What?"

"Will you agree to be my witness?"

"These cutlets are all cold!" Pyotr Ivanych observed with dissatisfaction, pushing his plate away.

"Are you laughing, Uncle?"

"What do *you* think? How can one take such nonsense seriously? Wanting me to be your second!"

CHAPTER 6

"What do you mean?"

"You know very well – of course I won't."

"Very well, then I'll have to find some stranger who will be privy to my profound mortification. I would just ask you to undertake to talk to the Count and agree on the formalities…"

"I can't – I simply couldn't bring myself to make such an idiotic proposal."

"Then goodbye!" said Alexander, picking up his hat.

"What? You're really leaving – without even drinking any wine?"

Alexander was on his way to the door, but just before reaching it he sat down, utterly dejected.

"Who can I go to, who can I find to help?" he said quietly.

"Listen, Alexander," Pyotr Ivanych began, wiping his mouth with a napkin and moving an armchair up to his nephew. "I can see I'm really going to have to talk to you seriously. So let's proceed. You've come to me for help, and I will help you, but in a different way from what you think – and there's a condition: you must do as I say. Don't ask anyone to be your witness: it won't do you any good. If you start spreading the story of all this nonsense, everyone will get to hear of it and it will make you a laughing stock and, worse still, will cause you trouble. In any case, no one will agree, and if you should find someone crazy enough to accept, it would serve no purpose, since the Count will not fight you; I know him."

"He won't! Then he doesn't possess a shred of honour!" Alexander burst out in fury. "I never imagined he was so contemptible."

"He's not contemptible, just too intelligent."

"So, according to you, I must be a fool?"

"No, it's just that you're in love," said Pyotr Ivanych, choosing his words carefully.

"Uncle, if you're going to explain to me the pointlessness of a duel, and how it's nothing but an outdated custom, then I should warn you that you would be wasting your time; I'm not budging!"

"No; it has long been established that fighting is stupid in general; people are always fighting; there's no shortage of asses, and there's no way of making them see reason. All I want to do is to convince you that you in particular should not be fighting."

"I'm curious; how do you propose to do that?"

"Listen to me! Now tell me, who is it you are so angry with, the Count or that... Anyuta, or whatever her name is?"

"I hate him and despise her," said Alexander.

"Let's begin with the Count. Let's suppose that he accepts your challenge, and even that you find someone who's fool enough to act as your witness – what will be the result? The Count will kill you as easily as swatting a fly, and afterwards everyone will be laughing at you, and a fine revenge that will be! I know you don't want that to happen; what you wanted was to destroy the Count."

"No one knows who will kill whom!"

"Most probably he will kill you. I mean, you don't know the first thing about shooting, and by the rules the first shot is his."

"The outcome is in God's hands."

"Well, if that's the way you want it, God will rule in his favour. They say the Count can hit a bullet with a bullet at fifteen paces, so you think he will miss you on purpose? Let's suppose even that God would permit such ineptitude and injustice, and that you were to kill him by some fluke – where would that get you? Would it win you back the love of your beauty? No, she would hate you for it – and, what's more, you would be forced to join the army, and the end result would be that on the very next day you would be tearing your hair out in despair and your love for your darling would turn to ice on the spot."

Alexander shrugged his shoulders contemptuously. "Since you're so clever at expounding all this, Uncle," he said, "why don't you do some expounding about what I should do in my situation?"

"Nothing! Just leave things the way they are. This business is beyond repair."

"You mean leave him with happiness in his grasp, as the proud possessor?... Oh no! Do you think there's any threat that can stop me? You have no idea what I'm going through! You can never have been in love, if you thought you could stop me with this unfeeling homily... it's milk that flows in your veins, not blood..."

"Stop talking such rot, Alexander! This Maria or Sofia, or whatever, of yours – there are plenty more like her in the world."

CHAPTER 6

"Her name is Nadezhda."

"Then who is this Sofia?"

"Sofia... she's the one in my village," Alexander said with reluctance.

"Well, there you are," his uncle continued. "A Sofia there, a Nadezhda here, a Maria somewhere else. The heart is an immensely deep well, and it takes ages to grope your way to the bottom of it: it can continue falling in love even in old age..."

"No, the heart loves only once..."

"And you're just repeating what you've heard others say! The heart continues to fall in love until its energy gives out. It lives out its life, and just like everything else in a human being, it has a youth and an old age. If one love doesn't work out, it marks time and stays quiescent until the next one. If there's an impediment to that one, or a separation, the power to love remains undiminished until the one after that, and so on until finally the heart invests itself entirely in the one successful encounter to which there is no impediment, and then it slowly and gradually cools down. For some people, love works out the very first time, and they go around proclaiming that you can only love once. As long as a man stays youthful and healthy..."

"You keep on talking about youth, Uncle, which means material love..."

"I talk about youth because love in old age is a mistake, an aberration. And as for material love, it does not exist, or it is not love in precisely the same way that there is no such thing as one ideal love. Both body and soul must be partners in love, otherwise love is incomplete; we're not spirits and we're not beasts. But you yourself said: 'It's milk that flows in the veins, not blood.' Well, there you are: on the one hand, take blood in the veins – that's material; on the other hand, take pride, habit – that's spiritual. And that's love for you!

"Now, what was I saying?... Oh yes, about the army; furthermore, after all this business, your beauty won't let you come near her, so you will have done harm to both yourself and her – and for nothing, don't you see? I hope we've now said everything there is to say about one aspect of the matter. Now..."

Pyotr Ivanych poured himself some wine and drank it.

"What a blockhead!" he said. "The Lafite he brought was cold."

Alexander remained silent, his head lowered.

"Now, tell me," his uncle continued, warming the wine glass in his hands, "why is it that you wanted to wipe the Count from the face of the earth?"

"I've already told you why! Wasn't he the one who destroyed my happiness? He burst in like a wild beast..."

"Into the sheepfold!" his uncle interposed.

"He robbed me of everything," Alexander continued.

"He didn't rob you, he just came and took. Was he obliged to enquire whether your beauty was taken or not? I don't understand this idiocy which most lovers have been committing since the beginning of time, namely getting angry with a rival. Can there be anything more idiotic than 'wiping him off the face of the earth'? What for? Because she took a liking to him! As if he did something wrong, and as if it would make things better if we punished him! And this – what's-her-name – Katenka of yours, did she offer any resistance? Did she make any effort to avert the danger? No, she surrendered, and stopped loving you. There's no point in arguing – you won't get her back! To persist is sheer egoism! To demand faithfulness from a wife, yes, that makes sense. There's an obligation involved: that's something on which the material well-being of a family depends – and even then you can't demand that she love no one... but only that she... er... well, you know. Anyway, didn't you yourself hand her over to the Count on a plate? Did you even compete for her?"

"Well, here I am trying to do just that," said Alexander, leaping up from his seat. "But here you are trying to thwart my noble impulse—"

He was interrupted by his uncle. "Yes, but you want to compete with a club in your hands! We're not in the steppes of Kyrgyzstan. In the civilized world we have other weapons. You should have competed at the right time and in a different way, by fighting a different kind of duel with the Count in full view of your beauty."

Alexander looked at his uncle in bewilderment.

"What kind of duel then?" he asked.

CHAPTER 6

"I'll tell you in a moment. What have you been doing up to now?"

Alexander began to narrate the whole course of events with a mishmash of "ifs", "ands" and "buts", reservations and evasiveness – and grimaces.

"You see, it's you who are wholly to blame in all this," said his uncle, after listening and frowning. "You've blundered right, left and centre. Oh Alexander, why the devil did you come here? Was it really worth the ride? You could have got up to all this back there at home on the lake with your aunt. How could you have acted so childishly, throwing tantrums, flying off the handle? Bah! Who behaves like that these days? What if that Yulia – or whatever – of yours were to tell everything to the Count? But, thank Heavens, nothing to worry about on that score! If the Count had asked her, she was probably smart enough to say..."

"To say what?" Alexander hastened to ask.

"That she was just leading you on, and that you were in love with her, but that she didn't find you in the least attractive and got on her nerves – it's what they always say..."

"You really think that's what she actually said?" asked Alexander, growing pale.

"No doubt about it. Do you really imagine that she would tell him that you picked yellow flowers for her in the garden? How naive can you be?"

"So, what kind of duel with the Count?" Alexander asked impatiently.

"It's like this: don't be boorish with him, don't avoid him and don't sulk – in fact, go out of your way to be extra nice to him – ten times as nice to him as he is to you! And that – what's-her-name, Nadenka – did I get it right this time? – don't antagonize her with your reproaches, and be indulgent with her caprices. Don't make it appear that you notice anything, or even that you have the slightest suspicion of betrayal, as if you thought that was out of the question. You shouldn't have let them get so close as to permit intimacy, but somehow contrived artfully to block their chances of their being alone together. You should have stayed with them wherever they went and gone out with them, even on horseback. At the same time, you should subtly and tacitly have been challenging your rival to battle, and equipping yourself and bringing to bear all your mental resources for the fight. Your artillery barrage should have been your wit and cunning; and then, stepping up the fight, you should have exposed and probed your rival's weakness, quite inadvertently, and without meaning to, of course, and in the friendliest of spirits, however reluctantly and however much it went against the grain, so as to strip from him little by little that disguise in which a young man drapes himself for the benefit of an attractive woman. You should have made a point of noticing what it is that is particularly striking or dazzling about him and then focus your attack on precisely those attributes, explain them in simple terms, show that they are nothing out of the ordinary, just like the hero himself, who has simply been putting on a show in order to impress her. All this should have been done coolly, patiently and skilfully – now that is the kind of duel that should be fought today! But it's beyond you!"

Pyotr Ivanych drained his glass and immediately refilled it.

"To win a woman's heart by resorting to such low cunning and guile is contemptible!" Alexander retorted indignantly.

"Do you think resorting to the club is any better? At least, using guile as your weapon, you can salvage someone's affection for you, but brute force – I don't think so. Wanting to get your rival out of the way is understandable; to strive to preserve the love of the woman you love and to avert the danger and remove the threat is only natural, but to punish a rival simply because he has won a woman's heart is no different from kicking something you've bumped into and hurt yourself – it's what children do. Like it or not, the Count is not to blame! I can see that you understand nothing of the workings of the heart, and that is why you have had so little success in the field of love and your writing."

"The field of love!" said Alexander, shaking his head contemptuously. "But can any love earned by guile ever be honourable and lasting?"

"I don't know about 'honourable': that depends on what a person is looking for, but it doesn't matter to me; I don't have a very high opinion of love in general, as you know: I would just as soon do without it altogether, but as to whether it's more lasting – yes, it is. In matters of the heart, you can't act straightforwardly. It's a complicated device, and if you don't know which button to press, there's no telling how

CHAPTER 6

it may react. Get someone to love you in any way you want, but to keep it you must use your wits. Guile is just one of the mind's functions, and there's nothing at all despicable about it. There's no need to humiliate your rival or slander him: all you succeed in doing like that is antagonizing the woman you love... All you have to do is to strip him of all the gloss and glitter that bedazzle her, and show her that he is no hero, but just an average, run-of-the-mill human being. I believe that it is legitimate to defend a good cause by means of trickery – something which is not scorned in warfare. For instance, you wanted to get married, but what kind of a husband do you think you would make by throwing tantrums with your wife and threatening your rivals with a blunt instrument? And what would that make you?" Pyotr Ivanych pointed a finger at his forehead. "Your Varenka was twenty per cent smarter than you, when she suggested that you wait a year."

"But could I have used guile successfully, even if I had tried? No one who was as much in love as I was could have done that. Some people can sometimes feign indifference, and make a point of staying away for a certain number of days – and it works. But as for me, to pretend to calculate, when I couldn't look at her without having to catch my breath and without my knees trembling and giving way, when I was ready to suffer agonies just in order to see her... No! No matter what you say, it's a greater delight for me to love with all my heart and soul, regardless of the suffering, than to be loved without loving, or just loving half-heartedly, for amusement, as part of some repugnant game, and to toy with a woman and then dismiss her like some lapdog."

Pyotr Ivanych shrugged. "Well, go ahead and suffer, if that's what you like," he said. "Oh, the provinces. Oh, Asia! You should live in the East, where they still order women whom to love, and if they don't obey, they are drowned. No, here" – he went on, as if speaking to himself – "to be happy with a woman – that is, not in your way, like a madman, but sensibly – there are a number of conditions which have to be accepted: you have to mould a woman out of the girl according to a well-designed plan – or method, if you like – of your own, so that she understands and plays the role she has been assigned. You must confine her within an invisible circle, but not too tight a circle, where she becomes aware of the boundaries and stays within them; you must contrive to take possession not only of her heart – which is a slippery and elusive thing to keep a grip on – but her mind and her will, and subordinate her tastes and habits to your own, so that she sees everything through your eyes and thinks with your mind—"

"In other words, she should become the puppet or the unquestioning slave of her husband," said Alexander, cutting him off.

"But why? You have to arrange it so that nothing she does conflicts with her womanly attributes and virtues. Accord her freedom of action within her sphere, as long as you monitor vigilantly her every movement, every sigh and every action, so that each and every momentary mood change, outburst, the first sign of any feeling, always meets with the apparent equanimity, but ever watchful eye of her husband. You have to maintain constant vigilance, but without tyranny... and it must be done subtly and without her noticing; and in this way you will lead her in the desired direction... Oh, it's a hard and complicated schooling in a school run by a clever and experienced husband – and that's what it's all about!"

He coughed pointedly, and drained his glass.

"Then," he continued, "a husband can sleep peacefully even when his wife is not by his side, and can sit with his mind at ease in his study when his wife is sleeping..."

"So that's it, that's the famous secret of a happy marriage!" said Alexander. "Slyly taking control of a woman's mind, heart and will – and taking comfort in the thought and even priding yourself on the achievement... that's your happiness? And what happens if she does notice?"

"Priding oneself? No, there's no need for that."

"Judging by the carefree way you sit in your study," Alexander went on, "while my aunt is sleeping, I can guess who that man is—"

"Shh! Shh!... Don't say anything!" his uncle broke in, waving his arms. "It's a good thing that she *is* sleeping, otherwise... you never know..."

CHAPTER 6

At that moment the study door began to open slowly, although no one could be seen opening it.

A woman's voice could be heard from the corridor. "But the woman should never let on that she knows all about her husband's great school, but start her own little one, although never letting the fact slip out over a bottle of wine…"

Both Aduyevs rushed to the door, but by the time they reached it, nothing could be heard but the sound of rapid footsteps and the rustle of a dress dying away.

Uncle and nephew stood looking at each other.

It was the nephew who broke the silence. "Well, Uncle?"

"It's nothing!" said Pyotr Ivanych, frowning. "It was the wrong time to be boasting. Let it be a lesson for you; but better still, don't get married – or, if you do, choose a nincompoop: you'll never manage with a clever woman; my school is very demanding!"

He thought for a moment, and then slapped his forehead.

"I should have realized that she would know you had called so late," he said with annoyance, "and that a woman would never sleep knowing that two men were in the next room exchanging secrets, and that she would be sure either to send the maid or come herself… How stupid of me not to have foreseen it! And it's all because of you and that damned Lafite! I let my tongue run away with me! And it only took a twenty-year-old woman to teach me such a lesson…"

"Are you afraid, Uncle?"

"What have I to be afraid of? No, not at all! I just slipped up; no need to lose my cool: I just need to find a way out of my awkward position."

He started thinking again.

"She was just boasting," he said after a moment or two. "What kind of school can she possibly have – at her age! She was just reacting out of annoyance. But now she has noticed the invisible circle and will cook up some ploy of her own… Oh, how well I know a woman's mind! But we'll see…"

He smiled confidently and cheerfully, and the furrows disappeared from his brow.

"Only now I need a different approach," he added. "The old method is no damned good now. What I need to do is…"

He stopped himself suddenly in mid-sentence, looking apprehensively at the door.

"Anyway, I'll deal with that later," he went on. "Now let's attend to your business, Alexander. Where were we at? Oh yes, you wanted to kill your… er… what's-her-name, didn't you?"

"She's too far beneath my contempt," said Alexander, sighing deeply.

"So you see, you're already halfway cured. Or could I be mistaken? You're still angry, I think. But anyway, go on despising her: it's the best thing to do in your situation. Now there's something I wanted to say – what was it?"

"Oh, say it, say it for God's sake," said Alexander. "I can hardly think straight right now. I'm in pain; I'm at the end of my tether… Give me the benefit of your cold good sense. Tell me whatever you can that will relieve and ease the pain in my heart…"

"Well, if I were to tell you, you would probably go back there."

"Go back! The very idea! After everything that—"

"There are those who do go back even without that; give me your word that you won't!"

"I'll even swear it, if you want."

"No, your word of honour will do: it's more reliable."

"My word of honour!"

"Well, you see, now we've decided that the Count is not to blame…"

"All right, if you like, and then what?"

"Now, what is it you blame that… what's-her-name… for?"

"What do I blame Nadenka for?" Alexander retorted in amazement. "She's not to blame!"

"No! But for what? Tell me! There's no reason to despise her."

"No reason! No, Uncle, that's a wild exaggeration! Let's suppose the Count… well, he didn't know… but even so, no! And her? Then who is left to blame, me?"

"Well, you're getting closer; the fact is no one is to blame. Tell me, why do you despise her?"

"Because what she did is contemptible."

CHAPTER 6

"And what was that exactly?"

"Repaying me for my noble, boundless passion with such ingratitude."

"But where does gratitude come in? Did you love her just to do her a favour? To do her a service – so as to ingratiate yourself with her mother?"

Alexander looked at him, not knowing what to say.

"What you shouldn't have done was to reveal to her the full strength of your feelings. It makes a man less attractive to a woman when he opens up completely like that... You should have learnt more about her character first, and then have acted accordingly, instead of lying down at her feet like a lapdog. In any kind of relationship with another person, surely you must learn to know them? In that way, you would have discovered that there was nothing more to expect from her. She was acting out her affair with you to the hilt in just the same way as she is with the Count – and maybe with others... There's nothing more you can ask of her: she's incapable of moving further or higher – it's not in her nature; and you saw God knows what in her..."

"Then how come she was able to love someone else?" Alexander put in miserably.

"Ah, so that's what you're blaming her for! That's a good question, but it's one you should be asking yourself. Then why did *you* fall in love with *her*? Anyway, fall out of love as soon as possible!"

"Does that really depend on me?"

"Well, did it depend on her when she fell in love with the Count? You yourself claimed that it's impossible to stem the upsurge of feelings, but when matters reached that very point, now you ask why she fell in love! Why did this one die, and why did that other one go mad? – how can one answer such questions? Love has to end at some point, it can't go on for ever."

"You're wrong: it can. I feel that my own heart has this power, and that my love would be eternal..."

"Oh yes? And if her love for you had been stronger... well, you would have beaten a hasty retreat! That's the way it always is; and I'm someone who knows!"

"Even if she had to stop loving me," said Alexander, "why did it have to end like this?..."

"Why? Does it matter? Isn't it enough that you were loved, you revelled in it – and now it's over?"

"She gave herself to another!" Alexander went pale as he said it.

"Then would you have preferred her to fall in love with someone else and keep quiet about it, while you continued to believe that it was you she loved? Well, decide for yourself – what was she to do? Did she do something wrong?"

"Oh, I'll get my revenge on her!" said Alexander.

"You're ungrateful," Pyotr Ivanych continued. "That's wrong of you. No matter how badly a woman has treated you – betrayed you, lost her feeling for you or acted, as the poets say, 'perfidiously' – you can only blame nature; in a case like this, you can always try to view the matter from a philosophical perspective, or blame the world, life itself, whatever, but never encroach on a woman's personality in either word or deed. The weapon to use against a woman is indulgence, or at the outside the harshest weapon you should use is... indifference. These are the only weapons a decent man is entitled to use. Remember, for a year and a half you fell on everyone's neck from sheer joy, you were beside yourself with happiness – eighteen months of sheer uninterrupted pleasure! But whichever way you look at it, you're ungrateful!"

"But Uncle, there was nothing on earth more sacred to me than love – without that, life is unlivable—"

"I'm just sick of hearing such rubbish," Pyotr Ivanych broke in with annoyance.

"I would have worshipped Nadenka, and would have begrudged her no happiness in the world; I dreamt of spending my whole life with Nadenka, and see what happened. Where is that noble, overwhelming passion of which I dreamt? It degenerated into a stupid, stunted farce of sighs, scenes, jealousy, lies and pretence. God help me!"

"What made you imagine something which doesn't exist? Wasn't I the one who told you that the kind of life you've chosen to live up to now doesn't exist? As you see it, a man's only purpose in life is to be a lover, a husband, a father... anything else you simply didn't want to

CHAPTER 6

know about. Over and above that, a man is a citizen, has knowledge in some field, has a career – a writer, or a landowner, a soldier, a government official, an industrialist… But for you, all this is overshadowed by love and friendship… a kind of Arcadia! You've been reading too many novels, and spent too much time listening to your auntie down there in the backwoods, and that's why you arrived with these ideas of yours. Now you've come up with a new one – *a noble passion*!"

"Yes, noble!"

"Please, no more of that! Do you really believe in 'noble passions'?"

"What do you mean?"

"Just this. The word 'passion' means a feeling, a predilection, an attachment, which reaches a point where reason ceases to function. So where does 'noble' come in? I don't understand: it's sheer madness – not even human. In any case, why do you look at only one side of the medal? I'm talking about love – take a look at the other side, and you will see that love is not all bad. Just remember those moments of happiness when you practically deafened me…"

"Don't remind me, please don't remind me!" said Alexander, waving his arms. "It's easy for you to think like that, because you can rest secure in the affections of the woman you love. What I would like to see is what you would do in my place."

"What I would do? I would go somewhere to take my mind off it, like the factory. Would you like to go there tomorrow?"

"No: you and I will never see eye to eye," Alexander responded sadly. "Your views, far from reconciling me to life, actually alienate me from it. I'm miserable; my heart is chilled. Up to now, it has been my love that has kept my heart warm. That love has gone, leaving my heart in anguish; I'm afraid, and all is bleak…"

"You should get back to work."

"Everything you say is true, Uncle; you and others like you may be able to see it like that. But you are, by nature, a cold person, with a soul not given to strong emotion…"

"And you imagine that you're the one with a soul of such great power! Yesterday, you were in the seventh heaven of delight, yet it took so little to… When you are hurt, you just can't get over it."

Alexander retorted feebly, barely able to offer a defence, "You think, feel and talk like a locomotive moving smoothly, evenly and calmly along its rails – I can even see the steam you're puffing."

"I hope there's nothing wrong with that; it's better than jumping off the rails and tumbling into a ditch – which is what's just happened to you – and being unable to stand on your own feet. You talk about steam. Yes indeed! It's that very vapour which does credit to man. It's precisely the component of this invention which makes you and me human – any animal is capable of dying from grief. Dogs have been known to die on the graves of their masters, or to die suffocated by the intensity of their joy at seeing them again after a long separation. What on earth is the use of that? And you think that you're some kind of special being, a cut above the rest of us, someone extraordinary…"

Pyotr Ivanych looked at his nephew and stopped suddenly.

"What's this? You can't be crying?" he asked, and his face darkened – in other words, he was blushing.

Alexander said nothing. His uncle's last few words had knocked the stuffing out of him. He had nothing left to say in his defence: he was totally under the influence of his dominant feeling. All he could think of was his lost happiness, and that now it was another… and the tears poured down his cheeks.

"Come on! Control yourself! You should be ashamed!" said Pyotr Ivanych. "Be a man! If you must cry, for God's sake do it out of my sight! That's enough, stop it right now!"

"Uncle! Remember when you were young," Alexander gasped out between sobs. "Were you really able to stand up calmly and unmoved to the bitterest humiliation that fate can mete out? To live such a full life for one and a half years and suddenly to have it snatched away – and be left with nothing… And for me to have all my sincerity repaid with cunning, secretiveness and indifference – my God! Can there be any pain worse than this? It's easy enough to say about someone else, 'They've changed,' but to become the victim of it yourself! And what a change! How she started dressing up for the Count! And when I came to see her, she would turn pale; she could hardly speak… and the lies… no!"

The tears were coming thicker and faster.

CHAPTER 6

"If I had the consolation that it was circumstances which took her from me, or if I had done something unknowingly to make her leave me... even if she had died, then it would have been easier to bear, but no, no... it was someone else. It's unbearable, horrible! And there's no way for me to tear her away from that usurper; you have disarmed me... What am I to do? Tell me! I can't breathe, I'm in pain, in torment – I'm desolate... I'll shoot myself..."

He put his elbows on the table, covered his head with his hands and continued sobbing noisily.

Pyotr Ivanych felt helpless. He paced the length of the room twice and then stood in front of Alexander and scratched his head, at a loss for words.

"Drink some wine, Alexander," said Pyotr Ivanych as gently as he was able. "Well, perhaps..."

Alexander was unable to respond. His head and shoulders heaved convulsively: he could only sob. Pyotr Ivanych frowned, waved his hand and left the room.

"What can I do with Alexander?" he said to his wife. "His howling and wailing just drove me from the room – I'm at my wits' end."

"And you just left him like that?" said his wife. "The poor thing! Let me go in to him!"

"You won't do any good: that's just the way he is – just like his auntie, a real crybaby. I did my best to talk him round."

"Talk him round – that's all you did?"

"It worked: he ended up agreeing with me."

"Oh, I'm sure you did: you're very clever... and sharp!" she added.

"Thank God, if I am; I believe that's what was needed in this case."

"If you're right, why is he crying?"

"It's not my fault: I did everything I could to comfort him."

"And what was it you did?"

"I did plenty! I talked to him for a good hour – my throat practically dried up. I laid out the whole theory of love as plainly as possible, even offered him money... and supper too – not to mention wine..."

"And yet he's still in tears?"

"And what a racket he's making – and it's getting worse now!"

"Amazing! Let me go and try, and meanwhile try to think of a better method..."

"What, what do you mean?"

She slipped out of the room like a shadow.

Alexander was still sitting there, holding his head in his hands. Someone touched him on the shoulder. He raised his head. In front of him stood a young and beautiful woman in a peignoir and a cap *à la finnoise.**

"*Ma tante!*"* he said.

She sat down next to him, looked at him intently – the kind of look which only a woman can sometimes give you – gently wiped his eyes with her handkerchief and kissed him on the forehead. He pressed his lips to her hand, and they talked for a long time.

An hour later, he left the room deep in thought but with a smile, and slept soundly for the first time after many sleepless nights. She returned to the bedroom, her eyes reddened from tears. Pyotr Ivanych had been snoring for a long time.

PART II

Chapter 1

A YEAR HAD PASSED since the events and episodes described in the last chapter of Part I.

Alexander's mood of dark despair had been replaced by one of bleak dejection. He had given up his thunderous curses accompanied by the grinding of teeth against the Count and Nadenka, and had dismissed them with profound contempt. Lizaveta Alexandrovna consoled him with all the tenderness of a friend and a sister, and he was a willing beneficiary of her kind attentions. Like all others of the same temperament, he was happy to subject his own volition to the authority of another – and like them, he was someone who needed a nanny.

His passion had finally drained out of him, and his period of genuine mourning was over, but he was sorry to part with it, and made every effort to prolong it – or rather, he had created an artificial melancholy for himself, acted it out, adorned himself with it and wallowed in it.

There was something about the role of victim that he enjoyed. He was taciturn, dignified, glum, like a man – to use his own words – stricken by "a blow of fate". He spoke of his noble suffering, of his sacred, exalted feelings which had been manhandled and trampled in the mud – "And by whom?" he would add. "A hussy, a flirt and a despicable profligate, a mangy lion. Can it be that fate has put me in this world just to have everything that was finest in me sacrificed to this scum?"

Men would not forgive other men, nor would women forgive other women for such deceit, and would have lost no time in seeing that their deceivers came a cropper. But is there anything young people of opposite sexes wouldn't forgive each other?

Lizaveta Alexandrovna would listen patiently to his jeremiads and comfort him as best she could, and this was not at all distasteful to her, perhaps because there was something about her nephew which plucked at strings in her own heart, and because she heard in his complaints about love an echo of sufferings to which she was no stranger.

She listened greedily to the moaning and groaning of his heart, and responded to them with barely discernible sighs and hidden tears of her own. For the outpourings of her nephew's misery, feigned and melodramatic as they were, she even found words of consolation of a similar tone and register; but Alexander didn't want to listen.

"Please don't talk to me about that, *ma tante*!" he protested. "I don't want to defile the sacred name of love by using it to describe my relationship with that..." At this point, he would sneer contemptuously, and was ready, like his uncle, to ask, "Er... what's-her-name?"

"Anyway," he would add, in a tone of even greater contempt, "she can be forgiven; I was much too good for her and that count, and that whole pitiful and worthless crew; no wonder I remained a closed book to them."

Even after he had finished, that expression of contempt remained on his face.

"Uncle claims that I should be grateful to Nadenka," he continued, "but for what? What was noteworthy about that love? It was as banal and commonplace as they come; was there anything at all about it which rose above the pettiest and most vulgar of everyday squabbles? Was there anything in that love that could be seen as the slightest bit heroic or selfless? No, there was practically nothing she did without her mother knowing! Did she ever take a single step for me outside the social norms, outside what was socially correct? Never! A girl whose feelings could not include the merest spark of poetry."

"But what kind of love could you ask of a woman?" asked Lizaveta Alexandrovna.

"What kind?" replied Alexander. "I would demand of her that I occupy the first place in her heart. The woman I love should not notice or see any man other than myself. All other men should be insufferable. I alone would be on a higher level, more handsome" – and here he drew himself up – "better and nobler than all others. Every second lived without me would be to her a wasted moment. In my eyes and in my words alone would she find bliss, and know of no other source..."

Lizaveta Alexandrovna tried to hide her smile, but Alexander did not notice.

CHAPTER I

"For me," he continued with shining eyes, "she would be ready to sacrifice all, any petty advantage or profit, to cast off the despotic yoke of her mother, her husband, and flee, if necessary, to the ends of the earth, to withstand robustly any privation – and, finally, even to look death itself squarely in the face: that's what I call love! But that—"

"And how would you reward her for such love?" his aunt asked.

"How?" Alexander began, raising his eyes to the heavens. "Why, I would lie at her feet. Gazing into her eyes would be my greatest happiness. Her every word would be law to me. I would sing of her beauty, her love, to nature itself:

"With her, my lips would possess
Petrarch's language and that of love itself…*

"And didn't I show Nadenka the love of which I was capable?"

"So you simply don't believe in a feeling if it's not expressed in the way you want? A strong feeling can remain hidden…"

"Wouldn't you like to assure me, *ma tante*, that a feeling like my uncle's, for example, remains hidden?"

Lizaveta Alexandrovna's face suddenly reddened. Deep down, she had to agree with her nephew that a feeling that never actually manifests itself is somehow suspect, and maybe doesn't even exist, and that if it did exist it would force its way to the surface. Also that, apart from the love itself, its very setting possesses indescribable delight.

She began to review mentally the whole course of her married life, and plunged into deep thought. Her nephew's indiscreet remark had stirred up in her heart a secret which she had kept deeply hidden, and prompted the question – was she happy?

She had no right to complain: all the external conditions of happiness which the mass of the people strive for had been created for her as if they had been carefully planned. Contentment, even luxury now, and security in the future – all this spared her those trivial, oppressive cares which gnaw at the heart and constrict the breasts of the legions of the poor.

Her husband had worked tirelessly, and continued to work. But what was the ultimate goal of all this work? Did he work for the general good of mankind by performing the tasks set for him by destiny or merely for narrowly selfish reasons, to acquire the money and status that would earn him prestige among his peers and ultimately to avoid being trapped in poverty by circumstances? Only God knows. He was loath to talk about loftier goals, talk that he dismissed as so much hot air, and confined himself drily and simply to saying "Work is there to get done".

Lizaveta Alexandrovna was forced to the grim conclusion that neither she herself nor love of her was the sole purpose of all his striving and zeal. He had worked hard before their marriage, even before he had known his wife. He had never talked to her of love, and had never asked her about it. Whenever she raised such questions, he would evade the issue with a joke, a quip or by pleading sleepiness. Soon after they had met, he mentioned marriage, giving her to understand that love was to be taken for granted, and that there was no point in talking much about it…

He was against doing anything for effect – which was all very well, but he had no time for baring his own feelings, and didn't see the need for it in others. However, at any time, with a single word he could have stirred up in her the strongest feelings for him, but he remained silent and refrained. It was something that didn't even tickle his self-esteem.

She tried to make him jealous, thinking that that couldn't help but provoke an expression of love – nothing of the kind! He only had to notice her picking out some young man or other at a social gathering for him to invite him on the spot to visit them, be very friendly to him and praise his accomplishments to the skies, and would not hesitate to leave him alone with his wife.

Lizaveta Alexandrovna sometimes deluded herself into believing that perhaps Pyotr Ivanych's behaviour was all part of a strategy, and that this might be the essence of his secret method whose purpose was to keep her constantly in doubt, and in this way to maintain her love. But her husband's very first reference to love swiftly disabused her.

CHAPTER I

If he had also been ill bred, uncouth and callous, and a dullard, one of those husbands whose name is legion, one of those who can be deceived without any sense of guilt, so necessarily, and so comfortably for their own good and for that of the wife – those husbands who seem naturally disposed to let their wives look around to find a lover who is the polar opposite of their husband – then that would be a different matter, and she might have behaved as do most women in her circumstances. But Pyotr Ivanych was an intelligent and tactful man, a rare species. He was subtle, perspicacious and quick-witted. He understood all the vagaries of the heart and the turbulence of the emotions – but that was as far as it went. He kept in his head the complete textbook of the matters of the heart – but not in his heart. From all his opinions on the subject, it was clear that everything he had to say about it was, as it were, learnt by rote, but never actually felt. When he talked about the passions, what he said was accurate, although he never acknowledged that they might apply to himself. In fact, he derided them and dismissed them as errors and aberrations from reality, as if they were some kind of disease which would eventually be cured by the right medicine.

Lizaveta Alexandrovna was aware of his intellectual superiority over his peers and was tormented by it. "If he were not so intelligent," she thought, "I would be saved." His goals tended to be concrete ones – that was clear – and he insisted on his wife not living in a dream world.

"My God!" thought Lizaveta Alexandrovna. "Can he have married just so as to have someone to keep house and to equip his bachelor quarters with the proper decor and standards of a proper family home in order to improve his social standing? A wife in the most prosaic sense of the term – someone to keep house for him! Can he not grasp the idea that concrete goals must always include love? Yes, family responsibilities are indeed the concern of the wife, but can they be discharged without love? Nannies, wet-nurses can make the child they care for the centre of their lives, but a wife, a mother! Oh, if only I could acquire feeling even at the cost of great pain – every kind of suffering that comes with passion – simply in order to live a full life, to feel that I am alive instead of merely vegetating!"

She looked around at all the luxurious furniture and all the precious trinkets and toys in her boudoir – and all those comforts, with which in other marriages the hand of a caring husband surrounds his beloved wife, seemed nothing more than a callous parody of true happiness. She was the witness of two terrible extremes – represented by her nephew and her husband – the one passionate to excess, the other as cold as ice.

"How little either of them understands true feeling, just like most men! And how well I understand it!" she thought. "But what's the use? And what for? Oh, if only…"

She closed her eyes, and kept them closed for a few minutes. Then she opened them, looked around and heaved a sigh, resuming her usual calm expression. The poor woman! No one noticed, no one knew. It was almost as if these unseen, impalpable and nameless sufferings unaccompanied by wounds or blood – and she, all the while clothed, not in rags but in velvet – were a punishment for some crime or other. But with heroic self-restraint she kept her sorrow to herself, and still had enough strength to comfort others.

Soon Alexander gave up talking about his noble sufferings and his misunderstood and priceless love. He adopted a more general refrain. He complained about the tedium of life, the emptiness of his soul, the anguish that drained him. He constantly reiterated:

"I endured my sufferings,
I cast away my dreams…*

"And now I am being haunted by a black demon. Oh *ma tante*, it's with me all the time – at night, in the middle of a friendly chat, in the midst of revelry, at times of profound meditation!"

Several weeks passed in this way. You might think that in another couple of weeks this eccentric would have calmed down completely, and perhaps might even have turned into a respectable, that is to say, simply a normal member of the human race, just like everyone else. Not a bit of it! The peculiarity of his strange nature always managed to find an outlet.

CHAPTER I

Once he came to his aunt in an access of malevolence towards the whole human race. A word, a taunt, an opinion, a quip, whatever form it took, it was always aimed at people he should have respected. He spared no one. He even had it in for her and Pyotr Ivanych. Lizaveta Alexandrovna tried to delve into the reasons.

"Would you like to know," he said with quiet solemnity, "what upsets me and infuriates me now? Well, listen. I had a friend whom I hadn't seen for several years, and for whom I always had a soft spot. My uncle, when I first came here, made me write him a strange letter containing his favourite rules and way of thinking; but I tore it up and sent a different one, so there was no reason for it to affect our relationship. After that letter, we stopped writing to each other, and I lost track of my friend. So what happened? Three days ago, I'm walking along the Nevsky Prospekt and suddenly catch sight of him. I stood rooted to the spot: tremors of excitement ran through me and tears came to my eyes. I held out my hand to him, but was so overcome by joy that I couldn't utter a word – I couldn't catch my breath. He took my hand and shook it. 'Hello, Aduyev!' he said, as casually as if we had parted only the day before. 'Have you been here long?' He was surprised that we hadn't run into each other before this, and asked casually what I was doing, where I was working, and made a point of informing me that he had a great job and was happy with the work, his superiors and his colleagues as well as… everyone and everything… then he told me that he had no time because he was hurrying to a formal dinner party. Can you imagine, *ma tante*! Here we were, two friends, meeting for the first time after so long, and he was worried about being late for his dinner…"

"But perhaps they were waiting for him, and it wouldn't have been polite to—"

"Politeness and friendship? Then you agree, *ma tante*? Well, let me tell you something else – it gets better! He put his address in my hand: he said I should call on him the next day in the evening – and disappeared. I watched him walking off for a long time; I just couldn't get over it. This was a companion of my childhood, and a friend of my youth! How do you like that? But then I thought perhaps he was just postponing things until the next evening and would take the time for us to have a real heart-to-heart talk. 'Very well then,' I think, 'I'll go.' So I turn up. There were ten friends with him. True – he shook hands with me more warmly than the day before – but, without saying a word, proposed a game of cards. I told him that I don't play, and sat down alone on a divan, imagining that he would leave the card table and come over and talk to me. 'You're not playing?' he said in surprise. 'But what will you do?' Now, what kind of question is that? There I am waiting – one hour goes by, then another hour, and he still doesn't come over. I'm losing patience. First, he offered me a cigar, then a pipe, said he was sorry I wasn't playing, that I must be bored, and made an attempt to entertain me – can you guess how? He kept on turning to me and telling me how well or badly he was doing with each hand at the card table. I finally ran out of patience and went over to him and asked whether he had any intention of paying me any attention that evening. I was so furious that my voice was trembling. He seemed surprised, and gave me a strange look and said: 'All right, let's just finish the game.' As soon as he said that, I picked up my hat, intending to leave, but he noticed and said: 'We're almost finished – and then we'll have supper.' They finally finished, and he sat down next to me and yawned, and our friendly chat began. 'Was there something you wanted to tell me?' he asked, in such a flat monotone that I said nothing and just smiled at him dejectedly – whereupon he suddenly came to life and started plying me with questions. 'What's the matter? Do you need something, or can I offer you any help professionally?' and so on. I shook my head and said that I didn't want to speak to him about work, or how well we're doing materially, but about matters closer to the heart, the golden years of our childhood, the games we used to play, the pranks we got up to... and imagine, he didn't even let me finish! – and said: 'You're still the same old dreamer!' – and then changed the subject as if it were a waste of time, and started asking me seriously about my affairs, my hopes for the future, my career, and about my uncle. I was surprised, and couldn't believe that a man's nature could have coarsened to such a degree. I wanted to give it one last try, and fastened on the question he had asked me about my affairs, and began

CHAPTER I

to tell him about how I had been treated, and started to say: 'Listen to what some *people* did to me...' That alarmed him, and he interrupted me to ask: 'What? You haven't been robbed, have you?' – obviously thinking that when I said 'people', I meant 'servants'.* Just like my uncle; it was the only misfortune which came to his mind. How can a man become so insensitive? 'Yes,' I said, 'people robbed me of my soul...' – and I started telling him of my love, my ordeal, of my spiritual emptiness, and began to get a little carried away, thinking that the tale of my sufferings would warm his icy crust, and that his eyes hadn't yet forgotten how to weep. Suddenly he burst out laughing, and I saw that he had been holding a handkerchief in his hands. All the time I had been talking, he had hardly been able to contain himself. Finally, he couldn't hold it in any longer. I stopped, horrified.

"'It's too much, too much!' he said. 'Better have some vodka! And then we'll have some supper. Bring vodka!' he ordered. 'Come on, let's go!' he said. 'The roast... beef... great... roast beef.' He was laughing so hard, he could hardly get the words out. He tried to take my arm, but I tore myself away from the clutches of that monster and ran... That's what people are like!" Alexander concluded, waved his hand and left.

Lizaveta Alexandrovna felt sorry for Alexander: sorry for his ardent but misguided heart. She saw that with a different upbringing and a proper outlook on life, he would have been happy and capable of making someone else happy, but now he was the victim of his own blindness, and the aberrations of his own heart. He himself creates the pain in his own life. How to point his heart in the right direction? Where is the compass that can save him? She felt that only a tender, friendly hand was capable of tending that delicate flower.

She had already once succeeded in taming the restless impulses of her nephew's heart, but that was when it was a matter of love. In that area, she knew how to deal with a wounded heart. Like the skilled diplomat, she was the first to heap reproaches on Nadenka, and to cast her treatment of him in the worst possible light – and, by belittling her in Alexander's eyes, she finally showed him that she was unworthy of his love. In this way, she wrenched from his heart the agonizing pain he was suffering, and replaced it with the comfortable but not entirely justified feeling of contempt. Pyotr Ivanych, on the other hand, tried to justify Nadenka's behaviour – and by so doing, far from easing his pain, was actually making it worse, because he made him feel that it was the worthiest candidate who had been chosen.

The friendship, however, was a different matter. Lizaveta Alexandrovna saw that Alexander's friend, although at fault in Alexander's eyes, was right in the eyes of most people. Just imagine trying to convince Alexander of that! She couldn't bring herself to attempt that feat and appealed to her husband, believing, not without reason, that he would not be short of arguments against friendship.

"Pyotr Ivanych!" she said sweetly to him one day. "I have something to ask you."

"What is it?"

"Try and guess!"

"Just tell me, you know I can refuse you nothing. It's probably about the St Petersburg dacha; but isn't it rather early now?…"

"No!" said Lizaveta Alexandrovna.

"What then?"

"New furniture?"

She shook her head.

"I'm sorry, but I really don't know," said Pyotr Ivanych. "Why don't you just take this pawn ticket and do whatever you like with the proceeds? It's yesterday's winnings…"

He started to take out his wallet.

"No, don't bother, put your money back," said Lizaveta Alexandrovna. "What I am asking won't cost you a copeck…"

"Not taking money when it's offered!" said Pyotr Ivanych, putting back his wallet. "Unheard of! What is it you want?"

"Just a little of your goodwill…"

"Take as much as you want."

"Well, you see, the other day Alexander came to see me—"

"Oh dear! I don't think I'm going to like this!" Pyotr Ivanych cut in. "Well?"

"He's so depressed," Lizaveta Alexandrovna continued, "and I'm afraid of what he might do…"

CHAPTER I

"Now, what's the matter with him? He hasn't been let down by some other woman he's fallen in love with, has he?"

"No, it's about a friend."

"A friend! It gets worse by the minute. So, what about this friend? I'm curious, please tell me."

"It's like this."

And Lizaveta Alexandrovna proceeded to tell him everything that her nephew had told her. Pyotr Ivanych shrugged his shoulders emphatically.

"But what do you want me to do about it? You know how he is!"

"Just show him some understanding and ask him how he feels inside."

"No, you should be the one to ask him."

"Try talking to him – how shall I put it?... more sympathetically, instead of in your usual manner... Don't make fun of his feelings..."

"You're not asking me to cry, I hope?"

"Well, it wouldn't hurt."

"Anyway, what use would it be?"

"A great deal of use... and not just to him..." Lizaveta Alexandrovna muttered under her breath.

"What?" asked Pyotr Ivanych.

She said nothing.

"Oh, that Alexander, he's a real pain in the..." said Pyotr Ivanych, pointing to the neck in question.

"How exactly has he been such a burden to you?"

"What do you mean, 'how'? I've had to deal with him for six years now; if it's not that he's in tears and needs comforting, I also have to keep writing to his mother."

"Oh dear, you poor thing! How trying for you! What a frightful bother! To have to get a letter once a month from the old lady and throw it into the waste-paper basket without reading it – or actually to have to talk to your nephew! Of course, I know it means taking you away from your whist! Men, men! If there's a good dinner, Lafite with the gold seal followed by cards – then absolutely nothing or anybody else matters! And if it gives you a chance to pontificate and show how clever you are – then you're happy!"

"Just the way it is with you when you have the chance to flirt," Pyotr Ivanych retorted. "To each his own, my dear! So what else?"

"What else, you ask. Why, the heart, of course! But never a word about that."

"And I should think not!"

"Oh, we're so clever – not for us to bother with such frivolities, oh no! We're in charge of people's destinies. What matters to us is how much a man has in his pocket, or what decoration he wears in his buttonhole, and nothing else is worthy of our attention. We want everyone to be like them, and if among them there happens to be one single sensitive soul, capable of loving and being loved…"

"Well, he didn't exactly do a wonderful job of being loved by that… what's-her-name… Verochka or whatever?"

"Well, look who he is putting on an equal footing with him! It's one of fate's little jokes. It's almost as if fate were mischievously pairing up a tender, sensitive soul with a block of ice! Poor Alexander. His trouble is that his mind and heart are out of step with each other, and that's why he is condemned by people whose minds have outrun their hearts, people who favour reason over feeling whatever the situation…"

"But you must agree that that's the important thing, otherwise—"

"No, I will never agree with that, not for the world. It may be important there at your factory, but you're forgetting that people also have feelings…"

"Well, five, if you mean the senses!" said Aduyev. "I learnt that way back when I was learning my ABC."

"And how distressing that is!" whispered Lizaveta Alexandrovna.

"There, there, no need to get upset; I'll do whatever you say, but first you have to give me my instructions," said Pyotr Ivanych.

"Well, talk to him nicely…"

"Give him a talking to? Certainly, that's what I'm good at."

"Here you go with your 'talking to'! I want you to tell him as nicely as possible what to ask and expect of the friends he has now, and in particular that his friend's behaviour wasn't as bad as he thinks… Anyway, why am I telling you this? You're so intelligent, you know how to talk people round," said Lizaveta Alexandrovna.

CHAPTER I

At this last phrase, Pyotr Ivanych's brow crinkled.

"After all those heart-to-heart talks you must have had with him," he said irritably, "and all that whispering that went on, you still didn't manage to exhaust the topic of love and friendship – and now you want to get me involved…"

"But it will be for the last time," said Lizaveta Alexandrovna. "I'm hoping that after that he'll feel better about things."

Pyotr Ivanych shook his head doubtfully.

"Does he have any money?" he asked. "Perhaps he doesn't and, well…"

"Can't you think of anything except money! He would be ready to give up all the money he has for a pleasant word from a friend."

"Well, isn't that just like him! It doesn't surprise me. Once he gave money to a colleague in his department for just that kind of effusive outpouring… But someone's ringing, could it be him? What should I do? Tell me again – give him a talking to… or what else? Money?"

"What do you mean 'a talking to'? That way, you'll make things even worse. I asked you to talk to him about friendship, about matters of the heart – but don't be hard on him, be more considerate!"

Alexander entered, bowed silently and, equally silently, ate a hearty dinner, and between courses rolled scraps of bread into little balls and inspected the bottles and carafes without raising his eyes. After dinner, just as he was picking up his hat, Pyotr Ivanych spoke up.

"Where are you off to?" he asked. "Why don't you stay a while?"

Still silent, Alexander obeyed. Pyotr Ivanych tried to think how to approach the task in a more agreeable and more tactful manner, and suddenly burst out abruptly with: "I understand, Alexander, that your friend treated you rather off-handedly?"

At these unexpected words, Alexander's head snapped back as if he had been wounded, and he aimed a look full of reproach at his aunt. She too had been taken aback by this abrupt approach, and for a moment kept her head buried in her work, and then she too looked reproachfully at her husband, but he was in the double grip of digestion and sleepiness, and the two glances bounced off him.

Alexander responded to his question with the faintest of sighs.

"That really wasn't very nice of him. What kind of friend is that! He hadn't seen his friend for five years, and couldn't even bring himself to give him a hug when they met, and just casually invited him round one evening and asked him to play cards... and offered him food. And then even worse, noticing how miserable his friend was looking, he went on to ask him about what he was doing, and his circumstances and if there was anything he needed – what insufferable curiosity! And then on top of it all – the very height of insincerity! – he had the nerve to offer his services... help... maybe even money, but absolutely no thought of heartfelt outpourings. Terrible! Terrible! I would like to see this monster myself, bring him round for dinner on Friday. Oh, and ask him what stakes he plays for."

"I don't know," Alexander responded angrily. "Laugh away, Uncle; you're right: I'm the only one who is to blame. To trust people, to look for sympathy – from whom? To bare my heart – to whom? I was surrounded by meanness, cravenness, pettiness, but I held on to my faith in good, valour and constancy..."

Pyotr Ivanych's head had begun to nod in a kind of regular rhythm.

"Pyotr Ivanych!" Lizaveta Alexandrovna whispered to him, tugging at his sleeve. "Are you sleeping?"

"What, me sleeping!" he said, now fully awake. "But I heard everything you said: 'valour, constancy'. How could I have been sleeping?"

"Don't bother my uncle, *ma tante*!" said Alexander. "He won't go to sleep: it will upset his stomach, and God knows what will happen then. He may be the master of the universe, but he's also the slave of his stomach."

He tried to produce a bitter smile, but somehow it came out sour.

"Tell me what it was that you wanted from your friend? A sacrifice of some kind – like climbing up a wall, or throwing himself out of the window? What's your understanding of friendship – what does it mean to you?" asked Pyotr Ivanych.

"Don't worry, I'm not asking for any sacrifice now. It's thanks to my experience of people that my notion of friendship and of love has sunk to such a low level. Here are some lines I always carry with me and which have always seemed to me to convey the truest definition of those two emotions, and it is the way I have always understood them – and is what they should be. I now see that that notion was false: it slanders people and betrays a pitiful ignorance of their hearts. People are not capable of such feelings. But no! I repudiate these treacherous words."

He took his wallet out of his pocket, and from it two sheets of paper which had been written on.

"What's that?" asked his uncle. "Show me!"

"It's not worth it!" said Alexander, and was about to tear them up.

"Read them, read them!" said Lizaveta Alexandrovna.

"This is how two of the latest French novelists have defined true love and friendship, and I agreed with them, thinking that I would encounter these two entities in real life, and that I would find in them… whatever!" And with a gesture of contempt, he started to read: 'Do not love with that false, timorous amiability which lives in our gilt palaces, which surrenders to a handful of gold and which fears the ambiguous word, but with that powerful affection which repays blood with blood, which manifests itself in battle and bloodshed, amidst the roar of the cannon and the thunder of the storm, when friends kiss, mouth to powder-blackened mouth, and smear each other with blood when they embrace, and when Pylades lies mortally wounded, and Orestes takes leave of him with a faithful thrust of his dagger in order to put him out of his misery, swears a terrifying oath to avenge his death and, after honouring this oath, wipes away his tear and finds repose—'"*

Pyotr Ivanych broke into his own kind of restrained laughter.

"Who are you laughing at, Uncle?" asked Alexander.

"At the author, if he wrote that in all seriousness, and was speaking for himself – and also at you if that is really the way you understood friendship."

"And to you that was nothing but ridiculous?" asked Lizaveta Alexandrovna.

"Nothing but. And I'm sorry, but pitiful as well as ridiculous. And, by the way, Alexander agreed by allowing himself to laugh too. As he himself just acknowledged, this idea of friendship was false and slandered people – and that is a step in the right direction."

"But a lie only because people cannot rise to the level of friendship as it should be properly understood…"

"Well, if people are incapable of doing that, then that definition of friendship must be wrong…" said Pyotr Ivanych.

"But there have been examples…"

"They are exceptions, and exceptions are almost always bad. Bloodied embraces, terrifying oaths, thrusts of a dagger!…" And he burst out laughing again. "Now read what it says about love," he continued. "I'm not even sleepy any more…"

"Well, by all means, if it will give you another opportunity to have a good laugh," said Alexander, and proceeded to read the following:

"'To love means no longer belonging to yourself, to stop living for yourself, to live inside the skin of another, to concentrate all your human feelings, hope, fear, sorrow and pleasure, on a single object; to love means to live in perpetual—'"

"What the devil does all that mean?" Pyotr Ivanych cut in. "What a slew of words!"

"No, it's very good! I like it," said Lizaveta Alexandrovna. "Read some more, Alexander."

He continued reading: "'To know no limits to feeling, to devote oneself to a single being, to live and think only for its happiness, to find great heights in being brought low, pleasure in sorrow, and sorrow in pleasure, to give oneself up to every possible pair of opposite extremes, except love and hate. To love means to live in an ideal world…'"

At this Pyotr Ivanych shook his head.

Alexander went on: "'In an ideal world where radiance and splendour reign supreme, all radiance is splendour. In this world, the sky appears purer, nature more luxuriant; life and time are divided in two – presence and absence. There are two seasons – spring and winter: spring belongs to the former and winter to the latter, because no matter how beautiful the flowers and how pure the azure of the sky, in the time of absence the splendour of both is dimmed; in the whole world to see only one being, and in that one being embrace the whole universe… Finally, to love is to catch every glance of the beloved, as the Bedouin catch every drop of dew to moisten their parched lips; in the absence of that being, to be assailed by a swarm of thoughts, and in its presence to be unable to utter a single one; to strive to outdo each other in serving and pleasing—"

Pyotr interrupted him. "Stop, for God's sake, that's enough!" he exclaimed. "I can't take it any more! You wanted to tear it up? Then tear it up right now! What rot!"

Pyotr Ivanych even rose from his chair and started pacing back and forth in the room.

"Can there really have been a time when people thought and acted like that in all seriousness?" he said. "All these fabrications they cook up about knights and shepherdesses must surely be insulting to their memory? And what possesses them to play on and analyse so minutely the vulnerable strings of the human heart?... Love! To make it all sound so important..."

He shrugged.

"Uncle, why go so far afield?" said Alexander. "I feel this power of love in myself, and I'm proud of it. My misfortune is simply that I haven't met a being worthy of it who possesses the same gift and the same power..."

"'The power of love'!" Pyotr Ivanych repeated. "You might just as well talk about the power of weakness."

"That's something beyond you, Pyotr Ivanych," Lizaveta Alexandrovna put in. "You simply won't believe in the existence of such love even in others..."

"And what about you? Are you telling me that you believe?" said Pyotr Ivanych, going up to her. "No, of course not, you're just joking. He's just a child, and doesn't understand himself or anyone else; you would be ashamed to believe such a thing. Could you really respect a man if he loved you like that? No, surely that's not the way people love..."

Lizaveta Alexandrovna looked up from her work.

"Of course they do," she said quietly, taking him by the hands and pulling him towards her.

Pyotr Ivanych removed his hands from her grasp and pointed at Alexander, who was standing by the window with his back to them, and resumed his pacing back and forth.

"What's that?" he said. "You sound as if you've never heard how people love."

"'How people love'!" she repeated pensively and slowly resumed her work.

Fifteen minutes of silence ensued. Pyotr Ivanych was the first to break it.

"What are you doing now?" he asked his nephew.

"Well... nothing."

"Hardly enough. But do you read at least?"

"Yes..."

"Well, what?"

"Krylov's fables."*

"That's a good book – only that?"

"The only one for now, but my God, what portraits of people, and how true to life!"

"You do have it in for people. Could it be that it was your love for that... you know who I mean... which made you like this?"

"Oh, I've forgotten all about that foolishness. Recently I passed by those places where I had been so happy and had suffered so much, and thought that my memories would surely be heart-rending."

"Well, were they?"

"I saw the dacha, the garden and the fence, and my heart didn't miss a beat."

"Well, there you are, I told you so. But what is it you find so obnoxious about people?"

"I'll tell you what: their nastiness, their mean-spiritedness, their... my God! When you think of all of the worst human qualities which have sprung up where nature has scattered such wonderful seeds..."

"But why should that matter to you? Is it your wish to reform people?"

"Why does it *matter* to me? Don't you know how I have been spattered by that mud in which people wallow? Don't you know all that has happened to me – and after that not to hate, not to despise people!"

"But what has happened to you?"

"I've been betrayed in love, and been coldly and callously forgotten by friends... and now I'm totally disgusted and repelled by the sight

CHAPTER I

of people and the thought of living among them. All their thoughts, their deeds and dealings are built on sand. Today they are bent on a single goal: they rush, they knock others out of their way, they stop at nothing to gain their ends, they flatter, they grovel, they scheme; but the next day, they forget what it was they were after the day before, and they are off chasing something different. Today, they are flattering someone, but tomorrow they will be vilifying that same person; today they are hot, tomorrow they will be cold... No, wherever you look, life is terrible and disgusting! And as for people!..."

Pyotr Ivanych once again was on the point of nodding off in his armchair.

"Pyotr Ivanych!" said Lizaveta Alexandrovna, prodding him gently.

"You're depressed, yes, you're depressed! You must find some work," said Pyotr Ivanych, wiping his eyes, "then you won't be insulting people for no good reason. What exactly is wrong with the people you know? I mean, they're all decent types."

"Whoever you get hold of, you find they're all beasts out of Krylov," said Alexander.

"The Khozarov family, for example?"

"They're a pack of animals, the lot of them!" Alexander cut in. "One of them showers you with flattery in your presence and fawns upon you, but I've heard what he says about me behind my back. Another one commiserates with you today when your feelings have been hurt, but tomorrow he'll be commiserating with the person who insulted you; today, he'll be joining you in making fun of someone else, and tomorrow he'll be with that someone else, making fun of you... What scum!"

"And the Lunins?"

"And fine ones they are too! He himself is the very image of Krylov's donkey which the nightingale flew thrice seven leagues to get away from. And as for her, she looks like Krylov's 'good fox'..."*

"And what about the Sonins?"

"Well, what is there to say in their favour? Sonin is always offering good advice when you no longer need it, but just try to ask for his help when you're in trouble and he'll send you home without supper – just like the fox did to the wolf.* Don't you remember what a fuss he made of you when he wanted you to recommend him for a position? And now listen to what he is saying about you…"

"And I suppose you don't think much of Volochkov either?"

"He's worthless, and a vicious animal into the bargain!" said Alexander, and even spat.

"Well, that's telling them what you think of them!" Pyotr Ivanych observed.

"And what else can I expect from people?" said Alexander.

"Everything: friendship, love, a commission as a staff officer and money… And now conclude this gallery of portraits with our own, and tell me which animals are we, your aunt and I?"

Alexander offered no reply, but there flickered across his face an expression of barely perceptible irony, and he smiled. Neither the expression nor the smile escaped Pyotr Ivanych's notice. He exchanged glances with his wife, and she lowered her eyes.

"Well, what about yourself? What animal are you?" asked Pyotr Ivanych.

"I haven't done anyone any harm!" Alexander said with some pride. "I've always treated other people properly… I have a loving heart; I approach people with my arms wide open, and what do I get in return?"

"You see how ridiculous he can be!" Pyotr Ivanych appealed to his wife.

"You find everything funny!" she replied.

"And I never asked anything of people: no great acts of kindness, no magnanimity, no self-abnegation… I asked only what was my due, what I had the right to expect…" Alexander continued.

"So you are in the right? You've come out of the water completely dry. Well, just hold it there and I'll show you some fresh water…"

Lizaveta Alexandrovna noticed that her husband had adopted a harsher tone and was worried.

"Pyotr Ivanych!" she whispered. "Please don't…"

"No, it's time he heard the truth. I'll only take a moment. Tell me, Alexander, just now, when you condemned everyone you know as knaves or fools, didn't you feel in your heart the slightest stirring of conscience?"

CHAPTER I

"Why should I have, Uncle?"

"Because over a number of years you always got a warm welcome from these 'animals'. Let's suppose that with people from whom they had something to gain they did scheme and play dirty tricks, as you say; but with you they had nothing to gain, so what was it that made them offer you hospitality and affection? That's not nice, Alexander!" added Pyotr Ivanych seriously. "Someone else, even if he had noticed some bad behaviour on their part, would have held his tongue."

Alexander was furious. "I assumed that they would at least have shown some appreciation of your goodwill in introducing me," he replied, but now more humbly, and a little deflated, "and anyway these were only social acquaintances…"

"All right, let's talk about your relationships which were more than social. I've already tried to show you – although I don't know whether I was successful – that you were unfair to your… what's-her-name, Sashenka, is it? For eighteen months you were made welcome in their home – practically lived there from morning until night – and, what's more, that *despicable hussy*, whoever she was, gave you her love. I would have thought that that treatment doesn't deserve contempt…"

"Then why did she betray me?"

"Oh, you mean why did she fall in love with someone else? I thought we had settled that matter satisfactorily. And do you really think that, if she had gone on loving you, your own love for her would have lasted?"

"Yes, for ever."

"Well, it seems you understand nothing; but let's move on. You say that you have no friends, but I've always thought that you had three friends."

"Three?" Alexander protested. "I once had one friend, but even he—"

"Three," Pyotr Ivanych insisted. "Let's take it in chronological order. First, there is that *one* friend. Someone else who hadn't seen you for several years wouldn't have bothered with you at all, but he invited you to his home, and you went there with a sour face. He took enough interest in you to ask whether there was anything you needed, and offered his help and his good offices – and, I'm convinced, would have given you money – yes! And in our day and age, that is an acid test which many relationships would not pass... No, let me meet him, and I can tell you that he will prove to be a decent person... for all that you describe him as insincere."

Alexander just stood there, his head lowered.

"Now, who do you think is your second friend?" asked Pyotr Ivanych.

"Who?" said Alexander in bewilderment.

"Are you that ungrateful?" Pyotr Ivanych came back. "What about Liza! See, he doesn't even blush! And me, what am I to you, may I ask?"

"You're... a relative."

"A grand title! I thought perhaps I was – something more. This is not a good side of you: a character flaw which even in writing exercises at school is described as *rotten*, something you can't even find in Krylov."

"But you were always pushing me away..." Alexander said meekly, without looking up.

"Yes, whenever you tried to hug me."

"You laughed at me for showing my feelings..."

"But why, and what for?" asked Pyotr Ivanych.

"You followed every step I took."

"Well, there you are! That's exactly what I did! Where would you find such an attentive tutor as that? And why did I take all that trouble? I could say more about that, but it might sound too much like some kind of cheap reproach..."

"Uncle!" said Alexander, going up to him with both arms outstretched.

"Go back to your seat! I haven't finished yet," said Pyotr Ivanych coolly. "I would hope that you can now name your third friend yourself..."

Alexander looked at his uncle as if to ask: "But where is he?" Pyotr Ivanych pointed to his wife.

"There she is."

"Pyotr Ivanych," Lizaveta Alexandrovna broke in, "for God's sake, please stop showing us how clever you are!"

"No, and stop interrupting!"

"I think I'm capable of appreciating my aunt's friendship..." Alexander mumbled indistinctly.

CHAPTER I

"No, you're not: if you were, you wouldn't have been looking up at the ceiling to find her, but would have pointed straight at her. If you had felt her friendship, out of sheer respect for her qualities you would not have been so contemptuous of people in general, and in your eyes she would have made up for the shortcomings of the others. Who was it that dried your tears and whimpered together with you? Who offered you sympathy for all that nonsense you poured out to her? And what sympathy! It's a rare mother who could have taken so much to heart everything that affects you; even your own mother wouldn't have been able to. If you had felt that sympathy, you wouldn't have smiled ironically the way you did before, and you would have seen that there is no fox and no wolf here, but simply a woman who loves like your own sister."

"Oh, *ma tante*!" Alexander was distressed and totally destroyed by this rebuke. "Surely you can't think that I don't appreciate all that, and that I don't consider you a shining exception to that whole crowd. Oh, God no! I swear..."

"I believe you, I believe you, Alexander!" she responded. "Don't listen to Pyotr Ivanych; he's making a mountain out of a molehill, and only too pleased to have another opportunity to show us how clever he is. Stop it, for God's sake, Pyotr Ivanych!"

"Just a moment, just a moment, and I'll be finished – 'one more last utterance'!* You said that you do to others everything that your duty requires of you?"

Alexander still didn't utter a word and didn't raise his eyes.

"Now, tell me, do you love your mother?"

Alexander suddenly came to life.

"What kind of question is that?" he said. "Who else is there for me to love after this? I worship her, and would give my life for her..."

"Very well, then you must know that she lives and breathes only for you, and your every joy and every sorrow is her joy and her sorrow. She now counts time not by months or weeks, but by news from you and about you... Now, tell me, how long has it been since you last wrote to her?"

Alexander gave a start.

"Well three weeks... or so," he mumbled.

197

"No, four months! And how would you choose to have such behaviour described? And what kind of animal does that make you? Perhaps you would be hard put to find a name for an animal that is not to be found in Krylov."

"And so?" Alexander asked, suddenly frightened.

"And so, the old lady is grief-stricken."

"Oh no! My God, my God!"

"It's not true, it's not true!" said Lizaveta Alexandrovna, and ran straight to the desk to fetch a letter which she handed to Alexander. "She's not ill; she's just really upset."

"You're spoiling him, Liza," said Pyotr Ivanych.

"And you're being too hard on him. Alexander was in a situation which preoccupied him for a time…"

"To forget your mother because of a hussy – that must have been quite some situation!"

"That's enough – for God's sake, stop it!" she said meaningfully, pointing to her nephew.

Alexander, having read his mother's letter, covered his face with it.

"Leave Uncle alone, *ma tante*, let him let loose with his reproaches; I deserved worse: I *am* a monster!" he said, grimacing in desperation.

"Calm down, Alexander!" said Pyotr Ivanych. "There are a lot of such monsters around. You were carried away by this foolishness of yours and temporarily forgot about your mother – it's only natural; ; love for one's mother is a tranquil emotion. The only thing she has in the world… is you; that's why she is easily upset. There's no point in punishing you any further; I'll just quote some words from your favourite author:

"Instead of finding fault with your friends.
Why not take a good look at yourself?*

"In other words, you should be more tolerant of other people's weaknesses. Without that rule, life would be unlivable for oneself and others. That's all I have to say. And now I'm going to bed."

"Uncle, are you angry with me?" said Alexander, sounding deeply remorseful.

CHAPTER I

"How did you get that idea? Why would I try to upset you? I didn't speak out of anger. I was just trying to play the part of the bear in the fable 'The Monkey and the Mirror'. Put on a pretty good act, didn't I, Liza?"

At this, he tried to kiss her, but she turned away.

"I think I've carried out your instructions to the letter," Pyotr Ivanych added, "but you... Oh yes, I forgot one thing... what shape is your heart in now, Alexander?" he asked.

Alexander remained silent.

"You don't need money, do you?" Pyotr Ivanych asked again.

"No, Uncle..."

"He never likes to ask!" said Pyotr Ivanych, closing the door behind him.

"What will Uncle think of me?" asked Alexander after a moment's silence.

"The same as he did before," replied Lizaveta Alexandrovna. "Do you think everything he told you came from the heart in all sincerity?"

"But of course."

"Not at all. Believe me, all he was doing was showing off. Didn't you see how methodically he set about it? He set forth all the evidence against you in a certain order – first the weaker evidence, and then the stronger; he began by getting you to reveal the reason for your low opinion of people... and then... it was all part of his method! And now, I think he's even forgotten all about it."

"What intelligence! How well he understands life, people! And what self-control!"

"Yes, a lot of intelligence, and too much self-control," said Lizaveta Alexandrovna despondently, "but..."

"And you, *ma tante*, will you lose respect for me? But believe me, it's only the blows under which I've been reeling which could have distracted me... my God, my poor mother!"

Lizaveta Alexandrovna extended her hand to him.

"Alexander, I will never cease to respect the heart within you," she said. "It's your feelings which trap you into errors, and that's why I will always pardon them."

"Ah, *ma tante*, you are the ideal woman!"

199

"Just a woman."

Alexander was profoundly affected by his uncle's scolding and, sitting there with his aunt, he was assailed by tormenting thoughts. It seemed that the peace of mind which she had worked so hard and skilfully to restore in him had suddenly abandoned him.

She was worried – unnecessarily – that Alexander might respond by doing something damaging, and she was laying herself open to some barbed retort. She had also been doing her best to provoke a caustic quip at Pyotr Ivanych's expense.

But Alexander was deaf and dumb; it was as if a bucket of cold water had been poured over him.

"What's the matter with you? Why are you looking like that?" his aunt asked him.

"It's nothing, just that I feel down-hearted for some reason. Uncle has made me understand myself; he's a great explainer!"

"Don't listen to him; he's not always right."

"Don't try to make me feel better. At the moment I'm disgusted with myself. I despised and hated people, and now I despise and hate myself. You can hide from other people, but where can you hide from yourself? Everything has been reduced to dust and ashes – people, life itself, all futile, myself included…"

"Oh, that Pyotr Ivanych!" said Lizaveta Alexandrovna, sighing deeply. "He can make anyone feel wretched!"

"There's only one consolation in all this: at least I haven't deceived or betrayed anyone in love or friendship."

"People didn't appreciate you," said his aunt, "but believe me, there *will* be a true heart to appreciate you, I can guarantee it. You're still so young – just forget all this, and find some occupation. You have talent, so write… Are you working on anything at present?"

"No."

"Write!"

"I'm afraid, *ma tante*…"

"Don't listen to Pyotr Ivanych! Talk to him about anything you like: politics, agronomy, anything but poetry. He will never tell you the truth about that. Your readers will value you – you'll see… So you will write?"

CHAPTER I

"Very well."

"Will you start soon?"

"As soon as I can. Now that's my only remaining hope…"

Pyotr Ivanych had awoken refreshed, and came into the room fully dressed and carrying his hat. He in turn advised Alexander to return to work at his office and in the agricultural department of the journal.

"I will try, Uncle," replied Alexander, "but you see, I've just promised my aunt…"

Lizaveta Alexandrovna signalled to him not to say anything, but Pyotr Ivanych noticed.

"What did he promise?" he asked.

"To bring me some new music," she replied.

"No, that's not true. What was it, Alexander?"

"To write a novella or something…"

"So you still haven't given up on your belles-lettres; and you, Liza, are leading him astray – you shouldn't be!"

"I don't have the right to give up on it," Alexander responded.

"Who is stopping you?"

"Why should I voluntarily and ungratefully turn my back on an honourable vocation, my true calling? It's the one bright hope left in my life, and you want me to destroy that too? This is something I've been called to by something outside myself – and if I kill it, I'll be killing myself too…"

"So, please tell me, what exactly is it that has called you from the outside?"

"It's something that I can't explain to you, Uncle. It's something you simply have to understand by yourself. Is there anything in your life that has made your hair stand on end – other than a comb?"

"No!" said Pyotr Ivanych.

"Well, let me ask you this: have passions ever surged in your breast, has your imagination ever caught fire and seethed with visions of beauty which have demanded to be embodied in some form? Has your heart ever beaten in some special way?"

"This is sheer craziness! And anyway, what about it?"

"To someone who has never experienced these things, how can one possibly explain the urge to write, when some restless spirit bids you night and day, in your dreams and in broad daylight, 'Write, write!'?..."

"But you're no good at it, are you?"

"Enough, Pyotr Ivanych! Just because you yourself are no good at something, why discourage others?" said Lizaveta Alexandrovna.

"Forgive me, Uncle, for saying that you are no judge in these matters."

"Then who is? Her?"

Pyotr Ivanych pointed to his wife.

"She's doing this purposely, and you believe her," he added.

"Yes, and it was you yourself who, when I first arrived here, advised me to write, to try my hand..."

"Well, what of it? You tried, and nothing came of it – and you should have given up."

"Do you really mean to tell me that you've never found a single idea, or a single line of mine at all worthwhile?"

"Of course I have! You're not a fool; take any normal intelligent person who has written piles and piles of stuff: of course you would be sure to find a worthwhile idea or two. But that's just a matter of intelligence, not talent."

In her annoyance at this remark, Lizaveta swivelled in her seat.

"And all this beating of the heart, the fluttering, these ecstasies and so on and so forth – who doesn't experience them?"

"Well, you in particular, less than anybody, it seems to me," his wife remarked.

"What are you talking about? You must remember, there have been times when I have been delighted..."

"By what? I don't remember."

"Everyone experiences these things," Pyotr Ivanych went on, turning to his nephew. "Who has never been moved by the silence and the darkness of night, or the sounds of the oak wood, by a garden, a pond or the sea? If it were only artists who experienced these things, there would be no one to appreciate their work. But expressing these feelings in their work is another matter: for this you need talent, and

CHAPTER I

it doesn't appear that you have any. It's not something you can hide: it stands out in every line, in every brushstroke..."

"Pyotr Ivanych, it's time for you to go," said Lizaveta Alexandrovna.

"In a moment. You want to make your mark?" Pyotr Ivanych went on. "You have other ways of doing that. The editor is full of praise for you; he says that your articles on agriculture are excellent – and thoughtful – and that it all bears the mark of real erudition and is not the work of a mere journeyman. I was delighted. 'Well,' I thought, 'we Aduyevs really have heads on our shoulders.' You see, I'm not without my pride! You can excel just as well in your work, and earn the prestige of a writer..."

"Some prestige! A writer – about fertilizer!"

"To each his own; one man's fate is to soar in celestial heights, another's fate is to burrow into fertilizer and find treasure. I don't understand why one should look down on the humbler occupations – they all have their own poetry. Look, if you were to make a career and make money by your efforts, make a good marriage, like the majority... I don't understand what else you could want. Your duty done, a life spent with honour and honest work – that's where happiness lies, to my way of thinking. Look at me. I've risen to the rank of state councillor,* I'm an industrialist by profession, and if you were to offer me the title of Poet Laureate instead, I wouldn't take it!"

"Listen, Pyotr Ivanych, you're really late!" Lizaveta Alexandrovna broke in. "It's almost ten o'clock."

"Yes indeed, it's time. Well, goodbye for now. And these people, God knows why, think they are superior beings," he growled on the way out. "It's, well..."

Chapter 2

ALEXANDER RETURNED HOME from his uncle's, sat down in an armchair and started thinking. He remembered the whole conversation with his aunt and uncle, and took himself severely to task.

How, at his age, had he allowed himself to hate and despise people – to see and talk about their insignificance, pettiness and weaknesses, and to pick on each and every one of the people he knew – but forgotten to consider his own case? How could he be so blind? And his uncle had lectured him like a schoolboy, and had given him a thorough going-over – and moreover in the presence of a woman, all in order to get him to take a look at himself. What an impression his uncle must have made on his wife that evening! Nothing wrong with that, of course, it's only normal; the trouble was that this impression was made at his expense. Now his uncle had achieved once and for all an indisputable supremacy over him.

So now what had become, after all this, he thought, of the advantages of youth, freshness, mental and emotional ardour, when someone armed only with the asset of experience, but with a dried-up heart and without energy, could destroy him so casually and nonchalantly at every step? When would this struggle finally become an even one, and when would the pendulum swing in his favour? His assets were both talent and an abundance of spiritual strength… but his uncle was a giant in comparison. How confidently he argued, how lightly he brushed aside any contradiction and achieved his goal with humour, with a yawn, ridiculing feeling and passionate outpourings of love and friendship – ridiculing, in a word, everything for which the older generation tends to envy the young! As he mulled all this over in his mind he flushed with shame. He swore that he would watch himself very carefully and take the first opportunity to crush his uncle, and to show him that no amount of experience could replace what it was that had "come to him from outside himself" – and that, for all his preaching, from this

CHAPTER 2

moment on, not a single one of his cold, methodical predictions would prove to be true. Alexander would find his own path by himself, and would tread it not tentatively, but with firm and even strides. He was now no longer the person he had been three years ago. He had peered into the recesses of his heart and had learnt its secrets; he had scrutinized the interplay of the passions and ferreted out the secret of life – not, of course, without suffering – but had armoured himself against it for ever. His future was clear: he had risen in revolt; he had grown wings – he was no longer a child, but a man, striking out boldly into the future! His uncle would see how henceforth it would be his turn to play the role of the pathetic apprentice to his nephew, the master craftsman; he would discover, to his surprise, that there was another life, other attainments, other kinds of happiness than those offered by a banal career which he, his uncle, had chosen for himself and which he had attempted to foist on him, maybe out of envy. Just one more honourable effort and the battle was won!

Alexander had come back to life. He once again began to create a special world of his own, but one a little wiser than the first. His aunt supported him in this resolve, but discreetly, while Pyotr Ivanych was sleeping, at the factory or the English Club.

She would ask him about his work, and whether he was enjoying it. He would describe the work he was planning and seek her approval in the guise of her advice. She sometimes disagreed with him, but more often they agreed.

Alexander committed himself to his work as tenaciously as if it were his last hope. Beyond it, he assured his aunt, lay nothing but an arid steppe, without water, without vegetation, bleak and deserted. What kind of life awaited him there? It would be like interring himself in his own tomb!

From time to time the memory of his extinct love would come back to him and trouble him, but he would dismiss it and take up his pen and write a moving elegy. At other times, bitter resentment would well up in him and would stir up from the depths the hatred and contempt he had felt for people only a short time before – and before you knew it, some vigorous lines of verse had been generated by it. At the same time, he had been pondering and beginning to write a novella. It took a great deal of thought, feeling and sheer hard work, and about six months of his time. Finally it was finished, revised, and a fair copy had been made. His aunt was thrilled. This time the story was set not in America, but in some village in the Tambov province. Its characters were ordinary people: malicious gossips, liars and other kinds of scum in tailcoats, adulterous women in corsets and hats. It was standard fare, and everything was where it was expected to be – appropriate – and in its proper place.

"Now, *ma tante*, I can show this to my uncle?"

"Yes, of course," she replied. "On the other hand, maybe it would be better to get it published as it is, without showing it to him. He is bound to say something negative about it. You know he always treats it as childish nonsense."

"No, I'd better show it to him!" said Alexander. "After it has passed muster with you and has satisfied me, I fear no one's judgement, so why not let him see it?..."

So it was shown to his uncle. When he saw the manuscript, he frowned slightly and shook his head.

"What is this? Something the two of you have written together?" he asked. "What a lot you seem to have written, and in such tiny writing – what made you take all that trouble?"

"Wait before you start shaking your head," his wife replied. "First listen! Read it to us, Alexander. And you, pay attention: don't nod off and then pronounce sentence. You can find fault anywhere, if you're looking for it; try to be tolerant."

"No, why? Just be fair, that's all," Alexander interjected.

"Well, if I must, I'll listen," said Pyotr Ivanych, "but on one condition: don't read it soon after dinner, otherwise I can't guarantee that I won't doze off. Don't take it personally, Alexander, but any time someone reads something after dinner, it always makes me sleepy – oh, and another thing: if it's something worthwhile, then I'll tell you what I think; if not, I won't say anything, and you can take it however you like."

The reading began. Pyotr Ivanych didn't nod off once: he listened without once taking his eyes off Alexander, hardly even blinking, and twice even nodded approvingly.

CHAPTER 2

"You see!" said his wife in a half-whisper. "What did I tell you?"

He gave her a nod too.

The reading continued for two consecutive evenings. On the first evening after the reading, Pyotr Ivanych, to his wife's surprise, told them the rest of the story.

"How do you know?" she asked.

"Not that hard to guess! The idea is not a new one – it's been used thousands of times. No real need to continue the reading, but let's see how he handles the rest."

The next evening, when Alexander was reading the last page, Pyotr Ivanych rang, and his servant entered.

"I need to get dressed," he told him. "Get my things ready! I'm sorry, Alexander, for interrupting you, but I'm in a hurry, I'm late for my whist at the club."

Alexander finished reading, and Pyotr Ivanych was out like a shot.

"Goodbye for now!" he said to his wife and Alexander. "I won't be looking in again here!"

"Stop, stop!" his wife cried out. "Aren't you going to say anything about the story?"

"Didn't we have an understanding?" he replied, and made as if to leave.

"Sheer obstinacy!" she said. "He's just being obstinate – I know him. Don't pay him any attention, Alexander!"

"It's ill will!" thought Alexander. "He wants to drag me down into the mud and force me into his world. Of course, he's an intelligent man and owns a factory – and that's all, but I am a poet…"

"That's the absolute limit, Pyotr Ivanych!" his wife began, almost in tears. "Say something at least. I saw you nodding your approval, so you must have liked it. It's just that you don't want to admit it out of stubborn pride. How could I admit that I liked a mere story? Oh no, I'm too clever for that. Admit that it was good!"

"I nodded my head because it's clear from the story that Alexander is intelligent, but what was *not* intelligent was to have written that story."

"But really, Uncle, a judgement like that…"

207

"Listen, you're never going to believe me, so there's nothing more to be said; so why don't we nominate a mediator? I'll tell you what I'll do to settle it between us once and for all. I'll pretend I'm the author of the story and send it to a friend of mine who works at the journal, and let's see what he says. You know him, so you probably trust his judgement. He's a man of experience."

"Very well, let's see."

Pyotr Ivanych sat down at the desk and quickly wrote a few lines, and handed the letter to Alexander.

Late in life, I have decided to take up writing. No help for it: if you want to make a name for yourself, you turn to anything – even this – I must be crazy! So I've produced the story I've enclosed. Take a look at it, and if it's any good, publish it in your journal – for a fee of course, you know I don't like to work without pay. You may be surprised, and you won't believe it, but I'm even letting you sign my name, so you know I must be telling the truth.

Confident of a favourable response to the story, Alexander patiently awaited the reply. He was even pleased that his uncle had mentioned money in the note.

"Very clever indeed," he thought. "Mummy complains that the price of grain is down, and she's not likely to be sending any money soon, so this 1,500 would come in handy."

However, three weeks or so went by and still no reply had come. Finally, one morning a large package and a letter were brought in to Pyotr Ivanych.

"Ah, they've sent it back!" he said, giving his wife a mischievous look. He didn't open the letter or show it to his wife, although she begged him to. That very evening, before leaving for his club, he went to see his nephew. His door was not locked, and he entered. Yevsei was snoring, sprawled diagonally on the floor at the entrance. The candle was burning itself out and was in danger of toppling off the candlestick. He looked into the next room; it was in the dark.

"Oh, the provinces!" Pyotr Ivanych muttered.

CHAPTER 2

He shook Yevsei awake, pointed to the door and the candle, and threatened him with a stick. In the third room, Alexander was slumped at his desk, his head in his hands, also asleep. A sheet of paper lay in front of him. Pyotr Ivanych glanced at it – a poem. He picked up the sheet of paper and read the following:

> Springtime's beauty has passed,
> The magic moment of love has vanished,
> It slumbers in the sepulchre of my breast
> And no longer races through my blood like fire.
> Long since have I another idol built
> Upon her altar long abandoned,
> To it I pray... but...

"And now you're the one 'slumbering'! Pray, but don't laze!" Pyotr Ivanych said aloud. "It's your own verses that have worn you out! No need for any other sentence to be pronounced, you've sentenced yourself out of your own mouth."

"Ah, I see you're still against my writings," said Alexander, stretching. "Tell me, Uncle, honestly, what makes you so intent on stamping out my talent, when you have to admit..."

"Oh yes, you mean envy, Alexander. Judge for yourself: you will achieve fame, honour, maybe even immortality, while I will remain an obscure individual, and will have to be satisfied with the title of a useful labourer. But I too, after all, am an Aduyev. So, if you don't mind, give me some credit. I mean, what am I? I've lived my life quietly, unknown, I've performed my duties, and have been happy and even proud. A pretty humble destiny, wouldn't you say? When I die – that is to say, when I'm no longer feeling or aware – 'the strains of prophetic music will not chant my name in far-off times, posterity and the world will not swell with it,'* and no one will know that there once lived a Pyotr Ivanych Aduyev, privy councillor,* and that will be no comfort to me in my grave, if indeed my grave and I myself will survive in some form for posterity. How different for you! 'Spreading your rustling wings!' You will 'fly beneath the clouds'. As for me, I shall have to be satisfied only with the knowledge that among the numberless works of man there will be 'a tiny drop of my own honey' to quote your favourite author."*

"For God's sake, leave him out of this. Never mind whose favourite author he is! You just enjoy making fun of people close to you."

"Ah, making fun! Wasn't it when you saw your own portrait in Krylov that you dropped him? *À propos*! Do you know that I have your future fame and your immortality here in my pocket? Although I would prefer to see it containing your money – it's more reliable!"

"What fame?"

"It's the reply to my letter."

"For God's sake, give it to me right now! What does it say?"

"I haven't read it; here, read it yourself, aloud."

"Will you have the patience?"

"What is it to me?"

"What do you mean? Aren't I your own nephew? You must be curious at least. What indifference. It's your selfishness, Uncle!"

"Perhaps; I don't deny it. In any case, I know what it says. So read it!"

Alexander began to read in a loud voice, while Pyotr Ivanych tapped his boots with his stick.

The letter read as follows:

"Is this a hoax or something, my dearest Pyotr Ivanych? You writing novels? Come on, who's going to believe you? You wouldn't be trying to fool an old hand like me, would you? And if it, God forbid, were the truth, and you had indeed temporarily diverted your pen from those – in the most literal sense of the word – precious lines, each of which is worth its weight in gold, and instead of producing respectable results had come up with this novel I have in front of me, then I would have told you that the fragile products of your factory were a lot sturdier than this creation of yours."

Suddenly Alexander's voice became very faint.

"But I refuse to accept a suspicion that is so insulting to you," he continued softly and timidly.

CHAPTER 2

"Louder please, Alexander, I can't hear you," said Pyotr Ivanych. Alexander continued reading, only much more softly.

"Since you have some interest in the author of this novel, you would probably like to know my opinion. It is this. The author must be a young man. He is no fool. But for no good reason, he seems to be angry with the whole world. He writes in such a vindictive, embittered spirit. No doubt he is disillusioned. My God, how long are we going to have these people around? It's too bad that, because of a wrong-headed view of life, so many gifts are wasted in empty, fruitless dreams, in futile striving for things for which they are not destined."

Alexander stopped to get his breath back. Pyotr Ivanych lit a cigar and puffed out a cloud of smoke. The expression on his face was his usual one of total serenity.

Alexander continued to read in a muffled, almost inaudible voice:

"Pride, believing in dreams, premature romantic impulses, a closed mind, with their inevitable consequence, idleness, are at the root of this unfortunate condition. Learning, work, a concrete occupation – these are the things that can bring our sick and idle youth to their senses."

"All that could easily have been said in three lines," said Pyotr Ivanych, looking at his watch, "but in what is only a casual letter to a friend, he has written a whole dissertation! What a pedant! Do you want to read any more, Alexander? Don't bother; it's boring. I have a few things to say to you…"

"No, Uncle, let me drink the cup to the bitter dregs; I'll go on."

"By all means, if you want."

Alexander continued reading:

"This regrettable temperamental tendency manifests itself in every line of the novel you sent me. Tell your protégé that a writer only produces something worthwhile when he, firstly, is not being carried away by

some powerful impulse or passion. He should look at life – and people in general – in a calm and positive manner, otherwise he just ends up talking about himself – something which is of no particular interest to others. This failing dominates the whole book. A second and major condition – and, out of sympathy for his youth and his pride of authorship, I don't think you should tell this to the author, because, as we know, this is the most sensitive of all the different kinds of self-esteem – is that a writer must possess talent, of which there isn't the slightest trace in this book. I should say, however, that the language is correct and unblemished, and the author has style."

Alexander could hardly bring himself to finish reading.

"Finally, he gets to the point!" said Pyotr Ivanych. "After all that blather! Let the two of us talk over the rest together."

Alexander let his hands drop. He looked straight at the wall with glazed eyes in silence, like someone stunned by an unexpected blow. Pyotr Ivanych took the letter from him and read the following PS:

"If you insist on seeing this novel published in our journal, then for you, I suppose, it could be put in in the summer months, when no one much reads it, but forget about any payment."

"So, Alexander, how do you feel?" asked Pyotr Ivanych.

"Calmer than I would have expected," Alexander replied firmly. "I feel like someone deceived in every respect."

"No, as someone who has deceived himself, and has tried to deceive others too..."

Alexander had not been listening to that reservation.

"Can this have been a dream too? And did it betray me too?" he whispered. "It's a bitter loss! Well, it's not the first time I've deluded myself. But what I can't understand is why I should have possessed all those irresistible urges to be a writer..."

"Well, that's just it! Whoever invested you with those urges obviously forgot to include the creative gift itself," said Pyotr Ivanych. "I told you..."

CHAPTER 2

Alexander gave a sigh and was lost in thought for a moment. Suddenly he sprang into action and rushed around the room, opening all the drawers: he pulled out several exercise books, sheets and scraps of paper, and began to hurl them violently into the fire.

"Don't forget these!" said Pyotr Ivanych, pushing towards him a sheet of paper which was lying on the desk and contained the first few words of a poem.

"These are going too!" said Alexander in despair, as he hurled the verses into the fire.

"Sure you haven't forgotten anything? Take a good look around! Said Pyotr Ivanych, looking carefully around. "Best to finish the job all in one go. What's that bundle over there on top of the cupboard?"

"This is going too!" said Alexander, taking hold of it. "It's those agriculture articles."

"Don't burn them, don't burn those! Give them back to me!" said Pyotr Ivanych, reaching out for them. "Those are worth saving."

But Alexander didn't listen to him.

"No!" he said in a fury. "If I'm finished with the fine art of creative literature, I don't want anything to do with the hack work either, and even fate itself will never change my mind."

And the bundle went flying into the fire.

"You shouldn't have done that!" said Pyotr Ivanych, poking around with his stick meanwhile in the waste-paper basket under the desk to find anything else to throw in the fire.

"And what shall we do with the novel, Alexander? I still have it."

"Couldn't you use it to stick on the screens?"

"No, not now. Should I send for it? Yevsei! Asleep again! Pay attention, otherwise they'll steal my overcoat right under your nose! Go to my room right now, and ask Vasily for the thick exercise book in the cabinet on the bureau – and bring it here."

Alexander sat there, leaning his head on his hand and looking into the fire. The thick exercise book was brought in. Alexander, deep in thought, looked at the fruit of his six months of work. Pyotr Ivanych noticed what he was doing.

"Time to finish, Alexander," he said, "and then we can talk about something else."

"Into the fire with you too!" cried Alexander hurling the book into the stove.

They both watched it burn: Pyotr Ivanych no doubt with pleasure, Alexander sadly, almost in tears. The uppermost page started to shrivel and rise, as if an unseen hand were twirling it – its edges began to curl and turn black, twisted and suddenly flared up – and was followed swiftly by another page, then a third. Suddenly several pages at once rose up and caught fire in a bunch, while the page which followed them showed white for two seconds and then began to blacken around the edges.

However, Alexander was able to catch the words "Chapter Three" on it just before it disappeared. He remembered what he had written in that chapter and began to regret losing it. He rose from his chair and had already picked up the tongs in order to rescue the remains of his work. "Maybe there's still time…" was hope's faint whisper.

"Hold it! Let me try with my stick!" said Pyotr Ivanych. "Otherwise you may burn yourself with the tongs."

He prodded the exercise book right up against the coals at the back of the grate. Alexander stood there, hesitating. The thickness of the book made it burn more slowly. At first, it gave off a thick cloud of smoke; a flame would flicker spasmodically underneath it and lick its sides, leaving charred patches, and then disappear. There was still a chance of saving it. Alexander had already stretched out his hand when, at that very moment, the whole book burst into flames. In a minute it had burnt itself out, leaving behind nothing but a heap of black ash with threads of fire running along it in places. Alexander threw down the tongs.

"It's over!" he said.

"Over!" repeated Pyotr Ivanych.

"Phew!" Alexander exclaimed. "I'm free!"

"Now this is the second time I've helped you to clean up your flat," said Pyotr Ivanych, "and I hope it's the last…"

"No turning back, Uncle."

CHAPTER 2

"Amen!" said his uncle, placing his hands on his shoulders.

"Well now, Alexander, I advise you to write to Ivan Ivanych without delay asking him to send you some work in the agricultural department, and after all this foolishness, it's important that you now write something really good. He keeps on asking me, 'So what about your nephew?'"

Alexander shook his head glumly.

"I can't," he said. "No, I can't, that's all finished now."

"Then what do you plan to do?"

"What?" he asked, and after a moment's thought, added: "Nothing for now."

"It's only in the provinces that people get by without doing anything, but here... then why did you come here? I can't understand!... Well, leave that aside for the moment. I have something to ask you."

Alexander slowly raised his head and looked enquiringly at his uncle.

"Well," Pyotr Ivanych began, moving his chair closer to Alexander, "you know my partner Surkov?"

Alexander nodded.

"Well, you've sometimes come to dinner at my place when he's been there. The only thing is that all you've done is to look him over as if to suggest that there is something odd about him. He's a good fellow, but quite shallow. His chief weakness is... women. Unfortunately, he himself, as you will have noticed, is not bad-looking: high-coloured, sleek, his hair always curled, scented and dressed like a fashion plate; so he imagines that women find him irresistible – in a word, a fop! I wouldn't normally waste time talking about him, but here's the thing: the moment he takes a fancy to someone, he's off on a spending spree – surprises, gifts, treats, doing anything he can to cut a dash: new carriages, new horses... just throwing money away! He even ran after my wife, so there were times when I wouldn't bother to send a servant to buy theatre tickets: I could always rely on Surkov to come up with them. If I needed to trade in a horse, find something hard to get or take a trip to the country to inspect the dacha, you could send him anywhere you wanted – a treasure! No one could have been more useful: you couldn't find anyone like that for love or money. It's too bad! I deliberately did nothing to stand in his way, but my wife got tired of him, so I had to get rid of him. So he goes on one of his spending sprees and isn't getting enough interest from his bank. So he starts coming to me for money, and I refuse; then he starts talking about capital. 'What's your factory to me? There's never any ready cash,' he says. It would help if he got married, but no, he's not interested. He is only interested in making conquests in high society. He tells me that he 'must have an affair with someone in the nobility; I can't live without love.' What an ass! Almost forty, and can't live without love!"

Alexander was reminded of himself, and smiled ruefully.

"He's a great liar," Pyotr Ivanych went on. "Later I would reflect on what he was making such a fuss about. He boasted endlessly – he wanted people to talk about him, he claimed to be on friendly terms with this one and that one, that he had been seen in a box at the theatre with such and such, that in someone's dacha he had been alone with someone on the balcony late at night, that he had gone riding with her in some out-of-the-way place in a carriage or on horseback. In the meantime, it turns out that these so-called 'noble liaisons' – damn them! – cost a lot more than *i*gnoble ones. And that's the cause of all the trouble – the idiot!"

"But what's all this leading to, Uncle?" Alexander asked. "I don't see where I come in."

"You'll soon see. Recently a certain young widow, Yulia Pavlovna Tafayeva returned here from abroad. She's not at all bad-looking. Surkov and I were friends of her husband. Tafayev died while he was abroad. Are you with me now?"

"Yes, I am. Surkov's in love with the widow."

"Exactly, head over heels. So what comes next?"

"Next... I don't know..."

"You really don't! Well listen. Surkov has twice let drop that he will soon be in need of money. I can already sense what this means, but I can't tell which way the wind is blowing. I've tried to worm out of him why he'll be needing money. He started hemming and hawing, and finally came out with it and said that he wanted to decorate the flat on the Liteyny.

CHAPTER 2

"I was trying to remember what it was about the Liteyny that made Surkov choose it, and I recalled that it's where Tafayeva lives, directly opposite the place he has chosen. Now, I've given him some money on account. There's sure to be trouble ahead unless... you help me. Do you understand now?"

Alexander lifted his nose a little, looked at the wall and then up at the ceiling, blinked a couple of times and finally turned to look at his uncle, but without saying anything.

Pyotr Ivanych regarded him with a smile: he liked nothing more than to catch people being slow on the uptake and letting them know he had noticed it.

"What's wrong with you, Alexander? Still writing those stories?" he said.

"Ah, now I get it, Uncle."

"God be praised!"

"Surkov is asking for money; you don't have any, and you want me to..." He came to an abrupt halt.

Pyotr Ivanych had burst into laughter, and Alexander broke off in mid-sentence, regarding his uncle in bewilderment.

"No, you've got it wrong!" said Pyotr Ivanych. "Have you ever known me to be without money? Try to come to me any time, and you'll see! It's like this: Tafayeva reminded me through him that I knew her husband. I went to see her, and she invited me to call on her. I promised to do so, and said that I would bring you. Well, I hope you finally understand?"

"Me?" Alexander repeated, looking his uncle straight in the eye. "Yes, well of course, now I understand," he said, hurriedly completing his sentence, but not getting beyond the last word.

"So what is it that you've understood?" Pyotr Ivanych asked.

"For the life of me, Uncle, I haven't understood a thing! Wait a minute... perhaps you mean that she's got a nice home... and that it will be a distraction for me... because I'm bored?..."

"That's wonderful! So that's why I'm going to take you visiting people's homes, and all that remains is for me to tuck you in at night and cover your mouth with a handkerchief to keep away the flies! No,

217

you still haven't got it. Let me tell you the idea: it's to get Tafayeva to fall in love with you."

Alexander suddenly opened his eyes wide and looked at his uncle.

"You're joking, Uncle? That's absurd!" he said.

"When it comes to absurdities, you commit them with a flourish, but when something is simple and natural, then for you it's an absurdity. Explain to me just what's absurd about this. Consider how love itself is absurd – a compound of hot blood and pride… But what's the use of talking to you? In spite of everything, you still believe that people fall in love with that one and only person they're destined to, their kindred spirit!"

"I'm sorry; now I no longer believe in anything. Do you really think that people can fall in love with each other just like that?"

"It's possible, but not for you. But don't worry, I wouldn't assign you such a tricky task. Now, this is all you have to do. Cultivate her, be attentive to her and never give Surkov a chance to be alone with her – in short, plague him, get in his way! For every word he utters, you utter two; if he offers an opinion, you refute him, thwart his every move, defeat him at every step…"

"Why?"

"You still don't understand! It's because to start with you'll drive him out of his mind with jealousy and chagrin, and then he'll cool down. With someone like him the second phase will swiftly follow the first. He's unbelievably conceited. So the flat will not be needed, his capital will remain intact and the work of the factory will proceed normally… Well, you understand? This will be the fifth time I've played this trick on him; before, when I was younger and still unmarried, I did what I'm asking you to do myself, or sent one of my friends."

"But, I don't know her," said Alexander.

"And that's precisely why I'm taking you with me to see her on Wednesday. On Wednesdays she's at home for a few of her old friends."

"But if she returns Surkov's love, then I'm sure you will agree that he will not be the only victim of my blandishments and attentions."

"Are you serious? No, she's a sensible woman, and when she sees him for the fool he is, she'll stop paying him attention, especially

CHAPTER 2

with other people around: her pride wouldn't permit it. At the same time, there will be someone else around, more intelligent and better looking, and she will be ashamed and get rid of him. And that's why I have chosen you."

Alexander bowed.

"Surkov isn't dangerous," his uncle continued, "but Tafayeva invites very few people to her home, so that it's possible that in her small circle he might seem impressive and a man of intelligence. Personal appearance counts for a lot with women. He is a master of ingratiation, and so he is tolerated. Perhaps she is flirtatious with him, and he... you know. Even intelligent women like it when men behave foolishly with them – especially when it's expensive foolishness. However, for the most part, it's not the one who is playing the fool for their benefit whom they love, but someone else altogether... Many men don't see that, including Surkov – but you will be the one to open his eyes."

"But probably Surkov won't be there only on Wednesdays; on Wednesdays, I'll be able to frustrate him, but what about the other days?"

"Do I have to explain everything to you? Flatter her, act as if you're a little smitten with her, and after you've been there once, she'll start inviting you again on Thursday and Friday, when you can redouble your attentions. Then I'll step in and try to influence her, and somehow suggest that you really are... you know. She herself, at least this is my impression, is very sensitive... probably of a nervous disposition... so I should think not at all unresponsive to other people's expression of their feelings..."

"Is it likely?" said Alexander, thinking aloud. "Even if I could fall in love again... well and good! But if I can't... it won't work."

"Precisely! It *will* work for that very reason. If you *were* to fall in love, you wouldn't be able to pretend, and she would spot it right away, and would proceed to wrap both of you round her little finger. But for now... just concentrate on Surkov for me, I know him like the back of my hand. As soon as he sees that he's getting nowhere, he won't want to be throwing his money away, and that's all I want to achieve... Listen, Alexander, this is very important for me, and if you do this for me – you remember the two vases which you liked in the factory? They're yours, only you'll have to buy your own stand."

"Really, Uncle, surely you don't think that I…"

"Yes indeed, why should you put yourself out for nothing and waste your time? That would be a fine thing – I don't think! Those vases are beautiful. These days, no one does anything for nothing. When I do something for you, offer me a gift; I won't refuse it."

"It's a strange proposition!" said Alexander hesitantly.

"I hope you won't refuse to do this for me. I am also ready to do whatever I can for you; when you need money, come to me… So then, Wednesday! This business will take a month, two at the most. I'll let you know, and if it turns out not to be necessary, then forget it."

"All right, Uncle, I'm ready to do it, only it's a strange… I can't guarantee it will work… Now, if I *could* fall in love again, then… but otherwise, I don't…"

"And it's a good thing that you can't, otherwise it would ruin the whole thing. *I'll* guarantee it will be successful. Goodbye!"

He left the room. Alexander sat for a long time by the fire over those precious ashes.

When Pyotr Ivanych arrived home, his wife asked: "So what about Alexander – what about his story, will he continue to write?"

"No, I've cured him of that for ever."

Aduyev told her what was in the letter he had received together with the novel when it had been returned, and about how they had burnt everything.

"You have no pity, Pyotr Ivanych!" said Lizaveta Alexandrovna. "Either that, or you're incapable of doing the decent thing in whatever you undertake."

"And I suppose you did the right thing when you encouraged him to go on covering paper with his scribbling! Do you really think he has talent?"

"No."

Pyotr Ivanych looked at her in surprise.

"So why did you?…"

"So you still haven't understood, don't you get it?"

CHAPTER 2

He said nothing, and couldn't help recalling his scene with Alexander.

"What is there not to understand? It's all very clear!" he said, looking her straight in the eye.

"What is, tell me?"

"That… that you wanted to teach him something, only you wanted to let him down more lightly, in your own way…"

"Such a clever man! And still he doesn't understand. Don't you know why he was always so cheerful, healthy, almost happy? It was because he had hope. And it was that hope that I was keeping alive. Is it clear now?"

"So it was like this that you were stringing him along all the time?"

"I think it was permissible. And what was so good about what you were doing? You didn't have the slightest pity for him; you stripped him of his last hope."

"Stop right there! What last hope? There was still plenty of foolishness ahead."

"What will he do now? Keep on going round looking all forlorn?"

"No, he won't: he'll have other things on his mind; I've found work for him."

"What? More translating about potatoes? Do you really think that can satisfy a young man, especially one so ardent and passionate? All you want is to see him using his head."

"No, my dear, not about potatoes, but something to do with the factory."

Chapter 3

WEDNESDAY CAME. Twelve or fifteen guests had gathered in Yulia Pavlovna's drawing room. Four young ladies, two bearded foreigners whom the hostess had met when she was abroad and an officer formed the first group.

Sitting apart from them was an old man, apparently a retired officer with two wisps of grey hair under his nose and an array of ribbons in his buttonhole. He was discussing tax-farming prospects with an elderly gentleman.

In another room, an old lady and two men were playing cards. A young girl was seated at the piano with another girl who was chatting with a student.

The Aduyevs appeared. No one could enter a drawing room with such aplomb and with such composure as Pyotr Ivanych. Behind him, Alexander made a somewhat diffident entrance.

What a contrast! One, a whole head taller, slim, well built, with a strong and healthy appearance; his eyes and demeanour both bespeaking self-confidence. But it was impossible to divine anything at all about his character or his thoughts from anything in his glance, his movements or his words, so deeply was everything hidden by his sheer urbanity and self-possession. You had the impression that both his gestures and the expression in his eyes were carefully calculated. His pale, impassive countenance was that of a man whose impulses and passion were kept under control by a despotic mind, and whose very heartbeat was dictated by his head.

Everything about Alexander, by contrast, appeared to indicate a weak and delicate constitution. His facial expression wavered, and there was a sluggishness and lethargy, as well as a nervousness about his movements. His eyes were lustreless and reflected the sensations which were troubling his heart and the thoughts which were stirring in his mind. He was of average height, thin and pale – not naturally so, as in the case of Pyotr Ivanych, but as a result of constant inner turmoil. His hair grew not like the thickets on Pyotr Ivanych's head and cheeks, but hung from his temples and the back of his head – long, drooping and extraordinarily soft – in light-coloured, many-hued silken strands.

He was introduced by his uncle.

"My friend, Surkov, isn't here?" asked Pyotr Ivanych, looking round the room in surprise. "He's forgotten you."

"Oh no! I'm very grateful to him," his hostess replied. "He calls on me. You know, apart from friends of my husband, I have practically no other visitors."

"Where is he then?"

"He'll be here soon. Just imagine, he promised faithfully that he would get a box at the theatre tomorrow for my cousin and myself when they are said to be impossible to get... and off he went."

"He'll get one all right; I guarantee it. He's a genius at that kind of thing. He never fails me – even when connections and knowing the right people won't help. Where he succeeds in getting things, and how much he has to spend in the process, is a secret known only to him."

Surkov entered. He was freshly groomed, but every fold of his garments and every detail of his appearance proclaimed his determination to be the hit of the evening, to surpass the most elegantly attired man present, and indeed to outdo fashion itself. If, for example, the latest fashion called for tails to be worn wide apart, his tails would be worn so wide as to resemble the wings of a bird stretched to their limit; if collars were being worn folded outside, the collars he had ordered, when worn with his tailcoat, would make him look like a thief who had just been grabbed by his collar to prevent him getting away. He himself issued detailed instructions for his tailor to follow. When he appeared at Tafayeva's gathering, his stock was this time fastened to his shirt with a pin of such enormous size that it could have served as a cudgel.

"Well, did you get one?" the company chorused.

Surkov was on the point of answering but, seeing Aduyev and his nephew, stopped short and regarded them with surprise.

"We've got him worried!" Aduyev murmured to his nephew. "Well, well! He's carrying a cane; what can that mean? What's that you have there?" he asked Surkov.

"The other day, I was getting out of a carriage... and, er, stumbled, so I'm limping slightly," he replied, giving a little cough.

"Nonsense!" Pyotr Ivanych whispered to Alexander. "Look at the knob: you see that golden lion's head. Only a couple of days ago he was boasting to me that he had paid Barbier 600 roubles for it, and now he's here showing it off – a perfect example of what he does with his money. Now get in there and knock him off his perch!"

Pyotr Ivanych pointed through the window at the house immediately opposite. "Remember, those vases are yours, and look lively!" he added.

"Do you have a ticket for tomorrow's performance?" Surkov asked Tafayeva, approaching her ceremoniously.

"No."

"Allow me to present you with one!" he continued, and added the whole of Zagoretsky's reply from Griboyedov's *Woe from Wit*.*

The officer's whiskers quivered slightly as he smiled. Pyotr Ivanych gave his nephew a sidelong look, and Yulia Pavlovna blushed. She invited Pyotr Ivanych to join her in her box.

"Thank you very much," he replied, "but tomorrow I'm on theatre duty – but perhaps I can offer this young man in my place?..." he said, pointing to Alexander.

"I was going to ask him too; there are only three of us, my cousin, myself and..."

"He will take my place," said Pyotr Ivanych, "and if you need him, there's also this rascal."

He pointed to Surkov and said something quietly to her. At the same time, he stole two furtive glances at Alexander and smiled.

"Thank you," replied Surkov, "but it wouldn't have been a bad idea to suggest replacing me earlier, when there was no ticket, so that I could have thought how to have myself replaced."

"Oh, I'm so grateful to you for your kindness," said the hostess brightly to Surkov, "but I didn't invite you to join me in the box because

CHAPTER 3

you already had a seat in the stalls. You probably prefer to sit directly in front of the stage... especially at the ballet..."

"No, no, you're having a little fun with me: you don't really mean that; to make me give up a seat next to you – not for the world!"

"But I've already promised..."

"What do you mean? To whom?"

"Monsieur René."

She pointed at one of the bearded foreigners.

"*Oui, madame m'a fait cet honneur*,"* the one in question responded briskly.

Surkov gaped at him open-mouthed, and then turned to look at Tafayeva.

"I'll change with him; he can have my seat in the stalls," he said.

"Try."

The bearded gentleman gesticulated furiously.

"Thank you very much!" said Surkov to Pyotr Ivanych, looking out of the corner of his eye at Alexander. "I have you to thank for this."

"No need to thank me; perhaps you'd like to join me in my box – there's just my wife and I; it's been quite a long time since you've seen her. Perhaps you could try your luck with her?"

Discomfited, Surkov turned away from him. Pyotr Ivanych quietly left the room. Yulia invited Alexander to take a seat next to her and talked to him for the next hour. Surkov tried several times to butt into the conversation, but somehow never succeeded. He chimed in with something about the ballet, and was met with the answer "yes" instead of "no", and vice versa; clearly no one was paying him any attention. Then he abruptly changed the subject to oysters, claiming that he had eaten 180 for breakfast – but no one even responded with a glance. He touched on a number of other topics, but seeing that he was getting nowhere, picked up his hat and hovered around Yulia in an attempt to convey his displeasure to her as well as his imminent departure. But she didn't even notice.

"I'm leaving!" he said finally, and emphatically. "Goodbye!"

The words barely concealed his hurt feelings.

"So soon!" she answered calmly. "Do let me catch a glimpse of you in my box tomorrow, if only for a minute."

"What terrible insincerity! When you know that I would trade in a seat in paradise for a seat next to you."

"If you mean a seat in the gods in the theatre, I believe you."

Now he no longer wanted to leave. He had forgotten about his hurt feelings because of the friendly word she had uttered when he was about to leave. But everyone could see that the process of his leave-taking had been concluded and that he had no choice but to go. He did so, but kept looking back like a dog that wants to follow his master but is being waved away.

Yulia Pavlovna was twenty-three or -four years old. Pyotr Ivanych had guessed right. She was indeed of a nervous disposition, but that didn't prevent her from being at the same time a pretty, intelligent and graceful woman. She was, however, timid, sensitive and a dreamer like most women of a nervous disposition. Her features were fine and delicate, and her eyes spoke of a gentle and reflective nature, although with a lurking hint of sadness about them – not for any particular reason, except perhaps for her nervousness.

Her view of life and the world was not entirely favourable, and when she fell to thinking about her existence, she concluded that her presence in it was superfluous. But if, Heaven forbid, anyone should, even accidentally, let slip a remark about tombs or death, she would turn pale. The bright side of life escaped her notice. Out on a walk, she would choose a dark, overgrown path and view the joyful scenery with indifference. At the theatre, she always chose drama over comedy, and never the music hall; she closed her ears to the sounds of any cheerful song which happened to reach them, and never smiled at a joke. At times, her face wore an expression of languor – not one suggesting suffering or pain, but rather a kind of contentment. It was apparent that an internal struggle was going on with some kind of enchanting dream – a struggle which exhausted her. After this struggle, she would remain sad and mournful for a long time; then suddenly this mood would change unaccountably to one of sheer high spirits, which was not, however, out of keeping with her true nature – whatever it was that raised *her* spirits would not have raised the spirits of others. It was all a matter of nerves! To listen to those ladies talking, you would hear

CHAPTER 3

nothing but words like "fate", "sympathy", "unaccountable impulses", "inexplicable sorrow", "obscure longings" – and this was always the turn taken by their conversation, a conversation always ending with a sigh and, of course, nerves and smelling salts.

"How well you've understood me!" said Tafayeva to Alexander as they said goodbye. "No other man, not even my husband, could properly understand my character."

The fact is that even Alexander was pretty much like her, and that's what made it easy for him.

"Goodbye."

She gave him her hand.

"I hope that you will find your way here, even without your uncle," she added.

The winter came. Alexander usually dined at his uncle's on Fridays. But four Fridays had now gone by without him at dinner – nor did he come on the other days. Lizaveta Alexandrovna was angry, and Pyotr Ivanych grumbled that Alexander was making them wait for him for an extra half-hour – and for nothing.

However, Alexander was by no means idle during this time: he was busy carrying out his uncle's instructions. Surkov had long since stopped calling on Tafayeva and went round telling people that it was all over between them, and that he had "broken it off with her". One evening – it was on a Tuesday – Alexander returned home and found two vases on his table with a note from his uncle. Pyotr Ivanych thanked him for his friendly efforts on his behalf and asked him to dinner as usual the next day. Alexander started thinking – it was as if this invitation was somehow interfering with his plans.

The next day, however, he went to Pyotr Ivanych's an hour before dinner.

"What's the matter? We never see you any more. Have you forgotten us?"

His uncle and aunt plied him with questions.

"Well, you did it!" said Pyotr Ivanych. "You surpassed yourself. You were too modest. 'I can't,' he says, 'I won't succeed!' Won't succeed indeed! I've been wanting to see you, but you're impossible to catch. Anyway, I'm really grateful! Did the vases arrive safely?"

"Yes, they did; but I'm going to send them back to you."

"Why? Absolutely not! They're yours by right."

"No!" said Alexander firmly. "I won't accept your gift."

"Oh well, as you wish! My wife likes them; she'll take them."

"I didn't know, Alexander," said Lizaveta Alexandrovna with a mischievous smile, "that you were so skilled in these matters... I can't tell you..."

"It was Uncle's idea," Alexander responded in some embarrassment, "I didn't really... Well, he just told me what to do..."

"Oh yes, just listen to him; he really wasn't capable – couldn't do it by himself – he handled the business beautifully... I'm really very grateful. And that idiot of mine, Surkov, nearly went out of his mind. He really made me laugh. Two weeks ago he runs in to see me; he's beside himself; I could tell why right away, but I don't let on, and just keep on writing as if I've no idea what it's all about. 'So, tell me what's new?' He tries to smile, as if he's perfectly calm... but he can hardly keep back his tears. 'Nothing good,' he says, 'I have some bad news for you.' I looked at him, pretending to be surprised. 'What is it?' I ask. 'Well, it's about your nephew.' 'Well, what is it? You're frightening me – out with it quickly!' I say. At this point, he can't control himself any more and starts shouting; he's fuming. I backed away from him in my chair. He's reduced to spluttering. 'You yourself complained that he does practically nothing, and yet it's you who is training him to be idle.' 'Me?' 'Yes, you; who was it who introduced him to Julie? I want you to know that the very day after meeting that woman he starts using her pet name.' 'Well, what's wrong with that?' I say. 'What's wrong with it is that now he is there with her all day...'"

Alexander suddenly blushed.

"You see how people lie out of sheer malice, I thought," Pyotr Ivanych continued, watching his nephew. "Can you imagine Alexander sitting round there all day long! I didn't ask him about that. Well?"

Pyotr Ivanych regarded his nephew in his usual steady and expressionless manner, but Alexander felt positively scorched by his look.

"Yes, well I do sometimes... go round..." Alexander mumbled.

CHAPTER 3

"'Sometimes' – that's different," his uncle continued, "that's what I asked him; but not every day. I knew he was lying. I mean what could you possibly be doing there all day? You'd be bored."

"Not at all! She's a very intelligent woman with, er, an excellent education... She likes music..." Alexander mumbled indistinctly and disjointedly, and started scratching his eye – although he never usually scratched – and stroking his left temple. Then he got out his handkerchief and wiped his lips.

Lizaveta Alexandrovna gave him a stealthy but penetrating look, turned towards the window and smiled.

"Well, so much the better," said Pyotr Ivanych, "if you weren't bored. I was rather afraid that I had imposed on you an unpalatable task. So, I say to Surkov, 'Thank you, my dear fellow, for having my nephew's interests at heart, I'm much... obliged; only, aren't you exaggerating the problem a little? I mean it's not so terrible after all.' To which he replies, 'What do you mean, "not so terrible"? He has nothing to keep him occupied, a young man should be working...' So I say, 'Yes, it's really not so terrible, but what's it to you, anyway?' He says, 'What do you mean, "what's it to me?" He's up to all kinds of tricks in order to frustrate me.' 'Oh, that's what the problem is!' I say in order to tease him. 'He's telling Yulia all kinds of things about me. He's become thoroughly hostile to me. I'm going to teach that young milksop a lesson' – I'm sorry, I'm just repeating his words. 'Why', says Surkov, 'should he be feuding with me? And it's nothing but slander he's using against me. I hope you will bring him to his senses...' 'I'll take it up with him, I can assure you I will. Only, that's enough, don't you think? What has he done to annoy you?' Have you been giving her flowers? Is that it?" Pyotr Ivanych stopped again as if awaiting a reply. Alexander kept silent. Pyotr Ivanych continued: "'What I'm telling you,' he says, 'is the truth. He brings her bouquets of flowers every day. It's wintertime,' he says, 'I can't imagine what it must cost. I know what those bouquets mean. And here's a thought which occurred to me: you and he are related, and I know very well that family ties mean something; I mean, would you have gone to so much trouble for someone else?' 'Are you sure it's every day?' I ask him. 'But wait, I had better ask him;

for all I know you may be lying.' Indeed, he probably was lying, wasn't he? You couldn't possibly?..."

Alexander wished that the earth would swallow him up, but Pyotr Ivanych had no mercy and looked him straight in the eye, waiting for an answer.

"Well sometimes... I did actually bring..." said Alexander, his head lowered.

"Here we go again with 'sometimes'. Not every day – that would really be uneconomical. In any case, tell me how much all that cost you, I don't want to see you out of pocket on my account – in addition to all the trouble you've taken for me. So let me have the bill. Anyway, Surkov still had the bit between his teeth and wouldn't let go. 'They're always out somewhere or other,' he says, 'either out on a walk or for a ride in her carriage, just the two of them, wherever there aren't too many people around.'"

Alexander was a little discomfited by these words; he stretched his legs out from under his chair and immediately drew them back again.

His uncle continued. "I shook my head doubtfully. 'Oh, yes! I can just imagine him going out for walks every day,' I say. 'Ask around!' he says. 'I'd do better to ask *him*,' I said. It's not true, is it?"

"Well, a few times... yes... I did go for a walk with her..."

"So, not every day; I didn't ask about that; I knew he was lying. 'Well, what of it?' I tell him. 'Why is that important? She's a widow and she doesn't have any men who are relatives. And Alexander is a gentlemanly character, not a rake like you. So what if she does take him? I mean, she can't go alone?' He doesn't want to hear it. 'No,' he says, 'you won't fool me! I know. He's always with her in the theatre, and I'm the one,' he says, 'who manages to get the box – with God knows how much trouble at times, and there he is sitting in it next to her.' At this I couldn't contain myself and burst out laughing. 'It serves you right, you fool!' I'm thinking. 'Good for you, Alexander! There's a nephew for you!' Only I feel bad about your taking all that trouble for me."

Alexander was in torment. Large beads of sweat were dripping from his forehead. He could hardly hear what his uncle was saying and didn't dare to look at him or his aunt.

CHAPTER 3

Lizaveta Alexandrovna took pity on him. She shook her head at her husband, silently reproaching him for torturing his nephew. But Pyotr Ivanych persisted.

"Out of jealousy, Surkov was anxious to convince me," he went on, "that you were already head over heels in love with Tafayeva. 'Now, come on,' I say to him, 'I'm sorry, but you're lying; after everything that's happened to him, he's not going to fall in love. He understands women too well, and despises them…' Isn't that so?"

Alexander nodded without looking up.

Lizaveta Alexandrovna felt bad for him.

"Pyotr Ivanych!" she said in an attempt to shut him up.

"Yes, what is it?"

"Some time ago a servant came with a letter from the Lukyanovs."

"I know, thank you. Now where was I?"

"Once again, Pyotr Ivanych, you've gone and dumped your ashes on my flowers – it's a disgrace!"

"Don't worry, my dear, they say that ashes promote growth in plants; now what was I going to say?…"

"Isn't it time for dinner, Pyotr Ivanych?"

"All right, tell them to serve it! I'm glad you reminded me about dinner, because Surkov tells me that you, Alexander, dine there almost every day – and, he says, that's why you're never here on Fridays, and also, supposedly, that you spend whole days together, just the two of you, and God knows what other things he makes up. I got so fed up with him that I finally had to throw him out. And indeed it did turn out that he was lying. Today is Friday, and here you are!"

Alexander crossed his legs and tilted his head onto his left shoulder.

"I'm extremely, extremely grateful to you. You've done this favour to me both as a friend and as a member of the family!" Pyotr Ivanych stated. "Surkov is now convinced that he stands to gain nothing and has withdrawn from the fray. 'She,' he says, 'imagines that I will be pining for her; she is mistaken! And to think that I wanted,' he says, 'to decorate the whole of the ground floor between the windows – and God knows what else I had intended to do. Probably,' he says, 'she didn't even dream of what happiness was in store for her. I would,' he says, 'even have considered marrying her if she had succeeded in captivating me. Now, all that is over and done with. You, Pyotr Ivanych,' he says, 'gave me some good advice, and I'm saving both money and time.' Now the fellow is acting all Byronic, plunged in gloom, and isn't asking for money, and I can now say with him: 'All over and done with!' Your job is done, Alexander, and in masterly fashion, and I will enjoy peace of mind for a long time to come. Now you can take it easy, and you don't have to so much as look at her any longer; I can just imagine how boring it must have been!... But please forgive me... I will make it up to you somehow. When you need money, do come to me. Liza! Tell them to serve some good wine at dinner; we'll drink to the success of the plan."

Pyotr Ivanych left the room. Lizaveta Alexandrovna stole a look once or twice at Alexander out of the corner of her eye, but seeing that he wasn't saying a word, also left to give orders to the servants.

Alexander was sitting there as if in a trance, just gazing at his knees. Finally he raised his head and looked around him – no one else was in the room. He took a breath and looked at his watch – four o'clock. He picked up his hat immediately, waved his hand in the direction of the door through which his uncle had left the room and quietly, on tiptoe, looking warily all around him, made his way to the entrance hall, took his overcoat and rushed headlong down the stairs on his way to Tafayeva's house.

Surkov had not lied. Alexander was in love with Tafayeva. It was almost with horror that he had reacted to the first signs of this love. He was racked by fear and shame as if he had contracted some infection – fear that he would fall prey once again to all the caprices both of his own heart and that of the woman he loved – shame because of having to face other people, and especially his uncle. He would have given anything to be able to avoid confronting him. Why, it was hardly three months ago that he had been boasting so proudly that he had renounced love once and for all. He had even written an epitaph in verse to that unsettling emotion, which had been read by his uncle. And finally, he had publicly proclaimed his contempt for women – and suddenly here he was again prostrate at a woman's feet! Further proof of his infantile recklessness. Good God! When would he be able to free himself from his uncle's irresistible influence? Would his life never be free to take its own independent and unexpected course, but forever be determined by Pyotr Ivanych's predictions?

The thought reduced him to despair. He would have been glad to flee from this new love. But how could he? What a difference was there between his love for Nadenka and his love for Yulia! His first love was nothing but an unfortunate aberration of the heart which demanded to be fed, and at that age the heart was undiscriminating, ready to embrace whatever happened to come along. But Yulia! There's someone who is no longer a capricious youngster, but a woman in her prime, bodily weak, but with a spirit full of energy – for love; she is – nothing but love! There is no other imperative for happiness and life itself that she recognizes. To love – a mere trifle? It's also a gift. And in the matter of love Yulia is a genius. This was the kind of love of which he dreamt: a conscious, considered love, but at the same time powerful and oblivious to anything outside itself. "I'm not breathless with joy, like an animal," he said to himself. "My senses do not swoon, but something is going on inside me which is more significant, of a higher order; I am conscious of my own happiness; I can contemplate it; it is fuller, although perhaps quieter... How nobly, how unreservedly, how naturally Yulia has yielded to her feelings!" It is as if she had been waiting for a man with a deep understanding of love – and that man appeared. He had proudly taken possession of this rich heritage as its rightful owner and was humbly recognized as such. "What joy, what bliss," thought Alexander, on his way from his uncle to her, "to know that there is a being in this world which, wherever it may be, whatever it is doing, is mindful of us, and is focusing all its thoughts, endeavours and actions on one single point, one single concept: that of the beloved being! It's as if it is our doppelgänger. Whatever this being hears, whatever it sees, whatever it passes by, whatever passes by it – all is validated by the impression of that other self. It is an impression known to both – each of them has studied the other – and the impression, then validated in this way, is embraced and confirmed in the soul by its indelible features. That other self renounces its own sensations if they cannot be shared and accepted by the other. One loves what the other loves, and hates what the other hates. They live inseparably in a single thought, a single feeling; they have a single eye, a single hearing, a single mind, a single soul..."

"Sir, where is it on the Liteyny Prospekt?" asked the driver.

Yulia loved Alexander even more than he loved her. She was not even aware of the strength of her love and didn't spend time thinking about it. In the case of a first love – no problem, but there's no falling in love just like that the second time. The trouble was that her heart had developed an almost infinite capacity, fed as it had been by novels, and was geared not just to accommodate a first love, but the kind of romance which, while it can be found in some novels, does not exist in real life, and is always doomed to unhappiness precisely because it is not possible in practice. At the same time, Yulia's mind had not found in novels the proper sustenance, and was left behind by her heart. She was totally unable to conceive of a love that was tranquil and straightforward, and free from episodes of turbulence and emotional excess.

She would stop loving a man if he did not immediately "drop to her feet" when the occasion arose, if he failed to swear his allegiance "with the full force of his being", if he had the temerity not to "burn her and consume her with fire in his embrace", or dared to find time in his life for any other pursuit but loving her, or to drain the "cup of life" in any other way than drop by drop from her tears and kisses.

This was the source of the dream world she had created for herself. Let the slightest thing happen in the normal world which did not conform to the laws of that dream world, and her heart rose up in outrage and she was in pain. Her woman's organism, weak as it was by nature, was easily, even severely shaken. Her nervous system was often overwrought, and often brought to the point of total collapse. This is the reason for those inexplicable moods of despondency and depression and the gloomy outlook on life to which so many women are prone. It also explains why the harmonious, so cleverly constructed order of human existence, constantly developing according to immutable laws, makes them feel tethered by a heavy chain. That is why, in

CHAPTER 3

short, reality itself frightens them, and makes them invent a world like that of the Fata Morgana.*

Who was it who had striven to bend Yulia's heart so badly out of shape, and so prematurely, while neglecting to develop her mind? Who could it be? Well, it was that classical trio of pedagogues who, at the behest of her parents, had come and taken her young mind under their tutelage in order to reveal to it the "workings and causes of all things"* and rip aside the veil of the past and show that under us, over us and within us there lies... an onerous duty! However, there are three nations to whose lot has fallen the task of performing this feat. Her parents themselves renounced all responsibility for her education in the belief that their work had ended, when, relying on the recommendations of their good friends, they recruited a Frenchman, Poulet, to teach their daughter French literature and other subjects, and also a German, Schmidt – because that was the thing to do – for her to learn German, although without actually mastering it; and finally Ivan Ivanych, the Russian teacher.

"But they're all so unkempt," said the mother, "and always so badly dressed – even worse than our servants by the look of them, and sometimes they even smell of wine..."

"But how can we possibly do without a Russian teacher? Absolutely not!" the father decided. "But don't worry, I'll find some who are more presentable."

The Frenchman started work. Both father and mother danced attendance upon him. They invited him to the house as a guest and treated him with the greatest courtesy; he was "our dear Frenchman".

Teaching Yulia was easy for him. Thanks to her governess she could already chatter in French, and read and write French almost faultlessly. It remained for Monsieur Poulet only to set her compositions. He gave her a variety of subjects: "Description of the Rising Sun", "The Definition of Love and Friendship", "A Letter of Congratulation to Her Parents" or "An Expression of Sorrow on Parting with a Friend".

But through her window Yulia could only see the sun setting behind the house of Gurin, the merchant, and had never had occasion to part with a friend; as for love and friendship, this was her first inkling of these feelings. She would have to find out about them some time.

Having exhausted his repertoire of subjects, Poulet decided to start his pupil on one of those cherished slim exercise books, the front cover of which bore in capital letters the title: "*Cours de littérature française*". None of us will ever forget that exercise book. Yulia learnt French literature by heart – or at least the contents of that slim exercise book, although after three years she had forgotten it all; but pernicious traces of it remained. She knew who Voltaire was and foisted on him *Les martyrs*, and to Chateaubriand she misattributed the *Dictionnaire philosophique*.* She called Montaigne "Monsieur de Montaigne" and referred to him in connection with Hugo. She spoke at times of Molière as still "writing" for the theatre, and she had learnt the famous speech of Racine, "*À peine nous sortions des portes de Trézène*".*

In mythology she particularly liked the comedy played out between Vulcan, Mars and Venus.* She was tempted to take Vulcan's side, but when she learnt that he had a limp and was clumsy and was only a blacksmith, she transferred her support to Mars. She also liked the fable of Semele and Jupiter, and also the banishment of Apollo and his earthly escapades, and understood all of this in precisely the terms in which it was written, without suspecting that any other meaning was hidden in these tales. Whether her French tutor himself had any suspicion – God knows! In response to her questions about the religion of the ancients, he would wrinkle his brow and respond complacently, "*Des bêtises! Mais cette bête de Vulcan devait avoir une drôle de mine... écoutez,*" and then added, patting her hand, "*Que feriez-vous à la place de Venus?*"* She didn't answer, but for the first time in her life she found herself blushing for no apparent reason.

The French teacher finally concluded Yulia's education by introducing her no longer theoretically, but practically to the new school of French literature, and giving her to read works which at one time had caused a sensation: *Le Manuscrit vert*, *Les Sept Péchés capitaux*, *L'Âne mort** and a whole slew of books sweeping France and Europe at that time.

The poor girl hurled herself greedily into that boundless ocean. What heroes she discovered there – Janin, Balzac, Drouineau and a whole succession of great men! How paltry the tale of Vulcan now seemed compared with these divine images! Venus was reduced to innocence

CHAPTER 3

itself by these new towering figures. She greedily devoured this new school, and no doubt reads them to this very day.

While the Frenchman was moving so far ahead, the stolid German hadn't even finished teaching grammar, solemnly making up tables of declensions, conjugations and working out ingenious ways of remembering case endings, like telling his pupil that the particle *zu* always comes at the end of the Russian word for "end" – *kontzu* – and so on and so forth.

But when he was asked to teach literature, the poor fellow took fright. When he was shown the Frenchman's workbook, he shook his head and said that that couldn't be taught in German, but that there was Aller's reader, which contained the names of all the writers and their works. But he didn't get away with that, and the parents insisted that he introduce Yulia to various writers, as Monsieur Poulet had done.

The German finally promised, and returned home deep in thought. He opened the cupboard, or rather pulled off one of its doors entirely, and leant it against the wall, because the cupboard had long ago lost its hinges and its lock, and took out an old pair of boots, half a head of sugar, a bottle of snuff, a carafe of vodka and a crust of black bread, followed by a broken coffee grinder, a razor with a sliver of soap stuck to it and a brush in a jar of pomade, an old pair of braces, an oilstone for sharpening penknives and a number of other such odds and ends. Finally a book made its appearance, followed by a second, a third, a fourth – and, yes, a fifth, making up the whole set. He slapped them against one another, raising a cloud of dust as black as smoke, which gently settled on the pedagogue's head.

The first book was *The Idylls of Gessner*.* "*Gut!*" said the German and eagerly read the idyll of the broken jug. He opened the second book, *The Gothic Calendar for 1804*. He leafed through it; it contained the dynasties of the European monarchs and pictures of various castles and waterfalls. "*Sehr gut!*" said the German. The third was the Bible, which he put aside. "*Nein!*" he muttered piously. The fourth was the *Night Thoughts* of Young;* he shook his head and muttered "*Nein!*" The fifth was Weisse,* and the German smiled triumphantly: "*Da habe ich's*,"* he said. When he was asked: "What about Schiller, Goethe and the rest?" he just shook his head and replied with an emphatic "*Nein!*"

Yulia yawned as soon as the German started translating the first page of Weisse, and then stopped listening altogether. The only thing that remained in her memory from her German tutor was that the particle always came at the end, as in *kontzu*.

As for the Russian tutor, he was almost reduced to tears when he tried to explain to Yulia that a "substantive noun" or a "verb" was such and such a part of speech, and that a "preposition" was a different part of speech, but finally managed to get her to trust him and to learn the definitions of all the parts of speech by heart. She could recite all the prepositions, conjunctions and adverbs without stopping, and when the teacher asked her portentously, "What are the interjections which express 'surprise' and 'fear'?" she promptly, and without stopping to take a breath, listed six or seven of them. Her tutor was delighted.

She also knew some of the principles of syntax, but was never able to put them into practice, and was dogged by faults of grammar all her life.

In history, she knew of Alexander of Macedon, and that he had fought many wars and was supremely brave – and, of course, supremely handsome – but when it came to his historical significance, and that of his period, it never occurred to either her or her teacher even to wonder – nor, for that matter, did Kaydanov* have much to say about that.

When the parents raised the question of literature with the teacher, he brought in a heap of old and battered books. Among the authors were Kantemir, Sumarokov, as well as Lomonosov, Derzhavin and Ozerov.* Everyone was surprised; they carefully opened up one book, sniffed it and threw it out, and demanded something a little newer. The teacher brought in Karamzin. But who would think of reading Karamzin after the new French school! Yulia read *Poor Liza* and a few pages of *Travels*,* but gave it back.

The intervals between these classes for the poor pupil were numerous, and failed to provide any improving or healthy nourishment for the mind! Her mind began to go to sleep, while her heart began to sound the alarm. One day an obliging cousin turned up, and happened to bring with her a few chapters of *Onegin* and *The Captive in the Caucasus*,* among other books, and the young lady got her first taste

CHAPTER 3

of the charm of Russian verse. *Onegin* was learnt by heart and never left Yulia's night table. But the cousin was no better able to explain the significance and the merits of that work than her other teachers. Yulia took Tatyana as her model and mentally repeated to her own imaginary ideal the passionate lines of Tatyana's letter to Onegin, and her heartbeat ached and throbbed to the rhythm of those lines. Her imagination sought here an Onegin, or there some hero from the pages of the masters of the new school – pale, melancholy and disillusioned.

An Italian and another Frenchman were brought in to round off her education, and they lent harmonious dimensions to her voice and movements – that is to say that they taught her to dance, sing and play – or rather to dabble – at the piano, until marriage came along, but they didn't teach her music. So there she was at the age of eighteen, already with that constant pensive expression, an attractive pallor, a slender waist, small feet, and starting to be seen in society.

She was noticed by Tafayev, a man with all the attributes of the perfect match: a respectable rank, a sizeable fortune, and wearing a cross on his neck – in short, a man of substance with a promising career. He could not be described as a simple and amiable man – not by a long chalk! He was not easily taken advantage of, and was a forthright critic of the current state of Russia and of its economic and industrial shortcomings, and in his circle he was known as a man to be reckoned with.

The pale, pensive girl, because of her striking contrast with his solid temperament, made a strong impression on him. At social gatherings, he would leave the card table plunged in thought, most unusually for him, watching that almost ethereal wraith flit past him. When her languorous gaze happened to fall on him, something which never happened by design, he, a nimble gladiator in the arena of social conversation, was intimidated in the presence of this timorous young girl and, although anxious to say something to her, found himself tongue-tied. He found this vexing, and made up his mind to take more positive action through the intercession of older ladies.

The information which had reached him about her dowry was satisfactory. "A good match!" he thought to himself. "I'm only forty-five, and she is eighteen; with our combined fortunes more than just the two of us could live very comfortably. As for appearance, well, she is more than averagely pretty, and I am what is known as a fine figure of a man. People say she is educated. But so what? I too have had my share of education: I studied Latin and Roman history, and I still remember some. There was that consul… what was he called?… Well, to hell with it! I also remember learning about the Reformation… There were those lines of poetry: '*Beatus ille*…'* Now, what comes next? '*Puer, pueri, puero*'* – no, that's wrong; what the devil! I've forgotten everything. By God, it's true, we learn only to forget! I don't care what anyone says, take any one of these important, intelligent people: not a single one of them will be able to tell you who that consul was… or in what year the Olympic Games were held. So that really the only reason for learning things is for form's sake. So that people can tell by your look that you've been educated. Of course you're going to forget; I mean, later on, out in the world, no one is ever going to talk about these things, and if anyone should happen to do so, I think they would simply be shown the door. No, we're a good match."

So that's how it happened that, on taking her first step after her childhood, Yulia had stumbled into that grimmest of realities, your run-of-the-mill husband. He couldn't have been more different from those heroes conjured up in her imagination by the poets!

After spending five years in that loveless marriage, which she thought of as a tedious dream, suddenly she found freedom and love. She smiled, invited him into her passionate embrace, abandoned herself to her passion in the same way that a horse rider abandons himself to a fast gallop. He is carried away by the momentum of his powerful steed, oblivious to the ground he is covering. It's breathtaking; objects flash past him, the fresh wind smacks him in the face, his breast swells fit to burst from the heady feeling… Or like someone paddling a canoe, abandoning himself to the speeding current of his will: the sun warms him, he glimpses the green banks of the river flashing by, a wave slaps playfully at the side of the boat, whispering gently as it passes, and beckoning him farther and farther on, showing the way to the boundless expanse ahead. And he follows in its wake. No time to stop and consider what lies at the end. Will his mount race over a precipice, will

CHAPTER 3

that wave smash him against a rock? The wind effaces thought, the eyes close, the spell is overpowering... In just the same way, she was in thrall to that spell, and was just carried along farther and farther. At last she was able to savour life's poetic moments; she cherished the alternating delight and torment of her heart in turmoil, and freely sought the excitement of those moments, even devising her own moments of torment and delight. She craved love as people crave opium, and greedily swallowed the draught that was poisoning her heart.

Yulia was anxiously waiting. She was standing at the window, her impatience mounting with every moment. She was plucking the petals from a hibiscus and angrily flinging them onto the floor, her heart sinking – a moment of sheer pain. She was playing a mental game of question and answer: "Will he or won't he come?" She was summoning all her energy to concentrate exclusively on solving that riddle. When the answer came up "yes", she smiled; if "no", she went pale.

When Alexander approached, her face went pale and she sank into an armchair, in a state of nervous exhaustion. When he entered, it was impossible to describe the look she gave him, or the joy which irradiated all her features, as if they had been parted for a year, when they had seen each other only the day before. She pointed silently to the wall clock, but barely had he opened his mouth to apologize when, without even giving him time to utter a word, she believed him, forgave him and forgot all about the pain that the waiting had caused her, and gave him her hand. They both sat down on the divan and talked for a long time, sat silent for a long time, and looked at each other for a long time. If a servant hadn't appeared, they would have forgotten to eat.

What delight! Alexander had never even dreamt of such an abundance of "sincere, heartfelt outpourings". In the summer, when they left the town to walk together in the country, while the crowd were diverted by the sound of music or fireworks, the two of them could be seen in the distance, passing through the trees arm in arm. In the winter, Alexander came to dinner, and afterwards they would sit together by the fire long into the night. Sometimes they would order a sleigh to be harnessed and, after speeding through the dark streets, hurried back to continue their unending conversation beside the samovar. Everything happening around them, every passing thought and reaction was registered and shared between them.

Alexander was as scared of encountering his uncle as he would have been to put his hand in the fire. He sometimes went to see Lizaveta Alexandrovna, but she never succeeded in getting him to open up to her. He was always on edge because of the possibility that his uncle might catch him there and make another scene – and that is why he always cut his visits short.

Was he happy? With anyone else in similar circumstances one might have answered: "Yes and no." But with him, it was: "No." In his case, love always began with suffering. At those moments when he succeeded in forgetting the past, he could believe in the possibility of happiness, in Yulia and in her love. But at other times, in the heat of those "heartfelt outpourings" he always began to feel uncomfortable and, when he listened to her passionate and rapturous declarations, even felt afraid. He felt that at any moment she would change, or that another unexpected "blow of fate" would strike him and instantly destroy his wonderful world of bliss. For every minute of joy that he tasted, he knew that he would have to pay with suffering, and gloom would overwhelm him.

However, the winter passed, summer arrived, and love continued uninterrupted. Yulia's attachment to him grew ever stronger. She had not changed, and no "blow of fate" had been dealt; what happened was something quite unexpected. The expression in his eyes was brighter. He had grown accustomed to the idea that in love, lasting commitment was possible. "Only, this love is not so passionate," he thought to himself once when he was looking at Yulia, "although it's lasting, maybe even eternal. Yes, there's no doubt. Finally, Fate, I understand you! You are trying to reward me for my past sufferings, and steer me, after long wanderings, into a peaceful harbour. And that safe haven of happiness... is Yulia," he exclaimed aloud.

She shuddered.

"What's the matter?" she asked.

"Nothing, I just..."

CHAPTER 3

"No, tell me; you were thinking something?"

Alexander stood mute. But she insisted.

"I was thinking that for our happiness to be complete, something is missing..."

"What?" she asked anxiously.

"Nothing really, I just had a strange idea."

Yulia was perturbed.

"Oh, don't torment me: tell me now!" she said.

Alexander thought for a moment, and then, under his breath, almost as if he were speaking to himself, said, "To earn the right never to leave her for a minute, never to leave here and go home... to be with her everywhere and at all times. To be in the eyes of the world her rightful owner... and she, unblushingly and without constraint, will publicly claim me as hers... and that's the way it will be for life. And to be forever proud of this..."

Saying all this in such an elevated style, clearly enunciating every word, he reached the word "marriage". At this, Yulia quivered and burst into tears. She extended her hand to him with a feeling of inexpressible affection and gratitude, and they both suddenly burst into animated conversation. It was all settled. Alexander would speak to his aunt and ask for her help in this complicated matter.

They were beside themselves with joy. They set off for the town with no particular destination in mind and went deep into the countryside, searching for the first hill they could find, and spent the whole evening sitting on it watching the sun go down, thinking of what their future life together would be like; they thought they would confine themselves to a limited circle of friends, and avoid accepting or issuing invitations simply for form's sake.

They returned home and began to discuss how they would organize their future household, and which rooms would be used for what purpose. They even got down to discussing how to furnish the rooms and other things of that kind. Alexander proposed turning her dressing room into a study for himself, so that it could be near the bedroom.

"How would you like your study to be furnished?" she asked.

"I would like it furnished in walnut covered in blue velvet."

"That would be very nice, and would be easy to keep clean. Dark colours should always be chosen for a man's study; light colours get dirty fast from the smoke. And the little passageway between your future study and the bedroom I'll decorate with flowers and foliage – that will look so nice, won't it? And I'll put an armchair in there so that I can sit and read or sew and see you while you're in there."

"It won't be long now, and then we won't have to say goodbye like this," said Alexander as he prepared to leave.

She pressed her hand to his mouth.

The next day, Alexander went to see Lizaveta Alexandrovna to tell her what she had already known for a long time, and ask for her help and advice. Pyotr Ivanych was not at home.

"All right then!" she said, after hearing his confession. "You're no longer a boy, and you know your own feelings and can act accordingly. But don't be in too much of a hurry; get to know her properly."

"Oh, *ma tante*, if only you knew what qualities she possesses!"

"For example?"

"She loves me so much…"

"Of course, that is an important quality, but it takes more than that to make a marriage."

She then proceeded to make some general points about the married state: what the wife should be like, and what the husband should be like. "Only please wait. It will soon be autumn, and people will be coming back to town, and then I'll call on your fiancée; we'll get to know each other, and then I can really get to work. Don't leave her; I'm sure you will be the happiest of husbands."

She was very pleased.

How women love to see men get married! Sometimes they can even see that a marriage will have problems and is not likely to work. But for them the main thing is to get the couple married, and then what happens is up to the newly-weds. God knows why women take so much trouble over this.

CHAPTER 3

Alexander asked his aunt not to say anything to Pyotr Ivanych until the very end.

The summer fled by, followed by a never-ending gloomy autumn. Another winter began. Aduyev and Yulia still saw each other just as often.

It was as if she had worked out a strict timetable for the days, hours and minutes which they should spend together, and sought every possible opportunity for them to do so.

"Will you be going to your office early tomorrow?" she would sometimes ask.

"About eleven o'clock."

"Then come round at ten, and we can have breakfast together. What about not going to the office at all? After all, so what if you're not there?…"

"But how can I? I have to think of our country… my duty…" said Alexander.

"Oh, that's just wonderful! Just tell them that you're in love and that someone loves you. Hasn't your chief ever been in love? If he has a heart he'll understand. Or just bring your work and do it here – who's to stop you?"

Another time, she wouldn't let him go to the theatre, and on no account was he to go to see friends. When Lizaveta Alexandrovna called on her, she was in a state of shock when she set eyes on Alexander's aunt and saw how young and pretty she was. She had imagined her to be just another aunt – elderly and nothing much to look at – and here, if you please, was a young woman of twenty-six or -seven and a real beauty! She made a scene with Alexander, and stopped him going to his uncle's house so often.

But what was the significance of her jealousy and tyranny compared with that of Alexander himself? He was sure of her commitment, and saw that betrayal or a cooling of her ardour was simply not in her nature, but he was jealous – and jealous beyond reason! It was not the jealousy born of a surfeit of love – weeping, groaning, howling from the pain of an aching heart, trembling with fear of the loss of happiness – but rather a cold-blooded jealousy born of indifference and vindictiveness. He tyrannized the poor woman from love more than others tyrannized their victims from hatred. He would feel, for example, in the evening, when there were guests present, that she had not looked at him long enough, often enough or lovingly enough, and he would prowl around like a wild beast, and there would be hell to pay if by any chance Yulia happened to be standing near a young man, or any man for that matter, even if he didn't happen to be young – or it could even be a woman, or sometimes even an inanimate object. Then insults, caustic remarks, dark suspicions and reproaches would rain down on her, and right then and there she would have to defend and redeem herself, and make amends of every kind and owe him absolute obedience. She was not to speak to this one, she was not to sit there, or move in that direction, and was not to expose herself to the smirks and whispers of malicious onlookers, and be left blushing or with the blood draining from her cheeks, dying from embarrassment.

If ever she received invitations, before she responded she would first of all have to look enquiringly in his direction, and if he so much as wrinkled his brow, she would have to decline on the spot, looking pale and nervous. Sometimes he would give his consent, and she would get ready, dress for the occasion, and was just about to take her seat in the carriage when, suddenly and impulsively, on the spur of the moment, he would pronounce his deadly veto – and she would go back and change her clothes. Afterwards, he might beg forgiveness and propose that they should go – but how could she get all dressed up again and get the carriage harnessed? So they stayed where they were. His jealousy did not depend on whether the people concerned were good-looking, intelligent or talented, or even positively ugly: sometimes his jealousy was aroused simply because he didn't like the look of someone.

Once a guest from her side of the family arrived. It was an elderly, plain-looking man who spoke about the harvest and his business in the senate. Alexander was so bored with his conversation that he went into the next room. There was absolutely no reason for jealousy. Finally, the guest took his leave.

CHAPTER 3

"I understand that you are at home on Wednesdays; would you mind if I came to enjoy the company of your friends?"

Yulia smiled and was about to say, "By all means" – when suddenly a voice could be heard from the next room in a whisper louder than any shout: "No!"

Yulia, in her agitation, hurriedly changed her "By all means" into a "No" in response to her guest's request.

But Yulia tolerated this behaviour. She shut herself away from guests, went nowhere and sat alone with Alexander. They continued systematically to revel in their bliss. Having exhausted their stock of the usual and available pleasures, Yulia started to invent new ones to add variety to the wealth of pleasures which already existed in their world. And what gifts of ingenuity she displayed! But even these gifts ran out, and repetition set in. There was nothing left to experience or to wish for.

There wasn't a single place in the surrounding countryside which they had not already visited, or a single play they had not already seen, or a book they had not already read and discussed. They had studied each other's feelings, thoughts, merits and shortcomings, and there was nothing left which might interfere with the implementation of their plan.

The heartfelt outpourings became rarer. Sometimes they sat for hours without exchanging a word, but Yulia was just as happy to be silent.

Very occasionally she would ask Alexander a question, and would be content with a "yes" or a "no" as an answer – and if no answer was forthcoming, she would give him a long look, he would smile in return, and she would be happy again. If he should neither answer nor smile, she would start to search for meaning in the slightest movement, the slightest look, and interpret it in her own way. Then, recriminations would inevitably follow.

They had stopped talking about the future, because it made Alexander feel awkward and ill at ease – a feeling he himself was unable to account for – and he would try to change the subject. He began to spend more time lost in his own thoughts. The charmed circle to which he had been confined by his love began to come apart in places, and in the distance he began to catch glimpses, sometimes of the faces of his friends, reminding him of the wild times they used to have together, the glittering balls with their throngs of beauties, and at other times of the ever preoccupied and busy image of his uncle, and his own work which he had abandoned...

It was in this state of mind that he was sitting one evening at Yulia's. Outside, a snowstorm was raging. Snow was beating against the windows, and patches of snow were clinging to the panes. All that could be heard in the room was the monotonous sound of the table clock's pendulum swinging back and forth and the occasional sigh from Yulia.

For want of anything better to do, Alexander was looking round the room, and happened to see the clock – it was ten o'clock, and he would have to sit through another two hours; he yawned. His glance happened to fall on Yulia. She was standing, and leaning with her back to the fire, with her pale face bent towards her shoulder, following Alexander with her eyes, with an expression devoid of mistrust or interrogation, but full of blissfulness, love and happiness. To all appearances she was struggling with a secret feeling, a sweet dream, and appeared exhausted. She was so highly strung that the effect on her nerves even of blissfulness itself reduced her to a painful lethargy; for her bliss and torment were indissolubly linked.

Alexander reacted in a dry, restless manner, and he went to the window and started drumming on the glass with his fingers, while looking out into the street.

From the street could be heard the sound of voices mingled with the rumble of passing carriages. Lights were burning in every window, shadows darted here and there. It seemed to him that where the lights were brightest, a merry crowd of people were gathered, and that perhaps a lively exchange of thoughts was taking place and sparks of feeling were flying back and forth. Out there, life was being lived noisily and with enjoyment. And over there, behind that dimly lit window, there no doubt sat someone toiling over some productive, meaningful piece of work. It occurred to Alexander that for almost two years now he had been dragging out an idle, senseless existence – two years of his life just thrown away – and for what? Love! There and then, he began an assault on love.

CHAPTER 3

"What kind of love was this?" he thought. "Something somnolent and inert. This woman surrendered to her feelings without a fight, without an effort, defenceless, a helpless victim – a weak woman, without character! She bestowed the favour of her love on the first comer. If it hadn't been me, it could just as well have been someone like that Surkov – in fact, she had already begun to fall for him. Yes, no matter how much she might protest – I saw it with my own eyes! If someone a little more engaging and worldly-wise than myself had come along, she would have thrown herself into his arms... It's positively immoral! Who calls that love? Where is that notion of 'kindred spirits' proclaimed by sensitive souls? And weren't we drawn together as kindred spirits? – kindred spirits which, it seemed, would be merged for ever. But no, it wasn't to be! Who the devil knows why – impossible to explain!" he whispered in exasperation.

"What are you doing over there? What are you thinking about?" asked Yulia.

"Oh just..." he said, yawning, and sat down on the divan away from her, with one hand grasping a corner of an embroidered cushion.

"Sit a little closer!"

He stayed where he was and offered no reply.

"What's the matter with you?" she continued, moving closer to him. "You're unbearable today."

"I don't know," he said listlessly, "it's something... as if I..."

He had no answer for her, or even for himself. He hadn't yet really understood what was happening to him.

She sat down next to him and started talking about the future – and, little by little, regained her composure. She portrayed a future of a happy family life, with some humour at times, and concluded on a very affectionate note. "You are my husband! Look," she said, pointing around the room, "soon all this will be yours. You will be the master of this house, just as you are the master of my heart. Right now I am independent: I can do what I want, go wherever and see whatever I want, but then nothing here will be touched except at your command, and I myself will be bound by your wishes – but what a wonderful chain that will be! Forge it as soon as possible – but when?... My whole life

I have dreamt of such a man, of such a love… and my dream has come true… and happiness is at hand… I can hardly believe it. You know – I think I'm dreaming. Surely it's a reward for all my past sufferings?"

Alexander found it painful to listen to all this.

"But what if I stopped loving you?" he asked suddenly, trying to strike a humorous note.

"I would tear your ears off!" she replied, taking hold of his ear, and then sighed, reduced to a thoughtful silence even by this attempt at levity. He remained silent.

"But what *is* the matter with you?" she asked suddenly, with renewed vigour. "You don't say anything, you hardly listen to me, you won't look at me…"

She moved towards him, placed her hand on his shoulder and started to speak softly, almost in a whisper, about the same subject, only with less confidence. She recalled how they had first come together, the burgeoning of their love, its first signs and its first joys. She almost choked from the sheer strength of her feeling of blissfulness – two pink patches coloured her pale cheeks. Her cheeks grew redder, her eyes glittered and then grew languorous and half closed; her breast heaved more strongly from her breathing. Her words became more indistinct, and with one hand she began to toy with Alexander's soft curls, and looked into his eyes. He quietly removed her hand from his head, took a comb out of his pocket and carefully combed back into place the hair that she had disarranged. She stood up and stared at him.

"What is it, Alexander?" she asked, troubled this time.

"There she goes again. How do I know?" he thought. But said nothing.

"Are you bored?" she said suddenly, and her voice betrayed a suggestion of interrogation and doubt.

"Bored!" he thought. "Yes, that's just the right word! Yes! Excruciating, deadly boredom – which has been eating away at my heart for a month now! My God, what can I do? She talks about nothing but love and marriage. How can I get her to change her tune?"

She had sat down at the piano and played some of his favourite pieces. He paid no attention and continued thinking his own thoughts.

CHAPTER 3

Yulia's hands dropped. She sighed, wrapped herself in a shawl and sat down at the other end of the divan and regarded Alexander with a pained expression.

He picked up his hat.

"But where are you going?" she asked in surprise.

"Home."

"It's not eleven o'clock yet."

"I have to write to my mother, I haven't written for a long time."

"What do you mean, 'a long time'? You wrote to her only two days ago."

He remained silent: there was nothing he could say. He had indeed written, and happened to have mentioned it in passing, but had forgotten – and love doesn't forget the slightest thing. In her eyes, anything whatsoever connected with the object of her love was a matter of importance. The mind of someone in love weaves an intricate web of tiny observations, memories, conjectures about anything surrounding the loved one, everything that happens in his life, everything that affects him. For someone in love, a single word – nay, the merest hint – is sufficient; but why do I say a hint? Why, even a glance, the barely perceptible quiver of the lip, is enough to provoke a conjecture, which then becomes an observation, which in turn becomes a hard and fast conclusion, which ultimately ends up, processed by the mind of the lover, as an instrument of torture or a source of sheer bliss. The logic of those in love, sometimes fallacious, but sometimes amazingly correct, swiftly builds up a tower of conjecture, and suspicions, but even more swiftly does the power of love raze it to the ground; for this, sometimes nothing more than a single smile, a single tear, not to mention as many as two or three words, will be sufficient – and all suspicions will suddenly vanish. This kind of vigilance cannot possibly be lulled or eluded. People in love will at times suddenly take into their heads something which others would not even dream of in their sleep, and at other times simply do not notice what is going on under their very noses; at still other times they are perspicacious to the point of clairvoyance, or even short-sighted to the point of blindness.

Yulia sprang up from the divan like a cat and caught him by the arm.

"What does this mean? Where are you going?" she asked.

"It's nothing really, nothing. I just need some sleep. I haven't been sleeping well lately – that's all there is to it."

"'Haven't been sleeping well'! Why, only the other morning you told me that you had slept for nine hours, and that it even gave you a headache…"

Another failed attempt.

"Well, I do have a headache," he said, somewhat embarrassed, "and that's why I'm leaving."

"But after dinner you said that your headache had gone."

"My God! What a memory you have! It's intolerable! Well, the fact is that I just want to go home."

"What's wrong with my place? What's so special at home?"

She looked him straight in the eye, shaking her head doubtfully. Somehow or other he managed to pacify her and left.

"What if I don't go to Yulia's today?" he asked himself when he woke up the next morning.

He paced back and forth three times in the room. "Right! I'm not going," he said resolutely.

"Yevsei! I want to get dressed," he called. And he left to walk around the city.

"What a pleasure, just to walk by myself," he thought, "to go wherever I like, to read the signboards, look in the shop windows, to go here and there… it's wonderful. That's it exactly – freedom, in the broadest, highest sense of the word – to walk just by oneself!"

He tapped the stick on the pavement as he walked and greeted his acquaintances cheerfully. As he walked along Morskaya Street, he saw a familiar face in the window of one of the houses. The owner of the face waved to him and invited him in. He looked in. "Well, if it isn't the Dumais Restaurant!"

He went in, dined and stayed there until the evening, when he left to go to the theatre. After the theatre, he went out to supper. He did his best to avoid thinking about going home; he knew what awaited him there.

And indeed, on returning home, he found some half a dozen messages waiting for him on the table and a sleepy servant in the hall, who had

CHAPTER 3

been given orders to wait until Alexander came in. The next day he had to make his excuses. He pleaded some business at the office. And things were more or less smoothed over.

About three days later, the same scenario was played out between the two of them – and was subsequently repeated over and over again. Yulia grew thinner, never went anywhere and received no visitors, but she held her peace, because Alexander did not take kindly to reproaches.

About two weeks later, after Alexander had arranged to fix a day for going out on the town with some friends, on that very morning he received a note from Yulia asking him to spend the whole day with her and to come a little earlier. She wrote that she was not feeling well and was feeling low, and her nerves were suffering, etc. He was annoyed, and went to tell her that he was too busy to stay with her.

"Yes, of course: dinner at Dumais, the theatre and tobogganing – very important business…" she said listlessly.

"What does that mean?" he asked, offended. "It looks as if you've been keeping me under surveillance! I won't stand for that."

He rose, intending to leave.

"Don't go! Listen to me!" she said. "We need to talk."

"I have no time."

"Just for one minute – sit down."

He sat reluctantly on the edge of a chair.

With folded arms, she scanned his face anxiously as if trying to read there the answer to the question she had not yet asked.

He was squirming with impatience as he sat.

"Be quick! I don't have the time!" he said curtly.

She sighed.

"Don't you love me any more?" she asked, with a little shake of her head.

"That old song!" he said, smoothing his hat with his sleeve.

"And how sick of it you must be!" she replied.

He stood up and began to pace the room rapidly.

After a minute, a sob escaped her.

"That's all I needed!" he snapped, almost savagely, as he stood facing her. "As if you haven't tormented me enough!"

"You mean, I've been tormenting *you*!" she exclaimed, sobbing even more bitterly.

"It's intolerable!" said Alexander, preparing to leave.

"No! I'll stop, I'll stop!" she said hurriedly, wiping away her tears. "There! I've stopped crying, so please don't go, and sit down."

She tried to smile, but could not staunch the flow of tears down her cheeks. Alexander started to feel sorry for her. He sat down and started swinging his leg back and forth. One question after another crowded into his mind, and he came to the conclusion that he had cooled off, and no longer loved Yulia. But why? God knows. She loved him more and more every day – could that be the reason? Good God, what a contradiction! All the conditions for happiness existed. There was nothing to prevent it; it wasn't even as if another feeling was competing with his love, but he had simply cooled off. How strange life was! But how to comfort Yulia? Sacrifice himself? Drag out endless days of tedium with her – put on an act? No, that would be beyond him; but not putting on an act would mean facing tears every moment of the day, reproaches – a torment for both of them... Could he suddenly introduce Uncle's theory of betrayal and the ebbing of love? The very idea! Even without that, she was in tears anyway – so what was left?

Yulia, seeing that he had lapsed into silence, took him by the hand and looked into his eyes. He turned slowly away and gently removed his hand. Not only did he feel no attraction to her, but a cold and unpleasant shiver ran through his body at her touch. She redoubled her caresses, but he failed to respond, and his attitude became colder and more morose. She suddenly pulled her hand away and exploded. Her feminine pride, her wounded self-esteem, her shame, all welled up. She raised her head, stood erect, and her face reddened from sheer outrage.

"Leave my house!" she ordered him abruptly.

He turned and left without a word of protest, but as the sound of his footsteps died away, she rushed after him.

"Alexander Fyodorych! Alexander Fyodorych!" she called out.

He turned round.

"Where are you going?"

"But you just told me to leave."

CHAPTER 3

"And you were only too happy to do so. Stop!"

"I have no time!"

She took him by the hand, and once again poured forth a torrent of loving, passionate speech, pleas and tears.

He could not find within himself a glance, a word or a gesture of sympathy. He stood there like a block of wood, shifting from one foot to another. His cool indifference enraged her. There were floods of threats and reproaches. Who would have recognized in her the meek, nervous woman that she was? Her hair was in disarray; her eyes burned with a feverish glitter; her cheeks were flaming; her features were strangely distorted. "How ugly she is!" thought Alexander, regarding her with visible distaste.

"I will have my revenge," she said. "Do you think that it's so easy to get away with toying with a woman's life? You wormed your way into my heart with flattery, pretence – you took total possession of me – and then abandoned me when I no longer had the power to dismiss you from my memory... No! I will never leave you alone: I will hunt you down wherever you may be. You will never get away from me. If you disappear into the countryside, I'll find you; if you go abroad, you'll find me there – anywhere you go, I'll always be there. I will not part from my happiness so easily. My life means nothing to me now... I have nothing left to lose, but I *will* poison your life. I will be avenged, I will be avenged – there must be another woman. No, it's not possible that you have left me just like that... I will find her – just wait and see what I will do: I'll make your life a misery! What a pleasure it will be for me to hear of your destruction... I could kill you myself!" she screamed, beside herself with rage and fury.

"How stupid this is! How absurd!" thought Alexander, shrugging his shoulders.

Seeing that Alexander remained indifferent to her threats, she abruptly changed her tone. She quietened down and regarded him sadly and silently.

"Have pity on me!" she said. "Don't leave me; what will I do now without you? I won't be able to stand parting with you! Understand that women love differently from men: their love is stronger and more tender.

For women love is everything, especially for me. Other women like to flirt; they enjoy being out and about in society; they like the noise and the action. I have never taken to that. My character is different. I love quiet, seclusion, books, music – but more than anything on earth, I love you…"

Alexander could not conceal his impatience.

"Very well, you don't love me," she continued spiritedly, "but keep your promise. Marry me, just be with me… you will have your freedom; do whatever you want, love whoever you want. All I ask is to be able to see you sometimes, however rarely. For the love of God, have pity on me, have pity on me!"

She burst into tears, and could not go on. Her passionate outburst had exhausted her, and she flopped onto the divan, closed her eyes, gritted her teeth, and her mouth was distorted from its convulsions – she was hysterical. It was an hour before she came to herself and recovered. Her chambermaid was attending to her. Yulia looked around. "But where is he?…" she asked.

"He left!"

"Left!" she repeated despairingly, and sat there for a long time in silence and without moving.

The next day, message after message was dispatched to Alexander. He did not come, and sent no reply. It was the same the next day and the day after. Yulia wrote to Pyotr Ivanych, asking him to call on her regarding an important matter. She did not care for his wife, because she was young and attractive, and was Alexander's aunt.

Pyotr Ivanych found her practically at death's door, so serious was her condition. He spent two hours with her, and then went to see Alexander.

"So this is the one who's putting on a great act, yes?"

"What do you mean?" said Alexander.

"Look at him! As if it's no concern of his! He's the one who can't make a woman fall in love with him, and here he is driving this woman crazy!"

"I don't understand, Uncle."

"What is there to understand? Of course you understand! I've just been to see Tafayeva, and she told me everything."

"What!" said Alexander in total disarray. "She told you everything!"

CHAPTER 3

"Everything. How much she loves you! Aren't you a lucky fellow! And here you were in tears because you couldn't inspire passion; well, here's passion for you. You should be gratified! She's out of her mind with jealousy and rage, and sobbing her heart out... but why are you involving me in your affairs? Now you've started lumbering me with your women – that was all I needed! I've just wasted a whole morning on her. I thought it was going to be some serious business, perhaps about mortgaging the estate through the Board of Guardians... she had once mentioned it... but this is what it turned out to be about – some business!"

"Why did you go to see her?"

"She invited me, and complained about you. You should really be ashamed of yourself. How can you be so callous? You haven't shown your face for four days. It's no joke! The poor thing is dying! So, get over there right away!..."

"What did you say to her?"

"The usual: that you love her madly, that you've long been searching for a loving heart, that you absolutely love 'heartfelt outpourings' and that you too cannot live without love; I told her that she has nothing to worry about, and that you will come back to her. I advised her not to keep you on too tight a rein, and let you have a little fun now and again... otherwise, I said, you will tire of each other. Well, you know, the kind of thing one says on these occasions. She cheered up enormously, and it slipped out that you were supposed to get married, and that even my wife had a hand in all this – but not a word to me; that's women for you! Anyway, thank God, she's not without means! So the two of you will manage. I told her that you will definitely keep your promise... I also put in a good word for you out of gratitude for the favour you did me... I assured her that you love her 'so passionately, so dearly'—"

Alexander's face fell, and he cut him off. "Why on earth did you do that, Uncle?" he said. "I... I don't love her any more! I don't want to get married! My feelings for her have turned ice-cold. I'd sooner throw myself into the river than—"

"Well, well!" said Pyotr Ivanych, feigning surprise. "I can't believe my ears! Wasn't it you who said – don't you remember? – that you despise human nature, especially women's – that there is no heart in this world worthy of you? And what else was it you said?... I wish I could recall..."

"For the love of God, Uncle, don't say another word; you've reproached me enough: I don't need another lecture from you. Do you really think I'm so incapable of understanding on my own? My God! People, people!"

He began to laugh out loud, and his uncle joined in.

"Now that's my boy," said Pyotr Ivanych. "I knew that one day you'd be able to laugh at yourself – and here you are!"

And they both burst out laughing again.

"So tell me," Pyotr Ivanych continued, "now what's your opinion of that... what's-her-name... Pashenka, is it?... with that wart."

"Uncle, that's not nice!"

"No, I just mentioned it to find out whether you still despise her."

"Leave it alone, for God's sake, and instead help me to get out of this awful situation. You're so clever, such a clear thinker..."

"Ah, so now it's compliments, flattery! No, just go and marry her!"

"Not on your life, Uncle! I'm begging you, help me!"

"Precisely, Alexander; it's a good thing. I've known for ages what you've been getting up to..."

"You mean you've known all along?"

"Exactly, I've known about your affair from the very beginning."

"I suppose it was my aunt who told you?"

"Certainly not! It was I who told her. It was easy. It was written all over your face. But don't be upset. I've already helped you."

"How? When?"

"Just this morning. Don't worry, Tafayeva won't be bothering you any more..."

"But how did you do it? What did you say to her?"

"It's a long story, Alexander, and a boring one."

"But God knows what damaging things you might have said to her. She must hate me, and despise me now..."

CHAPTER 3

"What difference does it make to you? I've pacified her – that should be enough for you. I told her that you were incapable of loving someone, and that you were not even worth bothering about…"

"So how is she now?"

"Now she's actually glad that you've left her."

"What do you mean, 'glad'?" Alexander enquired.

"Just that: 'glad'."

"You mean you didn't detect in her even a trace of regret, of disappointment? She was totally unmoved? That's beyond belief!"

He was disturbed, and started to pace back and forth in the room.

"Glad and unmoved!" he repeated. "I don't believe it. I'm going to see her right now."

"There's people for you!" Pyotr Ivanych remarked. "And so much for the heart; a wonderful thing to live by! Wasn't it you who were afraid that she would come after you? Wasn't it you who asked for help? And now you're worried that she may not be dying from her grief at losing you."

"Glad and content," said Alexander as he paced back and forth, paying no attention to his uncle. "So she didn't love me! No grief, no tears. No, I *will* go and see her."

Pyotr Ivanych shrugged his shoulders.

"I'm sorry, but I can't just leave it like that, Uncle," Alexander added as he picked up his hat.

"Well then, go back to see her, but if you don't succeed in disentangling yourself, don't come back and badger me; I'm not getting involved again. The only reason I intervened in the first place was because it was I who got you into that situation. So that's it. Now, why are you looking so down in the mouth?"

"I'm ashamed to be living in this world!…" said Alexander with a sigh.

"And to be completely idle." His uncle added. "Enough of that for now! Come to dinner with us later, and we'll have a good laugh about this whole episode, and then we'll take a ride to the factory."

"How worthless and insignificant I am!" said Alexander after a pause. "I have no heart. I'm despicable, morally destitute!"

"And all because of love!" Pyotr Ivanych said, cutting him off. "What a stupid way of spending your time! You should leave that kind of thing to the Surkovs of this world. But you are a capable fellow, and could make a more valuable contribution. So no more running after women!"

"But you love your wife, don't you?"

"Yes, of course, I've become quite accustomed to her, but that doesn't prevent me from doing my work, Anyway, goodbye for now, and we'll see you later."

Alexander sat there, confused and gloomy. Yevsei tiptoed in with his hand inside the boot he was carrying.

"Excuse me, sir, but would you mind taking a look at this?" he said deferentially. "This is great polish: it shines like a mirror, and it only costs twenty-five roubles."

Alexander roused himself and looked uncomprehendingly at the boot and then at Yevsei.

"Get out, you fool!" he said.

"Should I send it to our village?" Yevsei persisted.

"Get out! I'm telling you, get out!" Alexander shouted, almost in tears. "Stop badgering me, you'll send me to my grave with your boots!... You're a barbarian!"

Yevsei made a prompt exit into the hall.

Chapter 4

"WHY DOESN'T ALEXANDER come to see us?" Pyotr Ivanych asked his wife after returning home one day. "It's been three months since I've seen him."

"I've given up hope of ever seeing him," she replied.

"What can be the matter with him? Not in love again, is he?"

"I don't know."

"Is he well?"

"Yes, he is."

"Please write and tell him I need to speak to him. There are changes going on at his office. I can't understand his lack of concern."

"I've already written to invite him a dozen times and he just says he has no time, when all he's doing is playing draughts with some strange types or going fishing; why don't you go round to see him yourself and find out what's going on?"

"No, I don't want to. Send one of the servants instead."

"Alexander still won't come."

So they sent a servant, who returned very quickly. "Well, is he at home?" asked Pyotr Ivanych.

"Yes, sir. He sends his greetings."

"What is he doing?"

"Lying down on his divan."

"You mean at this hour of the day?"

"He's always lying there, you see."

"Well, is he sleeping?"

"Oh no, sir. I thought at first that the young gentleman was sleeping, but his eyes were open, and he was staring at the ceiling."

Pyotr Ivanych shrugged his shoulders.

"Will he be coming here?"

"Oh no, sir. 'Give them my greetings!' he says. 'And give my uncle my apologies, and say that I'm not feeling too well.' And he told me to give you his greetings, madam."

"What's wrong with him now? Really, it's surprising! What's he turning into? Tell them to keep the horses harnessed. I'll just have to go round there myself – but this is really the last time."

And Pyotr Ivanych did find him on the divan. When he saw his uncle come in, he sat up, but stayed sitting down.

"You're not well?" asked Pyotr Ivanych.

"So-so…" Alexander replied, yawning.

"What are you doing?"

"Nothing."

"You have no trouble just doing nothing?"

"No trouble at all."

"There's talk today that Ivanov is leaving your office."

"Yes, he is."

"Who's going to replace him?"

"Nichenko, they say."

"And what about you?"

"Me, no."

"What do mean, 'no'? Why not you?"

"They didn't offer me the position. What can I do? I suppose I'm not the right man for the job."

"Come now, Alexander, you should get busy and go and see the director!"

"No," said Alexander, shaking his head.

"It looks as if you don't care?"

"I don't."

"But this is the third time you've been passed over."

"Who cares? So what!"

"Well, we'll see what you say when your former subordinate starts giving you orders, and you have to stand up and bow when he comes in."

"I'll just stand up and bow."

"And what about your pride?"

"I don't have any."

"But you must have some interests in life?"

"None at all. I used to have, but not now."

CHAPTER 4

"Impossible: old interests are replaced by new ones. How come you give up your interests, but others don't? Aren't you a bit young for that? Why, you're not even thirty…"

Alexander shrugged.

Pyotr Ivanych no longer had any wish to prolong the conversation. He would have dismissed the whole thing as sheer childishness, but he knew that when he got home there would be no way of avoiding his wife's questions, so he continued in spite of himself.

"Why don't you find some way of amusing yourself, seek some company?" he said. "Or find something to read?"

"I don't feel like it, Uncle."

"People are beginning to talk about you – things like 'You know, you're mooning because you're in love, God knows what you're up to, or you've started hanging around with some strange types…' My own guess would be that last one."

"Let them say whatever they want."

"Listen Alexander, joking aside, none of this stuff is important; see people or avoid them, seek company or do without it – none of that matters; but remember: you, like anyone else, have to make a career of some kind. Don't you ever think about that?"

"What do you mean, 'think about it'? I've already done it."

"What do you mean?"

"I've already mapped out my sphere of activity, and I intend to stay within it. Right here, I am the master, and this is where my career is."

"Laziness, in other words."

"Perhaps."

"You have no right to lounge around while you have your strength. Have you done what you set out to do?"

"I'm doing it. No one can accuse me of idleness. In the morning, I work at the office – and to do any more than that would be sheer extravagance, superfluous effort. Why should I exert myself?"

"Everyone exerts themselves in one way or another: one person because he considers it his duty to do whatever his ability allows him to do; someone else does it for money; another one does it because he wants to be somebody… Why should you be the exception?"

"Ambition, money! Especially money! What for? I'm fed and clothed. That's all I need."

"And badly dressed too!" his uncle remarked. "And that's all that you consider necessities?"

"Yes, exactly."

"But what about the intellectual and the higher pleasures – art for instance?…" Pyotr Ivanych was starting to say, mimicking Alexander's tone. "You can move forward, your goal is loftier, your calling is a nobler one… Have you forgotten that you strive for nobler goals?"

"Forget all that!" said Alexander, clearly provoked. "That's pretty strange talk, coming from you, Uncle! Was that for my benefit? If so, you're wasting your time. Yes, I did aim higher – and what came of it?"

"What I do remember is that right away you wanted to become a minister, and later a writer. But when you saw that the path to that lofty calling was a long and arduous one, and that to be a writer you needed talent, you beat a retreat. A lot of young men like you come here with these fancy ideas, but cannot see that what they have to do is right under their noses. But the moment they have to write a report or something – well, what do you see? They're just not up to it. Of course, I'm not talking about you: you've proved that you can knuckle down to your work and make something of yourself in time. Of course that's tedious and means a lot of waiting. When we want everything right away and it doesn't happen, we're down in the dumps."

"But I don't want to aim any higher: I just want to stay where I am. Don't I have the right to choose my work – whether it measures up to my abilities or not? What does it matter, as long as I do my work conscientiously and responsibly? If I'm criticized because my abilities don't justify higher ambitions, that wouldn't hurt me a bit, if it were the truth. You've said yourself that there is poetry in the humblest of occupations, and here you are reproaching me for choosing precisely that. Who is going to prevent me from climbing down several rungs of the ladder and stop at the rung which suits me best? I'm not interested in any higher-level occupation – are you listening? I'm just not interested!"

"I heard you! I'm not deaf yet. It's just that everything you say is feeble sophistry."

CHAPTER 4

"I don't care. I've found my place, and I intend to stay in it. I've found some simple unsophisticated people, and it doesn't matter if they're intellectually limited; I play draughts and go fishing with them – and it's fine! Even if, as you see it, I'll be punished for it and will be giving up the glittering prizes, the money, the honours, the importance – all those things which appeal so much to you, I renounce them for ever…"

"Alexander, it pleases you to pretend that you're content and indifferent to all those things, but there's a hint of bitterness in your words – in fact on your lips they sound more like tears than words. There's a lot of bile inside you, but you don't know who to vent it on, because you are the only one to blame."

"So what?"

"What is it that you want? Everyone must want something."

"I want people to stop trying to force me out of the dark place I have chosen, a place where I don't have to bother about anything and where I can live in peace."

"You really call that living?"

"In my view, the life you live is not living, therefore I'm right too."

"What you want is to remake life to suit your own wishes – yes, I can see it. In that life of yours, lovers and friends stroll hand in hand amidst rose bushes…"

Alexander said nothing.

Pyotr Ivanych regarded him in silence. He had lost weight once again. His eyes were sunken. His cheeks and his forehead were beginning to show premature wrinkles.

His uncle was suddenly afraid. He didn't really believe there was such a thing as psychological suffering, but feared that under this desolation there lurked some incipient physical illness. "Maybe," he thought, "the boy is going out of his mind, and then I would have to deal with his mother – all that writing back and forth – and before you know it she would even turn up here."

"Yes, I can see that you are disillusioned," he said, thinking at the same time: "What if I could restore his cherished old ideas to him? Wait a minute! I'll put on an act…"

"Listen, Alexander!" he said. "Your morale is very low. You must shake off this apathy. It's doing you no good. And where does it come from? Perhaps you've taken too seriously to heart the things that I've thoughtlessly said to you from time to time about love and friendship. I wasn't entirely serious when I spoke, and was really doing it to cool your ardour, which seems somehow out of place in our more practical times, especially here in St Petersburg, where everything is levelled down, fashions as well as passions, practical matters as well as pleasures – everything is carefully modulated, weighed, pondered and assessed… Everything now has had recognized recognized limits imposed on it. Why should one person be so visibly out of step with all the rest of us? Do you think that I'm really so unfeeling that I don't recognize love? Love is a wonderful feeling: there is nothing more sacred than the union of two hearts – or friendship, for example. It is my inner conviction that a feeling must be permanent, everlasting…"

Alexander burst out laughing.

"What is it?" asked Pyotr Ivanych.

"What's all this crazy talk, Uncle? Why don't you send for a cigar? We could have a smoke; you'll keep on talking, and I'll sit and listen."

"What *is* the matter with you?"

"Why, nothing. So you've decided to make fun of me! And to think you were once thought to be an intelligent man! Toying with me, as if I were a plaything – it's offensive! What was the use of that school, which I've now left? All that pontificating you went in for! As if I didn't have eyes in my head. It was all just a party trick, and I saw right through it."

"I see I've made a hash of it," Pyotr Ivanych thought to himself. "Better let the wife handle it."

"Come and see us – my wife would particularly like to see you."

"I can't, Uncle."

"It's not very nice of you to forget her."

"Maybe even downright bad, but for God's sake forgive me, and don't expect me any time soon. Give me some time, and I'll come."

"Well, have it your way," said Pyotr Ivanych, and he waved goodbye and went home.

CHAPTER 4

He told his wife that he was giving up on Alexander, and was leaving him to his own devices. He, Pyotr Ivanych, had done everything he could, and was now washing his hands of him.

After breaking free from Yulia, Alexander had launched himself into a frenzy of pleasures, frequently quoting a well-known poet:

> Pour, pour a glass of sizzling wine!
> And let the quiet stream of oblivion
> For a time, staunch the cruel torment of my soul.
> Let's return to where joy breathes,
> Where seethes the joyful maelstrom of gaiety and noise,
> Where life is not lived, but life and youth is spent
> Amidst frolics and games at the table of pleasure,
> For an hour carried away by the illusion of happiness.
> I am steeped in empty dreams,
> Reconciled with fate by wine.
> I will assuage my troubled heart.
> I will not allow my thoughts to soar
> And will not let my eyes gaze
> Upon the soft radiance of the heavens.*

He fell in with a gang of friends and their constant companion – the bottle.

They saw their reflections first in the foaming liquid, and later in the glossy surface of their patent-leather boots. "Away with sorrow," they cried as they caroused, "away with woe! Let's spend, destroy, incinerate and carouse away our life and youth. Hurrah!" Glasses and bottles were hurled to the floor and shattered.

For a time, freedom, rowdiness and carefree living made him forget Yulia and his disenchantment, but the endless round of dinners and restaurants, the same old faces with their muddy eyes, the same old mindless, drunken gibberish of the same companions day after day – not to mention his still chronically upset stomach – no, he decided, this was not for him. Alexander's delicate physical and psychological constitution was predisposed to a state of melancholy and depression, and these constant high jinks proved too much for him.

He fled from the "frolics and games at the table of pleasure" and ended up back in his room alone with himself and his neglected books. But his book tumbled from his hands, and his pen remained resistant to inspiration. Schiller, Goethe, Byron revealed to him only the dark side of humanity – the bright side he failed to notice: he had no time for that.

But how happy he had been in that room at one time! Then he had not been alone; there was a beautiful invisible presence which kept him company and hovered over him by day as he sat diligently at his work and kept vigil at his bedside by night. His companions there were his dreams: the future was cloaked in fog, but it was not the oppressive kind which brought foul weather in its wake, but more of a morning mist which heralded a bright dawn. Behind that mist something was hidden... happiness, most likely. But now? The room itself, and indeed his whole world, was empty – except for cold, and the bitterness of regret.

As he contemplated his life, interrogating his heart and his head, he found to his horror that not a single dream, not a ray of hope remained in either place. All that was now behind him: the fog had cleared – before him stretched raw reality, as boundless as the steppe. Oh God, the sheer immensity of that space! What a grim and joyless prospect! The past had perished, the future had been destroyed, happiness did not exist. All that was left was a nightmare – yet life had to be lived!

What it was that he wanted, he himself had no idea. It was as if his head was shrouded in fog. He didn't sleep, but was drifting in some kind of oblivion. Oppressive thoughts crowded into his head.

What was there that could divert him? Enthralling hopes – there were none! Carefree respites – no! He could foresee everything that lay ahead. Esteem, striving for honours? What did that offer him? Was it worth spending twenty, thirty years butting his head against the ice like a fish? Did that prospect warm his heart? Does your soul rejoice when there are some who bow and scrape in your presence, all the time thinking, "To hell with him!"?

CHAPTER 4

Love? Oh, not that again! He knew it inside out – and anyway he had lost the ability to love. His memory obligingly – and however ironically – brought to mind Nadenka, but not the innocent, open-hearted Nadenka – his memory was not that obliging – but unfailingly Nadenka the deceiver, together with that whole setting: the trees, the path, the flowers – and in the middle of it all that snake in the grass, with that smile which had become so familiar, with its tint of rapture and its hue of shame – but for another, not for him. He clutched at his heart with a groan.

"Friendship," he thought, "another kind of folly! I've been through it all. There's nothing new, and the past cannot be recaptured; yet life goes on."

He no longer believed in anyone or anything, he could no longer lose himself in pleasure; he would get a taste of it, like someone who tastes a favourite dish, but without relish, knowing that it will only be followed by tedium, and that nothing can fill that inner void. Believe in feeling? It always lets you down, causes you emotional agitation and leaves you with more scars than before. Looking at people linked by love, carried away by sheer rapture, he would smile ironically and think: "Wait until you come to your senses – that first rapture will soon give way to jealousy, reconciliation and tears. Living together, you will end up bored to death with each other and part – the two of you in tears. You will come together again – worse still. You are crazy! You will fight all the time, there will be jealousy, followed by momentary reconciliation, followed in turn by even fiercer brawling; so much for their love, their devotion! Yet together, foaming at the mouth, sometimes with tears of despair in their eyes, they persist in calling it 'happiness'! And as for that friendship of yours... throw down a bone and watch your dogs fight over it."*

He was afraid of wanting things, knowing that at the very moment when what you wished for is in your grasp, fate will snatch it from you and present you with something quite different, which you have absolutely no desire for – something utterly worthless to you; and even if, finally, fate does give you what you want, it is only after it has tormented you, exhausted you and humiliated you in your own eyes that fate tosses it to you, like a scrap of food to a dog, after making it crawl to that tasty morsel, gaze at it, sniff at it, drag it into the dust and stand on its hind legs; only then, at its master's command, "Take!..."

He was daunted by the fact that in life happiness and unhappiness alternated like the ebb and flow of the tide. Joy of any kind was something he did not anticipate, but he did view suffering as inevitable – no way of avoiding it. All were subject to the same law and, as he saw it, were assigned their due share of happiness and unhappiness. His own share of happiness had been exhausted – happiness which happened to be fraudulent and illusory. Only suffering was real, and lay ahead. It might mean illness, old age, loss of various kinds, maybe even poverty. All these "blows of fate", as his aunt used to call them back in the village, lay in store for him, but what about delight? His lofty poetic aspirations had let him down – instead an onerous burden, known as duty, had been laid on him! What remained were only the most banal of benefits – money, creature comforts and promotions... Who cares about such things? But oh, how depressing it was to contemplate life, to understand what it was, but not to understand why it existed!

He continued to brood, and saw no escape from his flurry of doubts. His experiences had only crushed him, but to no good purpose, and had not made his life any healthier, had not cleared the air in it, and had not shed light on it. He didn't know what to do. He tossed from side to side on the divan and started reviewing the people he knew – which made him feel even worse. One was making an excellent career, had earned a great reputation as an able administrator and had become something of a public figure; another had acquired a family and chosen a quiet life in preference to all the banal prizes the world had to offer: he envied no one and coveted nothing; a third one... But why go on? They had all made their mark in one way or another and had settled down, and were following a path they had clearly marked out for themselves.

"I am the only one who... but what exactly am I?"

He started to interrogate himself; could he have become an administrator, a squadron commander? Could he have settled for a family life? And he realized that he would not have been content with the

CHAPTER 4

life of any of the three. There was some kind of imp stirring within him, constantly whispering that all that was beneath him, and that he should be aiming higher. But where and how, he could not fathom. He turned out to have been wrong about becoming a writer. "But what to do? Where to start?" he kept on asking himself, but didn't know what to answer. His exasperation kept on gnawing away at him. "Well, let's say, even being an administrator, or a squadron commander... But no, it's too late for that. Have to go back to square one."

Despair simply squeezed tears out of his eyes – tears of exasperation, envy, hostility towards everyone – the most painful of tears. He bitterly regretted not having listened to his mother and having bolted from his remote backwater in the country.

"Mummy sensed in her heart the pain that was in store for me in the future," he thought. If I had stayed there, these restless impulses would have slumbered, never to be awakened; there would have been none of the turmoil and ferment of that other busy and many-faceted life. At the same time, I would have been visited by all the human feelings and passions – self-esteem, pride and ambition, but on a smaller scale – and they would only have affected me within the limited confines of our remote district – and would all have been easier to consummate. Number one in the district! Yes, everything is relative. If I had stayed, that divine spark of heavenly fire which burns in varying degrees in all of us would have flashed in me unnoticed and would have been swiftly snuffed out in that uneventful style of life, or would have been ignited by my attachment to my wife and children. My existence would not have been poisoned. I would have performed proudly the role assigned to me, and my path in life would have been a quiet one, seemingly simple and easy to understand: it would have been a life well within my powers, and I would have been equal to all its struggles. And love? It would have flowered into a full-blown blossom and filled my whole life. Sofia would have loved me in a quiet way. I would have lost faith in nothing, and plucked only roses, without ever encountering thorns. I would never even have felt any jealousy – if only for lack of competition. What was it, then, which drew me so powerfully and blindly into the far distance, into a fog, and into an unknown and unequal struggle with fate? And how wonderfully I understood both life and people then! And that's how wonderfully I would have understood them today, without really understanding anything. Then, I expected so much from life, without ever having taken a close look at it, and would still be there expecting something more to this very day. How many treasures I had discovered within me – and what has become of them? I have squandered them all over the place. I parted with my open-hearted sincerity, my first precious passion – in return for what? Bitter disillusionment; I learnt that everything is a sham, nothing endures, and that nothing and no one can be relied on – neither myself, nor others – and I grew wary of others and myself. In the grip of this negative world view, I was unable to appreciate the smaller things of life, and be content with them, like my uncle and others like him… And now!…"

Now, there was only one thing he wanted: to forget the past, to recover his peace of mind, to rest his soul. He distanced himself from life more and more, and observed it through sleepy eyes. In crowds, at noisy gatherings, he found only boredom, and fled from them, but the boredom followed him. He marvelled at the way people could enjoy themselves, constantly busy themselves with one thing or another, and every day find new interests to entertain them. It seemed strange to him that people weren't sleepwalking or crying the way he was, and that they preferred to chatter about the weather instead of how badly they felt and their sufferings – and even if they did, it would be about how badly their legs or some other part of their body felt – rheumatism, haemorrhoids and the like. It was only their bodies which could worry them, but never a word about what was troubling them in their minds and hearts! "What insignificant, empty creatures people are, more like animals!" he thought. Yet sometimes he would fall to thinking deeply along these disturbing lines: "There are so many of them, these insignificant people, and I am just one person – can it really be that… all of *them* are the empty ones… that *they* are wrong… and I?…"

At these times, it would occur to him that he alone might be in the wrong, and this thought would make him even more miserable.

He stopped seeing his old friends, and whenever a new person came anywhere near him he felt chilled to his marrow. After his

CHAPTER 4

conversation with his uncle, he sank even deeper into his apathetic stupor; it was as if his very soul had gone into hibernation. He was immured in a stony-faced indifference, and lived a life of total indolence, studiously distancing himself from anything that might remind him of civilization.

"It doesn't matter how you spend your life, so long as you live," he would say. "Everyone is free to understand life any way he wants; and then, when you die…"

He would seek the company of the embittered, the malevolent and malcontent, to unburden himself to them, and to hear them jeer at fate; or he would frequent his intellectual and social inferiors, mostly in the person of old Kostyakov, whom Zayezzhalov had wanted to introduce to Pyotr Ivanych.

Kostyakov lived in Peski and walked about in his street in a shiny leather hat and a dressing gown, using a handkerchief as a belt. He had a woman who cooked for him living in his flat, with whom he played cards in the evenings. Whenever a fire broke out he was the first on the scene and the last to leave. Whenever he passed a church where a funeral service was being held, he would elbow his way through the crowd to look at the face of the deceased and accompany the hearse all the way to the cemetery. Indeed, he was fascinated by ceremonies of every kind, both festive and solemn. He loved being an eyewitness to untoward events of every kind, like fights, accidental deaths, collapse of ceilings, etc., and took special pleasure in reading accounts of such happenings in the newspapers. In addition, he read medical textbooks, as he put it, "in order to find out what people had inside them". In the winter Alexander would play draughts with him, and go fishing in the country with him in the summer. The old man could converse on a range of subjects. When they were out in the country, he would talk about grain and other crops; by the river it would be about fish or shipping; in the street, he would comment on the houses, on building, materials and prices… but he never had anything to say about abstractions. He viewed life as a good thing when there was money, and vice versa. Someone of this kind posed no threat to Alexander, and was incapable of ruffling his feelings.

Alexander strove zealously to mortify everything spiritual or emotional in his make up, just as hermits make a practice of mortifying their flesh. In the office, he was taciturn, and when he ran into people he knew, he fobbed them off with just a couple of words with the excuse that he was in a hurry and took off. But his friend Kostyakov he saw every day. Either the old man would spend that day at Alexander's place or he would invite Aduyev home for cabbage soup. He had already taught Alexander how to brew his own liqueur, how to make hotpot and cook tripe. Then they would go somewhere in the neighbouring countryside not too far from the city. Wherever they went they would meet a lot of people Kostyakov knew. With the menfolk he would chat about everyday matters, and he would joke with the women – just like the clown he had been described as being by Zayezzhalov when he had offered to introduce him. Alexander was happy to let him do most of the talking, while he himself remained mainly silent.

He had already begun to feel that the ideas of the world he had abandoned now rarely visited him and revolved more slowly in his head – and, finding nothing in the vicinity to echo or resist them, never made it as far as his tongue and simply withered away without blossoming. His heart had grown wild and empty, like an overgrown garden which has been abandoned. He was within an ace of becoming totally fossilized, and in just a few more months… it would have been "goodbye!" But this is what happened.

Once Alexander and Kostyakov were out fishing. Kostyakov was wearing a long coat and a peaked cap, and had set up a number of rods of varying lengths on the bank of the river, and also ledger lines, with floats and bells of different sizes. He was smoking a short pipe and, without daring to blink, was keeping a close eye on the small regiment of rods and lines, including Aduyev's, because Alexander was leaning up against a tree, looking in the other direction. They had been standing there in silence for some time.

"Did you get a bite? Take a look, Alexander Fyodorych," Kostyakov whispered to him.

Alexander looked into the water, and turned back to Kostyakov, saying, "No, it was just a ripple that you saw."

CHAPTER 4

"No, look, look!" Kostyakov shouted. "Good God! It's a bite, yes, a bite! Come on, pull, pull! Don't let go!"

And indeed the float had disappeared underwater, pulling the line after it and dragging the rod from where it was planted among the bushes. Alexander grabbed the rod, and then the line.

"Easy, easy! Don't pull so hard!... What are you doing? Not like that!" Kostyakov shouted, promptly taking hold of the line.

"Goodness! What a weight! Don't jerk it! Just ease it in or you'll break the line. Like this; left and right, left and right, and bring it in to the bank! Step back! A little more! Now, pull, but don't tug – like this, like this!..."

A huge pike surfaced. It quickly coiled itself into a ring, its silvery scales sparkling, and lashed its tail back and forth, splashing both of them. Kostyakov turned pale.

"What a pike!" he shouted, awestruck, and stretched his arms out into the water. Stumbling over his rod, he caught hold of the pike with both hands as it twisted and turned out of the water. "Look! It's squirming like the devil! Wow! What a specimen!"

"Wow, indeed!" someone repeated behind him.

Alexander turned round. Standing two steps away stood an old man with a pretty young girl on his arm. She was tall, her head was uncovered and she carried a small umbrella. She was frowning slightly, and bending slightly forward, following intently Kostyakov's every movement, without even noticing Alexander.

Aduyev was startled by this sudden arrival, and let go of the rod. The pike dropped back into the water with a thud and, swinging its tail gracefully from side to side, hurtled deeper into the water, trailing the line in its wake. All this happened in a split second.

"Alexander Fyodorych! How could you?" Kostyakov shouted in a fury, and seized the line and pulled it back in, but was left holding the severed end of it – minus the hook and the pike.

All pale, he turned to Alexander, showing him the end of the line, and looked daggers at him for a minute in silence, and then spat.

"I'm never going fishing with you again, come hell or high water!" he snapped, and went off to his rods.

Meanwhile the young girl had noticed that Alexander was looking at her, and she blushed and stepped back. The old man, apparently her father, bowed to Aduyev, who bowed sullenly in response, threw down his rod and sat down about a dozen steps farther away.

"More trouble in the offing!" he thought. "Oedipus and Antigone,* all over again! Another woman! My God! They're everywhere – no getting away from them!"

"Some fisherman you are!" Kostyakov was saying, putting away his rods and giving Alexander a baleful look every now and then. "You, go fishing? You'd be better off sitting at home on your divan, trying to catch mice, but fishing? Forget it! How can you catch fish, when you let them slip through your hands? It was practically ready for us to eat, almost cooking on the stove! It would have been a miracle if you hadn't let it slip off your plate!"

"Are they biting?" asked the old man.

"Well, you see," Kostyakov replied, "here I had six rods going, and didn't even get a pitiful tickle from a lousy little ruff, but meanwhile over there – not surprising if it had been the ground line – but the one with the float – what a piece of luck! A pike weighing about ten pounds, and then he let it get away. People say 'the hunter makes his own luck'! Not in my book! Why, if it had tried to get away from me, I would have grappled with it in the water – as it was, the pike practically gave itself up, but we're asleep – and people like that call themselves fishermen! Is that what fishermen are like? Not on your life! A real fisherman, even if someone fires a cannon right next to him, doesn't even blink. That's a real fisherman for you! And *you* think you're going to catch fish!"

Meanwhile the girl could see that Alexander was in every respect a totally different kind of man from Kostyakov. He was dressed differently: his build, his age, his manner and everything else was different. She could tell that he had been well educated: there was a thoughtfulness about his face, a thoughtfulness with a trace of sadness about it.

"But why did he make off?" she wondered. "It's strange, I don't think there's anything about me to make people avoid me…"

CHAPTER 4

The girl stood erect proudly, lowered her eyelashes, and then raised them again, and gave Alexander an unfriendly look.

She was feeling annoyed. She took her father and walked haughtily past Alexander.

Her father bowed once again to Alexander, but the daughter did not even favour him with a glance.

"Let him know that we haven't the slightest interest in him!" she thought, stealing a covert glance at him.

Alexander, although he didn't actually look at her, couldn't help trying to look a little more attractive.

"How dare he! He doesn't even look back!" thought the girl. "The gall of him!"

But the very next day Kostyakov took Alexander fishing again, and thus found himself eating his own words.

For two days they kept their distance from each other. At first, Alexander would look around apprehensively, but when he saw no one near him, he relaxed. On the third day, he pulled out a huge perch, and Kostyakov grudgingly broke the silence.

"Yes, but it's still not a pike!" he said with a sigh. "Good luck came your way, but you let it slip through your hands; you won't get a second chance. And I still haven't got a bite. Six rods, and nothing."

"Why don't you ring those little bells?" said a peasant who had stopped on his way past to see how the fishing was going. "Maybe the fish will be attracted – you know – by what they think are church bells ringing?"

Kostyakov gave him a baleful look. "Shut up, you ignorant peasant!" he said.

The peasant moved off.

"You blockhead!" Kostyakov shouted after him. "What else can you expect from brutes like that! Go and jeer at one of your own kind – what a nerve!"

God help anyone who bothers a hunter just when he's not catching anything!

On the third day, while they were fishing in silence and watching the water intently, something rustled behind them. Alexander turned round and winced as if he had been bitten by a gnat. He saw the old man and the girl standing there. Alexander eyed them warily, barely responding to the old man's bow, although he had been expecting this visit. Normally he went fishing dressed very casually, but this time he had put on a new overcoat and tied a blue scarf around his neck. He had combed his hair and even curled it a little, and was looking altogether like a fisherman out of an idyll. After waiting for just the length of time required by politeness, he went off and sat under a tree.

"*Cela passe toute permission!*"* thought Antigone. She was furious.

"I'm sorry!" said Oedipus to Alexander. "Perhaps we're in your way?"

"No," said Alexander. "It's just that I'm tired."

"Any bites?" the old man asked Kostyakov.

"How can you expect to get a bite, when people are standing and talking right at your elbow?!" he replied truculently. "Some blighter walked right past me, blurted out something and brought me bad luck – and of course, hardly a bite since then. So I assume you must live somewhere around here?" he asked Oedipus.

"That's our dacha, just over there, with the balcony," he replied.

"Is it expensive, if you don't mind my asking?"

"Five hundred roubles for the summer."

"It looks like a good one, well appointed, and lots of buildings in the courtyard. It probably cost the owner 30,000."

"Yes, about that."

"Right; and this is your daughter?"

"She is."

"Lovely young lady! You're out for a walk?"

"Yes, we are; if you're living in a dacha, you go walking."

"Of course, naturally, you have to; the weather is good right now, not like it was last week – awful weather! God spare us! I expect it ruined the winter crop."

"It will recover, God willing."

"Let's hope so!"

"So you're not catching anything right now?"

"Not me; but take a look at what he's caught!" he pointed to the perch. "I have to tell you," he went on, "you won't believe his luck! It's

CHAPTER 4

too bad his mind isn't on it, otherwise we would never leave empty-handed. Imagine letting a pike like that get away!"

He sighed.

Antigone began to prick up her ears, but Kostyakov fell silent.

The old man and his daughter began to appear more and more regularly, and Aduyev favoured them with his attention. From time to time he even exchanged a word or two with the old man, but never a word with his daughter. At first she found it annoying, then she resented it, and finally it began to upset her. Now, if Aduyev had paid her some normal, polite attention, she would have forgotten about him – but, as it was, it had the opposite effect. It would seem that the human heart is nothing if not perverse; if it weren't for this, there would be no need for us to have hearts at all.

Antigone at first started contemplating some terrible plan of revenge, but as time went by she gradually abandoned it.

Once, when the old man and his daughter came by, Alexander after a while stood his rod up against a bush and went to sit in his usual place, listlessly regarding the father and daughter in turn. They were standing sideways on to him. He didn't notice anything special about the father – a white smock, nankeen trousers and a hat with a low crown and a wide brim lined with green plush. But when it came to the daughter on the other hand – how gracefully she leant on her father's arm! From time to time, the wind lifted her hair from her face, as if deliberately trying to display to Alexander the beauty of her profile and her white neck, slightly raised her silken mantilla to reveal her slender waist, or swirled around the hem of her dress to show off her little feet. She was simply gazing at the water.

For a long time Alexander couldn't take his eyes off her, and felt a feverish shiver running through his body. He turned away from the source of the temptation and began to slash the heads off flowers with a switch.

"Oh, I understand what's happening!" he thought. "If I gave way to my feelings, love would be there for the taking. That would be stupid! Uncle is right. But I won't be driven by sheer animal feeling alone: no, I haven't sunk that low."

"Could I try my hand at fishing?" the girl asked Kostyakov timidly.

"Yes, young lady, why not?" Kostyakov replied, handing her Aduyev's rod.

"Now there's a partner for you!" said her father to Kostyakov, leaving his daughter and starting to stroll along the bank of the river. As he left, he added, "Liza, don't forget to catch some fish for supper!"

For several minutes, there was silence.

"Why is your friend so down in the mouth?" Liza asked Kostyakov quietly.

"He's been passed over for promotion three times."

"What?" she asked, wrinkling her brow.

"It's the third time, apparently, that he didn't get his promotion."

She shook her head.

"No, can't be!" she thought. "That's not it!"

"Don't you believe me, young lady? I swear on my life! Do you remember that pike? That's why he let it slip through his fingers."

"Look!" she cried out in her excitement. "It's moving, it's moving!"

She gave a tug, but she had caught nothing.

"It broke away!" said Kostyakov, looking at the rod. "Didn't you see it snatch the worm? Must have been a big pike. But you haven't got the knack, young lady: you didn't let it get a good bite."

"You mean, you need skill even for this?"

"Just like in anything," he said, offering his stock response.

She was excited and turned round in a hurry, dropping her rod in the water in the process. But Alexander was already looking in the other direction.

"But what do you have to do to get the skill?"

"You need to get more practice," replied Kostyakov.

"Oh, so that's it!" she thought, as pleased as punch. "That means, I need to come here more often – I understand! Very well, I will, but I will be tormenting you, Mister boor, in return for all your rudeness."

Thus it was coquetry which conveyed Alexander's answer to her, even though on that day he didn't actually say one word more to her.

"God knows what on earth she'll be thinking!" he said to himself. "She'll be putting on airs, and putting on an act of some kind... so stupid!"

CHAPTER 4

From that day on, the old man and his daughter started coming every day. Sometimes Liza would come without her father, but with her nanny. She would bring some work with her, and some books, and sit under a tree, ostensibly quite indifferent to Alexander's presence.

Her idea was to hurt his pride – or, as she would put it, to "torment him". She would chat audibly with her nanny about household matters in order to give the impression that she didn't even see Aduyev. But he in actual fact didn't see her – or, if he did, would bow curtly, without a word. When she saw that this tactic was getting her nowhere, she changed her plan of attack, and a couple of times actually started a conversation with him; sometimes even borrowing his rod. Little by little Alexander started to be a little more talkative, but was careful not to say anything indiscreet. Whether this was a stratagem on his part, or whether, as he would put it, "nothing had healed his old wounds", the fact remained that he treated her and spoke to her without any warmth.

One day, the old man ordered a samovar to be brought to the riverbank. Liza was pouring tea. Alexander stubbornly refused the tea, saying that he did not drink tea in the evening.

What he was thinking to himself was, "This whole business of tea-drinking brings people closer and helps them to get to know each other – I won't do it!"

"What are you talking about? Why, only yesterday you drank four glasses!" said Kostyakov.

"No, it's in the open air that I don't drink tea," Alexander hastened to add.

"Rubbish!" said Kostyakov. "This tea is great, top quality – must have cost fifteen roubles. Pour me a little more, young lady – and a little rum wouldn't hurt!"

So rum was brought.

The old man invited Alexander home, but he flatly refused. Hearing him refuse, Liza pouted and demanded to know his reason for being so unsociable. But no matter how skilfully she steered the conversation round to this subject, Alexander even more skilfully dodged it.

This mysteriousness only excited Liza's curiosity, and perhaps even another feeling. Her face, which had previously been as clear as a summer sky, began to cloud over with concern and look troubled. Often she would look at Alexander with sadness in her eyes, and then lower them and look at the ground, as if she were thinking, "You must be unhappy! Perhaps you've been jilted… Oh, how happy I could make you! How well I would care for you… love you! I would protect you from fate itself, I would!…" and so on and so forth.

This is how most women think, just as most women deceive those who are taken in by this siren's song. Alexander appeared to notice none of this. He would talk to her as if he were talking to one of his friends, or his uncle, without that trace of affection which inevitably creeps into any friendship between a man and a woman, which makes the relationship between them something akin to friendship. That is why people say that friendship between a man and a woman is impossible, and that which is described as "friendship" is nothing more or less than either the beginning of love or the remains of it – or, indeed, ultimately love itself. But anyone observing the way Aduyev and Liza treated each other might have believed that this kind of friendship does in fact exist.

Only once did he show any sign of even partly opening up to her. He picked up from the bench a book which she had brought him, and leafed through it. It was *Childe Harold** in the French translation. Alexander shook his head, sighed and silently put the book down again.

"You don't like Byron? You have something against him?" she asked. "Byron is such a great poet – and you don't like him?"

"I haven't said a thing, and here you are attacking me," he replied.

"Why were you shaking your head like that?"

"Oh, just that it's a pity that book fell into your hands."

"Were you feeling sorry for the book or for me?"

Alexander remained silent.

"Why shouldn't I read Byron?"

"For two reasons," said Alexander after a moment's silence. He put his hand on hers in order to make his point more forcibly – or maybe because her hand was so white and soft, and began to speak

CHAPTER 4

softly and unhurriedly, running his eyes over her hair, her neck and her waist in turn. The longer he went on doing this, the louder became his voice.

"Firstly," he said, because you are reading Byron in French, and thus losing the beauty and power of the poet's voice. Just take a look at this pale, flat, insipid language. That's just the ashes of the great poet: it's as if his ideas have been watered down. And the second reason is that I wouldn't recommend that you read Byron because... well, he may set off vibrations within you which may never have been stirred otherwise."

At this point, he squeezed her hand firmly and expressively, as if by doing so he would lend weight to his words.

"But why should you read Byron anyway?" he continued. "Perhaps your life will flow along as gently as this stream; you see how small and shallow it is – too small to reflect the whole sky or the clouds; there are no cliffs around, no crags; it burbles merrily along – and barely a ripple ruffles its surface now and then. All it reflects is the foliage lining the banks, a patch of the sky and a cloud here and there... and this, most likely, is the course your life would take – but you go out of your way to court unnecessary trouble and turbulence; you prefer to look at life through a glass darkly... Leave it alone, don't read this kind of thing! Look at everything with a smile, don't look too far ahead, live for the day, don't seek to discover the dark side of life and people – otherwise!..."

"Otherwise, what?"

"Nothing!" said Alexander, appearing to recollect himself.

"No, tell me, you've been through some kind of experience, haven't you?"

"Where's my rod? I'm sorry, I have to go."

He looked a little put out at having expressed himself incautiously.

"No; one more thing," Liza put in. "I mean, a poet must try to elicit the reader's sympathy. Byron is a great poet: why are you against my sympathizing with him? Am I really so stupid, so shallow that I can't understand?..."

She was offended.

"Not exactly; sympathize with what's natural in your woman's heart; look for what's in harmony with it, otherwise there will be a frightful dissonance... both in your head and in your heart."

He shook his head, the gesture suggesting that he himself was a victim of this dissonance.

"One person will show you a flower," he went on to say, "and make you enjoy its fragrance and beauty; another person will only point out the poisonous pith in its chalice... and that flower will lose all its fragrance and beauty for you. He will make you feel sorry that that pith is there, and you will forget about the fragrance that is also present. There is a difference between those two people and the kinds of sympathy they will arouse in you. Don't look for the poison, don't try to dig for the root of everything that happens to us and around us, and don't try to acquire unnecessary experience – that is not what will make you happy."

He said nothing more. She had listened to him attentively and trustingly.

"Please go on, please go on," she said like a child in a classroom. "I could listen to you for days on end and comply with everything you say..."

"Me?" said Alexander without warmth. "Come now! What right do I have to influence you? I'm sorry I said what I said. Read whatever you choose... *Childe Harold* is a very good book, and Byron is a great poet!"

"No, stop pretending! Don't talk like that. Tell me, what should I read?"

He started recommending to her in a sententious and didactic manner various works of history and travel, but she said that she had had enough of all that in school. So then he proposed Walter Scott, Cooper* and some French and English writers, male and female, as well as two or three Russian authors, attempting in this way to display – quite incidentally, of course – his literary taste and refinement. That was their last conversation of that kind.

Alexander was anxious to escape. "What are women to me?" he thought to himself. "I'm incapable of love, I've put all that behind me."

CHAPTER 4

"That's all very well!" said Kostyakov. "But you'll find yourself getting married anyway, you'll see. In my time all I wanted to do was to play around with the young girls and even the older ones, but when the time came for walking up the aisle, I felt as if a stake was being driven into my head; like someone was frogmarching me to the altar!"

But Alexander didn't make good his escape. He felt his former dreams beginning to stir within him. His heart began to beat at a faster rate. He could not shake off the visions of Liza's waist, her small foot and her tresses, and life became a little brighter. For the last three days, it had not been Kostyakov who had invited him to go fishing, but it was he who had dragged Kostyakov there. "It's beginning all over again," Alexander said to himself, "but I'm resolved!" – and meanwhile hurried down to the river.

Every day, Liza waited impatiently for the arrival of the two friends, and every evening a cup of fragrant tea with rum was poured for Kostyakov. And it was to this stratagem that Liza at least partly owed the fact that the two friends never missed a single evening. When they were late, Liza and her father would walk part of the way to meet them. When bad weather kept the two friends at home, the next day they, as well as the weather, came in for endless recriminations.

Alexander thought and thought, and made up his mind to suspend these outings for a while for God knows what reason – he certainly didn't know himself – and didn't go fishing for a whole week; and nor did Kostyakov. Finally they started going again.

About a mile before they reached the spot, they met Liza and her nanny. The moment she spotted them, an involuntary scream escaped her, and her face turned red with embarrassment. Alexander bowed stiffly, but Kostyakov started in right away.

"Here we are, and I bet you didn't expect us," he said. "Yes," he said with a laugh, "I can see you weren't expecting us – there's no samovar! It's quite a while since we met last! Is anything biting? I was always wanting to come, but couldn't persuade Alexander Fyodorych; all he wanted to do was to sit at home – or should I say 'lie down'?"

She gave Aduyev a reproachful look.

"What does this mean?" she asked.

"What does what mean?"

"You didn't come for a whole week?"

"Yes, I believe it was a whole week."

"Why not?"

"No reason, I just didn't feel like it."

"Didn't feel like it!" she said in surprise.

"Yes, and what about it?"

She remained silent, but it seemed that she was thinking, "Can you really not have felt like coming?"

"I wanted to send Daddy into town to see you," she said, "but I didn't know where you lived."

"Into town – to see me? Why?"

"What kind of question is that?" she said indignantly. "Why? To find out what had happened to you; whether you were ill or something."

"But what's it to you?"

"What's it to me, my God!"

"Why 'my God'?"

"What do you mean, 'why'?... Well, I mean, I have your books..." She was at a loss for words. "Not to come for a whole week!" she finally added.

"You mean, I'm supposed to come here every day, no matter what?"

"Yes, no matter what!"

"But why?"

"Why! Why!" She looked at him mournfully, repeating the words "Why! Why!"

He looked at her. What was all this? Tears, consternation, joy and reproaches? She was pale, a little thinner, her eyes reddened.

"So that's it! And so soon!" thought Alexander. "I didn't expect it so soon!" Then he laughed out loud.

"Why? You ask. Listen!" she said. "Tomorrow I must talk to you; I can't today." Her eyes flashed with a kind of determination. Apparently she was preparing to say something important, but at that moment her father came up to them.

"Until tomorrow," she said. "Tomorrow, I must talk to you; my heart is too full right now... You will come tomorrow? Do you hear?

CHAPTER 4

You won't forget us? You won't drop us?..." And she ran off without waiting for an answer.

Her father gave Aduyev, and then his daughter, a searching look and shook his head. Alexander watched her departing figure. What he felt was a kind of mixture of regret and anger with himself for inadvertently putting her in such a position; the blood rushed not to his heart, but to his head.

"She loves me," he said to himself on his way home. "My God! How tiresome! How absurd! Now I can't even go there – and it's the place with the best fishing... so annoying!"

Meanwhile, deep down, it seemed, he wasn't really as dissatisfied as all that with the situation, and he cheered up and chatted with Kostyakov all the way home.

His imagination obligingly, and as if deliberately, painted for him a full-length portrait of Liza with her generous shoulders and her slim waist – not to mention her small foot. A strange sensation stirred within him, a shudder once again ran through his body, but fizzled out before reaching his heart. He analysed the sensation through and through.

"You have to be an animal," he muttered to himself, "for a thought like that to enter your mind... Oh! those bare shoulders, that bust, that... small foot... to take advantage of her trust, her inexperience... to betray that trust, yes, to betray, and then what? The same boredom, not to mention pangs of conscience – and what for? No, no, I won't let myself, I won't do it to her... I'm strong enough! I feel I have enough strength of character, enough honour within me... I will not fall so low... I will not seduce her."

Liza waited for him all day with a thrill of pleasurable anticipation, but after a while her heart fell, her confidence ebbed: she felt miserable, without understanding the reason, and almost stopped hoping that Alexander would come. But when Alexander had not arrived by the time they had arranged to meet, her impatience gave way to a feeling of unbearable despair, and with the last ray of sunshine, all hope disappeared. She burst into tears, sobbing bitterly.

The next day, she came to herself, and was cheerful the whole morning, but towards evening her heart began to ache even more, torn between hope and fear. Again no one came.

It was the same on the third and fourth days. But hope still drew her to the riverbank. It took only a boat to appear in the distance or for a couple of human shadows to dart briefly along the riverbank for her to be stirred into a state of joyous anticipation, only to end up depleted by the burden of tension. But when she saw that it was not them in the boat, and that the shadows were not theirs, her head would fall in bitter disappointment onto her breast, and the weight of her despair would grow even heavier. But only a minute later, a sneaking hope would whisper to her a specious but comforting excuse for their delay, and once again her heart would start beating with anticipation. But Alexander was taking his time, deliberately so, it seemed.

Finally, at a certain moment when, sitting under a tree and sick with anxiety, she had totally given up hope, she suddenly heard a rustling sound; she turned round and, shivering with fearful joy, found Alexander standing before her with his arms folded.

Her eyes brimming with tears of joy, she stretched out her hands helplessly towards him. He took her hand and, also in the grip of strong emotion, devoured her face greedily with his eyes.

"You've grown thinner!" he said quietly. "Are you ill?"

She shuddered.

"You've been away for so long," she said.

"Have you been waiting for me?"

"Have I?" she said with renewed vigour. "If only you knew!" And tightened her grip on his hands.

"I came to say goodbye to you!" he said, and stood there, watching to see how she would react.

She looked at him in fear and disbelief.

"It can't be true," she said.

"It's true!" he replied.

"Listen to me!" she began suddenly, looking nervously around her. "Don't leave, for the love of God, don't leave! I'm going to tell you a

CHAPTER 4

secret... Daddy can see us here from the windows – come with me to our summer house in the garden... it faces the fields, I'll take you there."

They started walking. Alexander could not take his eyes off her shoulders and her slim waist, and began to feel that feverish shiver again.

"What can be so important?" he wondered as he followed her. "After all, I was just... Anyway, I might just as well take a look and see what it's like there – that summer house... her father did invite me, so I could have gone quite legitimately and openly... But I'm no seducer, I swear, anything but, and I'll prove it. After all, I came here precisely to tell her that I was going... although I'm not actually going anywhere! Get thee behind me, Satan!" It was just as if the imp from Krylov's fable had suddenly appeared from behind the stove* and whispered to him, "But why did you have to come here to tell her that? There was absolutely no need. You could just as well have stayed at home, and in a couple of weeks she would have forgotten all about you..."

But to Alexander it seemed that he was acting nobly by appearing on the actual scene of his heroic act of self-abnegation to fight with temptation face to face.

His first trophy from this victory of his better self was the kiss he stole from Liza, and then putting his arms around her waist and saying that he would never leave her, and that he had just made that up in order to test her, and to find out if she had any feeling for him. Finally, to complete his victory, he promised to return the next day to meet her at the same time in the summer house. On his way home, he started thinking about what he had done, and turned hot and cold by turns. He was horrified and could hardly believe himself, and made up his mind not to return the next day – and turned up earlier than had been agreed.

That was in August. It was already getting dark. Alexander had promised to be there at nine o'clock, but arrived at eight, alone and without his fishing rod. He made his way furtively, like a thief, glancing around nervously, and then breaking into a sprint. But someone had beaten him to it and was sitting on the divan in a dark corner, out of breath from hurrying. Alexander had been ambushed. He opened the door quietly, with his heart in his mouth, and tiptoed his way to the divan, and silently reached for the hand – of Liza's father. Startled, he jumped up and made for the door, but the old man grabbed him by the hem of his coat, and pulled him down onto the divan beside him.

"What are you doing here, young fellow?" he asked.

"I was... er... going fishing," Alexander mumbled, hardly able to move his lips. His teeth were chattering. There was nothing at all fearsome about the old man, but Alexander, like any thief caught red-handed, was shivering feverishly.

"Fishing!" the old man repeated derisively. "Do you know what 'fishing in troubled waters' means? I've been watching you for some time now, and have finally got to know you for what you are; Liza, of course, I've known since she was in her cradle, a good girl and trusting, while you are nothing but a dangerous rogue..."

Alexander attempted to stand up, but the old man held him by the arm.

"Now, young fellow, no need to get angry! You pretended you were unhappy and made a pretence of avoiding Liza, but you led her on, made her trust you just in order to take advantage of her... are you proud of that? What would you call that kind of behaviour?"

"I swear on my honour that I did not foresee the consequences," said Alexander in a tone of deep conviction. "I had no intention of..."

The old man was silent for a few moments.

"Well, maybe that's what it was!" he said. "Maybe it wasn't out of love, but just for your own amusement that you befuddled the poor girl, without even knowing what would come of it yourself; if it worked, fine! If not, nothing lost! There are a lot of these young bloods in St Petersburg. Do you know how they are dealt with?"

Alexander sat with his head bowed. He didn't have it in him to defend himself.

"At first, I thought better of you, but I was mistaken, sorely mistaken. My word! How meek and mild you pretended to be! Thank God I found you out in time!... Now listen! There is no time to lose; before you know it, the foolish girl will be here to meet you. I was watching you yesterday. I don't want her to see us here together; you must leave and, of course, never come back. She will think that you've let her

CHAPTER 4

down, and that will be a lesson to her. You must make a point of never coming here again, so find another place to go fishing. Otherwise... Now clear out while the going's good... Think yourself lucky that Liza can still look me in the eye; I've been keeping a close watch on her the whole day, otherwise you would not be leaving by the same route... Goodbye!"

Alexander tried to say something, but the old man opened the door and practically shoved him out.

Alexander left, but in what state of mind I'll let the reader judge for himself – that is if you're not too squeamish about putting yourself in Alexander's place for a minute.

My hero's eyes were brimming with tears – tears of shame, tears of rage against himself, tears of despair...

"Why am I alive?" he asked aloud. "My life is disgusting, deadly! I'll... I'll... But no! If I wasn't strong enough to resist temptation... I will have the courage to put an end to this useless, shameful existence..."

He strode quickly to the river. It was black. Long, fantastic ugly shapes were skimming its waves. At the bank where Alexander was standing, the water was shallow. "This is not the place to do away with myself," he said contemptuously, and headed for the bridge about a hundred yards away. Alexander leant over the railings in the middle of the bridge and looked at the water. He mentally bade farewell to life, sent his sighs to his mother and his blessing to his aunt, and even his forgiveness to Nadenka. Tears were streaming down his cheeks from the powerful emotions gripping him... He covered his face with his hands... There's no telling what he might have done if the bridge hadn't suddenly started to sway under his feet. He looked around. "My God!" He was on the brink of an abyss. His grave yawned beneath him; half of the bridge had broken off, and was drifting away... barges were passing by; one more minute – and it was goodbye! Mustering all his strength, he made a desperate leap... onto the other side. He landed, gasping for breath, and clutched at his heart.

"Got a fright, did you, sir?" the watchman asked him.

"What do you mean? Didn't you see? I nearly fell right into the water," Alexander replied, his voice trembling.

"God help us! You never know what may happen next," said the watchman, yawning. "Why, only the other summer, a young gentleman *did* fall in."

Alexander made his way home, still clutching his heart. From time to time, he stopped to look at the river and the now divided bridge, and then quickly turned away with a shudder and walked on all the faster.

Meanwhile Liza, dressed as attractively as possible and accompanied by neither father nor nanny, went to sit under the tree every evening until late at night.

As the days went by, night fell earlier and earlier, but she continued her waiting; there was never a sign of the two friends.

Autumn came. The riverbank was strewn with yellowing leaves shed by the trees. The green of the foliage had faded; the river had turned the colour of lead, and the sky was always grey. A cold wind blew, accompanied by constant drizzle. The river and its banks were deserted. The sound of lively singing, laughter and animated conversation was no longer to be heard. Boats and barges no longer journeyed back and forth. Not a single insect was left to rustle in the grass or a single bird to chirp in the trees. Jackdaws and crows heightened the sense of desolation with their cries, and fish had stopped biting.

Liza continued to wait; she still needed to talk to Alexander to tell him her secret. She still sat on the bench under the tree in her wadded jacket. She had grown thin, and her eyes were sunken; she wore a scarf wrapped around her face, and that is how her father found her one day.

"Let's go home; no more sitting here!" he said, frowning and shivering with cold. "Look at you – your hands have turned blue; you're frozen stiff. Liza, do you hear me? Let's go!"

"Where to?"

"Home; we're moving to the city today."

"Why?" she asked in surprise.

"What do you mean, 'why'? It's autumn; and we're the only ones left here in our dacha."

"But, really," she said, "it will be so nice here in the winter; do let's stay!"

"What on earth has got into you? That's enough! Let's go!"

CHAPTER 4

"Wait!" she begged him. "The good days will come back again."

"Listen!" her father replied, patting her cheek and pointing to the spot where the two friends had come to fish. "They're not coming back…"

"Not… coming back?" she repeated. She was crestfallen, but from the way she said it, it could have been taken as a question. She offered her hand to her father, and quietly, her head bowed, set off home, looking back from time to time.

Aduyev and Kostyakov had long since resumed fishing, but somewhere on the other side of the river.

Chapter 5

LITTLE BY LITTLE ALEXANDER SUCCEEDED in forgetting Liza, as well as that unpleasant encounter with her father. He had recovered his peace of mind and was in good spirits, and often laughed at Kostyakov's feeble jokes. He was amused by his companion's view of life. They had even made plans to build a cabin on the river, a little farther out, where the fishing was better, and live out the rest of their days there. Alexander was once again spiritually mired in the mud of narrow horizons and the banalities of everyday life. But fate had remained vigilant, and prevented him from being sucked under.

In the autumn he received a letter from his aunt with an urgent plea to escort her to a concert, since his uncle was unwell. There was to be a performance by an outstanding artist of European renown.

"What? A concert," said Alexander, seriously alarmed. "A concert – with that same old crowd and all that glitter, trumpery, dissembling and pretence... No, I won't go."

"I bet that's going to cost you five roubles into the bargain," said Kostyakov, who happened to be with him at the time.

"The tickets cost fifteen roubles, as a matter of fact," said Alexander, "but I would willingly pay fifty roubles to get out of it."

"Fifteen!" Kostyakov exclaimed, throwing up his hands. "What crooks! May they rot in hell! They come here to fleece us, to rob us blind. Damned scroungers! Don't go, Alexander Fyodorych! Forget it! Now, if it were something worth having, something you could put on the table, something to eat, that would be another thing, but just to sit and listen – and for fifteen roubles! Why, you could buy a foal for that money!"

"Sometimes, people pay even more just to spend a pleasant evening," Alexander remarked.

"Spend a pleasant evening! Well, if that's the case, why don't we go to the bathhouse? We'll have a great time! Whenever I don't know what to do with myself, that's where I go – it's terrific! You go at six o'clock

CHAPTER 5

and leave at twelve; in between you warm yourself up, have a scrub down. Sometimes, you get to meet interesting people: a clergyman, a merchant, an officer; you get to talk about trade, or maybe the last trump... and you wish you didn't have to leave. Some people simply don't know the right place to go in the evening for a good time!"

But Alexander went anyway. With a sigh, he dragged out last year's tailcoat and pulled on white gloves.

"Five roubles for the gloves – that makes twenty, doesn't it?" Kostyakov calculated, who was helping Aduyev to dress. "Twenty roubles, just like that, thrown away on a single evening – just to listen to something, for God's sake!"

Alexander had got out of the habit of dressing formally. In the morning, he went to the office in his comfortable civil-service uniform. In the evening, he changed into his old frock coat or his overcoat. He was not comfortable in a tailcoat. In one place it was too tight, in another place it wasn't tight enough, and his neck was too hot in the satin stock.

His aunt was very pleased to see him, and felt grateful that he had taken the trouble to emerge for once from his seclusion, but not a word was uttered about what kind of life he was leading or what he was doing.

Having found a seat for Lizaveta in the auditorium, Aduyev was leaning against a column behind some broad-shouldered music lover, and started to feel bored. He discreetly covered up his yawn behind his hand, but had hardly closed his mouth before a thunderous burst of applause greeted the appearance of the artist. Alexander didn't even bother to look at him.

The orchestra began to play... After a few minutes, the sound of the music began to die away. The last few notes were joined by some other barely audible sounds, lively and playful to start with, and suggestive of children at play; the only voices which could be heard were those of children playing some noisy game. Then the voices grew more harmonious and mature, suggesting a spirit of carefree youth, bold and full of life and energy. Next, the voices slowed their tempo, became softer, as if conveying the tender outpouring of love, an intimate conversation, and as they died away, gradually faded into a passionate whisper and dwindled into silence...

No one dared to move a finger. The vast audience was frozen speechless, until it breathed a single "Ah!" in perfect unison, which travelled like a whisper around the auditorium. The audience began to stir, but was stilled by the new sounds which could be heard and which gradually merged into a single crescendo, and then splintered into a thousand cascades crowding and pressing in on one another, roaring and filling the air with their jealous recriminations, and seething with furious passion – the ear was not quick enough to absorb the tumult – and abruptly the sounds vanished, as if the instrument had exhausted itself and lost its voice. The bow drew forth now a muffled, intermittent groan, and then tearful and plaintive sounds, all of them breathing a last lingering, anguished sigh. A heart was breaking, as if singing a song of love betrayed and hopeless longing. The voices seemed to be singing of all the pain, all the suffering of the human soul.

Alexander was trembling. He raised his head and, through his tears, peered over his neighbour's shoulder. A thin German, bending over his instrument, stood before the audience, keeping it in his powerful thrall. He finished playing and casually wiped his hands and mopped his brow with a handkerchief. The audience burst into a roar and frenzy of applause. Suddenly this artist acknowledged the audience in his turn, bowing humbly in gratitude.

"And here he is bowing to *them*," thought Alexander, timidly regarding the thousand-headed Hydra, "and standing so tall before them!"

The artist raised his bow, and in an instant there was total silence, and what had been a crowd of jostling individuals a moment before, once again was transformed into a single body. New sounds filled the air – majestic and solemn, the kind that made the listeners sit up straight, their heads held high, their noses raised; they made chests swell with pride and inspired dreams of glory. The orchestra made its entrance in a muffled undertone, like the murmur of a crowd heard from a distance. Alexander turned pale, and his head dropped. Those sounds seemed specially designed to bring back to him and explain the whole of his past life, with all its bitterness and disillusionment.

Someone said, pointing at Alexander, "Look at that one over there, see how he looks! I can't understand how anyone can let his feelings

CHAPTER 5

show so openly; why, I've heard Paganini* play, and didn't even bat an eyelid."

Alexander silently cursed his aunt for inviting him, and also the artist himself, but most of all he cursed fate itself for not allowing him to remain oblivious.

"And what's the purpose of it anyway, what's the point?" he thought. "What does fate want from me? Why remind me of my weakness, the futility of a past that cannot be brought back?"

He escorted his aunt back home, and was on the point of leaving to return to his own apartment, when she held his arm to stop him going.

"Are you sure you won't come in?" she asked reproachfully.

"No."

"Why not?"

"It's late now, maybe some other time."

"And you won't even do this for me?"

"For you, least of all."

"But why?"

"It would take too long to explain. Goodbye!"

"Just half an hour, Alexander, do you hear me, that's all I'm asking. If you refuse, that can only mean that you've never had any affection for me whatever."

She spoke with such feeling, and with such persistence, that Alexander simply didn't have the heart to refuse, and he followed her inside, his head lowered. Pyotr Ivanych was sitting in his study.

"Do you really mean to tell me that I deserve such disregard from you, Alexander?" said Lizaveta Alexandrovna, after seating him by the fire.

"You're mistaken, it's not disregard," he replied.

"What does that mean? What would you call it? How many times have I written to you, asking you to come and see me, and you didn't come, and in the end even stopped replying to my notes?"

"It's not disregard..."

"Then what is it?"

"Doesn't matter!" said Alexander. "Goodbye, *ma tante*."

"Wait! What is it I've done to you? What's the matter with you, Alexander? Why are you being like this? You're indifferent to everything, never go anywhere, and the people you *do* consort with are wrong for you."

"Well, that's the way it is, *ma tante*: it's a way of life that I prefer, a quiet life – and I like it: it suits me…"

"Suits you? And you find that that kind of life and that kind of people meet your intellectual and emotional needs?"

Alexander nodded.

"Don't pretend, Alexander! You're deeply hurt in some way, and don't want to talk about it. Before, you always found someone to confide in about your troubles; and you knew that you would always find comfort, or at least sympathy – but now you really don't have anyone?"

"No one."

"There's no one you trust?"

"No one."

"You mean you don't remember your mother from time to time… and how much she loves you… and her affection? Hasn't it occurred to you that even here there may be someone who loves you, perhaps not like her, but at least like a sister, or even more, like a friend?"

"Goodbye, *ma tante*!" he said.

"Goodbye, Alexander; I won't keep you any longer," said his aunt, her eyes brimming with tears.

Alexander started to pick up his hat, but put it down again and looked at Lizaveta Alexandrovna.

"No, I can't leave you like this; I can't bring myself to do that!" he said. "What are you doing to me?"

"Try just for a minute to be the old Alexander again. Tell me everything, trust me…"

"I simply can't keep silent when I'm with you. I'll tell you everything that's in my heart," he said. "You ask why I hide from people, why I'm indifferent to everything, why I won't see even you. Why? I must tell you that life has become sickening to me, so I have chosen a way of life in which life intrudes least. There's nothing I want, nothing I am seeking, except peace and quiet, and peace of mind. I've tasted the emptiness and worthlessness of life, and thoroughly despise it. 'Anyone who has lived and thought cannot but despise people in his heart.'* Activity,

CHAPTER 5

busyness, worries, diversion – I've had enough of all of that. There's nothing I strive for, nothing I'm looking for. I have no goals, because whatever people strive for or achieve – in the end it's nothing but a will-o'-the-wisp. For me, joy is a thing of the past: it has no appeal for me. When I'm with educated people, I become more aware of life's dissatisfactions, but when I'm by myself, far from the madding crowd, I am benumbed – and in that trance, whatever may happen, I notice neither people nor myself. I do nothing, and see neither other people's actions nor my own – I'm at peace, totally indifferent; there's no such thing as happiness, and as for unhappiness, it cannot touch me…"

"That's terrible, Alexander!" said his aunt. "To have turned your back on everything at your age!"

"Why are you so surprised, *ma tante*? Step back from the horizon which is now too close to you, and too confining, and take a more detached view of life, of the world – and what do you find? What was wonderful yesterday is worthless today; what you wanted yesterday, you don't want today; yesterday's friend is today's enemy. Is it worth troubling yourself about anything – to love, to become attached to anything, to quarrel, to make up – in a word, to live? Isn't it better to let your mind and your heart go to sleep? I sleep – that's why I don't go anywhere, especially not to see you. I would fall asleep once and for all, but you would awaken my heart and my mind, and propel me once again towards the abyss. If you want to see me cheerful, healthy, perhaps alive, even what my uncle calls happy, then leave me where I am right now. Let's be content with this much excitement, and let my dreams fade – let my mind ossify, my heart turn to stone, my eyes forget how to shed tears, and my lips forget how to smile – and then in a year or maybe two, I'll come back to you, ready for any test: then you will no longer be able to awaken me, no matter how hard you try, but right now—"

He made a gesture of despair.

"Look here, Alexander," his aunt broke in eagerly, "in just one minute, you've changed; there are tears in your eyes. You're still the Alexander you once were, it's no good pretending: don't try to contain your feelings, let it all out…"

"Why? It won't do me any good! I'll just be in even more pain. This evening has destroyed me in my own eyes. I have seen clearly that I have no right to blame anyone for my misery. I've ruined my own life. I dreamt of becoming famous, God knows on what grounds, and neglected my work; I made a mess of my humble career, and now it's too late to remedy my past mistakes. I scorned the common herd, despised those people – and that German with his profound and powerful spirit, and his poetic nature, has not renounced the world, and doesn't scorn ordinary people; he welcomes their applause and is proud of it. He understands that he is a barely noticeable link in the endless chain of humanity. He knows everything that I know; he has known suffering. Did you hear him tell the story of his life in those sounds that he was making, including his joys and sorrows, his happiness, his world-weariness? He understands grief. How small I was made to feel today, worthless in my own eyes with my anguish and suffering! He awakened in me bitter self-knowledge: that I am proud – and weak. Why oh why did you invite me? Goodbye, let me go!"

"How can you blame me, Alexander? Could I really have awakened this bitterness in you?... I, of all people?"

"But that's just the point: your angelic, kind face, *ma tante*, your gentle way of speaking, the affectionate touch of your hand – all of that touches and confuses me; I just want to cry because I want to live again – it's so painful... but why?"

"What do you mean, 'why'? Come and stay with us permanently, and if you think that I am the least bit worthy of your friendship, that means that you will find consolation in another woman, I'm not the only one of my kind... You will be appreciated."

"Oh yes! Do you think that it will always be like this – consoling me? Do you think that I'm going to trust the fact that I'm moved and touched for the moment? You are of course a woman in the very best sense of the word; you have been born to bring joy and happiness to a man; but can that happiness be relied on? Is there any guarantee that it is lasting, and that today or tomorrow fate won't turn even this happiness upside down? – that's the question! Is there anything or anyone that one can trust? Isn't it better to live without any hopes, without

CHAPTER 5

vicissitudes, and expect nothing – and since you're not looking for joy, you will never have to mourn any losses?"

"There's no escaping fate, Alexander, and even where you are now, it will still track you down..."

"That's true, except that it's only where I am now that fate can't get a laugh out of me, but I can more easily get a laugh out of fate; for example, a fish gets away just as you're stretching your hand out to reach it, or it starts raining just when you're about to go out of town, or the weather's good, and you don't feel like going... it's laughable!..."

Lizaveta Alexandrovna had run out of objections.

"You will get married... you will fall in love..." she ventured tentatively.

"Get married! You can't be serious! Do you really think that I'm going to entrust my happiness to a woman, even if I were to fall in love with her – not that that's going to happen? Or do you really think that I would undertake to make a woman happy? No, but I do know that we would deceive each other, and would be deceiving ourselves. Uncle Pyotr Ivanych and experience have taught me that..."

"Pyotr Ivanych! Oh yes, he has a lot to answer for," said Lizaveta Alexandrovna with a sigh, "but you didn't have to listen to him... and you could have been happy in marriage..."

"Yes, certainly I could have back in the country, but now... No, *ma tante*, marriage is not for me. I can't put up a pretence now, when I stop loving and am no longer happy – nor could I turn a blind eye if my wife were just putting on an act: we would both be playing a game... the same way you and Uncle do..."

"You mean us?" Lizaveta Alexandrovna was astonished and dismayed.

"Yes, the two of you! Tell me, are you as happy as you once dreamt you would be?"

"No, not as happy as that... but happy in a different way from what I had imagined, in a more realistic way, perhaps even happier – but does any of this matter?" Lizaveta Alexandrovna replied in her embarrassment. "And you too..."

"More realistic! Oh *ma tante*, this is not you speaking: you're just echoing Uncle! I know what happiness is in his book: more rational,

I'll grant him, but happier? For him everything is happiness: there is no unhappiness for him. But never mind him! No! There's nothing left for me in life: I'm tired, tired of life…"

They both fell silent. Alexander glanced at his hat; his aunt was trying to think of something to persuade him to stay.

"But what about talent?" she said eagerly.

"Come, come, *ma tante*, you must feel like making fun of me! Have you forgotten the old saying: 'Don't kick a man when he's down'? I don't have any talent, none at all. I have feeling, and I was carried away; what I thought was creativity was just a dream, but I wrote anyway. Just recently I came across some old misbegotten attempts of mine, and when I read them, I simply had to laugh. Uncle was quite right to goad me into burning every last one of them. Oh, if only I could bring back the past, I would make very different use of it."

"Don't give up on yourself entirely!" she said. "Every one of us has been given a heavy cross to bear…"

"What's this about a cross?" said Pyotr Ivanych as he entered the room. "Hello, Alexander, are you the one with the cross?"

"Pyotr Ivanych was stooping and could hardly put one foot in front of the other as he walked.

"Yes, but not the kind of cross you're thinking of – I was talking about the heavy cross that Alexander has to bear."

"So what is this cross of his?" Pyotr Ivanych asked, lowering himself with immense care into his armchair. "Ouf! That really hurts! What did I do to deserve this!"

Lizaveta Alexandrovna went over to help him into the armchair, placed a cushion behind his back and drew up a stool for him to rest his legs on.

"What's the matter with you, Uncle?" Alexander asked.

"You see what a cross *I'm* bearing! It's my lower back," he groaned. "This is one hell of a cross! And this is my reward for all those years of hard work! My God, how it hurts!"

"Well, it's your own fault for spending so much time sitting; you know what the climate is like here," said Lizaveta Alexandrovna. "The

CHAPTER 5

doctor told you to walk more. But no: you spend the morning writing and the evening playing cards."

"So you want me to walk around the streets with my mouth wide open, gawking like an idiot, just wasting time?"

"And this is your punishment."

"There's no way of avoiding it, if you want to apply yourself to your work. Who doesn't suffer from lower-back pain? It's virtually a mark of distinction of anyone who is serious about his work... Oh God! Can't straighten my back. So, Alexander, what are you up to?"

"The same as usual."

"Oh! So you won't be having lower-back pain. How surprising!"

"What's so surprising? Aren't you partly to blame for his becoming so..." said Lizaveta Alexandrovna.

"Me? Well, that's a nice one! *I* was the one who taught him to do nothing!"

"Precisely, Uncle, you shouldn't be surprised," said Alexander. "You did a great deal to create the circumstances which made me what I am – not that I'm blaming you. It's my own fault that I wasn't sensible enough – or, I should say, wasn't able to make proper use of what you taught me, because I wasn't prepared for that. Perhaps you're partly to blame because you were well aware of my character from the very first, and instead of trying to change it, a man of your experience should have realized that it was impossible... You created an inner conflict in me between two competing views of life and were unable to reconcile them – and what was the end result? I ended up wallowing in doubt – a total mess, Uncle!"

"Oh! My back!" Pyotr Ivanych groaned. "It was precisely out of that total mess that I was trying to create something worthwhile."

"Yes, but what did you end up doing? You painted a picture of your version of it, all its naked ugliness – and when I was still at that stage of life when I should have been seeing only its bright side."

"What I was trying to do was show you life as it really is, instead of allowing you to fall prey to the idea that it's the exact opposite. I remember the kind of young fellow you were when you came here from your home in the country; I really thought I had to warn you that you couldn't be like that here. I may have saved you from a lot of foolishness and a lot of mistakes – which, if it weren't for me, you would still be making – and what mistakes!"

"Perhaps. But there was just one thing you left out of the picture, Uncle – happiness. What you forgot was that it is a man's delusions, dreams and hopes that make him happy – not reality…"

"That's crazy talk! Something you brought with you from somewhere on the border with Asia. In Europe, we've long since ceased to believe in that kind of thing. Dreams, fancy ideas, illusions: that's fine for women and children, but a man must face the facts of life for what they are. Is there anything in your view which is worse than being deluded or cheated?"

"Yes, Uncle, but whatever you may say, happiness is a tapestry woven from illusions, hopes and trust in people, confidence in oneself and also love and friendship… and you have drilled it into me that love is nonsense, a mere façade, and that it's easier, or even better, to live without it, and that passionate love is no great accomplishment and does not make us superior to animals…"

"And remember how you wanted to find love: writing bad verse, and all that preposterous talk, and that Grunya of yours – if that's her name – all of which would bore anyone to death. And that's the kind of thing you thought would captivate women?"

"Oh, and what do you think works?" Lizaveta Alexandrovna asked drily.

"God! My back feels like someone's stabbing me!" Pyotr Ivanych groaned.

"You also dinned it into me," Alexander continued, "that there is no such thing as deep devotion or true affinity: there is just habit…"

Lizaveta Alexandrovna watched her husband silently and intently.

"You must understand – the fact is that I was telling you that so that… you know… Ouch! My back!"

"Yes, you were telling that," Alexander went on, "to a twenty-year-old youth for whom love was everything, and whose every action, every goal, revolved around that emotion, and for whom… love alone was the be-all and end-all of existence."

CHAPTER 5

"You must have been born two hundred years ago!" Pyotr Ivanych mumbled. "In some Never-Never Land."

"You expounded to me," Alexander persisted, "your theory of love – deception, betrayal, indifference... and why? I knew all about that before I first fell in love, and so, even when I was in love, I started analysing it, like a student dissecting a body under the guidance of his professor, and instead of seeing the beauty of its anatomy, he sees only muscles and nerves..."

"Nevertheless, I remember, that didn't prevent you from losing your head over that... what's-her-name... Dashenka, was it?"

"But you didn't allow me to go my own way and find myself betrayed; otherwise I might have seen in Nadenka's betrayal of me an unfortunate happenstance, and would have waited until such time as I would have no need of love, but you came up right away with your theory and convinced me that it was something which was bound to happen. So at twenty-five years of age I had lost my faith in happiness and in life itself, and my heart had dried up. As for friendship, you rejected it and called it too a matter of habit, and even described yourself, probably in jest, as my best friend, because, after all, you had successfully proved that there was no such thing as friendship."

Pyotr Ivanych listened while rubbing his back with one hand. He entered his objections nonchalantly like a man who thought that he could demolish his opponent's accusations with a single word.

"And you understood friendship very well," he said. "What you wanted from a friend was that same comedy which we are told was played in ancient times by those two fools... what were their names? – where one of them agreed to take the place of the other as a hostage, and then the other one came back to see him.* If everyone behaved this way, the whole world would become one great madhouse!"

"I loved people," Alexander continued, "I believed in their virtues, I saw them as my brothers, was ready to reach out and embrace them warmly—"

"Yes, of course, what could be more important! I remember your embraces," Pyotr Ivanych broke in. "I grew heartily sick of them."

"And you made it very clear how little you thought of them. Instead of guiding my heart in my attachments, you taught me to analyse, to examine, to be on my guard against people; I followed your advice – and stopped loving them!"

"How was I to understand you? You know how impulsive you are; I thought that it would only make you nicer to them. I do know them, so I didn't start hating them…"

"So, you're telling me that you love people?" Lizaveta Alexandrovna asked him.

"I've… got used to them."

"Got *used* to them!" she repeated tonelessly.

"And he would have too," said Pyotr Ivanych, "but he had already been spoilt rotten back there in the country by his aunt and those yellow flowers, and that's why he has found it so hard to evolve."

"But afterwards I still believed in myself," Alexander began again. "You showed me that I was worse than others, and I learnt to hate myself."

"If you had taken a more detached view of things, you would have seen that you were neither better nor worse, and that was what I was asking of you; and then you wouldn't have started hating others or yourself, and would have learnt to be able to take human weaknesses in your stride, and be a little more attentive to your own. Now, I know what I'm worth, and see that I'm not a good person, but I confess, I do love myself."

"Oh, so when it comes to yourself it's 'love', and not 'getting used to'!" Lizaveta Alexandrovna remarked coldly.

"Oh, my back really hurts!" Pyotr Ivanych groaned.

"And finally, at one fell swoop, without warning, without pity, you destroyed my most cherished dream. I thought I had inside me a spark of poetic talent: you ruthlessly made it clear to me that I wasn't born to be a high priest of the fine arts, and painfully extracted that splinter from my heart and offered me work that I detested. If it hadn't been for you I would have been writing—"

"…and would have become known to the public as a writer with no talent…" Pyotr Ivanych cut in.

CHAPTER 5

"What do I care about the public? I was doing it for myself, I would have attributed my failures to malice, envy and ill will, and would eventually have resigned myself to the conclusion that there was no point in continuing, and would have taken up some other activity of my own accord. So why are you so surprised that, now that I know all there is to know, I have lost heart?"

"Well, what do you have to say?" asked Lizaveta Alexandrovna.

"I've no wish to say anything; what can one say in response to such nonsense? Am I to blame for the fact that when you came here, you imagined that you would find nothing but yellow flowers, love and friendship, and that all that people do here is either write poetry or listen to it – and here and there, just for a change, they try their hands at prose? I tried to make you understand that people everywhere, and especially here, have to work even until their backs ache... that there are no yellow flowers, just money and promotions – which is a lot better! That's all I wanted you to understand! I didn't despair of your ever coming to understand what life is like, especially as it is currently understood. I've seen for myself that even you have come to understand that life has few flowers and little poetry to offer, and have come to imagine life to be a great mistake – and that since you see this, you are entitled to spend your time being bored, while others cannot see this, and therefore enjoy life to the full. Well, what is it that dissatisfies you, what is it that you lack? Someone else in your place would be thanking his lucky stars. You've been spared poverty, ill health, and nothing really tragic has happened to you. So what is it you don't have? Is it love? You feel you haven't had your fair share? You've been in love twice, and your love has been returned, but you've also been let down, so you've broken even. We've concluded that you do have friends, the kind of friends that not many people have – real friends! Of course, they won't necessarily go through fire and water for you, and they're not too keen on being hugged, but then nothing could be more stupid than that – and you should finally get that into your head! On the other hand, you can always be sure of getting advice, help and even money from them... Don't you count them as friends? Eventually you will get married, and you'll have a career and make a good living – it's just a matter of applying yourself. Just do what everyone else does, and fate won't pass you by – you'll come into your own. It's ridiculous to imagine yourself to be special and important, when that is not what you were meant to be. So what have you got to be so miserable about?"

"I don't blame you, Uncle, quite the contrary: I can appreciate your intentions, and I thank you for them from the bottom of my heart. But what can you do? They weren't fulfilled. But don't blame me either. We didn't understand each other – and that was the tragedy. What can, and does appeal to you and one or two others, does not happen to appeal to me…"

"Me and one or two others! No, you've got it wrong, my dear fellow! You really think I'm the only one who thinks and acts the way I tried to teach you? Look around you, look at most people, the 'common herd', as you like to call them, and not those who live on their country estates – it will be a long time before this will apply to them. No, look at the educated, modern majority who think and act; what is it that they want, what are they striving for? How do they think? And you will see that it's exactly what I tried to teach you – and what I asked of you. I didn't just make all of this up."

"Then who did?" asked Lizaveta Alexandrovna.

"The age we live in."

"So we're all bound to follow the dictates of this modern age of yours," she asked, "all of which are sacred and true?"

"Yes, all sacred!" said Pyotr Ivanych.

"Oh, really! So we must do more thinking than feeling? Not follow the promptings of our hearts? Stifle our impulses? Never give way to, or trust, our 'heartfelt outpourings'?"

"Yes," said Pyotr Ivanych.

"Everything we do should be strictly by the book, and we should place less trust in people, treat everything as unreliable and live just for ourselves?"

"Yes."

"And isn't this also sacred: that love is not the most important thing in life, and that we should love our work more than the person we love most – that we can't count on anyone's devotion – that we should

CHAPTER 5

believe that love will grow cold and end in betrayal or as a habit – and that friendship is nothing but habit. Isn't this all true?"

"It's always been true," replied Pyotr Ivanych. "Only, before, people didn't want to believe it, but now it has become axiomatic."

"And is this sacred too: that everything must be examined, scrutinized and thought through – and that there's no room for forgetting ourselves, dreaming a little, letting ourselves be carried away even by an illusion, just to make ourselves happy?..."

"Yes, it's sacred because it's sensible," said Pyotr Ivanych.

"And is it also true that in dealing with those dearest to you, you should let your mind be your guide – your wife, for instance?..."

"My back has never given me such trouble before – how it hurts!" said Pyotr Ivanych, writhing on his chair.

"Ah! So when it comes to your back, ours is still the good age to be living in – unquestionably!"

"It is indeed, my dear; caprice, impulse achieve nothing, but wherever there is good sense, a good reason, experience, gradual evolution, that's what makes for success, and everything strives for perfection and the good."

"Maybe there is some truth in what you say, Uncle," said Alexander, "but it does nothing to comfort me. According to your theory, I know everything, I see everything through your eyes; I'm a graduate of your school – but just the same, life is dreary, a burden, intolerable... Why is that?"

"Because you're not used to the way things are now; and you're not the only one: there are still those who have been left behind; they are the 'victims', they are really pitiful. But what can you do? We can't hold back the vast majority just for the sake of a handful of people. For everything you've just accused me of," said Pyotr Ivanych after a moment's thought, "I have just one major justification. Do you remember that, when you first arrived here, after a five-minute conversation with you, I advised you to go back home? You didn't want to. So why should you attack me now? I predicted then that you would never adapt to the way things are now, but you chose to rely on my guidance and asked for my advice... and spoke loftily of the latest advances in human thought, of the aspirations of mankind... the practical spirit of the age – well, there you are! I couldn't babysit you from morning to night – why should I have? I couldn't cover your mouth at night with a cloth to protect you from the flies, or make the sign of the cross over you as you slept. I talked sense to you, because that's what you asked me to do, and what was the result? Well, that's certainly not my problem. You're not a child, and not a fool, and are capable of thinking for yourself... Instead of getting on with your work, what did you do? You went around whining about some girl throwing you over, moaning and groaning about parting with a friend, suffering from spiritual emptiness, or being overwhelmed by your feelings; well, what kind of life is that? It's sheer torture! Just take a look at the youth of today – fine young people! Hives of intellectual activity and energy – and how nimbly and easily they deal with all that tommyrot, known in your outdated language as 'spiritual anguish', 'suffering' and who the hell knows what else!"

"You're very glib when it comes to making your case!" said Lizaveta Alexandrovna. "But aren't you sorry for Alexander?"

"No, I'm not. Now, if he were suffering from backache, I would be. That wouldn't be pure fancy, a daydream or poetry, but something that really hurts." He winced again.

"Well, couldn't you at least tell me what to do now, Uncle? How would you apply your intelligence to this problem?"

"What to do? Why, yes, go back to your country estate!"

"Go back home!" said Lizaveta Alexandrovna. "Are you out of your mind, Pyotr Ivanych? What would there be for him to do?"

"To the country!" said Alexander, and both of them looked at Pyotr Ivanych.

"Yes, back to the country, and you can see your mother and console her. I mean, you're looking for a quiet life, and here everything upsets you. And what could be less upsetting than what you have there? Your aunt, the lake. Yes, go! And who knows? Maybe... you know... Ouch!" He clutched his back.

A couple of weeks later, Alexander handed in his resignation and came to say goodbye to his uncle and aunt. Alexander and his aunt

CHAPTER 5

were silent and sad. Her eyes glistened with tears. Pyotr Ivanych was the only one to speak.

"No career, no fortune!" he said, shaking his head. "Was it really worth coming all this way, just to put the name of Aduyev to shame?"

"That's enough, Pyotr Ivanych!" said Lizaveta Alexandrovna. "I'm fed up with hearing about your career."

"But, my dear, to have spent eight years doing nothing!"

"Goodbye, Uncle; thank you for everything, everything…"

"No need to thank me! Goodbye, Alexander. Don't you need money for the journey?"

"No thank you, I have enough to get by."

"What is this? He will never take money from me! This time, it really infuriates me. Well, take care, have a safe journey!"

"Aren't you sorry to see him go?" said Lizaveta Alexandrovna.

Grudgingly, Pyotr Ivanych conceded, mumbling, "Well, I did… get used to him. Remember, Alexander, that you do have an uncle and friend – you hear? And if you ever need a favour, a job, or some of that 'filthy lucre', don't hesitate to come to me: you can always count on all three."

"And if you should need sympathy," said Lizaveta Alexandrovna, "comforting in distress, a warm friend who's always there for you…"

"And don't forget the 'heartfelt outpourings'," added Pyotr Ivanych.

"So remember," Lizaveta Alexandrovna continued, "that you have an aunt and a friend."

"Well, my dear, he has all that in the country – everything he needs: flowers, love, outpourings and even an aunt."

Alexander was deeply moved, and unable to utter a word. As he said goodbye to his uncle, he reached out to hug him, although not so spontaneously as he had eight years before. Pyotr Ivanych, instead of giving him a hug, just took him by both hands and squeezed them harder than he had eight years before. Lizaveta Alexandrovna dissolved in tears.

"Whew! That's a weight off my shoulders, thank God!" said Pyotr Ivanych after Alexander had left. "Even my back seems to feel better!"

"What did he do to you?" his wife mumbled through her tears.

"What did he do? Why, it was sheer torture – even worse than the trouble I have with my workers. If they give me trouble, they get a thrashing, but with him, with Alexander, what can you do?"

Lizaveta Alexandrovna spent the whole day in tears, and when Pyotr Ivanych asked about dinner, he was told that the table hadn't even been laid, and that the mistress had shut herself up in her study and had not summoned the cook.

"It's that Alexander again! Always Alexander!" said Pyotr Ivanych. "Nothing but trouble when he's around!"

He went on grumbling and growling until he finally left to dine at the English Club.

The next morning the coach rumbled slowly out of the city, taking with it Alexander Fyodorych and Yevsei.

Alexander poked his head out of one of the windows, doing everything he could to put himself in a mournful state of mind, and finally settled for a silent soliloquy. They passed by hairdressing salons, dental clinics, dress shops and the mansions of the wealthy. "Goodbye!" he said, shaking his head and clutching his own thinning hair. "Farewell, city of fake hairpieces, false teeth, cloth imitations of nature, round hats – city of polite disdain, affectations and futile busyness! Farewell, magnificent graveyard of deep, strong and warm emotions! I spent eight years looking modern life in the face but with my back turned to nature, so nature turned its back on me: I squandered my life force and grew old at the age of twenty-nine; but there was a time… Farewell, farewell, you city,

"Where I suffered, where I loved,
Where I buried my heart."*

"I reach out to embrace you, you broad fields, and you, you blessed villages and meadows of the land of my birth; take me to your bosom, that I may come to life and rise from the dead with my soul!"

At this point he read Pushkin's poem, "The barbarian artist with his sleepy brush" etc.,* wiped the tears from his eyes and withdrew inside the carriage.

Chapter 6

It was a fine morning. The surface of the lake, already familiar to the reader, in the village of Grachi, was barely ruffled. An onlooker would have to screw up his eyes because of the blinding glare of the sun's rays, and – emerald and diamond by turns – the sparks and glints shooting off the water.

The weeping birches were dipping their branches into the water. Patches of sedge had settled here and there along the banks, trying to conceal the big yellow flowers on the broad green leaves floating on the water. At intervals, feathery clouds scurried through the sky, and the sun seemed to turn its back on Grachi, momentarily leaving the lake, the wood and the village in the shade, while somewhere in the distance it was still shining brightly. The cloud would pass, and the lake would glitter again, and the fields be bathed in its golden rays.

Anna Pavlovna had been sitting on the balcony since five o'clock. What had summoned her – the sunrise, the freshness of the air or the dawn chorus of larks? It was none of those things! She had been unable to take her eyes off the road which went through the wood. When Agrafena came to collect the keys, Anna Pavlovna could not spare her a glance, and handed her the keys without looking up or even asking why she needed them. The cook came in – and again, without looking up, she issued a whole series of instructions. Orders had been given to prepare the table for ten people for the next day.

Anna Pavlovna was left alone again. Suddenly her eyes shone. Every nerve within her was focused on seeing: a dark dot had appeared on the road. Someone was coming, slowly and silently. Drat! It was a cart coming down the hill. Anna Pavlovna frowned. "Looks like the evil one is bringing someone this way!" she complained. "But no, it's not passing by: they're all coming straight towards us."

Reluctantly, she sat down again and trained her eyes on the wood, quivering with anticipation, blind to everything around her – and there was a lot to see around her. The scenery had changed considerably. The midday air, baked by the scorching rays of the sun, had become oppressive and suffocating. Then the sun set. The light disappeared, and the wood and the villages beyond it were swathed in a seamless blanket of an ominous blackness.

Anna Pavlovna came to and looked up. "My God!" What appeared to be some monstrous living creature was moving from the west, an ugly black blotch with a coppery tint around its edges, and advancing rapidly towards the village and the wood, spreading what seemed to be enormous wings from its sides. All of nature turned sullen. The cows hung their heads, the horses waved their tails, inflated their nostrils and snorted and shook their manes. The dust stirred up by their hooves lay heavily on the ground only to be scattered by the wheels. A storm cloud approached menacingly. Soon a distant rumbling was moving closer.

Everything went quiet, as if expecting something extraordinary. What had become of those birds which usually sang and darted around in such lively fashion before the sun went down? And those insects with their buzzing and humming in the grass? Everything had gone into hiding and was holding its breath: it seemed that even the inanimate objects shared the ominous premonition. The trees had stopped swaying and brushing one another with their twigs: they had straightened up, and only rarely did they bend their heads towards each other as if they were whispering warnings of the impending danger. The storm cloud had already blotted out the horizon and had taken the form of an impenetrable, leaden canopy. In the village everybody began to rush for the shelter of their homes. There followed a moment of solemn silence everywhere. A fresh breeze heralded the arrival of the storm, and blew a chill into the faces of travellers; as it passed, it rustled the leaves, slammed doors of the villagers' huts, stirred up the dust on the street and died away in the bushes. A whirlwind of a storm followed in its wake, slowly propelling a column of dust ahead of it. It burst into the village, breaking off some rotten planks from the fence and tearing off a thatched roof in its path, lifted the skirts of a peasant woman carrying water home and chased chickens along the street with their tails in the air.

CHAPTER 6

The storm passed. Silence again. Everything was in a state of panic, trying to hide. Only a stupid ram had felt nothing coming and was nonchalantly chewing its cud right in the middle of the street, looking around him and wondering what all the fuss was about; a single feather and a blade of straw whirled along the street hurrying to catch up with the whirlwind.

Two or three drops of rain began to fall, and there was a sudden flash of lightning. An old man got up from his seat on the mound outside his door and rushed his grandchildren inside; his wife crossed herself and hurriedly closed the window. There was a peal of thunder, which drowned out all human noise and rumbled dramatically and majestically through the air. A startled horse broke away from its tethering post and galloped into the fields with its tether flying from its neck, and its owner in hopeless pursuit. Meanwhile the driving rain poured down in torrents more and more heavily, drumming with increasing energy on roofs and windows. A small white hand fearfully poked out onto the balcony the object of its loving care – a bunch of flowers.

At the first peal of thunder, Anna Pavlovna crossed herself and left the balcony.

"No – obviously no point in waiting any longer today," she said with a sigh, "he must have stopped somewhere because of the storm, probably for the night."

Suddenly, the rumbling of wheels could be heard, not from the wood but from the other side. Someone was entering the courtyard. Aduyeva's heart missed a beat.

"How could they have come from that direction?" she wondered. "Did he want to surprise me? But no, they couldn't have come that way."

She didn't know what to think, but soon everything was made clear.

A minute later Anton Ivanych came in. His hair was beginning to turn white, and he had put on weight; his cheeks were plumper from inactivity and overeating, and he was wearing the same old frock coat and wide trousers.

"I've been waiting and waiting for you, Anton Ivanych," Anna Pavlovna began. "I began to think you weren't coming – I'd almost given up."

"How could you think such a thing about me, dear lady? It might be true if it were a matter of calling on anyone else, yes! But I don't go calling on just anyone – you're the exception. I was held up through no fault of my own; right now I'm having to get around with just one horse. It was at Pavel Savich's christening that the piebald got lame. An evil spirit put it into the coachman's head to take the old door from the barn and lay it over the ditch – those people are too poor and don't have a spare plank. Anyway, there was a nail or a hook of some kind in that door – only the Devil knows! The horse took one step and stumbled over the edge, and I nearly got my neck broken – curse them! So the horse has been lame since then. Such skinflints! You wouldn't believe, dear lady, what their house is like. People are treated better in the almshouse; but in Moscow at the Kuznetsky Bridge, they think nothing of spending 10,000 in a year!"

Anna Pavlovna was too distracted to listen to him, and just gave a nod when he had finished.

"Did you know I had received a letter from Sashenka, Anton Ivanych?" she broke in. "He wrote that he would be coming around the twentieth – I was beside myself with joy."

"Yes, I heard, dear lady. Proshka told me, and at first I couldn't understand what he was saying, and I thought he had already arrived: I was so happy that I broke into a sweat."

"God grant you health, Anton Ivanych – you love us so much!"

"Of course I do! I mean, I used to carry Alexander Fyodorych in my arms; he was like one of my own."

"Thank you, Anton Ivanych, God bless you! I haven't been sleeping, and have been keeping everyone else up. What if he were to arrive, and there we are, all sleeping – what a welcome that would be! Yesterday and the day before, I went down to the wood on foot; I would be going there now, but I'm just feeling too old – it's a curse! And I'm exhausted from lack of sleep. Sit down, Anton Ivanych, you're wet through; wouldn't you like something to drink or a little something to eat? You could wait for dinner perhaps, but it wouldn't be until late – we have to wait for our dear guest of honour to arrive."

CHAPTER 6

"Well, yes, then, perhaps a bite to eat. Although I must confess that I've already had breakfast, in a manner of speaking."

"How did you manage that?"

"I stopped by at Maria Karpovna's. I had to, you see, more because of the horse than for myself: it needed a rest. It's no joke going twelve versts without stopping in this heat! So I had a bite since I happened to be there. It's a good thing that I didn't listen to them and stay longer, although they urged me to, otherwise we would have been stuck there the whole day because of the storm."

"And how is Maria Karpovna?"

"Well, thank God! She sends her greetings."

"Thank you, and that daughter of hers, Sofia Mikhailovna – how about her hubby?"

"She's fine, dear lady – a sixth baby on the way. It's expected in a couple of weeks. They asked me to come around that time. You wouldn't believe how poor they are – it's painful to see. You'd think the last thing they'd want is more children, wouldn't you? But no, they keep on."

"What are you saying?"

"I swear to God! Their doorposts are all crooked; the floor sags under your feet, the roof leaks and there's no money to pay for repairs, and all they put on the table is soup, cheese curds and mutton; yet they never tire of inviting me!"

"Yes, the same thing with that one – she was after my Sashenka!"

"The nerve of her, dear lady! After a fine young man like that! I can hardly wait to set eyes on him – what a handsome fellow! I have a hunch, Anna Pavlovna; I wouldn't mind betting that he's engaged to some princess or countess, and is coming to ask for your blessing and ask you to the wedding."

"Oh, come now, Anton Ivanych!" said Anna Pavlovna, absolutely delighted.

"No, I mean it!"

"Oh, my dear fellow, may God give you health! Oh yes, it slipped my mind; I wanted to tell you, but I clean forgot. I kept trying to think what it was; it was on the tip of my tongue; would you believe, it just slipped my mind completely. Would you like to have some breakfast first, or should I tell you now?"

"As you please, dear lady, you could even tell me during breakfast; I can assure you that I won't miss a single crumb... I mean 'word', that is."

"Well, here's the thing," Anna Pavlovna began, after breakfast had been brought in and Anton Ivanych was safely seated at the table, "I dreamt..."

"But you mean you're not having anything to eat yourself?" Anton Ivanych asked.

"Oh no! I couldn't eat a thing right now! It would stick in my throat. The last few days I haven't even been able to finish a cup of tea. So, I dreamt that I was sitting just like this, and right in front of me Agrafena is standing with a tray, and I'm saying to her in my dream, 'Agrafena, how come you're standing there with an empty tray?' She doesn't say anything, but just stands there staring at the door. So I'm thinking – in my dream – 'Goodness me! What can she be staring at like that?' So I start looking in the same direction myself, and as I'm looking, who should suddenly come in but Sashenka, looking very sad; he comes up to me and says, for all the world as if he's really there, 'Goodbye, Mummy, I'm going somewhere over there far away,' and points to the lake, 'and I won't be coming back,' he says. 'Where is it you're going, my dear?' I ask, with my heart sinking. And it's like he's not saying anything, but giving me a strange, mournful look, and I'm asking him again, 'Where have you come from?' and my darling sighs and points again to the lake and whispers, 'From the whirlpool at the bottom, from the water sprites.' I'm all shaken up – and I wake up. My pillow is soaked with tears, and I can hardly wake up from the dream; I'm sitting up in the bed and crying my eyes out. I got up and lit the lamp in front of the Kazan Holy Mother of God,* our Protector, praying that in her mercy she will keep him safe from all trouble and misfortune. I can't tell you the anxieties that overwhelmed me! I couldn't understand what it all meant. Maybe something happened to him? Such a terrible storm!..."

"My dear lady, it's a good sign when you cry in your sleep," said Anton Ivanych, knocking an egg against the side of the plate. "It means he will definitely be here tomorrow."

CHAPTER 6

"I was thinking that maybe we should go down to the wood to meet him after breakfast; we could make our way there somehow, although it's suddenly become very muddy down there."

"No, something tells me he won't come today!"

At that very moment the distant sound of a bell was wafted on the breeze, and then instantly died away. Anna Pavlovna stopped breathing.

"Oh!" she exclaimed, heaving a deep sigh of relief. "I was just thinking…"

The sound could be heard again.

"My God! Couldn't it be the bell?" she said rushing out to the balcony.

"No," replied Anton Ivanych, "it's the foal which is grazing right near here with a bell tied to its neck. I saw it on my way here. I gave it a fright to stop it straying into the rye. Why don't you tell them to hobble it?"

Suddenly the sound of the bell could be heard, this time as if it were coming from right under the balcony, and getting louder and louder.

"Good Lord! That must be it, it's coming here! He's here, he's here!" Anna Pavlovna screamed. "Hurry, Anton Ivanych! Where are the servants? Where's Agrafena? Where *is* everyone? It's as if he were arriving at some stranger's house. My God!"

She was in a state of total confusion – and the bell was ringing as loud as if it were inside the room.

Anton Ivanych leapt up from the table.

"It's him, it's him!" he cried out. "And there's Yevsei on the coach box! Where's the icon, where's the bread and salt? Bring them quick! I don't have anything to greet him with on the porch! How can I, without bread and salt? It would be a bad omen! Why is everything so disorganized here! No one is prepared! And look at you, Anna Pavlovna, just standing there – why don't you go out to greet him? Hurry!"

"I can't!" she said, struggling to bring out the words. "My legs won't move." And with these words she collapsed into an armchair. Anton Ivanych snatched a hunk of bread from the table, put it on a plate along with a salt cellar and looked as if he was about to fly out of the room.

"Nothing is ready!" he complained. But before he could move towards the door, in burst three menservants and two housemaids.

"He's coming! He's coming! He's here!" they were shouting, as pale and terrified as if robbers were breaking in.

They were followed in by Alexander himself.

"Sashenka, my love!" exclaimed Anna Pavlovna, but stopped suddenly and regarded Alexander in bewilderment.

"But where's Sashenka?" she asked.

"It's me, Mummy!" he replied, kissing her hand.

"You?"

She stared at him.

"Is it really you, my dear?" she said, hugging him tightly. Then she took another look at him.

"What's happened to you? Are you ill?" she asked in a worried voice, without letting go of him.

"I'm fine, Mummy."

"Fine! What has happened to you, my darling? This isn't the way you looked when you left?"

She pulled him to her and burst into tears, kissing his head, his cheeks and his eyes.

"What's happened to your hair? It was like silk!" she asked, speaking through her tears. "Your eyes sparkled like two little stars; your cheeks were red as blood and as white as milk, like a ripe apple! Evil people must have robbed you of your beauty and my happiness out of envy. But wasn't your uncle watching out for you? And I thought I was entrusting you to the care of a responsible person! But he didn't know how to care for this precious treasure, my darling!"

The old woman wept and covered Alexander with kisses.

"It seems that tears in a dream are *not* a good omen," Anton Ivanych thought to himself.

"But, my dear lady, why are you weeping and wailing over him, as if he were dead?" he whispered. "It's a bad omen."

"How are you, Alexander Fyodorych!" he said. "It was God's will that we should meet again in this life."

Without speaking, Alexander offered him his hand. Anton Ivanych went to check that all the luggage had been brought in, and then proceeded to summon the whole household to come and greet the

CHAPTER 6

young master, but they had already congregated in the entrance and the hallway. He lined them all up and issued instructions about who was to kiss his hand, his shoulder or the hem of his garment, and what they should say to him in the process. One of the lads he simply threw out, telling him not to come back until he had washed his face and wiped his nose.

Yevsei, with a leather strap around his waist and covered in dust, was greeting the servants. He distributed gifts he had brought from St Petersburg – a silver ring for this one and a birchwood snuffbox to that one. When he saw Agrafena, he stood rooted to the spot and regarded her in silence with a stupefied grin of delight. She gave him a sidelong distrustful glance which in spite of herself was transformed in an instant into a radiant smile, and she burst into laughter. On the verge of tears, she suddenly turned away with a frown.

"Why don't you say something?" she said. "Standing there like a dummy; can't you even say hello?"

But he couldn't find anything to say, and went up to her with that same stupid grin on his face. She fended off his attempt to hug her.

"Look what the Devil dragged in!" she said indignantly, stealing the odd look at him – but there was a smile in her eyes which betrayed her delight.

"I suppose those St Petersburg girls turned your head as well as the young master's? Look at those whiskers you've grown!"

He took a small cardboard box out of his pocket and gave it to her. It contained bronze earrings. Then he pulled out of his bag a package in which a big headscarf was wrapped. She took both gifts and, without giving them a look, stuffed them into a cupboard.

"Show us what you got, Agrafena Ivanovna!" some of the other servants asked her.

She rounded on them. "What is there to look at? Nothing you haven't seen before! Get out, all of you, what are you doing standing around here?"

"This is for you too!" said Yevsei, handing her another package.

"Show us what's in it!" she was urged.

Agrafena tore off the wrapping, and several packs of used, but still almost new, playing cards spilt out.

"That's all you could find to bring?" said Agrafena. "You think I have nothing else to do, except play cards? What gave you the idea that I wanted to play cards with you?"

She put the cards away as well. An hour later, Yevsei was already installed in his old place, between the stove and the table.

"Lord! How quiet it is here!" he said, stretching out and pulling in his legs by turns. "This is the life! Not like St Petersburg – it's like being sentenced to hard labour up there! What about a bite to eat, Agrafena Ivanovna? I've had nothing to eat since the last staging post."

"Still up to your old tricks? Here then! The way you wolf it down, anyone would think that they starved you there."

Alexander visited all the rooms, and then went into the garden, where he stopped for a moment at every bench and every bush. His mother was by his side.

Whenever she looked at his pale face, she gave a sigh, but was afraid to cry in front of Anton Ivanych. She plied Alexander with questions about his life in St Petersburg, but was unable to find out why he was so pale and thin, and why he had lost so much hair. She offered him food and drink, but he refused and said he was so tired from the journey that all he wanted to do was sleep.

Anna Pavlovna inspected the bed to see if it was properly made, and scolded the maid for making it too hard; she ordered her to make it again while she watched her, and wouldn't leave the room until Alexander was safely tucked in. She crept from the room on tiptoe, and sternly admonished the servants not to speak or even to breathe aloud, and not to wear their boots while moving about the house. Then she gave orders for Yevsei to be sent to her. Agrafena came in with him. Yevsei knelt and kissed Anna Pavlovna's hand.

"What happened to Alexander?" she asked with menace in her voice. "Just look at him!"

Yevsei said nothing.

"Why don't you say something?" said Agrafena. "It's your mistress who's talking to you!"

CHAPTER 6

"Why has he got so thin?" said Anna Pavlovna. "And what happened to his hair?"

"It's not for me to know, madam: it's the master's business!"

"Not for you to know! But you must have noticed something?"

Yevsei didn't know what to say and kept silent.

"A fine one you found to trust!" said Agrafena, looking fondly at Yevsei at the same time. "It would have been a different matter if you had found a respectable person! What were you doing there? Answer your mistress! You'll be in for it later if you don't!"

"It's not as if I wasn't doing my job, madam!" said Yevsei timorously, looking back and forth between his mistress and Agrafena. "I served my master faithfully and loyally; if you would care to ask Arkhipych…"

"Who is Arkhipych?"

"He was the porter where we were."

"You see what nonsense he's talking!" said Agrafena. "Why bother listening to him, madam? You should lock him in the cowshed – that would loosen his tongue!"

"May the Lord strike me dead on the spot if I didn't do everything I was told to do!" said Yevsei. "I'll take the icon down from the wall!…"

"Oh yes, you're clever with words!" said Anna Pavlovna. "But when it comes to doing something, you're nowhere to be seen! I can see just how well you looked after my darling – you even let him ruin his health! That's what you call 'looking after'! Just you wait!… I'll show you!"

"How can you say I didn't look after him, madam? After eight years, only one of the master's shirts is missing, and I've even kept all his old ones."

"And what became of that shirt?" Anna Pavlovna said angrily.

"It never came back from the laundress. I reported it to Alexander Fyodorych, so that he wouldn't have to pay her, but he didn't say anything."

"What a creature!" said Anna Pavlovna. "Simply couldn't keep her hands off some good linen!"

"Me, not look after him!" Yevsei continued. "Everyone should be lucky enough to have someone like me to work so hard for him. Sometimes the young master would want to lie in, and I had to run to the baker's…"

THE SAME OLD STORY

"What kind of rolls did he eat?"

"White – the good kind."

"Yes, I know they were white, but was it shortbread?"

"What a dolt!" said Agrafena. "Doesn't even know how to talk properly – and he thinks he's a Petersburger!"

"No, it wasn't: it was Lenten bread," Yevsei replied.

"Lenten! You scoundrel, you murderer, you villain!" said Anna Pavlovna, purple with rage. "Didn't even enter your head to buy him shortbread rolls – and you were supposed to be looking after him!"

"But, madam, he didn't ask for them."

"Didn't ask for them! My darling doesn't care: he just eats whatever he's given. And you didn't even give it a thought? Didn't you remember that he always ate shortbread rolls when he was here? Buying Lenten rolls indeed! I suppose you spent the money on something else? You haven't heard the last of this! Now what else, tell me!"

"Well, after his morning tea," Yevsei went on, now intimidated, "he would go to the office, and I would clean his boots; I'd spend the whole morning on them, and clean them all over again – sometimes even three times. In the evening, he would take them off, and I'd clean them again. How can you say, madam, that I didn't look after him? I've never seen any other gentleman wearing boots shined like that. Pyotr Ivanych's boots weren't shined as well, and he had three servants!"

"But why does he look like this?" said Anna Pavlovna, somewhat mollified.

"Probably because of the writing, madam."

"Did he do much writing?"

"Oh yes, every day."

"What was he writing? Some kind of documents? What were they?"

"Documents, I should think."

"And you didn't try to stop him working so hard?"

"Yes, I did, madam. 'Don't sit there so long, Alexander Fyodorych,' I would say, 'perhaps you should take a walk; the weather is so good, and a lot of people are out and about. What's all this writing? You'll strain your heart, and your mother will be cross…'"

"And what did he say?"

CHAPTER 6

"Get out of here, you fool!"

"And he was quite right!" Agrafena interjected.

At this, Yevsei turned to look at her, and then turned back to look at his mistress.

"And what about his uncle: didn't he do anything to try to restrain him?" asked Anna Pavlovna.

"Restrain him, Madam? Why, he would come in, and if he found him doing nothing, he would really go for him. 'How can you just sit there doing nothing?' he would say. 'You're not back home in the country now; here you have to work, and not just lie around! All you do,' he says, 'is dream!' Then he really lets him have it…"

"How do you mean, 'lets him have it'?"

"He goes on about 'the provinces'… then they get into a real argument – and you wouldn't believe the language!"

"Curse him!" Anna Pavlovna said, and spat. "Let him have his own kids and insult them! When he should have tried restraining him, he… God in heaven! Merciful Lord!" she exclaimed. "How can you rely on anyone, if even your own flesh and blood are more dangerous than wild beasts?! Even a dog protects its puppies, and here is an uncle who mistreats his own nephew! And you, you dummy, couldn't ask his uncle not to lambast your master like that, and kindly leave him alone! Let him berate that creature he's married to! No, he's found his target! 'Work, work!' Let him work *himself* to death! He's no better than a dog – God forgive me! Like he's found a slave to work for him!"

This was followed by a moment of silence, broken only when Anna Pavlovna went on to say:

"When did Sashenka start looking so thin?"

"It was three years ago," replied Yevsei. "Alexander Fyodorych started moping around, didn't eat much, started getting thinner and thinner – just like a candle that's melting."

"Why was he 'moping'?"

"God knows, madam. Pyotr Ivanych talked to him about it; I could hear what he was saying, but it was beyond me – couldn't make head or tail of it all."

"But what was it that he was saying?"

Yevsei thought for a minute, apparently racking his brains trying to remember, and moving his lips.

"There was some word that they were using – but I've forgotten it."

Anna Pavlovna and Agrafena watched him, and waited impatiently for him to continue.

"Well?" said Anna Pavlovna.

Yevsei still remained silent.

"Well, say something, you scatterbrain!" Agrafena urged him. "The mistress is waiting."

"I think there was something about 'dis' er... 'ill... usioned'," Yevsei finally managed to get the word out.

Anna Pavlovna looked at Agrafena in bewilderment, and Agrafena looked at Yevsei. Yevsei looked back at them both, but had nothing to add.

"So what was it you were trying to say?" Anna Pavlovna asked.

"'Disi... disillusioned', yes that was it exactly – I remember!" Yevsei replied with great confidence.

"Something terrible must have happened – what could it have been? Lord above! Was he ill or something?" Anna Pavlovna asked in alarm.

"Oh dear, madam! Could it mean that he was under a spell of some kind?" Agrafena was quick to say.

Anna Pavlovna went pale, and spat.

"Bite your tongue!" she said. "Did he go to church?"

Yevsei was at a loss for words.

"I wouldn't say, madam, that he was very keen on going," he said hesitantly. "Well, you could almost say he didn't go at all... You see, the ladies and gentlemen there don't really go to church much."

"So that's why!" Anna Pavlovna said with a sigh, and crossed herself. "Obviously my prayers were not enough. That dream didn't lie: my darling did come from the whirlpool at the bottom of the lake!"

Anton Ivanych entered the room.

"Dinner's getting cold, Anna Pavlovna," he said. "Isn't it time to wake up Alexander Fyodorych?"

"Good God! Absolutely not!" she responded. "He didn't want to be woken up. 'Go and eat by yourself,' he said. 'I have no appetite. I'd

CHAPTER 6

better go to bed,' he said. 'I'll feel better after I've slept; maybe I'll feel like eating this evening.' Don't be cross with me, Anton Ivanych, I'm an old woman! I'm going to light the lamp near the icon and pray. I don't feel like eating while Sashenka is sleeping, so why don't you go and eat by yourself?"

"Very well, dear lady, I'll do as you say; you can count on me."

"Now, would you mind doing me a favour?" she continued. "You are our friend, and so devoted to our family. Please have a word with Yevsei, and try to wring out of him why Sashenka has become so glum and thin, and what happened to his hair. You're a man, so it's easier for you... Did someone upset him there? I mean there are so many bad people around... Find out everything you can!"

"Very good, dear lady, I'll question him thoroughly, and I'll get to the bottom of whatever it is. So please send Yevsei to me; I'll be having my dinner. Oh hello, Yevsei!" he said, sitting down at the table, and tucking in his napkin behind his tie. "How are you?"

"'How are you,' sir? You mean what was it like in St Petersburg? Not so good. I see you've filled out a bit in the meantime."

Anton Ivanych spat.

"Don't put the mockers on me, my fellow – you never know what trouble is round the corner!" he said, and began on his cabbage soup. "So, how was it there then?" he asked.

"All right, but not that good."

"How was the food? Pretty good, I suppose? What did they give you?"

"What indeed? Just some galantine from the shop, and some cold pie – and that's your dinner!"

"You mean, in the shop, or in your own kitchen?"

"No one cooked there. There, unmarried gentlemen don't keep a table."

"Come off it!" said Anton Ivanych, putting down his spoon.

"No, really! Even my master had food brought in from the tavern."

"Only gypsies live like that! And you expect people not to get thin! Here, have something to drink!"

"Thanks very much, sir! Here's to your health!"

No one spoke, and Anton Ivanych continued eating.

"How much are cucumbers there?" he asked, putting a cucumber on his plate.

"Forty copecks for ten."

"I don't believe it!"

"It's true, I swear. Why should I be ashamed to tell you – and sometimes salted cucumbers are brought from Moscow."

"Well, what do you know! Good Lord! Who wouldn't lose weight!"

"Where would you find a cucumber like that in that place?" Yevsei continued, pointing to a cucumber. "Not even in your dreams! Absolute rubbish! No one would even give them a look here; but *there* the gentry eat them. It's a rare home where they bake their own bread. As for storing cabbage, corning meat and soaking mushrooms – it's not something they do there."

Anton Ivanych shook his head, but said nothing because his mouth was full to bursting.

When he had finished chewing, he asked, "So what do they do?"

"You can get everything at the shop, and what they don't have, you can get at the butcher's nearby. If they don't have what you want, there's always the confectioner's, and if even they don't have it, then go to the Inglitz shop – but the French have everything!"

Silence.

"Well, and how much is suckling pig?" asked Anton Ivanych, loading his plate with almost half of one.

"I wouldn't know; we didn't buy any – it's kind of expensive, about two roubles, I think."

"Wow! No wonder people get thin! What a price!"

"The better class of gentlemen don't eat much of that: it's mostly the office clerks."

More silence.

"So, how was it for you there; pretty bad, was it?"

"You wouldn't believe how bad! You know what the kvass is like here – well, the beer there is even more watery. And after drinking the kvass, you feel your stomach is upset all day long! The only good thing they have there is the boot polish – that's some boot polish! You can't take your eyes off it! And what a great smell! You could almost eat it!"

CHAPTER 6

"You can't be serious?"

"I swear to you!"

Silence.

"So that's what it's like then?"

"That's right."

"And the food was lousy?"

"Lousy. Alexander Fyodorych ate practically nothing – almost gave up eating – not even a pound of bread for dinner."

"Well, of course he's got so thin! It's all because everything's so expensive, isn't it?"

"Yes, that and because they don't have the habit of eating until they're full every day. Those gentlemen don't eat, so much as snatch a bite here and there once a day – and that, only if they have time, between five and six – sometimes even after six, and even then it's just a quick snack – and that's it! For them, eating is something you do only when you've done everything else you have to do."

"What a way to live!" said Anton Ivanych. "Never mind getting thin, it's a wonder you didn't die! And it's the same all the time?"

"Well, no: on holidays these gents sometimes get together, and you wouldn't believe how they eat. They go to some German tavern and order up – would you believe? – a hundred roubles' worth. As for drink – God help us! – it's even worse than with people like us! And Pyotr Ivanych occasionally invited guests. They would sit down at the table sometime before seven and wouldn't leave it until after four in the morning."

At this, Anton Ivanych simply goggled.

"You really mean they were eating all that time?"

"Yes, the whole time!"

"That would have been quite a sight! Not like us at all! So what do they eat?"

"Well, there's really nothing to see, sir. You don't even recognize what you're eating; God knows what those Germans put in their food – you're afraid of putting it in your mouth. Even their pepper is different. They pour into their sauce something from those imported bottles. Once Pyotr Ivanych's cook invited me to eat some of the food he had cooked for him. I was nauseous for three days afterwards. I saw there was an olive in the food, and thought it would be like the olives we have here. I took a bite – and there it was – a tiny fish right inside it! It tasted awful, and I had to spit it out. I tried another one – same thing. They were all the same – the hell with the lot of you!"

"You mean they serve them like that on purpose?"

"God knows! I did ask – all the fellows just laughed. They said, 'They're born like that, get it?' First came a hot course, quite normal, served with pies – but about the size of a thimble; you pop half a dozen of them in your mouth, start chewing, only to find you've already swallowed them without knowing it – they dissolved… Straight after the first course, they suddenly serve a sweet course, then beef, then ice cream, then some kind of greens, and finally a roast… couldn't eat that stuff!"

"So your stove was never lit? Of course, anyone would lose weight on that diet!" said Anton Ivanych, getting up from the table. "We offer thanks to thee, O God," he began aloud with a deep sigh, "who filled the earth with heavenly blessings… What am I saying? My tongue ran away with me; I mean 'earthly blessings' – and do not deprive me of your heavenly kingdom.

"Clear the table! The mistress and the young master will not be eating. This evening prepare another suckling pig… or do you have a turkey? Alexander Fyodorych likes turkey, and he must be getting hungry. And now bring some fresh hay to the attic for me; I'm going to take a nap for an hour or so, but wake me up in time for tea. If Alexander Fyodorych stirs… well, you know, wake me up."

After his nap, he went to Anna Pavlovna.

"So, Anton Ivanych, what do you have to tell me?"

"Nothing, dear lady, I just want to thank you so much for your hospitality… and I had such a nice nap – the hay was so fresh and smelt so good…"

"You're most welcome, Anton Ivanych! So, what does Yevsei say? Did you ask him?"

"Of course I did! I found out everything – nothing to it! The problem will soon be solved. It's all because, let me tell you, the food was so bad there."

CHAPTER 6

"The food?"

"Yes, judge for yourself. Cucumbers, ten for forty copecks. Suckling pig, two roubles. The food all comes from the confectioner's – never enough to fill your stomach. Of course people are going to get thin! Don't worry, dear lady, we'll put him back on his feet now that he's here, and get him healthy. Just give the order to prepare a little more birch liquor. I'll give you the recipe – I got it from Prokof Astafich. Give him a glass or two in the morning and in the evening – and before dinner too. You can use holy water… do you have any?"

"Yes, I do; you brought some yourself."

"Oh yes, so I did. And make sure the food is fattening. I ordered suckling pig or turkey for supper."

"Thank you, Anton Ivanych."

"Not at all, dear lady! Perhaps you would care to order some chickens with white sauce?"

"Yes, I will…"

"No need to trouble yourself. What am I here for? I'll take care of it. Let me…"

"Yes, please do, you're such a help, like a father to this family."

He left the room, but she started thinking.

Her woman's instinct and her mother's heart told her that it was not food which was the real reason for Alexander's despondent mood. She tried to draw it out of him indirectly by dropping hints and in a roundabout way, but Alexander didn't take the hints and remained silent. Two weeks went by in this fashion. A lot of suckling pigs, chickens and turkeys came Anton Ivanych's way, but Alexander remained just as glum and thin as ever, and his hair didn't grow back.

Finally, Anna Pavlovna made up her mind to have it out with him.

"Listen, my dear Sashenka," she said to him when the opportunity presented itself. "You've been living here for a month now, and I haven't seen you smile once. You move around like a storm cloud, looking down at the floor. Is it that you don't find any satisfaction on your home ground? It looks as if life was better for you when you were away, and now you're pining for that life? It's breaking my heart to see you like this. What happened to you? Tell me what it is you're missing – whatever it is, I'll make sure you get it. Has someone upset you? I'll see that they'll pay for it!"

"Don't worry, Mummy," said Alexander, "it's nothing really! It's just that I've grown up, matured and am thinking about things more: that's why I'm a little glum…"

"And what about being so thin and losing your hair?"

"I can't explain why, there's no way I can tell you everything that happened in eight years. Quite possibly my health *has* suffered a little…"

"Where does it hurt?"

"Here and here," he said pointing to his head and his heart.

Anna Pavlovna felt his forehead with her hand.

"No fever," she said. "What could it be? A shooting pain in the head?"

"No… it's just…"

"Sashenka, let's send for Ivan Andreich."

"Who is Ivan Andreich?"

"The new doctor; he came about two years ago – a real expert. He never prescribes any medicine. He gives tiny grains that he makes himself – and they help. Our Foma had some stomach trouble: he was screaming with pain for three days. The doctor gave him three grains – the pain disappeared like magic! Let's get you some treatment, my darling!"

"No, Mummy, that won't help; it will go away by itself."

"So why are you moping like this? You must have had some bad experience – what was it?"

"It was just…"

"What is it you want?"

"I don't know myself – I'm just miserable."

"Heavens above! It's a total mystery!" said Anna Pavlovna. "You say you like the food, you have every comfort, a good position. Could it be – I wonder? And you're listless! Sashenka," she said quietly after a pause, "isn't it time you… got married?"

"What do you mean?! No, I'm not getting married."

"I have my eye on a girl – a little doll, rosy-cheeked, and so delicate, absolutely gorgeous, a real beauty! And such a beautifully slim waist and a slim figure. She was at boarding school in the city. She owns

CHAPTER 6

seventy-five serfs and is worth 25,000 roubles and comes with a splendid dowry. Her people were in business in Moscow, and she comes from a good family... So, Sashenka, what about it? I've already had coffee with her mother, and just casually dropped a hint. She showed every sign of being delighted..."

"I'm not getting married," Alexander repeated.

"You mean never?"

"Never."

"Merciful God! Where will this all end? People are people, everyone except you – God knows what you are! And what joy it would bring me if God would grant me grandchildren to make a fuss of. Believe me: marry her and you will grow to love her..."

"I will not grow to love her, Mummy, I've done with love."

"How could you have? You haven't even been married. Who were you in love with there?"

"A girl."

"How come you didn't get married?"

"She betrayed me."

"How do you mean, 'betrayed'? You weren't married to her?"

Alexander said nothing.

"What kind of young women can they be in St Petersburg, if they fall in love before marriage? Betray! How disgraceful! She had happiness within her grasp and couldn't appreciate it! Despicable! If I ever met her, I would spit in her face. Is that how your uncle was looking after you? Who could she have preferred to you? If only I had been there! Anyway, she's not the only girl in the world: you'll find someone to love another time."

"I did fall in love with someone another time."

"Who was it?"

"A widow."

"So how come you didn't marry her?"

"I was the one who betrayed *her*."

Anna Pavlovna looked at him and didn't know what to say.

"Betrayed her!..." she repeated. "Obviously a shameless hussy!" she added. "A real den of debauchery, God forgive us! Love before marriage, without the sacraments of the Church, unfaithfulness. When I think of all the terrible things that go on in this world, the end of the world must be at hand! But tell me, isn't there anything I can do for you? Perhaps the food isn't to your liking – I can send for a cook from the town…"

"No, thank you, everything is fine."

"Perhaps it's dull just being by yourself; I could ask some neighbours to call."

"No, no, please don't bother, Mummy. It's nice and quiet here: it's fine, it will soon pass… I still haven't got my bearings."

And that was all that Anna Pavlovna could get out of him.

"No," she thought to herself, "without God, there's no way forward." She asked Alexander if he would go to Mass with her in the next village, but he overslept twice, and she couldn't bring herself to wake him. Finally she asked him to go one evening to the night service. "I suppose so," he said, and they went. His mother entered the church quickly and stood right next to the choir. Alexander stationed himself near the door.

The sun was setting, and its slanting rays played on the golden frames of the icons or lit up the dark, severe images of the saints and blotted out with their brilliance the weak and tremulous flickering of the candles. The church was almost empty; the peasants were at work in the fields. But in a corner near the exit, a few old women were huddled together wearing white headscarves. Some others, looking forlorn with their cheeks resting on their hands, were sitting on the stone step of a side altar, from time to time emitting loud sighs of distress – whether for their sins or for their domestic problems, God alone knows. Others again fell to the ground and prostrated themselves, and lay there for hours praying.

A fresh breeze blew in through the iron grating into the window, lifting the cloth on the altar and rustling the grey hairs of the priest, turning the page of a book here and there and snuffing out a candle. The footsteps of the priest and the sexton rang out on the stone floor of the empty church. The sound of their voices echoed cheerlessly among the columns. Up in the dome, jackdaws cawed and sparrows

CHAPTER 6

chirped, flying back and forth from one window to another, the flapping of their wings and the tolling of the bells sometimes drowning out the service...

"As long as a man's life forces are hard at work," Alexander was thinking, "as long as his desires and passions are driving him, his feelings are fully engaged, and he shuns the calming, important, solemn process of contemplation to which religion leads, and he seeks consolation in it only when his forces are spent and exhausted, his hopes are crushed, and he is burdened with age..."

Little by little, the sight of these familiar objects began to evoke memories within him. In his mind, he revisited his childhood and youth – the time before he left for St Petersburg. He remembered how, when he was a child, he repeated the prayers after his mother. How she taught him about the guardian angel who guards the human soul and wages a constant struggle with the Evil One; he remembered how, pointing at the stars, she explained that they were God's angels, who watch the world and keep count of the good and evil deeds of people, and how these divine beings weep when a person's evil deeds outweigh his good deeds, and how they rejoice when the good outweighs the evil. She would point to the distant blue of the horizon and tell him that that was Zion... Alexander sighed as he awoke from these memories.

"Oh, if only I could believe all this once again!" he thought. "The beliefs of my childhood are lost, but what have I learnt since that is new and certain? Nothing. What I have found is doubt, mere talk, theories... I have ended up further from the truth than ever. Why all this clash of opinions, all this hair-splitting? My God! When the heart is no longer warmed by the heat of faith, how can one hope to be happy? Am I any happier now?"

The service ended. Alexander returned home even more despondent than he had set out. Anna Pavlovna had no idea what to do. Once he woke up earlier than usual, and heard a rustling at his bedside. He looked round: an old woman was standing over him and whispering. She disappeared as soon as she saw that she had been noticed. Under his pillow Alexander found a herb of some kind, and an amulet had been hung around his neck.

"What does this mean?" Alexander asked his mother. "Who was that old woman who came into my room?"

Anna Pavlovna was embarrassed.

"That... was Nikitishna," she said.

"Who is this Nikitishna?"

"Well, my dear, you see... I don't want you to be angry..."

"What is this all about? Tell me!"

"She helps a lot of people, they say. She just whispers over water and breathes on someone sleeping – and it all goes away."

"Two years ago," said Agrafena, "a fiery serpent used to fly down the widow Sidorikha's chimney at night..."

At this point Anna Pavlovna spat.

"Nikitishna," Agrafena continued, "cast a spell on the serpent, and it stopped coming."

"So what happened to the widow Sidorikha?" asked Alexander.

"She gave birth, but the child was all black and skinny, and it died after two days."

Alexander burst out laughing, perhaps for the first time since his arrival.

"Where did you find her?" he asked.

"Anton Ivanych brought her," Anna Pavlovna replied.

"Why are you so willing to listen to that fool?"

"A fool! Oh, Sashenka, how can you? It's a sin! Anton Ivanych a fool! How can you say such a thing? Anton Ivanych is our benefactor, our friend!"

"Then take this amulet and give it to our 'friend and benefactor' – let him wear it round his neck."

From then on, he always locked the door when he went to bed at night.

Two or three months went by. Little by little, the seclusion, the quiet, the domestic life and all the comforts that went with it helped Alexander to put some flesh back on his bones. Idleness, freedom from care and the absence of any moral disturbances gave him the peace of mind that he had sought in vain in St Petersburg. While he was there, in flight from the world of ideas and the arts, confined within stone walls, he wanted only to sleep like a mole, but he was constantly troubled by surges of

CHAPTER 6

envy and frustration. Everything that happened in the worlds of science and art, the emergence of every new celebrity, confronted him with the question: "Why not me, why is it never me?" In St Petersburg, at every turn he would be forced to make invidious comparisons by the people he met. There – he was so often found wanting; there, it was as if he was facing a mirror in which he saw all his weaknesses reflected, and there... was the inexorable figure of his uncle constantly deriding his way of thinking, his idleness and his totally unwarranted dreams of glory. There – was a world of sophistication and refinement and an abundance of talent, in which he played no part. And finally, there – people tried to subject life to certain conditions, to bring its dark and enigmatic side into the light, leaving no room for feeling, passion or dreams, and robbing life of its poetic enchantment, wanting only to stamp it out – a dry, dull, uniform and oppressive pattern...

But here – what freedom! Here – he was better, cleverer than the rest! Here – he was idolized by everyone for versts around. Furthermore, here – confronted by nature at every step, his soul was nourished by peaceful and restful impressions. The babbling of the brooks, the whisper of the leaves, the chill and at times the very silence of nature inspired thought and aroused feeling. In the garden, in the fields and in the house, he was visited by memories of his childhood and youth. Anna Pavlovna, sitting by his side, would sometimes seem to divine his thoughts. She helped him to revive his memory of certain trifling details of life which were dear to him, or simply spoke of things which he had forgotten.

"Look at those lime trees," she said, pointing to the garden, "they were planted by your father. I was pregnant with you. I would sit here on the balcony and watch him. He would work and work away and look at me, with sweat pouring from him in torrents. 'Ah! You're here?' he would say. 'That's what makes it such a pleasure to work!' And then he would go back to work. And there is the meadow where you used to play with the other children. You always got so angry – any little thing that rubbed you the wrong way, and you would cry blue murder. Once, Agashka – the one who's married to Kuzma now; his is the third cabin from the village fence – happened to shove you – your nose was all bloody and bruised. Your father gave her such a thrashing – I had a hard time getting him to stop."

Alexander mentally supplemented these memories with others: "It was on that bench over there under the tree," he thought, "that I used to sit with Sofia – I was so happy then. And over there between the two lilac bushes, she gave me my first kiss." And all that he could see so clearly. He would smile at these recollections and spend hours sitting on the balcony, watching the sun rise or set, listening to the bird chorus, the lapping of waves on the lake and the humming of the unseen insects.

"My God! How good it is here!" he said under the influence of these tender impressions. "Far from the hurly-burly, from that petty existence, from that anthill where people

"In droves behind the fence,
Breathe not the early morning chill,
Nor the vernal fragrance of the meadow.*

"How tired you get of living there, and how your soul reposes here, in this simple, uncomplicated, unpretentious life! Your heart is reborn, your breast breathes more freely, and your mind is not tormented by painful thoughts, and its endless battle with the heart: here they are in perfect harmony. There's nothing your mind needs to dwell on. Free from care, without troubling thoughts, your heart and mind at rest, and with only the mildest quickening of the pulse, does your gaze flit from the wood to the ploughed field, and from the field to the hill, finally losing itself in the endless blue of the sky."

Sometimes he crossed over to the window which gave onto the courtyard, the street and the village. A different picture altogether – like a painting by Teniers, full of bustling family life.* Barbos sheltering in the shade of his kennel, stretched out with his head resting on his paws. The hens in their dozens greeting the morning, and clucking as they chase each other around, while the cocks fight. A flock of sheep is being driven to the field along the village street. Sometimes, the forlorn sound can be heard of the mooing of a stranded cow which

CHAPTER 6

has been left behind by the herd, standing in the middle of the street and looking in all directions.

Peasants – men and women – were on their way to work, carrying rakes and scythes on their shoulders. Occasionally a gust of wind would snatch two or three words of a conversation and carry them up to the window. Over there, a peasant's cart was rumbling over the bridge, followed lazily by a hay wain. Blonde, unkempt children, lifting their smocks, were wandering over the meadows. As he watched this scene, Alexander began to appreciate the poetry of "the leaden sky, the broken fence, the wicket gate, the dirty pond and the trepak folk dance".* He had exchanged his fashionably cut frock coat for the loose and comfortable garment worn around the house. The ever-watchful eye of his loving mother kept track of every part and every moment of this peaceful domesticity – in the morning, in the evening, at the table and at leisure.

She could never get her fill of the pleasure of watching Alexander fill out, the colour returning to his cheeks, and his eyes beginning to glow with life. "His hair won't come back, of course," she said. "It was like silk."

Alexander often went for walks in the surrounding area. Once he met a crowd of women and young girls on their way to pick mushrooms in the wood. He went with them and spent the whole day there. When he returned home, he commended a girl called Masha for her agility and skill, and Masha was taken into the household to "attend the master". He would sometimes ride out to watch the work in the fields and saw at first hand what he so often used to write about for the journal. "How often we were wrong in what we wrote…" he thought, and shook his head, and he began to take a deeper and closer interest in the subject.

Once, when the weather was bad, he thought he would try to do a little work. He sat down to write, and was quite pleased with the first results. He needed a certain book for reference purposes, and wrote away to St Petersburg for it to be sent. He set to work in earnest, and sent away for more books. Anna Pavlovna tried to dissuade him from writing in order to prevent him from "overstraining his heart", but he wouldn't hear of it. She sent in Anton Ivanych. Alexander wouldn't listen to him either, and continued to write. Three or four months later, and not only had he not lost weight, but he had actually put on some, and Anna Pavlovna's mind was at rest.

Eighteen months had passed in this manner. Everything would have been fine, except that towards the end of this time Alexander started to brood again. It wasn't that he had any special wishes – and even if he had, they would have been easily granted: they did not fall outside the confines of his home life. Nothing in particular bothered him: no worries, no doubts, yet he was bored. Little by little he began to feel stifled by the tight domestic circle in which he was confined. His mother's coddling became tiresome; he was fed up with his work, and was no longer captivated by nature.

He would sit in silence by the window, regarding his father's lime trees without interest, and was irritated by the lapping of the lake. He began to reflect on the reason for this new mood of despondency, and found that he was missing – St Petersburg?! The further removed he became from his past, the more he began to regret it. Blood still ran hot in his veins, and his heart was still beating; his soul and his body craved activity... A new problem. My God! He almost wept over this revelation. He had thought that his despondency would pass, that he would get used to living in the country, get into the habit... but no: the longer he lived there, the more depressed he became, and the more he longed to return to that maelstrom which he now knew so well.

He had come to terms with his past, and he thought of it fondly. His hatred, his mournful look, his sullenness, his unsociability, had all diminished because of the seclusion in which he had been living and the thinking he had done. He saw the past in a clearer light and the treacherous Nadenka almost in a new and brighter light. "But what am I doing here?" he said irritably. "Why am I going to waste? Why am I allowing my gifts to moulder? Why not let my work make an impression there? I've become wiser. My uncle is no better than me. Surely I can make my own way? Of course, I haven't been successful so far: I've been fighting the wrong battles – but, never mind, I've finally woken up – the time has come! But how upset Mother will be if I leave! But still, I have to leave; I can't stay and rot here! There, others have

CHAPTER 6

made their way in the world... And what about my own career, and my fortune? I alone have dropped behind... and what for? And why?" He rushed around in his consternation, and didn't know how he was going to be able to tell his mother that he was leaving.

But his mother saved him the trouble – by dying.

This is finally what he wrote to his uncle and aunt in St Petersburg. To his aunt:

Before I left St Petersburg, ma tante, you sent me on my way with tears in your eyes and some precious words which have engraved themselves on my memory. You said, "If you should ever feel in need of warm friendship, sincere sympathy, then there will always be a corner in my heart for you." The time has now come when I have finally understood the full value of those words. The claims that you so generously granted me on your heart promise me peace of mind, quiet, consolation and tranquillity, and perhaps even happiness in my life. Three months ago my mother passed away. I will say no more about that. From my letters you will know what she meant to me, and you will understand what I have lost in her... I am now leaving this place for ever. But where would a solitary wanderer like me head for, if not for whatever place you happen to be? Just tell me one thing: will I find in you the same person that I left eighteen months ago? Perhaps you have erased me from your memory? Would you agree to assume the tedious task of healing a new and grievous wound with that same friendship which has more than once rescued me from distress in the past? I am investing all my hope in you as well as in your powerful ally – activity.

This must surely be a surprise to you? And you must find it strange to hear this from me, and to read these lines written in such a calm and uncharacteristic style. But don't be surprised, and don't be afraid. The man who comes to you will not be deranged and will not be a dreamer – nor will he be bitter or provincial: just a man like so many others in St Petersburg, the kind of man I should long since have become. Please make a point of preparing my uncle for this. When I look back on my life, I feel embarrassed and ashamed for myself and others, but it couldn't have been otherwise. Look how long it took me to wake up! Not until I was thirty! St Petersburg was a harsh school for me, but that together with the thought I have been giving to the matter back at home in the country have made my destiny quite clear to me. Having put a considerable distance between myself and my uncle's lessons and my St Petersburg experience, I have been able to make sense of both since I have been here away from the hurly-burly, and now see things as clearly as I should have done at the time. I also see how pitifully and foolishly I strayed from the direct path to my goal. I am now at peace. I'm no longer tormented or harassed by doubts – but I'm not satisfied with that. It may be that this tranquillity still stems from sheer egoism. However, I have the feeling that very soon my outlook on life will become still clearer, to the point where I will discover a new source of tranquillity – and a healthier one. Right now I still can't help regretting that I have reached that Rubicon where, alas, youth ends and the time comes for reflection, careful consideration and analysis of life's setbacks – a time for being aware. It may be that my opinion of people and life hasn't changed much, but I no longer nurse so many hopes and desires – in brief, I've lost my illusions. Accordingly, there is not so much room left for mistakes, or allowing myself to be deceived. And from a certain standpoint that's very comforting! So now I see the future more clearly: the worst is behind me; I'm less afraid of turmoil, because there's less opportunity for it. The worst turmoil is behind me, and I couldn't be more thankful for it. I'm ashamed to remember how, when I thought myself a victim, I used to curse my fate – and life itself. Curse! How pitifully childish and ungrateful! As I later realized, suffering cleanses the soul and makes a man tolerable both to himself and others – it exalts him. I now acknowledge that not to partake of suffering is not to partake of the fullness of life. There are many important issues inherent in suffering which we probably cannot expect to resolve while we are here. I see in turmoil and trouble the hand of Providence, which faces man with an endless task – to keep moving forward, to aim higher than his appointed goal while struggling at every turn against illusory hopes, against painful impediments. I see too that this struggle and this turmoil are

CHAPTER 6

a necessary part of life, and that without them life would not be life, but stagnation, sleep... When the struggle is over, before you know it, life itself is over: a man has worked, loved, experienced pleasure, suffered, done what he had to do – in other words, he has lived!

Do you understand the way I see it? I have emerged from the darkness, and now see that the whole of my life so far has been nothing but a kind of difficult preparation for the present journey, a tortuous apprenticeship for life. Something tells me that the rest of the journey will be easier, less turbulent, clearer. Light has been shed on dark places, difficult knots have come untied by themselves. Life is coming to seem like a blessing, and not a curse. Soon I will once again be saying "How good life is!" But I won't be saying it as a youth intoxicated by the pleasure of the moment, but rather in total awareness of life's true pleasures and pains. So, even death itself is not frightening: it presents itself as a beautiful experience rather than a nightmare. Now, finally a breath of unaccustomed tranquillity has wafted into my soul; the infantile grievances, the pinpricks of wounded self-esteem, the childish temper tantrums and comical anger against the world and people, just like the dog who got angry with the elephant – it's as if none of this ever happened.

I have made friends again with those whom I had long ago discarded – with people both here and in St Petersburg; it's just that they, I note in passing, are a little more difficult, coarser and more ridiculous. But I'm not angry with them, both here and in St Petersburg, and I'm even less likely to be so in the future. Here is an example of my new tolerance. There is a character called Anton Ivanych who is always coming round, and we entertain him. This time it was, according to him, "to share my grief", and tomorrow he'll be going to a neighbour's wedding – "to share their joy" – and while he's there, he'll be offering his services to someone as their wise woman. But neither grief nor joy ever prevents him from dropping in on everyone for meals four or five times a day. I see that he couldn't care less whether it's a death, a birth or a wedding, but I don't find him repugnant – he doesn't bother me... I tolerate him, and don't throw him out. A good sign, don't you think, ma tante? What will you say when you see what I have just written in praise of myself?

To his uncle:

My uncle, who could not be nicer or kinder – or should I say, "Your Excellency"?

You can't imagine how delighted I was to learn that your career has been crowned with well-deserved success; your fortune you acquired long ago. And here you are with the rank of actual civil councillor* and a director of Chancery!

May I make so bold as to remind Your Excellency of a promise you made when I was leaving: "When you need a position, an occupation or money, come to me!" is what you said. Well now, I need both a position and an occupation – and, of course, I will be needing money. Yes, this poor provincial dares to ask for accommodation and work. What fate will this request meet? Will it be the same fate once met by Zayezzhalov's letter when he wrote asking for your help in some case of his?

As for "creative endeavour", which you were unkind enough to mention in one of your letters... wasn't it wrong of you to bring up such long-forgotten follies, which I blush to think of even now? Oh, Uncle – oh, Your Excellency! Who hasn't been young once and a little foolish? Who has never had some strange, so called "cherished" dream which was fated never to come true? Take my neighbour on the right, who imagined himself to be a hero, a giant – a veritable Mighty Hunter... who wanted to astound the world with his exploits; he ended up as a retired warrant officer who never saw combat, and now peacefully grows potatoes and sows turnips. The neighbour on my left dreamt of revolutionizing Russia and the whole world on his own terms, and after working as a clerk in the law courts for some time, moved down here, and still hasn't even managed to repair his fence. I thought that I had been endowed from on high with a creative gift and wanted to reveal to the world new and unheard-of secrets, without suspecting that those secrets weren't actually secrets,

CHAPTER 6

and that I was no prophet. All of us were ridiculous – but tell me, who, without blushing for himself, is entitled to pillory and hold up to ridicule these youthful, noble, impetuous, although not entirely modest dreams? Who has not, at one time or another, harboured unattainable ambitions or imagined himself a hero performing feats of valour, whose praises would be sung and whose glory would be of epic proportions? Whose imagination has not been carried away to bygone heroic and fabulous times? Who has not been moved to tears by lofty thoughts and intimations of beauty? If there is such a person, let him cast a stone at me – I do not envy him. I blush for my youthful dreams, but I honour them: they testify to a purity of heart; they are a sign of the nobility of a soul aspiring to the good.

You, I know, will not be swayed by these arguments; you need pragmatic, practical arguments – well, here is one for you. Tell me how would a person's potential ever come to be recognized and developed if the young were to suppress their own budding propensities, if they did not give free rein to their dreams and were instead slavishly to toe some line that had been laid down for them, without putting themselves to the test? Ultimately, isn't it a law of nature that youth should be troubled, hot-blooded, sometimes even wild, foolish, and that, equally, the dreams of everyone must subside with time, just as my own now have subsided? Were you in your own youth immune from such failings? Try to remember: rummage in your memory. I can see from where I'm sitting how you, with your calm, unflappable expression, are shaking your head and saying, "No, nothing of the kind!" But allow me to unmask you; in love, for example, would you recant? No, you wouldn't. But I am in possession of the evidence. Remember, I was able to investigate the scene of the crime. The drama of your amours was played out before my very eyes, and its theatre was – the lake. Yellow flowers still grow along the shore: one of them duly dried and preserved. I have the honour to enclose and present it to Your Excellency as a sweet memento. But there is even a more deadly weapon to aim at your assaults on love in general, and mine in particular – namely a document! Are you frowning? Well, it's quite a document! Are you growing pale? I filched this precious tattered relic from my aunt's no less withered bosom and carry it with me as everlasting proof against you and as protection for myself. You may well tremble, Uncle! Furthermore, I am privy to all the details of your love story: my aunt regales me with them every day, at tea in the morning, at supper and as sleep approaches – complete with every interesting detail. I am including all this precious material in a special memoir. I will not fail to hand it over to you in person, along with my writings on agriculture which I have been working on for the last year. For my own part, I feel it is my duty to assure my aunt that your "feelings" – as she calls them – for her have remained unchanged. When I have the honour of receiving from Your Excellency a favourable response to my request, I will be honoured to present myself to you with a gift of dried raspberries and honey together with some letters which my neighbours have promised to supply me with in accordance with their needs – except for Zayezzhalov, who died before the end of his trial.

Epilogue

This is an account of what happened to the principal characters in this novel four years after Alexander's return to St Petersburg.

One morning Pyotr Ivanych was pacing back and forth in his study. This was no longer the old, cheerful, well-built, slim Pyotr Ivanych with his uniformly calm expression, standing straight with his head held high and proud. Whether it was because of age or circumstances, he seemed to have let himself go. His movements were not as agile, his look not as firm and self-confident, and a lot of grey had crept into his side whiskers and temples. It was apparent that he had celebrated his fiftieth birthday. He walked with something of a stoop. What was particularly strange was to see on the face of this impassive and calm man – as we knew him formerly – an expression something more than just worried, but actively depressed, although it still conveyed his essential character.

He seemed to be in a state of bewilderment. He would take a couple of steps and then stop suddenly in the middle of the room, or walk rapidly back and forth between the opposite corners of the room. It looked as if he had suddenly been visited by an unaccustomed thought.

In an armchair near the table there was seated a shortish, portly man wearing a cross around his neck, and a tightly buttoned tailcoat. He was sitting with one leg crossed over the other. The only thing lacking was a big gold-knobbed cane in his hands, that traditional cane which used to be the clue by which a reader immediately identified a doctor. Perhaps, this mace-like appurtenance was also appropriate to his role as a doctor. With it, when not otherwise occupied, he would go for a stroll, and with it he would sit for hours at the bedside of a patient, offering comfort, with the expression on his face doing duty for two or three different roles: those of physician, practical philosopher and family friend – to name but three. But this was all very well in expansive and spacious circumstances, where people rarely fall ill, and where a doctor is more of a luxury than a necessity. But Pyotr Ivanych's doctor was a St Petersburg doctor, who did not know what it was to travel on his own two feet, although he actually prescribed constitutionals for his patients. He was a member of some council, the secretary of some society, a professor, and was the doctor for a number of official institutions. He also provided medical services to the poor, and was an indispensable presence at all consultations; he also had his own extensive practice. He never took off his left glove, and would never have taken off his right glove had it not sometimes been necessary to take a pulse; he never unbuttoned his tailcoat, and practically never sat down. On this occasion, out of sheer impatience, he had been crossing his left leg over his right, and his right over his left in turn. He had been waiting to leave for quite some time, but Pyotr Ivanych had not yet said a thing.

"What is to be done, doctor?" he asked, stopping suddenly in front of him.

"Go to Kissingen,"* replied the doctor, "it's the only thing left to do, since these attacks of yours have started to recur too frequently—"

"But why are you only talking about me?" said Pyotr Ivanych, interrupting the doctor. "I'm talking to you about my wife. I'm past fifty, but she is still in her prime, and she has a life to live; and if her health has already begun to decline at this time..."

"What's all this talk about decline?!" the doctor remarked. "I was simply telling you of my apprehensions about the future, but right now there is nothing... I was simply trying to say that her health... or her indisposition, but as it is... well, not exactly a normal condition..."

"Doesn't it amount to the same thing? You just slipped in that comment, and you've also forgotten that since I've been watching her closely every day, I've been discovering more and more disquieting changes, and for the last three months I haven't had an untroubled moment. I don't know why I didn't see it earlier – I just don't understand! My official duties and other business are taking up too much of my time, and undermining my health... and now, it seems, hers too."

He resumed his pacing of the room.

EPILOGUE

"Have you questioned her today?" he asked, after a pause.

"Yes, but she hasn't noticed anything wrong with her. At first, I supposed that the reason might be physiological; she has had no children… but, apparently not! Perhaps the reason is purely psychological…"

"That makes it easier," said Pyotr Ivanych.

"But perhaps there really is nothing wrong. There are definitely no suspicious symptoms. What I think is that you have been staying too long in this swampy climate. Go to the south, expose yourself to new impressions, and then see what happens. Spend the summer in Kissingen, take the waters, and then Italy in the autumn, and Paris in the winter. I can assure you that the accumulation of mucus, irritability… won't be a trace left!"

Pyotr Ivanych was hardly listening to him.

"A psychological cause!" he muttered in an undertone, and shook his head.

"Let me tell you why I mention a psychological reason," said the doctor. "Anyone who didn't know you, might suspect that there were worries, or rather, not worries… but rather frustration of some kind; sometimes people have certain needs, something is missing… I just wanted to leave you with this thought—"

"Needs, frustration!" Pyotr Ivanych broke in. "Everything she desires is taken care of; I know all her tastes and habits. As for needs, hm! You've seen our home, you know how we live?"

"You have a wonderful home," said the doctor, "marvellous… your cook, your cigars. But how come that friend of yours who lives in London… has stopped sending you sherry? I haven't seen him here this year for some reason…"

"Fate is so treacherous, doctor! Could it really be that I haven't been as careful as I should with her?" Pyotr Ivanych began more heatedly than usual. "I've always weighed everything so carefully, I believe, and every step I've taken… No, somewhere along the line something went wrong. But where? With all the success, with the career I've had… I don't know!"

He waved his hand and continued to pace.

"Why are you so upset?" said the doctor. "There's nothing at all dangerous. I can only repeat what I said the first time: that organically she is perfectly healthy, and there are no threatening symptoms. Some anaemia, a little run down – but that's all!"

"Nothing to worry about then!" said Pyotr Ivanych.

"Ill health is a bad thing, not a good thing..." the doctor went on. "It's not that she's the only one. Take those outsiders who live here – what do you see when you look at them? So get away from here! And if you can't get away, do something to bring her out of herself; don't just leave her to sit at home: try to please her, take her places, provide more exercise for her body and spirit – they are both in a state of unnatural stagnation. Of course, in time it may affect her lungs, or..."

"Goodbye, doctor! I'm going to see her," said Pyotr Ivanych, and hurried to his wife's sitting room. He stopped at the door, quietly parted the curtains and gave her an anxious look.

She... well, what was it that the doctor had noticed particularly about her? Anyone seeing her for the first time would have found in her a woman like many others in St Petersburg. Pale, it is true, lustreless eyes, her blouse hanging loosely and evenly about her narrow shoulders and flat chest, her movements slow, almost sluggish. But rosy cheeks, the glitter in the eye, the liveliness of movement are hardly the hallmarks of *our* beauties. Neither Phidias nor Praxiteles* would have found here a Venus for their chisels. No, plasticity of beauty is not to be sought among our northern beauties: they are not statuesque, they are not given to the poses of antiquity, in which the beauty of Greek women were immortalized – indeed, the very material into which these poses were moulded is not to be found here; nor are those flawless and perfect contours of the body... Sensuality does not flow from their eyes in a hot stream; their half-opened lips do not glisten with that innocently voluptuous smile that issues from the torrid mouths of the women of the south. Our women have been endowed with another, higher form of beauty. The sculptor's chisel cannot capture that gleam of thought in the features of their faces, that struggle of the will with passion, or the interplay between those ineffable utterances of the soul with the numberless subtle shades of wilful ambiguity, of feigned artlessness, anger and kindness, hidden joys... and sufferings – all those momentary flashes of lightning bursting forth from the concentric circles of the soul...

EPILOGUE

However that may be, the fact is that anyone seeing Lizaveta Alexandrovna for the first time would not notice any sign of discomposure. Only someone who had known her before and remembered the freshness of her face, the gleam in her eyes which had once made it difficult to discern their colour, drowned as it was by the luxuriant ripplings of its light, and who remembered her plump shoulders and shapely bosom, would look on her now with dismay – and his heart, if he were not without feeling for her, would tighten with pity, as perhaps Pyotr Ivanych's heart did now, however reluctant he might be to admit it to himself.

He entered the room quietly and sat down beside her.

"What are you doing?" he asked.

"I'm checking the household accounts," she replied. "Would you believe, Pyotr Ivanych, last month we spent almost 1,500 roubles on food alone – it's outrageous!"

Without saying a word, he took the ledger from her and put it on the table.

"Listen," he began, "the doctor says that if I stay here, it will be bad for my health; his advice is to go abroad and take the waters at a spa. What do you say?"

"What do you want me to say? On something like this, what the doctor says is more important. If that's what he advises, you have to go."

"What about you? Would you like to go?"

"I suppose so."

"But perhaps you would prefer to stay here for a while?"

"All right, I'll stay here."

"Well, which is it?" Pyotr Ivanych asked, with a trace of impatience.

"Make whatever arrangements you like for both of us," she replied in a tone of resigned indifference. "If you say so, I'll go – if not, I'll stay."

"You mustn't stay here," said Pyotr Ivanych. "The doctor says that the climate here isn't good for your health either."

"Where did he get that idea from?" said Lizaveta Alexandrovna. "I don't feel there's anything wrong with my health."

"A long journey," said Pyotr Ivanych, "might also be too tiring for you; perhaps you would like to stay for a while with your aunt in Moscow, while I'm abroad?"

"All right, then I suppose I'll go to Moscow."
"Or else we could both go to the Crimea for the summer?"
"All right, let's go to the Crimea."

Pyotr Ivanych was losing patience. He stood up and started pacing back and forth the way he did in his study, and then stopped in front of her.

"So it doesn't matter to you one way or the other where you are?"
"No, it doesn't."
"Why not?"

Without replying, she picked up the ledger from the table.

"It's up to you, Pyotr Ivanych," she said. "We have to cut down, I mean, 1,500 just for food…"

He took the ledger from her and threw it under the table.

"Why are you so preoccupied with that?" he asked. "Or are you worried about money?"

"Why shouldn't I be? I'm your wife, aren't I? You taught me yourself… and now you're rebuking me for doing it… I'm just doing my job."

"Listen, Liza!" said Pyotr Ivanych after a short pause. "Are you trying to go against your true nature, suppress your true instincts?… That's wrong! I've never tried to coerce you; you don't expect me to believe that this stuff" – he said, pointing to the ledger – "interests you. Why do you impose these constraints on yourself? I allow you total freedom…"

"My God! What do I need freedom for?" said Lizaveta Alexandrovna. "What would I do with it? You have always been so good at arranging everything for both of us that I've got out of the habit of thinking for myself – so just keep on doing what you've always done, and I won't have any need of freedom."

They both lapsed into silence.

"It's been a long time," began Pyotr Ivanych, "since I've heard you ask for anything, express any wish, or even a whim."

"I don't need anything," she said.

"But don't you have any special… private wishes?" he asked earnestly, looking straight at her.

She was hesitating whether to answer or not.

Pyotr Ivanych noticed her hesitation.

EPILOGUE

"Tell me, for God's sake, tell me! Your wishes will be mine, they will be the law, and I will respect it."

"Very well," she replied, "if you're willing to do that for me, then abolish our Fridays… I can't stand those dinners…"

Pyotr Ivanych stopped to think.

"As it is, you live in seclusion," he resumed, "and when our friends stop visiting on Fridays, you'll be in total isolation. But all right, if that's what you want, that's what I'll do. But what will you do then?"

"Just hand over to me your accounts, your books, your affairs, and I'll deal with it all," she said, and reached under the table to retrieve the ledger.

Pyotr Ivanych took this to be a poorly disguised pretence.

"Liza!" he said reproachfully.

The ledger remained under the table.

"What I was thinking was: why don't you revive some old acquaintanceships which we've completely given up? I'd like to give a ball – that would be a way of doing it. You would enjoy yourself, you could start going out yourself…"

"Oh, no! Not that!" Lizaveta Alexandrovna exclaimed in a fright. "For God's sake, don't do that! A ball… How could you think of such a thing!"

"But what are you so afraid of? You're still young enough to enjoy a ball; you can still dance…"

"No, Pyotr Ivanych, please don't start all that!" she said spiritedly. "Having to worry about what to wear, what accessories, entertaining a crowd of people, going out – God help us!"

"So you mean you want to spend the rest of your life going around in this smock?"

"Yes, if you don't mind, I would never take it off. What's the point of getting all dressed up? And think of the expense: all that fuss and bother, all for nothing."

"You know what?" Pyotr Ivanych suddenly put in. "I understand that this winter Rubini* is going to perform here – a whole season of Italian opera; I've reserved a box for us – what do you think?"

She said nothing.

"Liza!"

"There's no point..." she said timidly. "I'm afraid that too would be too much for me... I get tired..."

Pyotr Ivanych bent his head, went over to the fireplace and, leaning against the mantelpiece, looked at her with an expression of – how shall I say? – sadness – no, not sadness, rather alarm, concern and fear.

"Where, Liza, does it come from, this..." he began, but could not go on – he couldn't bring himself to utter the word "indifference".

He continued to look at her for a long time without speaking.

In her lifeless, dim eyes, on her face, totally devoid of the animation of thought and feelings, in her apathetic pose and sluggish movements, he glimpsed the reason for this indifference – the word he had been afraid to utter. He had already guessed the answer when the doctor had hinted to him about his apprehensions. He had even then started to see things clearly and begun to suspect that in systematically barring his wife from any irregularities in her behaviour which he thought might threaten their marriage, he was at the same time denying her anything in his own behaviour and attitudes which might make up for the loss of those, perhaps illicit, satisfactions which might be available to her outside her marriage, and that her home life was nothing less than a fortress which by his methods had been made impregnable to temptation from the outside, while inside, it was patrolled and barricaded against all legitimate expressions of feeling...

He was quite unaware that despite himself, his by-the-book approach, and lack of warmth in his dealings with her, had come to amount to a kind of cold tyranny – and a tyranny over whom? Why, the heart of a woman! The price he paid for this tyranny was wealth, luxury and all the superficial and what he imagined to be the appropriate components of happiness – a terrible mistake, and all the more disastrous because he did this not out of ignorance, not out of a merely rudimentary understanding of the human heart – he did understand it – but rather because of negligence and his self-centredness! He forgot that she had no job or career, didn't play cards, had no factory, and that the best food and wine meant very little to a woman – yet that was the kind of life which he had imposed upon her.

EPILOGUE

Pyotr Ivanych was well meaning, and he would have given anything to make amends – if not out of love for his wife, at least because it was the right and fair thing to do. But how to make amends? He had spent more than one sleepless night since the doctor had told him of his apprehensions regarding his wife's health, trying to find ways and means of reconciling her heart with her present situation and repelling those forces which were destroying her. And that was precisely what he was thinking about as he stood by the fire. He could not help wondering whether some deadly disease might already have taken root in her as a result of the drab and empty life she had been living...

His brow broke into a cold sweat. He was busily trying to devise ways and means, but felt the key must lie more in the heart than the head. But where was he to find that key? Something was telling him that if only he could bring himself to fall at her feet, fold her lovingly in his arms and tell her with passion in his voice that he lived only for her, and that she was the sole purpose of all his work, his busyness, his career, his accumulation of wealth, and that his mechanical way of treating her was driven only by the fierce, unremitting and zealous desire to secure his place in her heart... He understood that the effect of such words would galvanize her corpse back to life, back to flourishing health and to happiness, and that there would no longer be any need to go and take the waters.

But to speak and to prove are two quite different things. In order to prove, there must be a passion to do so, but when he looked into his soul, Pyotr Ivanych could find no trace of passion. He felt only that his wife was indispensable to him – which was true – but unlike the other things in life which were indispensable to him, she was only indispensable out of habit. It was possible that he would not be averse to dissembling, and playing the role of lover, for all that it was ridiculous for a man of fifty suddenly to start speaking the language of passion; but to pretend to a woman that you are passionately in love with her when you aren't? Would he be able to muster enough heroism and ingenuity to carry the burden of this act through to the point at which the cravings of her heart would be satisfied?

But what if the wound inflicted on her pride would prove a death blow to her when she noticed that something which several years before would have been a magic potion was being served up to her now as medicine? No, in his usual meticulous fashion, he had carefully weighed and pondered this belated step, and had decided against it. There was something that he had thought of doing along the same lines, but in a different way, since it had now become possible and necessary. For three months now, he had been toying with a thought which at first had seemed absurd, but right now – it was different! He had been keeping the idea for an emergency. Well, the emergency was at hand, and he decided to carry out his plan.

"If this doesn't work," he thought, "then I give up! Come what may."

Pyotr Ivanych strode resolutely to his wife and took her hand.

"You know, Liza," he said, "what role I play in my department; I am considered the most effective official in the ministry. This year, I am being put up for promotion to privy councillor, and I am certain to get it. However, don't think that this is as far as I will get in my career: I may go still higher... and I would have..." She looked at him in surprise, wondering where all this was leading.

"I have never doubted your abilities," she said. "I am convinced that you won't stop halfway, and will get to the very top..."

"No, I won't; in a day or two, I am going to offer my resignation."

"Your resignation?" she asked in astonishment, and sat up straight.

"Yes."

"Why?"

"Listen to what I'm going to say! As you know, I have settled up with my partners, and I'm no longer the sole owner. It's making me a clear profit of up to 40,000 with no effort on my part. It's like a well-oiled machine."

"Yes, I know, but what of it?" asked Lizaveta Alexandrovna.

"I'm going to sell it."

"What are you talking about, Pyotr Ivanych? What's got into you?" she said in growing astonishment, looking at him fearfully. "What's all this about? I'm bewildered, I don't understand..."

"You really don't?"

"No!" Lizaveta Alexandrovna was perplexed.

"Can't you understand that when I see how bored you are, and how your health is suffering… from the climate, I want to put my career and my factory to good use, and take you away from here, and devote the rest of my life to you?… Liza! Did you really think that I was incapable of self-sacrifice?" he added reproachfully.

"So this was all for my sake?" said Lizaveta Alexandrovna, now beginning to think clearly. "No, Pyotr Ivanych," she said incisively, and sounding worried. "For God's sake don't make any sacrifices for me. I won't accept them – do you hear me? Absolutely not! That you should stop working, stop succeeding, stop making money – and just for me! God forbid! I'm not worth it. Forgive me; I have never measured up to you, I'm too worthless, too weak to be able to appreciate and value your lofty goals and your noble achievements… I was not the right woman for you."

"More magnanimity!" said Pyotr Ivanych, shrugging his shoulders. "My mind is made up, Liza."

"Oh, God! What have I done! I was cast like a stone in your path – I stand in your way. What a strange fate is mine!" she added, almost in despair. "If I don't want to, don't need to live, why doesn't God take pity on me and take me? To be an obstacle in your path…"

"You're wrong to think that my sacrifice is a heavy one for me. I've had enough of this meaningless life! I want to rest, I want some tranquillity, and where can I find that except by your side? We are going to Italy."

"Pyotr Ivanych!" she said, almost in tears. "You are a good, well-meaning man… and I know what you are doing now is putting on an act of feigned magnanimity… but perhaps this sacrifice is useless, perhaps it has come too late, and here you are throwing away everything that matters to you…"

"Spare me! Liza, don't pursue that line of thought, otherwise you will discover that I am not made of iron," Pyotr Ivanych cautioned her. "I repeat: I want to stop living only by my head, I'm not entirely dried up inside."

She gave him a long, questioning look.

"But... do you really mean it?" she asked after the pause. "Do you truly want to rest, and you're not giving it all up just for me?"

"No, for myself too."

"Because if it's for me, I'm not worth it, not worth it..."

"No, no! I'm not well, I'm tired... I need to rest."

She gave him her hand. He kissed it with feeling.

"So we're going to Italy then?" he asked.

"Very well, we'll go," she said tonelessly.

For Pyotr Ivanych, it was as if a weight had dropped from his shoulders. "We'll see what happens!" he thought.

They sat there for a long time, not knowing what to say to each other. It's not clear who would have broken the silence if the two of them had been left alone. But the sound of hurried footsteps was heard in the next room, and Alexander appeared.

How he had changed! He had filled out and lost hair, but how ruddy he had become! With what dignity he sported his paunch and the decoration around his neck! His eyes shone with pleasure. He kissed his aunt's hand with particular warmth and shook his uncle's hand.

"Where have you just come from?" asked Pyotr Ivanych.

"Guess!" he replied suggestively.

"You're looking very lively today?" said Pyotr Ivanych enquiringly.

"I'll bet you can't guess!" said Alexander.

"Once, ten or twelve years ago, I seem to remember, you rushed in here just like this," said Pyotr Ivanych, "and broke something of mine... and I guessed right away that you were in love, but now – surely not that again? No, it can't be, you're too sensible to..."

He glanced at his wife and held his tongue.

"Are you still trying to guess?"

His uncle looked at him, thinking hard.

"Surely not... you're getting married?" he offered tentatively.

"You've got it!" Alexander exclaimed jubilantly. "Congratulate me!"

"Really! Who to?" his uncle and aunt asked in unison.

"To Alexander Stepanych's daughter."

"Are you serious? I mean, that's a wealthy bride!" said Pyotr Ivanych. "And her father – no problem there?"

EPILOGUE

"I've just come from there. Why wouldn't her father give his consent? Quite the contrary. He had tears in his eyes when I asked for her hand, hugged me and said that now he could die in peace – and that he knew he was entrusting his daughter's happiness to the right person. 'Only,' he said, 'be sure to follow in your uncle's footsteps!'"

"He said that? You see, your uncle still counts for something here!"

"And what did the daughter say?" asked Lizaveta Alexandrovna.

"Well… you know how it is with these young women," replied Alexander. "She didn't say anything, and just blushed; and when I took her hand, her fingers were waggling in my hand as if she were playing the piano – they were trembling."

"And she didn't say anything?" said Lizaveta Alexandrovna. "And you really didn't take the trouble of asking her what she felt before formally proposing? It didn't matter to you? Why are you getting married?"

"What do you mean, 'why'? Can't hang around for ever! I'm fed up with being alone. The time has come to put down roots and settle down, get a home of my own, and do my duty… My bride to be is pretty and rich… and Uncle is here to tell you the reasons to get married – he's got it all worked out…"

Pyotr Ivanych, without letting his wife see him, signalled to Alexander with a wave of the hand to leave him out of it and keep quiet, but Alexander didn't notice.

"But perhaps she doesn't care for you?" said Lizaveta Alexandrovna. "Maybe she can't love you – what do you say to that?"

"Uncle, why don't you explain? You would do it better than I can. Look, let me use your own words," he went on, failing to notice that his uncle was squirming where he stood, and was coughing in an attempt to stifle what was coming next. But Alexander continued: "If you marry for love, love passes, and you just continue out of habit, and if you don't marry for love, the result is just the same: you get used to your wife. Love is one thing, and marriage is another, and the two things don't always coincide, and it's better when they don't. That's right – isn't it, Uncle? I mean, that's what you taught me…"

He looked at his uncle and came to a sudden halt, seeing the baleful look he was getting from him. His mouth wide open in consternation, he looked at his aunt, and then back again at his uncle, and closed it. Lizaveta Alexandrovna shook her head dolefully.

"So, you're getting married then?" said Pyotr Ivanych. "Well, it's the right time. Good luck to you! And there you were on the point of doing that when you were twenty-three."

"Well, I was young then, young!"

"Precisely – it was your youth."

Alexander thought for a moment, and then smiled.

"What is it?" asked Pyotr Ivanych.

"Nothing, a weird thought just occurred to me…"

"What?"

"When I was in love," said Alexander, trying to arrange his thoughts, "marriage eluded me…"

"And now you're getting married, love is eluding you," his uncle added, and they both burst out laughing.

"So it follows that you are right, Uncle, in thinking that it's habit which is the main thing…"

Pyotr Ivanych gave him another ugly look, and Alexander shut his mouth, not knowing what to think.

"Getting married when you're thirty-five is the right thing," said Pyotr Ivanych. "You remember how you went into convulsions here, kicking and screaming that uneven marriages outrage you, that the bride is dragged in like a sacrificial victim decked out in flowers and diamonds, shoved into the arms of an older man – most likely, ugly and bald. Let's have a look at *your* head!"

"It was youth, youth, Uncle! I didn't understand what it was all about," said Alexander, smoothing his hair with his hand.

"Yes, what it's all about," Pyotr Ivanych continued, "and do you remember back then when you were in love with that, what was her name, Natasha, was it? You were in a frenzy of jealousy, outbursts, heavenly bliss… What became of all that?"

"Come, come, Uncle, that's enough of that!" said Alexander, blushing.

"What about all those tears, that tremendous passion?"

"Uncle!"

"What? So you've given up those 'heartfelt outpourings' and are no longer picking those yellow flowers! You're 'fed up with being alone'…"

"Oh, if that's the way it is, then I can prove that I am not the only one to have been in love, ranting, raving, jealous rages, all those tears… allow me – I have here a written document…"

He took a wallet out of his pocket, and after some time spent sorting through the papers it contained, pulled out a tattered, dilapidated and yellowing sheet of paper.

"Here, *ma tante*, is evidence that my uncle wasn't always such a prudent, derisive and pragmatic man. He was quite at home with 'heartfelt outpourings', and it wasn't on crested writing paper in special ink that he gave vent to them. I've been carrying this scrap of paper around with me for four years now, waiting for the chance to expose my uncle. I had almost forgotten about it, but you yourself just reminded me."

"What's all this nonsense? I don't understand," said Pyotr Ivanych, looking at the piece of paper.

"Well, take a look."

Alexander put the sheet of paper right in front of his uncle's eyes. Pyotr Ivanych's face suddenly darkened.

"Give it to me! Let me have it! Alexander!" he barked, and tried to snatch it from him. But Alexander was too quick for him, and whisked it away.

Lizaveta Alexandrovna was watching them with curiosity.

"No, Uncle, I'm not giving it to you – until you confess, right here in my aunt's presence, that you were once in love, just as I was, just as everyone was… otherwise I'm handing it over to my aunt as a constant rebuke to you."

"That's vicious!" Pyotr Ivanych shouted. "What are you doing to me?"

"So you won't?"

"All right, all right; I was in love. Now give it to me!"

"Not yet! You first have to confess to jealous tantrums, ranting and raving."

"All right, I ranted and raved, there were jealous tantrums…" he said, frowning.

"And the tears?"

"No, there were no tears."

"Wrong! My aunt told me – admit it."

"I can't get the words out, Alexander – maybe now I will cry."

"*Ma tante*, here is the document for you."

"Let me see what it is," she said, reaching for it.

"Yes, I cried, I cried! Now give it!" Pyotr Ivanych howled in desperation.

"By the lake?"

"Yes, by the lake."

"And did you pick yellow flowers?"

"Yes, I did. Isn't that enough for you? Give it to me!"

"No, not quite. Give me your word of honour that you will consign my youthful follies to eternal oblivion and stop casting them in my teeth."

"My word of honour."

Alexander gave him the sheet of paper. Pyotr Ivanych seized it, lit a match and burned it.

"At least tell me what it says," said Lizaveta Alexandrovna.

"No, my dear, I'll never tell, even on the Day of Judgement," replied Pyotr Ivanych. "I can't believe I ever wrote it – impossible!"

"It *was* you, Uncle!" Alexander retorted. "I suppose I could say what is in it – I've learnt it by heart: 'My angel, I adore you…'"

"Alexander! This will make us sworn enemies!" Pyotr Ivanych roared in anger.

"There he goes, blushing guiltily, as if he's committed a crime – and for what! For his first tender love," said Lizaveta Alexandrovna, shrugging her shoulders, and turned away from them.

"It's when you're in love for the first time that you do so many foolish things," said Pyotr Ivanych softly, almost furtively. "With the two of *us*, there were never any 'heartfelt outpourings', flowers, walks by moonlight… but you love me just the same…"

"Yes, I have… got very used to you," Lizaveta Alexandrovna responded distractedly.

Pyotr Ivanych started stroking his whiskers pensively.

"Well, Uncle, isn't that the way you wanted it?"

Pyotr Ivanych winked at him as if to say, "Shut up!"

"Pyotr Ivanych can be forgiven for thinking and acting like that," said Lizaveta Alexandrovna. "He's always been that way, and I don't think anyone knew him any different, and it wasn't from you, Alexander, that I ever expected such a revelation…"

She gave a sigh.

"What are you sighing for, *ma tante*?" asked Alexander.

"For the old Alexander," she replied.

"You mean you would really have preferred me to remain the way I was ten years ago?" Alexander countered. "Uncle was right when he described all that as foolish dreaming…"

Lizaveta Alexandrovna's expression began to turn grim, and Alexander fell silent.

"No, not the way you were," replied Lizaveta Alexandrovna, "ten years ago, but four years ago. Do you remember the letter you wrote me when you were back home in the country? That is the way I like to remember you!"

"I think I must have been a dreamer then too," said Alexander.

"No, you weren't dreaming. It was then that you began to understand what life was about. Then you were at your best – noble, perspicacious… Why didn't you stay like that? Why were you only like that on paper, but not in practice? That was something of beauty, which shone like the sun appearing from behind a cloud – but only for a moment…"

"So what you mean, *ma tante*, is that now, I'm not… perspicacious, not… noble…"

"God forbid! Not at all! No, now you are perspicacious and noble… but in your own way, not in mine…"

"What can I do, *ma tante*?" said Alexander with a loud sigh. "That's just the way it is. I'm moving with the times – mustn't fall behind! I agree with Uncle; I'll quote him—"

"Alexander!" his uncle interrupted him, sounding furious. "Let's go to my study for a moment; there's something I need to say to you."

They went to the study.

"What on earth possessed you to talk like that about me?" said Pyotr Ivanych. "Can't you see what a state my wife is in?"

"What do you mean?" said Alexander in alarm.

"Don't you notice anything? The fact is that I'm leaving my work at the ministry, giving up my business, everything, and taking her to Italy."

"What do you mean, Uncle?" Alexander exclaimed in astonishment. "This is the year of your promotion to privy councillor…"

"But you see, the privy councillor's wife is in a bad way…"

He paced back and forth in the room sunk in thought.

"No, this is the end of my career!" he said. "It's all settled. I'm not destined to go any further… so what?" He waved his hand. "Why don't we talk about you instead?" he said. "It seems you're following in my footsteps…"

"That should please you!" Alexander interjected.

"Yes, indeed!" Pyotr Ivanych continued. "In a little over thirty years' time – collegiate councillor,* a substantial salary from your work at the ministry, you'll be making a lot of money from your outside activities, and you're marrying into money at just the right time… Yes, we Aduyevs know what we're doing all right! You take after me, although so far without the backache…"

"Well, I do get twinges here from time to time," said Alexander, touching his back.

"All of that is splendid – except, of course, for the backache," Pyotr Ivanych continued. "I must confess I didn't expect you to turn out well when you first arrived: your head was in the clouds, full of other-worldly speculation… Now that's all past – thank God! My advice to you is to continue to follow in my footsteps, except…"

"Except what, Uncle?"

"Well, I wanted to give you some advice… about your future wife…"

"What do you mean? I must say I'm curious."

"Well, perhaps not!" said Pyotr Ivanych, after a pause. "I'm afraid it might make things worse. Just do what you think best; you may just happen to get it right. So let's talk about your marriage instead. I hear that your bride comes with a dowry of 200,000 – is that right?"

"Yes, the 200,000 is from her father, plus the 100,000 left by her mother."

"So that makes 300,000!" Pyotr Ivanych exclaimed, sounding almost alarmed.

"Yes, and what's more, just today her father said he will now be transferring ownership of all his 500 serfs to us in return for giving him an annual allowance of 8,000. He'll be living with us."

Pyotr Ivanych jumped up from his armchair with unaccustomed agility.

"Stop! Stop!" he said. "I can't believe my ears; did I hear you right? Tell me again, how much?"

"Five hundred serfs plus 300,000 roubles," Alexander repeated.

"This isn't a joke, is it?"

"Why would it be a joke, Uncle?"

"And the estate – it's not mortgaged, is it?" Pyotr Ivanych asked quietly, without moving.

"No."

His uncle folded his arms and regarded his nephew for several moments with great respect.

"So, a career and a fortune!" he said, almost to himself. "And what a fortune! And right out of the blue! You've achieved everything, everything! Alexander!" he added proudly and jubilantly. "It's my blood that runs in your veins. You are a true Aduyev! I can't believe I'm saying this, but give me a hug!"

And they embraced.

"This is the first time, Uncle!" said Alexander.

"And the last!" replied Pyotr Ivanych. "This is a special occasion. And once again you don't need any of that filthy lucre from me. But come to me if the need should ever arise."

"I'm sorry, but it so happens that I do need some – I have a lot of expenses. So if you can spare 10 or 15,000…"

"After all this time, this is a first!" proclaimed Pyotr Ivanych.

"And the last, Uncle. It's a special occasion!" said Alexander.

Note on the Text

The text in the present edition is based on *Обыкновенная История*, published in Moscow in 1977 by Gosudarstvennoe izdatel'stvo khudozhestvennoi literatury (first edition published in 1960).

Notes

p. 31, *bel homme*: "Handsome man" (French).

p. 37, *Mr Zagoskin and Mr Marlinsky*: The Russian writers Mikhail Zagoskin (1789–1852) and Alexander Bestuzhev (1797–1837), who wrote under the pseudonym Marlinsky after being exiled to the Caucasus for his involvement in the Decembrist revolt of 1825.

p. 37, *On Prejudice by Mr Puzin*: A reference to a book by Polikarp Ivanovich Puzin (1781–1866), published in St Petersburg in 1834.

p. 42, *un chez-soi*: "A place of one's own" (French).

p. 46, *the Bronze Horseman… poor Yevgeny*: The *Bronze Horseman* is a statue of Peter the Great (1672–1725), tsar of Russia 1682–1725 and founder of the city of St Petersburg, by the French sculptor Étienne Maurice Falconet (1716–91). It takes its name from an 1833 poem about the statue by Alexander Pushkin (1799–1837), in which a young man, Yevgeny, survives a flood in the city only to find that the woman he loved was killed, and then curses the statue, which comes to life and pursues him.

p. 54, *Pushkin's demon*: A reference to Pushkin's short poem 'The Demon' (1823), whose narrator's youthful idealism, elevated feelings and love of the beauty of nature turn to despair, doubt and cynicism under the influence of a mysterious malevolent being.

NOTES

p. 69, *Schiller*: The German poet Friedrich von Schiller (1759–1805).

p. 94, *among fields and forests primeval*: From the opera *Pan Tvardovsky* (1828) by Alexei Verstovsky (1799–1862), with libretto by Mikhail Zagoskin (see first note to p. 37).

p. 102, *Soupe julienne and à la reine, sauce à la provençale, à la maître d'hôtel*: The three French dishes listed here are a chopped-vegetable soup, "queen's soup" (made with chicken and cream) and a provençale dressing (made with tomatoes, garlic and olive oil).

p. 109, *Mémoires du Diable... Soulié's books*: The prolific French novelist and dramatist Frédéric Soulié (1800–47) wrote a large number of sensation novels, the most famous being *Mémoires du Diable* (*Memoirs of the Devil*, 1837–38).

p. 121, *why should only the opinions of others be sacrosanct?*: A line from the satirical comedy in verse *Woe from Wit*, written in 1823 by the Russian diplomat and author Alexander Griboyedov (1795–1829), much of whose dialogue has become proverbial in Russian.

p. 132, *Peau de chagrin*: A novel by the French novelist and playwright Honoré de Balzac (1799–1850), published in 1831, about an impoverished young man who is given a magical ass's skin that has the power to grant his wishes. It is published in English as *The Wild Ass's Skin*.

p. 135, *opodeldoc*: A balm invented by the Swiss physician Paracelsus (c.1493–1541) consisting of soap, camphor and herbal essences.

p. 136, *I won't allow a seducer... flowers*: From Pushkin's verse novel *Eugene Onegin* (1825–32) VI, 17, 6–12, with some alterations.

p. 145, *Quelle idée!*: "What an idea!" (French).

p. 155, *what a pathetic species, worthy only of laughter and tears!*: From Pushkin's poem 'The Commander' (1835).

p. 172, *à la finnoise*: "In the Finnish style" (French).

p. 172, *Ma tante*: "My aunt" (French).

p. 177, *With her, my lips... that of love itself*: Pushkin, *Eugene Onegin*, I, 49, 13–14.

p. 180, *I endured my sufferings, / I cast away my dreams*: The opening of a lyric by Pushkin of 1821.

p. 183, *thinking that when I said 'people', I meant 'servants'*: The word for "person" was also the word used for "servant" at this time in Russia.

p. 189, *when Pylades lies mortally wounded… wipes away his tear and finds repose*: In Greek mythology, Orestes is the son of Agamemnon, who kills his own mother, Clytemnestra, and her lover, Aegisthus, to avenge the death of his father. In some versions of the story Orestes is aided by Pylades, the son of King Strophius, with whom he was raised. The close friendship of Orestes and Pylades is proverbial.

p. 192, *Krylov's fables*: Ivan Andreyevich Krylov (1769–1844) was the author of fables satirizing Russian society.

p. 193, *Krylov's donkey… Krylov's 'good fox'*: In Krylov's fable 'The Ass and the Nightingale', a donkey advises a nightingale to sing more like his friend the rooster, in response to which the nightingale flies away. In 'The Good Fox', a fox urges birds of various species to care for three orphaned redcap chicks, whose mother was killed by a hunter. When, as the fox is speaking, the three chicks fall down at his feet in their weakened state, he promptly eats them.

p. 193, *just like the fox did to the wolf*: In Krylov's fable 'The Wolf and the Fox', a fox offers a starving wolf hay to eat without revealing that he has stored away a supply of meat for himself. The wolf, who is interested in meat, not hay, consequently goes to bed without any supper.

p. 197, *one more last utterance*: Words spoken by Father Pimen at the beginning of Scene 5 of Pushkin's historical play *Boris Godunov* ('Night: A Cell in the Chudov Monastery'), which was published in 1831 but not performed until 1866.

p. 198, *Instead of finding fault… good look at yourself?*: From Krylov's fable 'The Monkey and the Mirror', about a monkey who, on seeing his own "hideous" reflection in a mirror without realizing that he is looking at himself, comments to his friend the bear on the ugliness of others. The words quoted here are the bear's reply.

p. 203, *the rank of state councillor*: Under the system introduced by Peter the Great in 1722, Russian civil and military positions were organized according to a "Table of Ranks". There were fourteen ranks, or grades, the first being the highest. Pyotr Ivanych's rank, that of state councillor, is the fifth on this scale.

NOTES

p. 209, *the strains of prophetic music... will not swell with it*: A free quotation from the Third Canto (ll. 190–91) of Pushkin's narrative poem *Ruslan and Lyudmila* (1820). On his quest to rescue his bride Lyudmila, the knight Ruslan finds himself on a deserted battlefield, surrounded by corpses, and speculates that he himself might one day share the same fate, and that his heroic deeds will go unsung.

p. 209, *privy councillor*: Pyotr Ivanych is here anticipating his promotion to the third rank on the Russian Imperial scale.

p. 210, *Spreading your rustling wings... to quote your favourite author*: Pyotr Ivanych here quotes from another of Krylov's fables, 'The Eagle and the Bee', in which an eagle watches a bee's honey-making labours and pities him, as his work is lost among that of his thousands of fellows and consequently unrecognized and unsung by the world. The eagle, in contrast, inspires fear and awe as soon as he spreads his wings and takes to the air. The bee replies that he is happy to work for the common good, and that he is consoled by the thought that he has made a contribution, however small.

p. 224, *Zagoretsky's reply from Griboyedov's Woe from Wit*: In Act III, Sc. 9 of Griboyedov's play, the socialite Zagoretsky arrives at Famusov's ball and presents the daughter of his host with tickets for a sold-out theatre performance, bragging about the difficulties he had in laying his hands on them.

p. 225, *Oui, madame m'a fait cet honneur*: "Yes, madam has done me this honour" (French).

p. 235, *Fata Morgana*: A kind of mirage in which distant objects are distorted, often beyond recognition, and sometimes appear to be floating in mid-air above the horizon. Such mirages were originally seen in the Strait of Messina between Italy and Sicily and named after Morgan le Fey, a sorceress from Arthurian legend, who was believed to be luring sailors to their deaths with these "castles in the air".

p. 235, *workings and causes of all things*: A quotation from the sixth 'Satire' by the Moldavian-born Russian diplomat and poet Antiochus Kantemir (1708–44).

p. 236, *She knew who Voltaire was... misattributed the Dictionnaire philosophique*: The point here is that Yulia gets the authorship the wrong way round: the prose epic *Les Martyrs* (1809) is by the French Romantic writer François-René de Chateaubriand (1768–1848) and the encyclopaedic *Dictionnaire philosophique* (1764) is by the French Enlightenment historian and philosopher Voltaire (1694–1778).

p. 236, *She called Montaigne... des portes de Trézène*: Yulia has learnt about the French writers Michel de Montaigne (1533–92), considered the inventor of the essay, Victor Hugo (1802–85), known for novels such as *Notre-Dame de Paris* (1831) and *Les Misérables* (1862), Molière (1622–73), author of comic plays such as *Le Misanthrope* (1666) and *Le Bourgeois gentilhomme* (1670), and Jean Racine (1639–99), author of tragedies such as *Phèdre* (1677), in which the speech referred to here occurs.

p. 236, *the comedy played out between Vulcan, Mars and Venus*: As related in Homer's *Odyssey*, the goddess Venus, who was married to Vulcan, god of fire, had a passionate affair with Mars, god of war. On learning of his wife's infidelity, Vulcan forged in his smithy a net made of chains in which to ensnare the lovers.

p. 236, *Des bêtises! Mais cette bête de Vulcan... à la place de Venus?*: "Such nonsense! But this beast of a Vulcan must have had a strange appearance... listen... What would you have done in Venus's place?" (French).

p. 236, *Le Manuscrit vert, Les Sept Péchés capitaux, L'Âne mort*: *Le Manuscrit vert* (*The Green Manuscript*, 1832) is by Gustave Drouineau (1798–1878), *Les Sept Péchés capitaux* (*The Seven Deadly Sins*, 1847–49) by Eugène Sue (1804–57) and *L'Âne mort et la femme guillotinée* (*The Dead Donkey and the Guillotined Woman*, 1829) by Jules Janin (1804–74).

p. 237, *The Idylls of Gessner*: The Swiss painter and poet Solomon Gessner (1730–88) was the author of pastoral prose poems, published as *Idyllen* (1756–72).

p. 237, *the Night Thoughts of Young*: The English poet Edward Young (1683–1765) was the author of *Night Thoughts* (1742–45), a long poem about death.

p. 237, *Weisse*: The German Enlightenment writer Christian Felix Weisse (1726–1804), best known for his writing for children.

p. 237, *Da habe ich's*: "Now I have it" (German).

p. 238, *Kaydanov*: Ivan Kuzmich Kaydanov (1782–1843), who taught Pushkin at the Imperial Alexander Lyceum in Tsarskoye Selo, near St Petersburg, and was the author of several secondary-school textbooks on world history.

p. 238, *Kantemir, Sumarokov, as well as Lomonosov, Derzhavin and Ozerov*: All writers associated with Russian literary classicism: Antiochus Kantemir (see second note to p. 235); the playwright Alexander Petrovich Sumarokov (1717–77); the scientist and author Mikhail Vasilyevich Lomonosov (1711–65); the poet Gavrila Romanovich Derzhavin (1743–1816); and the dramatist Vladislav Alexandrovich Ozerov (1769–1816).

p. 238, *Karamzin… Poor Liza and a few pages of Travels*: Nikolai Mikhaylovich Karamzin (1766–1826) the leader of the Romantic movement in Russia, is best known for his twelve-volume *History of the Russian State* (1816–29). He was the author of the novel *Poor Liza* (1792) and the non-fiction work *Letters of a Russian Traveller* (1791–92).

p. 238, *The Captive in the Caucasus*: A narrative poem by Pushkin of 1822.

p. 240, *Beatus ille*: The beginning of the second of the *Epodes* by the Roman poet Horace (65–8 BC): "*Beatus ille qui procul negotiis*" ("Happy is he who is far from the business of the world").

p. 240, *Puer, pueri, puero*: Tafayev here starts declining the Latin word for "boy".

p. 267, *Pour, pour a glass of sizzling wine… Upon the soft radiance of the heavens*: From the poem 'Desire for Peace' (1825) by the poet, theologian and founder of the nineteenth-century Slavophile movement Alexei Stepanovich Khomyakov (1804–60).

p. 269, *throw down a bone and watch your dogs fight over it*: A reference to Krylov's fable 'Doggy Friendship', in which two dogs swear eternal friendship, but then immediately forget their promise to each other when a single bone is thrown their way.

p. 276, *Oedipus and Antigone*: In Greek mythology, Antigone was the daughter of Oedipus.

p. 278, *Cela passe toute permission!*: "This goes beyond all that is permitted!" (French).

p. 282, *Childe Harold*: That is, *Childe Harold's Pilgrimage*, a narrative poem by Lord Byron (1788–1824).

p. 284, *Walter Scott, Cooper*: The Scottish novelist Sir Walter Scott (1771–1832), who virtually invented the historical novel in Britain in works such as *Waverley* (1814) and *Ivanhoe* (1819), and the US novelist James Fenimore Cooper (1789–1851), famous for tales set on the American frontier such as *The Last of the Mohicans* (1826).

p. 289, *the imp from Krylov's fable... appeared from behind the stove*: In Krylov's fable 'A False Accusation', a Brahmin secretly cooks an egg on a candle flame on a fast day. When he is caught by his superior and tries to claim that the Devil tempted him to do it, an imp appears and accuses him of slander.

p. 297, *Paganini*: The Italian violinist and composer Niccolò Paganini (1782–1840).

p. 298, *Anyone who has lived and thought cannot but despise people in his heart*: Pushkin, *Eugene Onegin* I, 46, 1–2.

p. 305, *that same comedy... the other one came back to see him*: A reference to the Greek legend of Damon and Pythias, an exemplar of true friendship and loyalty. According to the story, when Pythias was sentenced to death by the Syracusan king Dionysius I, his friend Damon agreed to take his place in prison so that Pythias could return home one final time. This act of loyalty so pleased Dionysius that he decided to spare Pythias.

p. 312, *Where I suffered, where I loved... Where I buried my heart*: Pushkin, *Eugene Onegin* I, 50, 13–14.

p. 312, *"The barbarian artist with his sleepy brush" etc.*: The first line of Pushkin's poem 'Rebirth' (1819): "The barbarian artist with his sleepy brush / Blackens the master's painting."

p. 318, *the Kazan Holy Mother of God*: A reference to *Our Lady of Kazan*, or the *Theotokos of Kazan*, a Russian Orthodox icon representing the Virgin Mary that, according to tradition, was discovered in the city of Kazan in 1579.

p. 338, *In droves behind the fence... fragrance of the meadow*: From Pushkin's narrative poem *The Gypsies* (1827).

p. 338, *like a painting by Teniers, full of bustling family life*: The Flemish painter David Teniers the Younger (1610–90) was famous for his representations of peasant life.

p. 339, *"the leaden sky... the trepak folk dance"*: From an abandoned chapter of Pushkin's *Eugene Onegin*, known as 'Onegin's Journey' (stanza 18), originally intended to go between the seventh and final chapters.

p. 344, *actual civil councillor*: Pyotr Ivanych has been promoted from the fifth to the fourth rank on the Russian Imperial scale. See note for p. 203.

p. 348, *Kissingen*: Bad Kissingen, a spa town in Bavaria.

p. 350, *Phidias nor Praxiteles*: The ancient Greek sculptors Phidias (fifth century BC), who created the Elgin marbles and the statue of Zeus at Olympia, one of the Seven Wonders of the Ancient World, and Praxiteles (fourth century BC), who was best known for a statue of Aphrodite (or Venus), of which only copies survive.

p. 353, *Rubini*: Giovanni Battista Rubini (1794–1854), a renowned Italian tenor.

p. 364, *collegiate councillor*: The sixth rank on the Russian Imperial scale. See note for p. 203.

Translator's Ruminations

A Brief Guided Tour
around the Translator's Workshop

Some hidden reefs and shoals not apparent on the surface of the water to the passengers on deck – or the readers of a translation – but which have to be navigated carefully by the helmsman – or translator – to ensure the passengers' smooth sailing.

UNANSWERED – AND UNANSWERABLE – QUESTIONS

Grappling with a work of classical literature poses one extra difficulty for a translator – the author of the work is no longer available for questioning.

It must be a rare work of fiction which has not raised questions of various kinds in the minds of its readers. With authors who are alive and available, a translator can seek clarification on any point which raises doubts, defies comprehension or would deepen the translator's understanding of context, background and characters' motivations. Apparent inconsistencies may also arise, especially in a work which has been written over an extended period of time – sometimes over several years. In this connection, it is worth recalling that before the advent of word processing, and even the now extinct typewriter, books were written by hand, and checking several hundred handwritten pages with all their marginal annotations, insertions and deletions for inconsistencies would have been a task of an entirely different order of difficulty in mid-nineteenth-century Russia.

One such question would be: "Ivan Alexandrovich, why did you choose this title for the book?"

THE TITLE

Goncharov gave this novel the title of *Обыкновенная История*, literally "Ordinary story" (Russian doesn't use articles), traditionally translated as *A Common Story*. Since he gave all his three novels titles beginning with the two letters *Об–* (*Ob–*), it might be thought that that helps to explain this title. However, that theory is undermined by the fact that this was his first novel, and his choice of these two letters is thus unlikely to have been influenced by the fact that his two later novels also bore titles beginning with those letters.

I don't believe any direct evidence has emerged to explain his reason for beginning all three titles with "Ob–", although it has been surmised that because his first novel was so successful, he might have stuck with these two letters for some talismanic reason – as some kind of good-luck charm – in the same spirit in which some professional athletes make a point of wearing the same talismanic garment which they wore for their first successful performance.

However that may be, it still leaves unsolved a deeper mystery, namely why he called it *A Common Story* at all. If one were to canvass the opinions of ten people who had read the book, and asked them what they thought was "common" or "ordinary" about the story, I wonder how many of those opinions would be the same. Of course, the answers offered by Goncharov's Russian-speaking contemporaries would be much more illuminating, relevant and valid than those of today's English-speaking readers of a translation, who might very well find a great deal about the geographical, historical and social setting of the story anything but "ordinary" – and, of course, it was anything but those aspects which the author had in mind when he chose the title. Goncharov's contemporaries would not have been sidetracked in that way. What was it about the story as such, rather than its setting, that influenced the author in his choice of title, and that he thought was "ordinary"?

The only inkling I have been able to glean, which might shed some light on what he meant by the title, was from one of the numerous passages of dialogue between Alexander Aduyev and his uncle Pyotr Ivanych.

Alexander has come to see his uncle, and is bursting to tell him how he has fallen in love and is delirious with happiness. Pyotr Ivanych has neither the time nor the patience to hear him out, and proposes in order to save time that *he* should tell that story to Alexander instead of the other way round. Alexander is totally baffled.

His uncle then proceeds to recount in some detail the sequence of events leading to his nephew's state of seventh-heaven bliss with such devastating accuracy that Alexander's first thought is to accuse his uncle of spying on him. Pyotr Ivanych dismisses that accusation and explains:

> "It stands to reason; *it's been the same old story since Adam and Eve* – with slight variations. Once you know the character of the dramatis personae you can predict the variations."

UNFORESEEN / UNFORESEEABLE RECURRENCE

An example. When the expression "*искренние излияния*" ("*iskrenniye izliyaniya*"; dictionary definition: "sincere outpourings") occurs for the first time, you, the translator, try to find the best solution in that instance. Subsequently, it recurs time and again and you realize that it has taken on a talismanic significance, and has become a leitmotif, and you have to reappraise it in this new light. *But* you don't remember how you translated it previously, and – because there was no way of predicting the frequency of its recurrence or its importance as a leitmotif, it never occurred to you to keep a record of it. In that case, you have to go back, search for and gather together all occurrences, and ensure that they are all given the identical translation – which may or may not be the one you originally decided on. So, you must decide either to bring all the subsequent choices into line with that, or to find a translation which better accords with the use made of that expression by the down-to-earth and pragmatic Pyotr Ivanych to mock and deride his nephew's high-flown and florid locutions, along with his idealistic illusions and the conduct that accompanies them.

QUOTATIONS

What to do about quotations in general? Is it part of the translator's task to track down their origins – author and work? Well, the author whose work you are translating didn't provide this service to *his* readers, so why should you? Since your author didn't feel it necessary to do so, it can be inferred that he felt he was safe in assuming that the quotation in question would have been familiar to *his* readers. Should then the readers of the translation, who can largely be assumed *not* to be familiar with them, be left without this information, which would help to level the cultural playing field for them? Or should the translator take that extra step and supply it for them? This step, however, may be the beginning of the slippery slope of crossing the frontier into editorializing or exegesis, and should be left to the discretion of publishers and their editors, especially taking into account that the reader is also left in the cultural dark by the far greater number of opaque *allusions* – which inevitably crop up in a work aimed at a readership in an alien culture, and also far removed in time.

Readers of contemporary fiction translated into English rarely enjoy the benefit of such cultural playing-field-levelling information. Whether they actively feel the lack of it is a moot point. It may well be that what is true in so many other areas of life is also true here – namely that when you are not conditioned to expect something, you don't miss it if you don't get it. A case in point is the recent smash-hit bestseller trilogy by Stieg Larsson, *The Girl with the Dragon Tattoo*, so smoothly translated , and so free of the distractions just described, that it would not surprise me if a large number of readers of its English version were virtually oblivious to the fact that it was *a translation* that they were reading, in spite of the fact that it contains many allusions to Swedish life and culture which would elude them. Interestingly, its original title, *Men Who Hate Women*, was for some reason clearly considered inappropriate for English-speaking readers.

If it should be objected that I am comparing apples with oranges, I would concede only that, in fact, the comparison is between different varieties of apple.

QUOTATIONS IN VERSE – WHICH OCCUR FREQUENTLY IN *THE SAME OLD STORY*

The extra problem posed is not the same as the problem which faces a translator who undertakes the entirely different task of translating the whole of the original poem from which these passages have been taken.

The choice is essentially between a version in prose or in verse.

However, in the case of these isolated excerpts, it is clear to me that priority should be given to presenting the *sense* of the passage to your readers so that they can understand its relevance to the surrounding context. Any attempt to render the passage in verse in order to preserve the style, charm, humour, beauty, quirkiness or any other aesthetic value of the original – especially if it rhymes – would inevitably be at the expense of the sheer meaning and relevance of the quotation to its context.

"BEING FAITHFUL TO THE ORIGINAL"

An elevated and noble-sounding precept, but like so many such, it tends to crumble under closer inspection and disintegrate under a microscope. To wit.

One reader wrote to offer a commendation of the *Oblomov* translation, but with a gentle sting in its tail, he asked: "Can it be true that an illiterate servant girl could quote Alexander Pope? She says: 'For fools rush in where angels fear to tread'. No doubt, Goncharov knew this; has he put 'it' in the wrong mouth?"

An adequate response to this comment, on the face of it a perfectly legitimate one, means spelling out, or peeling off, the layers of a translator's thought processes as he or she mediates between what some describe as "remaining faithful to the original" and what fewer have described as "faithfully serving the readers", by transmitting something that will make perfect and accessible sense to them in their own language, will not jar, stop the flow or leave the reader puzzled or baffled, while remaining "faithful" to the author's *thought*, as well as, in this case, couched in the original epigrammatic or proverbial form chosen by the author.

By "it" did that reader mean the saying he quotes in English? If so, there is no evidence whether Goncharov knew "it" or not, since his original Russian expression "Для дураков закон не записан" ("*dlya durakov zakon nye zapisan*") literally translated becomes: "For fools [the] law is not written." This expression is a sawn-off version of a longer "winged utterance", as such locutions are known in Russian, in the same way that "As fools rush in" is a sawn-off version of *its* original. Illiterates, be they servants or not, girls or not, are probably just as likely to make use of figures of speech, proverbs and other "winged utterances" as any other native speakers of their language. English speakers grow up absorbing and using a great number of them which originated in the Bible and the works of Shakespeare, without necessarily having read, or being able to read, either.

When it comes to rendering "sayings", many – often conflicting – factors enter into the equation, and the result is always a trade-off. Some "purists" or "extremists" might advocate staying "faithful to the original". A recent, oft-quoted example would be the rendering of a certain original Russian expression as "drinking up his trousers", which has been justified precisely by invoking the precept of "faithfulness to the original", although its actual effect is simply that of dumbfounding any "literate English servant girl" who may happen to be reading it. She might, of course, be comforted to learn that it was "faithful to the original" ("*пропил брюки*" – "*propil bryuky*"). An equally extreme example of following this precept would be to translate *literally* into Russian the expression "he's lost his marbles" or a figurative expression which was once used at the United Nations about President Reagan's tax proposal: "Everyone was wondering whether he was going to run or pass, but in the end he punted", sowing no little consternation among the interpreters.

It seems to me that the *reductio ad absurdum* of this approach would be simply to transliterate the whole text of a Russian original into the reader's native alphabet – what could be more "faithful" or "closer to the original"?

Here is a further example of a literary translation problem of a different order, which challenges (or should challenge) the translator.

Translating the *ipsissima verba* (that is, the "raw material") of the original, even correctly, is often a far cry from delivering it in "processed" form – that is, in a form which makes sense of those words to a contemporary English-speaking reader – and as close as possible to the sense in which they would have been understood by the Russian-speaking contemporaries of the author.

At a certain point in the story, the author tells us that in the aftermath of a failed love affair which leaves an embittered Alexander in its wake, he, Alexander, has written a novella which, according to Goncharov, is about "ordinary people", and depicts them as liars, cheats, dissemblers and hypocrites with, apparently, no redeeming features. The sentence immediately following this is a comment by the author – which, translated literally and correctly, reads: "Everything was appropriate, and in its proper place."

How does this apparent contradiction square with the sentence it follows?

And: "What on earth are readers of the translation going to make of it?"

I have canvassed the opinions of one or two native Russian speakers, and they read into the words a certain irony on the part of the author, Goncharov, at the expense of Alexander, the author of the novella, and may in fact be a "put-down" – in spite of the fact that the actual words, taken at face value, amount to commendation rather than a snide criticism.

In the event, my judgement call, or trade-off, was to leave the *ipsissima verba* exactly the way they are. Any other course would have been tantamount to an editorial comment or a lengthy footnote along the very lines of what I have just written.

"STRAIGHTFORWARD RUSSIAN WORDS" – AND "STRAYING FROM THEM"

A reviewer of *Oblomov* wrote: "Purists may object that Pearl has strayed too far from what are often straightforward Russian words." Again, the only way of responding to this comment is to invite the "purists" into the labyrinth of the translator's thought processes as he deconstructs the seemingly innocent and unexceptionable expression "straightforward Russian words".

Clearly, here the reviewer is dissociating himself from this stricture. Whether the three words in question are his own, or the words of one of the "purists", they require a great deal of elucidation, and would benefit greatly from reference to specific examples. Part of the problem lies precisely in the use of the word "words". To put it briefly, the stricture implies that it is individual words that have to be translated, rather than a sequence of words in the form of a phrase or a sentence – especially in the course of literary translation, rather than, say, the Canadian weather forecast – one of the first machine translations (between English and French) to survive the process intact and usable. How one translates individual "words" depends heavily in their immediate as well as their larger context.

Furthermore, the notion of "straightforward" is not at all "straightforward".

Even such an apparently "straightforward" word as an everyday concrete object like "*кран*" ("*kran*") not only warrants half a dozen equivalents in my Russian-English dictionary, but even there its immediate context changes and determines its translation. No doubt the first English word that would come to any translator's mind would be "tap", but even this does not go without saying because of the peculiar feature of "English" as the world's dominant language. "Tap" would not be the word that would come to an American translator's mind. It would be "faucet". I have no idea what it would be in the case of a Caribbean, Australian, Philippine or Indian translator.

As to the "immediate context" factor, my dictionary offers the following examples: "*пожарный кран*" ("fire cock"), "*водоразборный кран*" ("hydrant"), "*плавучий кран*" ("floating crane"), "*подъёмный кран*" ("hoisting crane"). A translator would have to travel very far afield to come up with the correct term for *kran* in all these different "immediate contexts".

At the opposite extreme (whatever may be thought to be the opposite of "straightforward") are chameleon, or "blank-cheque" words like "*условный*" ("*uslovniy*"), "*вообще*" ("*voobshche*") and "*деятель*" ("*deyatyel*"), which cannot possibly offer an obvious, "straightforward" English equivalent. For "*uslovniy*", dictionaries usually offer a choice of three "words" – "conditionally", "provisionally" and "conventionally", which could not be further from being exhaustive. On my list of "blank-cheque" words (that is, words whose "amount" is waiting to be filled in according to context value), "*uslovno*" is one of the "blankest", along with "*voobshche*". Would the failure by a translator to translate "*voobshche*", as "in general" or "on the whole" (as Tass translators did as a matter of course – and wrongly – in Soviet times), or "*uslovniy*" as "conditional", "provisional" or "conventional", be regarded accordingly as "straying too far…"? Dogs can only be described as having "strayed too far" if they have broken free of the leash by which they have been tethered, but the distance they are "free" to travel depends on the length of their leash. In the case of "straightforward Russian words", the length of the leash varies – and varies considerably – depending on how "straightforward" they really are, not to mention the immediate context in which they are embedded. With a word like "*тоска*" ("*toska*"), even the tersest of Russian-English dictionaries can hardly offer fewer than seven "equivalents". Smirnitsky has sixteen! And, it must be said, even these do not cover the whole spectrum of the nuances of this all-encompassing emotion or mood to which the Russian "soul" is so sensitive – and prone.

As an example of how unstraightforward a "straightforward Russian word" can become when it comes to translating it for readers or an audience, here is a case in point.

THE "ПРОСТОКВАША" ("PROSTOKVASHA") PROBLEM

As a Russian word, this one is about as straightforward as they come.
And the problem?
First of all, it took this translator a good forty minutes of research to come up with its "straightforward" meaning in English, namely one of the many variations on the theme of "soured milk" which bulk so large in Russian cuisine.

But, since it was the one and only dish being served by his hostess for his supper to an honoured guest of higher social rank who was showing a promising interest in her unmarried daughter, it was hard for me to believe that this meal really consisted entirely of some form of soured cream. However, all my sources concurred in this definition, and I felt that readers of the translation would also find such ungenerous and grudging hospitality a baffling incongruity, especially since the Count, the guest in question, is then described as eating it with a hearty appetite.

Further research revealed that it would not have been at all uncommon, in that society and at that time, for this dish *alone* to be served as the last meal of the day – partly, I believe, on the grounds that this kind of dairy product was good for the digestion. Feeling, as I did, that a lengthy footnote to this effect would be too much of distraction to the reader, I decided to compromise with a word which, although on the archaic side, would at least be recognizable to the reader – if only because of Miss Muffet – and was at least in close culinary and semantic proximity to "*prostokvasha*".

Now that food has reared its ugly head, something should be said about some of the other...

SPECIFICS OF EVERYDAY LIFE

In nineteenth-century Russia, people travelled in a wide variety of vehicles, practically none of which have counterparts in the English-speaking world today – except for trains in the latter part of the century. Since these conveyances are for the most part mentioned purely for the narrative purpose of getting the dramatis personae from one place to another, and it is clear that they have wheels (runners in winter) and are drawn by horses, and are driven by coachmen rather than their owners, and come in almost as bewildering a variety as the cars we travel in today, I believe that readers rarely need to be told anything else about them. If they *did* need to know, only an illustration, or a paragraph-length description would serve the none-too-relevant purpose.

They also wore a wide variety of garments, only some of which happen to coincide with or resemble what today's English speakers are wearing, while there are other items of clothing which simply have no counterpart today in the target culture, partly because of climatic differences, partly because of changes of fashion and mores, and partly because modern English-speaking countries have long since shed their peasantry.

DIALOGUE

...which is one of Goncharov's great strengths, and which figures prominently in this novel, poses distinctive problems of its own.

To mention but one: sometimes, in dialogue, Russian can be very elliptical and laconic, but an interlocutor of the relevant time and place would have enjoyed the benefit of the speaker's tone, intonation, gestures, facial expression and body language in order to capture the full flavour of the words themselves. Therefore, in order to offset that disadvantage, and to maintain equivalence, more – sometimes many more – words have to be used in the translation.

* * *

Have you ever found yourself reading a book for the second time, and noticing things you missed the first time – as happens with plays and films? And it's not just the things that you consciously skipped – or skimmed – the first time!

I had read this book several years before, but in the course of translating it, I was astonished to discover that my memory of it was not only impressionist, but positively pointillist – actually, more like a particularly porous sieve!

I come away from this experience with the profound conviction that you haven't really read a book unless you've translated it!

Acknowledgements

My heartfelt gratitude to Margarita Razenkova, whose unstinting, tireless, loyal and painstaking assistance went far beyond the call of duty.

Many thanks to Victor Prokofiev, Oleg Semyonov and Marina Kuzina for their corroboration and guidance at moments of doubt.

And belated thanks here, instead of at the right time and in the right place, to my good friend, Jennifer Klopp, for her contribution to my work on *Oblomov*.

The publisher would like to thank the Institute for Literary Translation, Russia – in particular Evgeniy Reznichenko and Maria Skachkova – for making this project possible.

ALMA CLASSICS

ALMA CLASSICS aims to publish mainstream and lesser-known European classics in an innovative and striking way, while employing the highest editorial and production standards. By way of a unique approach the range offers much more, both visually and textually, than readers have come to expect from contemporary classics publishing.

LATEST TITLES PUBLISHED BY ALMA CLASSICS

209 Giuseppe T. di Lampedusa, *Childhood Memories and Other Stories*
210 Mark Twain, *Is Shakespeare Dead?*
211 Xavier de Maistre, *Journey around My Room*
212 Émile Zola, *The Dream*
213 Ivan Turgenev, *Smoke*
214 Marcel Proust, *Pleasures and Days*
215 Anatole France, *The Gods Want Blood*
216 F. Scott Fitzgerald, *The Last Tycoon*
217 Gustave Flaubert, *Memoirs of a Madman* and *November*
218 Edmondo De Amicis, *Memories of London*
219 E.T.A. Hoffmann, *The Sandman*
220 Sándor Márai, *The Withering World*
221 François Villon, *The Testament and Other Poems*
222 Arthur Conan Doyle, *Tales of Twilight and the Unseen*
223 Robert Musil, *The Confusions of Young Master Törless*
224 Nikolai Gogol, *Petersburg Tales*
225 Franz Kafka, *The Metamorphosis and Other Stories*
226 George R. Sims, *Memoirs of a Mother-in-Law*
227 Virginia Woolf, *Monday or Tuesday*
228 F. Scott Fitzgerald, *Basil and Josephine*
229. F. Scott Fitzgerald, *Flappers and Philosophers*
230 Dante Alighieri, *Love Poems*
231 Charles Dickens, *The Mudfog Papers*
232 Dmitry Merezhkovsky, *Leonardo da Vinci*
233 Ivan Goncharov, *Oblomov*
234 Alexander Pushkin, *Belkin's Stories*
235 Mikhail Bulgakov, *Black Snow*

To order any of our titles and for up-to-date information about our current and forthcoming publications, please visit our website on:

www.almaclassics.com